Blood Ties

David Adams Richards

ISBN 0 88750 249 0

Design by Michael Macklem

Printed in Canada

PUBLISHED IN CANADA BY OBERON PRESS

For Alden Nowlan

July 1967

Mass was over now and they started up the road together with the heat coming down on them, pressing down, except Orville stayed ahead of them, his young spindly legs moving as quickly as they could. When they were halfway Allison stopped and offered them a drive. Orville kept on walking—a little quicker as if to get home before the car.

"I think it looks like rain," Allison said.

"I think it will," Maufat said. He sat in the back seat between her and Irene, his knees together, his hands on his knees. "I'm going to have to get a car I think."

Allison's wife had the baby on her lap.

The heat was a wet heat and could be felt in the car, could be seen out the car windows in the drain, the weeds slanted motionless, almost dripping with it.

"Do you have to serve the picnic, Irene—I had trouble with the baby—I didn't hear because of him."

"Yes your name was called; our name was called."

"I don't want to serve," Cathy said.

Her mother looked around behind Maufat's shoulder and stared at her. She looked down and across to where her father's dirt-black fingernails were scratching at the legs of his pants.

They drove past Orville. He didn't turn at all to notice them so they kept on driving. Cathy turned to wave but he didn't answer it, and he turned his head to look along the side of the drain where the weeds were slanting and waiting in the thick heat, and where the thick smell of summer seemed to be. It seemed to be only there along the side of the ditch. Then it began to rain, slow at first but by the time they pulled into the drive it was raining hard.

The field looked black with it.

"He'll get drenched," Irene said.

"Now thank you," her father said.

Because she ran from the gate into the porch she got wet, almost soaked through the blouse, it came that quickly, making the field slant under with the weight of it. She felt the chill of the rain on her when she went into the porch, kicking from the door the case of bottles that leaned against it. The chill stayed with her when she went inside. Outside all was darkening, the trees blowing with the rain and the flat, rutted surface of the drive turning to puddles and mud. She ran upstairs unfastening her skirt as she went, singing to herself, the rain dripping down from her, and the small streaks of mud she had tracked in. As she sang the words came up from her throat louder and louder. She pushed open the door to her room and went to the small grey window that slanted at an angle at the side of her bed. Out there on the roadway she could see him coming, walking close to the drenched woodlot on the opposite side. He had his head down and his hands in his pockets and he didn't run, not the way anyone would be expected to run in a rain like that. The sound of the rain beating and splashing and pumping from the broken clouds. Thunder—the roadway deserted except for him walking alone. She lay on the bed and pulled the magazine out from under her and began to read, her lips moving slowly with the words.

"Are you coming?" her mother said.

She looked up. Her mother stood at the doorway, unchanged, with her white sunless hand resting against the side of the wall.

"And put that away—it's Sunday; you've just received—so put that away."

She dropped the magazine to the floor and stood, changing out of her Sunday clothes with her back to her mother. He was coming up the drive now still walking in that manner—his long thin legs thrusting out, covering his shoes with mud.

"Not really," she said.

"That woman has to be fed and changed."

"I had wanted to go swimming."

Out on the beach the sand would be black wet, the waves would come in and the seaweed would wash up saturated and grey. The waves would come up and splash the reef, and far down below it, the *slip*. The beach would be empty.

"You can't go swimming now."

She watched him coming and then he was gone around by the porch and she heard the door swing open and she heard her father grunting to him, but she heard nothing from him.

She turned around and with her throat filling that way she couldn't speak for a moment. She didn't want to go. They would roll her over and take her like a child and change her—time and again, every day, time and again. She had wanted to go swimming—the long hot beach, the water, the thick rich mill smell coming down over it, the sky purple-blue with heat and mist.

6

"He took my radio again—he has it in there every day—he took it again. It's my radio. I should be able to keep my own darn radio. He takes it every darn day," she said.

Her mother looked at her. Her sunless hand against the wall.

"She has to be fed and changed. No more than an hour—no more than an hour and a half. She'll go to sleep then."

They went down the stairway together, her mother a step ahead of her, the knee-length dress of her mother and her mother's stockings with a run in both legs, the white calves bulging out. She had such thin little hands and such thick legs now, not the legs she used to have. There was a time before, a time when her legs were as pretty as her hands. Cathy watched her on the stairway moving down.

"He takes my radio all the time—all the time, so that's it! That's it! From now on you'll see a padlock on my door. Even if we had ordinary doors I wouldn't mind. So that's it. Padlock on my darn door from now on."

The rain wasn't so hard now. After supper she would go to the beach because it would be clear by after supper. But the flies after a rain swarmed terribly. Even now she thought she saw a clearing in the far sky. To sit in her room all afternoon and wait for the clearing—reading and smoking cigarettes. He sat in the living-room staring at nothing.

"Padlock from now on, Orv; the heck with you. You put my radio back—and stop taking my stuff like that, that's all I have to say."

He turned his head away and his eye closed, and then in one motion he lay down across the couch, with his shoes still on dangling over the arm.

"Did you track mud in here?" Irene said.

"No!" He never opened his eye.

"Well, be careful of tracking mud in here—I see some stains here—look, it's all marked up. It is! Did you do that?"

He didn't answer.

"Did you do that?"

"No," he never bothered to open his eye.

"Yes, well you better put my radio back—soon as you go upstairs put it back," Cathy said, looking at the mud marks ground into the carpet, already spot-streaked and faded and dirty. "Are we going now?" she said.

"Soon, soon," Irene answered going into the kitchen.

Maufat was in the kitchen with his chair pulled up between the stove and the table. He had pushed the plastic fruit dish to the side, and at the side of it he had his beer placed, and on his left the ashtray and cigarettes. He had his cards dealt out and was looking in perplexity over them, grunting now and then to himself, and picking the beer up now and then to drink it.

"Five on your red six," Cathy said coming over to him.

He turned around with his mouth full and shook his head until he swallowed. His face soured.

"I know—I know; now you'll ruin everything. I want to get it myself—if I can't get it myself I ain't gonna play."

She turned to her mother.

"When are you starting dinner?"

"After—when she's fed and changed and comfortable. Laura can come over with me this evening. You only have to come with me now."

The sky wasn't clearing; it had been a mistake to think it was. Irene stood nearest the window waiting for it to abate, for it to draw back into itself. That is how Cathy thought of it all—she thought that the clouds drew closer together and then the rain drew back into it. Thunder came. Her father never picked up the five for the red six. Not yet. He kept flipping the cards in groups of threes over and over again. He put an ace up and then the deuce upon it. He would have to put them all up now. Lightning came. She counted; each second was a mile away and she counted seven seconds—thunder came. The lightning was in the forest above where the leaves were thick with the saturation; where the twisted sunless branches were black with the saturation.

"We could run over," Irene said.

When the lightning came again it seemed to whiten the sky, making a pure white out of those grey clouds from whence it came, making white the mud. the usually scum-red mud of the drive. She had walked over and stood behind her mother to watch it coming. If they left now and ran across by the field-path they would make it in a matter of minutes but it was the field high with the wet grass that would soak through her slacks.

"I don't care," she said.

She turned and went inside again and grabbed Orville's jacket from the rack.

"I'm taking your jacket."

He grunted and opened his eye. She could see the faintest smile coming from him before he turned his back to her.

So they went out into the rain. Irene had Maufat's black leather rain jacket with the hood and she trudged out in front of her daughter, her step marks visible in the mud, indistinguishable after a few seconds in the downpour. Cathy kept close behind her. They went eyes down, weighed down and pushed by the onslaught, as heavy as beasts in the onslaught. Like her mother trudging ahead of her, as heavy as Allison's cow; one slow movement ahead of the other. She never ran. Why didn't she run? Why didn't she run?

"Run, Mom."

Irene didn't answer and each time Cathy lifted her eyes she felt the rain, felt it even though Irene's figure was half protecting her, the black rain jacket and the grey-black sky.

They entered through the bushes behind the swings, an opening where two small red pine grew on opposite sides. When they went through the branches soaked her, and the bushes directly after, their leaves full green with the wetness. They were on the path now and the field with its thigh-high growth on both sides of them. Thunder again.

"Run, Mom—Irene, run, Irene!"

Her mother trudged harder into the rain.

Ahead in the distance was the charred black chimney of the old house, the clouds seeming to be so close as to touch it, the storm raging against it, the half-open shutters at its front slapping, though she couldn't hear the sound of them, only the sound of her own warm breathing and then, the rain and wind. They were halfway across the field now, and moving no faster though she had called out for her mother to run. The path was narrow and could be crossed only at single file; unless she wanted to run through the high grass and then out beyond her mother she could go no faster than her mother did.

She waited until they were almost to the end of the path and then she went, out into the thick, thigh-high grass running, the thick uncomfortable wetness. The house was far away, across the dirt road, across the coloured walk. Irene trudged never looking, comical and absurd in the rain jacket that hung season after season on a nail in the porch, so that it was as if that was where it should always be. And she wearing it and it smelling of railway—of the tracks and the soot and the grease of the cars, though he never wore it now, or hardly ever. But the smell and the taste and the look of it was always the same. Always, even during that night when Alton took it and began to open bottles with the hooks on it, the foam of the beer spurting out against it and making it even blacker. It never lost its smell—it never ceased to remind her of all the dirt and all the men that her father worked with, though she had never seen any of them face to face; and all the trains and the track going out for miles, bright white steel rusted on the underneath, and of her father himself.

She ran, her mother never looked. The grass and burdocks and spear-roses stuck out against her, catching at her as she ran. She ran looking across to Irene. There was no thunder now, only the rain. But it was all slippery—more so than the path, and when she had passed at a distance of a few yards and began to turn back toward it, she slid, her one leg sliding out and the other buckling under, and felt herself spinning around and falling sideways—into a small clump of stinging nettles. She went down into them sideways and her hands reaching went into them. She cried out and Irene coming up to her on the path stopped and waited.

"Are you hurt?" she said.

Cathy lifted herself and came out onto the path ahead of her mother, wringing her dirt-wet stinging hands one against the other, still feeling in herself the emptiness of the space when she was falling like that and the thud of when she hit. And the nettles now taking effect in her hands burned at her skin.

"Are you hurt?"

Her eyes were watering a little and her mother's soft grey eyes looked out from under the black hood at her, the rain dripping that way from the hood and down about her sunless face. Her eyes were watering a little but she laughed weakly and then moaned weakly at the end of her laughter.

"I fell in those darn nettles."

"Your face—not your face?"

"No, my hands," she said rubbing them still, harder now, one upon the other.

She turned from her mother and walked ahead of her the rest of the way, across the dirt road, now wet and puddled in its ruts, and across the coloured walk, the stones more and more distinguished by the rain, and into the large rear porch of her grandmother's home—the quiet soundless porch emptied of all that used to be there, emptied of the vases and chairs and tables and the life those objects gave. Emptied of all except the ancient sewing-machine that sat upon its small pine table by the end of the far wall, its turning wheel motionless and its foot-pedal missing.

"He shoulda took that too," Cathy said.

Irene didn't answer. She opened the door to the kitchen and Cathy went inside, taking off her jacket and throwing it over a chair. It was a much larger kitchen than their own. It at one time had supported a much larger family. She rubbed her hands together one across the other and shivered with the wetness of her body.

"How are you today?" she said.

She knew that there would be no answer. When was the last real answer given she couldn't remember. But she knew that she must say something, or even without knowing it at all spoke, perhaps through kindness not for the woman but for her mother or herself. But she knew that there could be no answer, no more than the face lifting, tilting slightly sideways at their entrance as if jerking her head upwards at something completely unexpected. The sad human face jerking and bobbing, the radio on the windowsill and she in a chair with cushions by the stove.

"Was she there this morning?"

Irene nodded.

"She's been there since before church?"

Irene nodded again.

Sundays were always the worst. Irene went to the cupboard and took two small cans of baby food. She had left her rain-jacket on and worked opening the cans without even noticing it. Cathy brought a towel from the bathroom and dried her face. Her hands were still stinging so that she kept rubbing them over and over again, the small distinct red specks beginning to appear on the itch. She took the towel and rubbed it across her short brown hair, short brown hair pinned at the side of her face, but even doing this she kept her gaze on the woman working in the rain-jacket and the older woman sitting mutely in the chair.

"Are you going to feed her right away?"

Irene didn't answer. She emptied the cans into a saucer and turned, her hood still hanging at the back of her head, her grey eyes serious and concerned.

"You get some warm water on those hands."

The old one sat there watching—staring at them but not staring, aware yet unaware of who or what was in the room with her at that instance. As if when they both left she would still be staring. No matter whether after they changed her, they put her to bed and set the radio beside her she would still be staring.

Irene went over. She took the plastic spoon and dipped it into the mush and bent over slightly. The old one opened her mouth slightly.

She made no attempt to take the spoon. Irene shoved it through the small dark crevice her parted lips made.

"Oh I can't do this," she said. She straightened and put the food down, taking her jacket off after she did so. Then she went back to it, back to the saucer and spoon. The woman chewed and swallowed as innocently as a child, sometimes with a soft unmistakable gurgling in her throat, the only voice she had.

She washed the itch with soap and warm water. The sting didn't diminish, the rain outside hadn't as yet diminished. She watched a car turn on the highway far down below her home.

"That must be Laura now," she muttered. Her mother didn't answer, her grandmother answered only in the eating and swallowing of the food.

She turned and went over.

"Do you need any help?"

"Not yet—I can do this."

"What do you want me to do then—I mean why am I here?"

"We have to put her upstairs—you know that; we have to take her up there after."

It was always *that*. She crossed from the kitchen, crossed through the dining-room and inside. Here she sat on the sofa and stared through the window, the drapes only half opened, the patterns the rainfall made streaking against the pane. And across the field was the back end of her house, the back section of the porch. Above the porch was his room. He was up there now, up there alone in the quiet of his room, listening to his father cough and mutter to himself as he turned the cards over and over again. Listening to all that alone with his candles. She knew about the candles. She had written it into her diary when she had first found them stuffed behind his sleeping-bag there in his open closet. She had written:

"Orville takes candles!"

"Orville takes candles!" into her diary, without him knowing that she knew; and as yet he didn't know that she knew. But sometimes she smelt the burning of candles late at night, or even sometimes during the day when nobody was upstairs except him in his room and she in hers, reading the stories in the magazines that she had piled underneath her bed. The unmistakable rich dripping smell of church wax burning in his room. She said nothing.

She sat quiet, her legs crossed, one wet leg over the other. Her mother made the only sound in the kitchen, nothing of the sound of the old mute woman leaning toward the cushions on the chair. Nothing of the sound of the house, nor even of the rain anymore—it had stopped. She wanted a cigarette. Her mother must have known when she had started smoking, her mother, in fact, must have known now, dusting out her room the way she did. She wanted a cigarette, nothing more than that; to watch the house and smoke. Some day she would walk down the stairs with a cigarette in her hand, walk into the kitchen with it burning and that would be that. Her mother would say nothing, no more than anyone. She would say:

"You've started I see—you shouldn't you know."

But that would be all; it would be no more, no less. Nothing more. Some day she would do that. She felt that if her mother knew anything she kept it to herself, like she kept to *herself* the candles in his room.

But even before, before when it was hazy that day with the frost lying off the ice and the river; they said, "The river will jam," because it had thawed so early and the snow like brown slush with the mud. And the air so warm with the thaw one could walk without a coat. She was outside and Karen was with her and she was walking and then she felt it. She knew what it was even then, even before the slightest hint of what it was had ever been told to her. But it was there now and she felt it, felt it something like sweat inside her. She said:

"I gotta go."

"Where?"

"Home, I gotta go home."

Karen stood there, the thaw around her and the soft warm air. She was younger—she was only eleven. She stood there for a moment and Cathy walked on ahead but not quickly until Karen said:

"I'll come with ya."

And then she said:

"No—I'll see ya."

Then with Karen still standing there she broke into a run as fast as anything and all around her was the sweet warm breeze of the thaw. The trees warm with budding and she ran into the porch and into the kitchen. Irene was there putting doughnuts into the fat and as soon as Irene saw her she must have known. She said: "What's wrong?"

"I need a bandage I guess."

And then Irene was frightened of something—of herself. Then she said:

"Come here, I'll get you something, okay?"

And Cathy said "Okay" and her mother never watched her with her eyes, kept avoiding her altogether. But they both knew what it was, how it would be hereafter. Then the next day there was a small pamphlet on her bed.

The rain was over now, and then with only a short pause the first sun came after it, like something sprouting. It hit the window she was watching from and the field all at once. The grass and bushes brightened all at once. It would get warm now and then after supper it would be clean and good and warm enough to swim. Her mother was in the kitchen but she couldn't have still been feeding—the feeding must have been over like the rain, and the old woman must have been comfortable again, but not so comfortable as when they would take her and change her and put her upstairs in her own room with her own things in it. At least he hadn't taken them as yet; but yes he would—he being older than Irene and all thought surely it was his right to take them—his right to do whatever he wanted to do; but didn't he help now, she thought. Oh yes, didn't he help out half carrying her around, half keeping her alive just by sitting up nights with her like Irene.

Her mother was at the garbage. She could hear the sound of the bag being lifted from the tin container in the porch and then when her mother came in the door swung closed and the windowpane in the door rattled a little.

"Cathy."

"What?"

"Could you take this out. The rain's almost over. Are your hands stinging?"

"No," she kept rubbing them together, monotonously, methodically one against the other. The sun had cleared the sky and all about seemed to be brighter—the gravel brighter on the dirt drive into the place.

"Well could you take this out behind then?"

"Yes," she said. She didn't move for a moment.

"Cathy, I'm holding it."

"Yes yes yes."

She went into the kitchen and her mother was holding it, one edge with both her hands so that the other edge slanted. The old woman watching and the radio on the windowsill; the fly crawling above it on the pane.

She took it and went outdoors. The sun was out warm on her wet slacks. She cut behind the house and through the dense foliage that grew where the old barn used to be, where the planks and wet boards from the rain intermingled with the weeds and high grass that had grown above them so that the eye could hardly tell where they were at all. Only the feet half tripping could tell where they were. The air was sweetened with the summer again that the rain had brought out all the more, which came to her all at once as she walked back. Low clumps of spruce at the edge of the field where the old fence logs tilted over.

She walked beyond them and into another field, smaller and dotted with mustard weed, dotted with the sharp smell of the weed growing bright yellow about her in the sun. The sun hot on her hair again drying the short brownness of it. She walked over to the edge of this field and threw the bag of cans into a pile of others. The cans were brown and rusted as if they had been left there years ago by some person who had little or nothing to do with herself. The air was hot now and she paused for a moment. Around her the silence, the cans silent, intermingled one with the other and with the day so bright and the short mutilated lilac that grew around them, that they had trampled down over the space of these three years to make a place for the cans and the emptied bottles of useless medicine, the bottles all sizes and shapes—all looking strangely a part of the sun and the day. Her legs were uncomfortable again from the grass.

It was strange the way it was; the very taste of those cans, their smell mingling with that of the lilac, the spruce. The rich *deceased* smell of them casting off something that was so much a part of them. Like the wind sometimes blowing the smell of sulphur this far downriver and it lying over the water, purple blue, creating a mist all its own.

It was the black flies that drove her back to the house.

Irene was washing one of the old woman's nightdresses in the sink. Cathy stood with her back to the door watching. The purple of the cloth of the dress coming in and out of the water, the smell of the bar of soap her mother used to rub at the stains, the noise of the rubbing of the fabric together, and her mother's hands wet and whitened even more, rising and falling from the water and back as she did the work. The old woman sat, moving slowly the top of her body back and forth. Her eyes were half closed and over her right eye the giant white mole looked even more gigantic, as if it were that that weighed down the eye. Cathy watched her moving in the chair.

"Are we going to put that on her?"

"No—there's another one up there."

"Did she eat it all?"

15

"Mostly."

The old one sat limp again. Her eyes popped open like the popping of something unexpected, like she had just this minute realized that there were those in the room speaking. Both eyes popped large and grey and scared, at Cathy at the door, behind the door at something outside, at the porch and at nothing all at once.

"When he comes over does he feed her at all or sit up with her at all?"

"Who?"

"Lorne—you know who."

"I don't know. It doesn't matter."

"No, nothing matters—as long as you spend your money and everything and are over here all the time and everything."

Irene rubbed the fabric; her white hands withered and reddish and whitened even more by the soap and the brownish water.

"No, nothin matters," Cathy said again moving her right foot ahead of her left, and feeling the dampness of her jeans clinging to the back of her thigh. "No, nothin—you come over here to watch her and he comes over to here to steal all the stuff."

"He's not stealing all the stuff. He took some things because Betty wanted some things for the new room. When Mom dies they'll be his anyway."

"And yours too."

Irene said nothing. The old woman watched saying nothing. It was he who came over here and took the furniture and she let him and Maufat let him. Maufat didn't do a thing to stop him and she didn't do anything to stop him. It was as much theirs anyway.

"It's as much ours as his anyway."

"He came over here last week and Betty comes over here every other day."

"Sure," she said quietly.

"I can't do a darn thing about it—what do you want me to do, start a fight?" Irene said raising her voice. "Start a fight in the family like a fightin Frenchman just cause they're taking some useless tables? Is that what you'd do?"

"No, that's not what I'd do."

"Well then?"

"Well nothing—the hell with them then. I don't care, let them burn the darn place down for all I care."

Irene said nothing. She drained the water out and lifted the heavy material sopping in both her withered hands and began to wring it from one end to the other over the sink. Light came in through the small window curtains above the sink and shattered against the table leg on the inside.

Cathy went over and took hold of the other side. The heat of the light came in through the curtains and broke against her face. There were cars on the road now travelling to the beach because the rest of the day would be warm and good to swim.

Her mother took the nightgown and went into the porch to hang it from the back line.

"Are we taking her up then?"

"Yes." Irene came back through the door, her grey eyes low, watching the woman motionless in the chair by the stove.

"Now then," Cathy said moving into the centre of the floor.

"Yes."

Cathy went over to the woman first and stood a little to the side of her looking down at her balding head, the red pinkness of the skull under the frail white hair.

The woman did not look to either of them because she was looking at her own hands now, the swollen disjointed wristbone of her right hand sticking out prominent with both her hands together that way, not really folded together but joined and resting on her lap. She was staring at them but not really seeing them at all. The small stains of yellow food mush at the corners of her mouth.

When Irene came over and stood opposite at the right side of the old woman Cathy moved a little closer. Irene bent over and took the hands slowly off the cushion that lay across the woman's lap and the woman started, bobbed her head up and opened her mouth a little, looked around from one side of her to the other. Her face was narrowed and with her mouth opened that way, frightened. Frightened like the bird that day falling from its nest and Orville, instead of putting it back when Cathy asked him, ran and got his gun and shot it in the naked back with a pellet. Between the bone joints of the wings, and the bird turned its head around and looked at them that way, its beak opened. Frightened. And Cathy yelled, "Put it back up, Orville, put it back up," but instead he took a rock and threw it on the bird and the bird threw its naked wings out and burst at the naked belly.

"She's not remembering anything today," Irene said.

"How are you?" Cathy said as if talking to someone else's child.

"Lift her here," Irene said bending over and putting one of her hands under the old woman's shoulder. "Not too hard—wait, not too hard

17

now, Cathy."

"I never do," she whispered. "I never do."

Irene lifted a little faster, a little more self-assured, with one hand under the shoulder and the other resting on the arm.

Cathy did the same, following the movement of her mother closely, the pressure that her mother gave, until the old woman was lifted from the cushion on the seat. It was wet from where she had sat so long upon it—all morning even before church. Irene said nothing.

"Turn her slowly, Cathy—she'll walk with you if you turn her slowly." Her voice had dropped evenly to a whisper, the sound of her voice as slow and as carefully light as the pressure and the movement itself. The old one let her head drop, the red pinkish patch at the roots of her balding head, the hair so white and smooth and fine in the sunlight that came through now to break against it.

They turned her slowly, one on either side of her, and walked through to the dining-room and then turned left again.

"Turn her slowly now, don't push her around, now turn her slowly."

She sighed. Irene said nothing. The old one's head seemed weighted. They turned her left and began to walk just as slowly, ever so slowly so that it was tiring for her just to move, through to the small hallway and then into the washroom. Irene shut the door. The pink tile of the bathroom walls, because Maufat last winter spent two months doing it over, because Irene had said:

"Don't you think it needs to be done, perhaps Lorne can help you do it." He did it alone because Lorne said he couldn't help—though he came over once or twice in the nights when Betty came with Irene. So he uprooted the floor and redid the walls. Sometimes Cathy came over and watched him work when he was working alone with the sound of *her* upstairs.

"Where's Lorne?"

"Don't know."

"Well Mom said he was supposed to help."

"Don't know."

He did it himself, liking to work alone.

The sky was blue now, the clouds cast off, the bright outside light casting itself on the pink. He always liked to work alone anyway. What was the good of it anyway—Irene saying that it had to be done? She watched out the window when they lowered her onto the flush and the bright plastic curtains came down and hit the new tile and fluttered a little against it. She leaned against the closed door. The sky was so perfectly blue now.

"Get me that face-cloth there."

She reached over and handed her one off the rack.

"The one in the sink—run some warm water over it—not too hot, just warm water."

She stepped over and ran the water, half seeing the old woman's head bobbing as the light came in against the pink walls and the pink of her balding head.

"She's all chapped here."

She ran the water faster and then slowed it down and rinsed out the cloth, handing it to Irene. Then she turned away again, almost seeing herself turn away, as if it was the proper thing to do—for the old woman, for the privacy of the old woman, her grandmother, and herself. And as if it were something her mother wanted, expected. She turned sideways and stared at the new brown shower-curtain shoved back at the side of the tub.

"You have to help me now lift her again."

She turned. Her mother patiently staring.

"She isn't remembering anything today," Cathy said looking down at her.

They lifted her again and moved at the same slow pace back through the hallway and into the living-room.

"Watch how you turn," Irene said.

The sun was good now. The living-room clean and bright with the chair coverings pressed and straightened on the arms of the chairs. When they came to the bottom of the stairs they stopped. Her mother took a somewhat firmer hold of the shoulder that seemed to pull upwards a little. Cathy did the same. They remained standing there motionless for a moment.

"Okay, have you got her—try to get her to move her feet with you—I don't want her to trip up on those stairs, so when you move your feet try to get her to move her feet. Ready—because you have to start now first—ready?"

They started moving up. The bad leg dragged behind. It made her heavier, clumsier to move with. Perhaps she didn't want to go up now that they were moving. The bad leg went rigid after four steps. They had to balance her more carefully. They waited.

"She's all chapped—she must be in pain."

"I'm scraping my arm on the banister, if we could just move her over," Cathy said.

They moved her over. Then they started up again. The bad leg still drawing behind as if she were making an attempt to stay down. They stopped on the eighth step and rested. There was a smell of the wet heat of the upstairs. The hallway window had been half opened all this time. They moved her to the top of the stairs, then along the hallway and into the room. Irene's forehead was wet and her grey-brown hair dropped limp over it, and her grey eyes were large and waterless.

The room was dark and smelled of medicine and powder. The brown rosary rested on the dresser, and a picture of her husband pinned at the side of the mirror, and another full-length picture framed on the wall above the bed, and a string of neck beads lying across the night-table.

Irene's grey eyes were waterless and dry, but sweat stood out on the skin of the hollows, and the dampness of the limp locks of the grey-brown hair.

"Set her here."

"On the bed?"

"On the bed for a while."

They turned her evenly and carefully and placed her onto it, the mattress sagging with the light rigid weight of her body. Irene took one of the bed pillows and placed it at her lap and the old woman placed her arms upon it. Then her body sank upon the bed, becoming more relaxed.

The chair faced the window. Outside the hollow where the backyard slanted, where the barn used to be, and the thick foliage growing up from it now. Outside the raspberry bushes growing across the old wagon and against the side of the back shed. Outside the sky blue and the thick grass wetted from the storm.

The white laced curtains were pinned back, neat and clean; but the dust on the window ledge had not been cleaned off in a long time. It had gathered and clustered together over the ledge and the window stick that lay upon it. The pane itself was streaked with fingermarks, where someone a while ago had put their palms against it when trying to raise the window. The driblets of rainwater were fast drying on the outside.

"Could you get it out of the second drawer then?"

Irene was undoing the woman's dress buttons. The old woman put her hand up when the pillow was lifted away and put her dry hands over Irene's knuckles. The disjointed bone of the old woman's wrist. Cathy turned and went to the dresser. The picture of a strong-looking man standing against the side of a house—the house somewhere, she did not know where. His hat was clutched in his right hand, and the limbs of the tall maples at the side of it were as faded as the half-discernable face of someone staring from the window on the inside, looking out at that moment, expecting something to happen. Of the picture of that silent man being taken. Dozens of times she had taken the picture down, dozens of times she had gone over to look closely at the picture above the bed, each time wanting to know whose face it was. The half-discernable face staring into the day.

Now she only glanced at it and turned her eyes away—to the mirror itself, to the reflection of Irene in the mirror taking the left arm of the old woman and pushing it out of her dress. Then she took the night-dress out of the second drawer and went over again.

"Do you need me to help?"

"If you could just hold her up a little—no, now by the head and shoulders—there. No, now put your hand farther down on her back and hold her up more."

She turned her eyes away, to the floor, to the brown mat upon it. The old one was trying to cry because she was gurgling like that again. Her mother took the dress off. It was soiled.

"You didn't bring the cloth up."

She didn't answer.

"Well, get the cloth again, will you—and bring up that red towel, will you?"

"Water?"

Irene didn't answer.

Cathy went downstairs again and into the washroom. She ran the water warm and took the small pan and the bar of soap and the towel. Then she made her way up again, walking slowly so as not to spill it over. She went into the room with her mother standing over the bed, with the old one upon it naked. She didn't look.

"You're going to have to help me take this sheet off—can you help me do that?"

She lifted the woman by the shoulders carefully. Irene took the sheet ends and tried to slide it down under her. The pink balding spot upon the top of the head—the hair so fine white when the sunlight came through it. The small round scarring sores on the body. She didn't look.

"I should've remembered to do this before this—I should've re-membered."

"Sometimes I don't know why," Cathy said.

"Why?"

"Nothin," Cathy said.

Her mother took the soiled sheet away and threw it to the floor with the dress.

"We're not going to do that," Irene said.

She didn't answer. It was as if she was guilty of something. She stared at the floor where the sheet was crumbled in a mass.

"I should have remembered to take the sheet away before we ever set her down."

They laid her down properly again. Her mother took a white single sheet and covered the top half of her body. Then she took the cloth and began to bathe the lower part. Then when she finished drying the lower part she shifted the sheet and began to bathe the upper. The old woman's eyes were closed again—the white giant-looking mole.

"How are you?" Cathy said.

Then her mother finished and began to dry the upper. Then she took the powder. It smelled of the heat, the room. When she was finished she took the nightdress and held it out, undoing the lace at the top of it.

"Lift her head now—careful now."

They put it over her head and down about her, propping her arms through one at a time, and then down about her, covering her legs.

"Are you going to sit with her?" Cathy said.

"A while—here now, we'll put this blanket about her and place her in the chair."

They lifted her from the bed again and turned her and let her sink into the chair. Then Irene took the bed pillow and put it over her lap. The old white hands lying across the white pillow-casing and the sun on the white mole of the woman's eye and on the chair.

"Get that comforter in the hall."

She went out and took it off the railing and came back, glancing at the picture above the bed.

"Where was that taken?"

"What?"

Irene took the comforter and placed it around her, under the pillow at her lap.

"The picture."

"I don't know—they got a bear that day, it was before they went back with a team to haul it out—but I don't know whereabouts."

"Do you want the rosary?"

"Yes give her the rosary."

"So you don't know who that person is in the window then?"

Irene took the rosary and placed it in the old one's hands. She began to fidget with it in her hands.

"What?"

"That person—some woman I think staring out of that house?"

"Oh no—it was upriver anyway—50 years ago anyway. He shot the bear and when they brought it home Lorne was the baby then. So I wasn't even born then but Lorne wouldn't go near it. I mean the bear skin. He wouldn't go near it."

"Leave it to Lorne," Cathy said.

Irene said nothing, the hollow of her eyes were no longer sweating, her dry face seemed to stiffen because she had been talking. She looked about quickly.

"Did you get the radio?"

Cathy went downstairs and picked up the radio. She ran back up with it and placed it on the dresser and turned it on loudly so that the old one in her half-deafness might have a chance to hear it.

There was a minister speaking but she left it on. The minister would be off soon and then there'd be music.

"Well, I'm going now."

Irene nodded her head. She pulled the three-legged stool from the corner closet and sat upon it near the chair where the woman was sitting. She reached out her hand and took the hand in hers, and when she did the eyes opened and stared into nothing.

"I'll start supper," Cathy said.

She left and went downstairs. The blue sky from the kitchen window looked strong with the heat and there was a slight rainbow now fading above the tree-line, over the far sideroad. "Yes," she thought, "I'll have to get Karen and get some strawberries soon."

Then she heard the sound of the music. It was music now, no longer the minister's voice and then in a moment the sound of the old woman's good foot tapping against the floor.

The night sky was pale, black over the tree-line; the roadway still hot, the heat dying as the pale sky was dying. In the ditches at the sides of the highway it was drying, the rocks turning back from the wet brown to the pale summer white, that on the burning days the heat reflected from almost like bottle glass. There was no breeze yet and the weeds rose statue still, rose out into the silence, as silent as the highway itself, with only the soft glimmering of moisture at their stems.

She went all summer barefooted. Now that she had waited an hour she had started. Crossing the highway she went alone by the path that branched off the church road. The path still held the moisture in its dirt, so that clay dirt clung at the bottoms of her feet. The large white beach towel was thrown across her shoulder and she held it with her brown right hand as she walked. She was singing. Her mother said:

"Did you phone Laura?"

"Yes."

"Will she come over?"

"Yes, she said in an hour."

"Poor old soul, I hate to bother her that way—I hate to. I wish— are you going to the beach?"

"Yes."

"Wait an hour—I don't want you drowning—you wait."

"I'm waiting."

"Is Orville going too?"

He was lying there—he didn't answer. "Orville," she said. "Orville, are you coming?" He shook his head with one toss of it, the long blond bangs at the front falling over his eye. "Don't then—don't," she said.

The tide was high. As she walked along the beach it came up wetting her feet, her ankles throwing the seaweed green and wet against her legs like a covering. It was the wet warm salt of it as she moved downward, toward the cliffs and breakwater. The breakwater white, twelve feet high and vegetation growing between its cracked boards, some of them already splitting though it was a new one built only four years ago when they widened the shore road. But the ice when the bay froze came up against it, grated against it, the purple cold of the ice and the sea breeze coming in from the far open channel and the snow-white mist blowing up over the white purple of the ice. The cliffs hanging with icicles like a slide. The sky dark.

The sky was white pale now, the sun still in it though not so strong anymore. The breeze blew in at her as she walked. She passed the cliffs carefully, her toes spread because that was the way Orville had said it was easiest to do—"When you go along the cliff spread your feet stupid —stupid." *She had stared up at him from the water her left hand cut. Then she had laughed because he called her stupid because he was stupid.* She spread her toes and her brown hands grasping each separate dented chink of the rock. Where the ice was in the winter, where the swallows darted above it now, spiraled and set in the wind.

She came out across it and glanced at a slight angle downward at the

24

beach to where they were. She wanted to raise her arm and wave to them, to tell them she was coming. The fire was lighted, its grey smoke smouldering out toward the bay, out into the sky, lifting then losing itself in the sky. She couldn't smell it yet. Yet the smell itself was the deep haunting warmth of the smell of summer.

She didn't raise her arm nor did she shout. She was watching until she came to the last boulder that jutted out and from *their* side of the beach seemed to make a face of a man jutting out, the incline of the cliff its humping shaggy back. The boulder was drenched, the large waves hitting and splashing up over it. She stood on the boulder, her hands free, her feet spread. For a second she stood balanced on it— and then she jumped. Out past the log that leaned up against it, out far enough to fall free of everything and to land in the sand, still wet under the top coating that the afternoon sun had cleaned and dried.

"Hello," she shouted.

They waved their arms. They were still gathering for the fire, but the fire was going strong now and down below that, far down below the slip, the lighthouse, large and sea-white and desolate in the twilight.

The small chill of the breeze from the water. Edmund was dragging a log from the sand dune toward her, his right strong hand on the rusted spike.

"Where's Orv?"

He was bigger and stronger looking. If anyone saw them both that knew neither he would be the older. The log made a path behind him, he holding it in his right hand against his thigh.

"You'll get cut up."

"Where's Orv?"

"Home."

She passed him and kept walking toward the fire.

"Doesn't that boy do nothin—doesn't he do nothin?"

She didn't answer. She moved toward the fire looping the towel around her arms. The warm strong smell of it sparking and moving outward. The bay was darkening—she could not see the island when she looked out and she knew when she went out into it there would be the dark soundlessness of it around her. She would step out into it up to her thighs before she went under—she always did that, to feel it around her thighs, and when she went under it would be black and warm. Edmund would yell, "Eels—eels."

"We have beer—it's warm," Angela said.

"Where?"

"We put it in the water—six—they gave it to us."

The smoke drifted back and forth so that she could smell the smoke when she came up to stand beside Karen, smell it full every so often in her face.

"Who?"

"Where were you this afternoon?"

"With Annie."

"How is she now?"

"She wasn't remembering anything today." She stared at the fire, already the coal chunks on the under side of the burning wood. Edmund came with the log, his thin white legs looking red when the shadow of the blaze hit them. He threw the log against it but he wasn't strong enough. He wasn't strong enough because the log hit and the sparks splintered and the log rolled off toward the water.

"You stupid ass," Karen said. She jumped back rubbing her eyes. "You stupid ass."

"If you'da helped me—if you'da helped me," he said.

He was looking at his hand. He went to the log once more, rolling it back. "I cut me goddamned hand," he said.

"Who?" Cathy said.

"A whole bunch down from town," Angela said. Karen watched Edmund rolling back the log. Then she helped him lift it. Jerard came out over the black boulder yelling.

"You'd better go home," Karen said.

"I'll wash it in the water—goddamn hand," he said.

"Who was it?" she said.

"Oh that John guy—and Andy Turcotte—and that Kevin guy. They came down again and then when they were leaving John took the beer and said—guess what he said: 'Give this to my little Cathy.' They were all drunk and little Miss Primrose was pissed off."

"Who?"

"Oh that Julie one that's always hanging onto Andy because he has his old man's car."

"Oh," she said. She stared at the fire. It was brighter now because the sky was darker. The sky was bright red now above the burn. "I don't even know him," she said.

"Well, he said it—but he was drunk and Kevin was drunk, and he wanted to jump off the breakwater."

"John wanted to," Karen said.

"That's what I mean—but little Primrose didn't say a thing—just kept staring at Andy—wouldn't even talk to us."

"Oh," she said. She took her cigarettes from where they were held tight against her shorts and her stomach.

Then she threw off her shorts and top, laying them on her towel, and walked away from the warmth of the fire. Small flies swarmed on the beach away from the smoke of the fire.

"I'm going in—coming?"

The waves came up and splashed against the brownness of her legs, the swelling waves large against her. "I'm going in," she yelled again.

She went under into the wet opening her eyes underneath it, and reaching her hands forward seeing only the cool black before her. Then she came up and turned toward the fire.

"Watch for eels," Edmund yelled. "Watch for eels."

"Why don't you two boys go home?" Karen yelled. "Why don't you—why don't you; you don't see Orville hanging around us now do you—do you?"

2

Leah had come in again tonight.

She came up from the beach slowly, her hair damp with the water still, the salt on her still. It was late and when she saw the lights on she wondered, because the lights were never on this late. And then coming closer she saw the car parked at the rear of the back porch door, and then closer still she distinguished her father through the kitchen window with his back turned, and she knew that Leah was there.

She was waving her towel against the sky and when she saw the lights and then the car she stopped waving it, letting it fall limp and white in the moonlight and strike the road behind her.

"Leah's here again," she said. "Leah's here again."

It was after one. The moonlight over the trees, coming down over them silently and the road straight and silent and sparsely lighted, the warmth still on it in the dark.

The warmth still on the house side but the voices hardly audible as she came up to it, and when she went in, silence, her father stirring one hand along the railing by the kitchen sink.

Then it picked up again:

"Well, I don't know," Irene said.

"Well, I do—I do," Maufat said. He was holding the railing with his right hand, the pulse beating silently in it, the bones and muscles tight.

"Oh yes now sure," Irene said. "Start a hullabaloo because of it, sure now that's not going to get no-one nowhere."

He took his beer up and drank from it, his face rigid with a certain hate that flared whiter the more he drank, the relentless swallowing in his throat.

He put the bottle down and moved away from the sink and pulled out a chair at the kitchen table. No-one spoke again for a few moments. Leah must have been talking a lot already and she must have been crying—her eyes wet, the purple mascara running, her bold hard eyes wet and red with the blood in them. She stared up at Cathy and nodded half-smiling—as if she must smile no matter what or how. The well-formed angry lips.

"So where were you?" Maufat said.

"At the beach."

"No damn business being out this late."

"I was only with Angela and Karen. I was only with them swimming—Orville should have come—he should have."

Maufat took up another beer and snapping it open began to drink. Irene stared at nothing, into the pale green kitchen wall, green the colour of a damp day, green like the first shoots that come out.

"Well I don't know," she said. "You'd think he'd have more sense than that for sure. A child six years old."

Leah took up the vodka again and poured out another, and then took it up without pouring the mix into the glass and drank. She never flinched, only her eyelids moving slowly as she downed the thing. Her hair was fair and tight back on her head. Then she took the mix and drank. Irene stared at her, a contorted expression across her sunless face. "You aren't going to start that up again, are you?"

"What?"

"You aren't going to let him start making you drink again, are you?"

"He'll never make me do anything again—never that bastard will."

"Well then, good," Maufat said.

"What did he do—start on Ronnie again?" Cathy said.

No-one answered her. The radio came down low from Orville's room, where he was now, where he was all evening, where he always was.

"Then he said he was going to shoot himself," Leah said. Her hands fidgeting with the label, the long painted fingernails tearing at it, making a scratching sound.

"He wouldn't have the guts to shoot himself," Maufat answered, taking the bottle up again to finish it.

"Shhh," Irene said.

"Well I mean it," he added. "I mean it, beating up on a boy that way—no sense. He got no sense and he got no guts either."

"Well he took the gun; he took the shotgun out and went back behind Lester's field there and into the woods. And Lester and old Maude out looking at him because they heard the commotion and all, and he taking the shotgun and putting the clip full—right full as if he'd miss with the first one. And then I watched him crossing over the field—but I weren't going to go after him, no sir. He expected me to chase him—I wasn't. He coming in and throwing Ronald against the stove for no damn reason."

"Against the stove," Cathy said.

"He had to have stitches above the eye—Leah had to take him up," Irene said.

"Against the stove as if he were a goddamn dog," Leah said. Her voice was breaking out, her fingernails still scratching at the label, her face twisted down sadly. "As if he were a little goddamn dog!" Her voice was broken now but it was not pathetic, it came out strong and harsh and through her teeth that way, came out as if she were trying to hold it in, hold back.

It seemed; it seemed as Maufat said once when they were going upriver to a picnic and at the last moment Leah and Cecil cursed and swore at each other so much that Lorne decided to leave without them, it seemed that "Those two ain't right for each other; they got married too young for sure." It seemed that way, as Maufat said. She and he cursing each other over and over on the front lawn, she holding the baby crying in her arms.

Stitches! "Leah gets awful depressed, awful darned depressed," as Irene said. And now her eyes blood red and dripping with mascara. She took the bottle up again and drank without pouring it into the glass this time, without the mix this time again. "But there's more to Leah than there is to him," as Irene said. "There's more to her and she gets awful darned depressed—when the baby come, do you remember —her mind wasn't on it and she wouldn't quit smoking at all, remember, and it was hard enough for her to quit drinking—the doctor had to order her twice, remember!"

As Irene said, and now they were at it again—the heat of Leah's face flushing up as she swallowed the vodka straight. Then she took up the orange drink for a chaser and swallowed it.

"Where is he now?" Cathy said.

"He's in there on the couch sleeping."

"No, I mean Cecil."

There was silence. The shadow of her frame resting almost distant on the green wall behind her, the shadow of the pint bottle half emptied. Cathy moved to the table also. The reflection from the naked bulb splittering its small light upon the table-cloth.

"You should put that away now," Irene said.

Maufat reached down for another beer, the last in the case, and with his right foot kicked it farther under the table.

"And you should put that away," she said again, though he opened it anyway and stared ahead to the window that looked out into the night, the oil barrel and the field.

"You know when he went back to Lester's field I was scared, I didn't know he was serious or not because he gets awful mad at times, like when he threw Ronnie against the stove he weren't himself, he come in the house there and looked mad even before he started talking. Then he started saying he weren't going back to work and if I tried to make him he'd go out west with Shelby. I didn't say a thing, I brushed past him with water for the sheets and then he got real mad cause he expected me to get mad. So like I told you he dumped the water over the floor and then started swearin and I started swearin and then he did it to Ronnie. But when he took the shotgun I got scared. Because you never know what he's going to do, you never know from one minute to the next with that temper of his, you just never know. I got scared but the hell with him I've had enough of that—I weren't going to chase him, nosirree. He couldn't get me to chase him—not like he used to—not runnin around caterin to him. That bastard what he is!"

"But where is he now then?" Irene said, her face whiter under the light.

"Leah, where is he now?"

"Well, he goes out tramping past me with that shotgun of his—the clip full. I watched from the window. When he went past me I said: 'Go on shoot yourself then I don't care go on then' and he said: 'Oh don't you worry shit-arse don't you worry.' Then I rushed over to Ronnie and put an ice-pack on it. I didn't think it was as bad as it was, that bastard. But then I started worrying cause you just never know and you shouldn't tempt anybody about those things. It would have made me look awful bad now if I hada tempted him into it. So he goes across Lester's field. Trampin right across it and swingin the shotgun back and forth, and Lester and Maude standin right there. I don't know he must have said 'hello' to them when he passed, because they sorta nodded in that funny way of theirs. And then looked at each other. But when he goes into the woods I got scared. It was still raining a little and the field that he crossed was wet, so for some reason I started getting these crazy thoughts that maybe he'd really do it. And then Ronnie's cut wasn't healin and I knew I had to take him up so I went out and got the car started and then come in and got him and brought him out with a blanket wrapped around him."

And she took the bottle up again, with nothing in her eyes now except something vague and distant, something she was remembering that was as pale as the green wall, that had taken the fire from her and the colour from her. But then suddenly, when she had finished pouring the drink, she began to laugh. Her face changed again, and she tilted back her head and chair and began to laugh. Maufat looked at Irene. He took the bottle and drank again. His eyes were narrow, looking. It was the narrow perplexed look of her father, like her father when he wouldn't put the five on his red six, when he would rather play it out himself, and the look of her mother, half-frightened.

"Well then Leah, what happened?" Irene said. "Leah what happened!"

Because she didn't laugh right. It wasn't right. It was first long and then short—it broke and was silent and then it started again as she tipped the chair back in place and stared at the colourless liquid in the glass, the thickness of it in the glass. Then she became silent as she stared; her lips tightened, quivering a little as they did so.

"Soon as I got Ronnie to the car I heard a shot, and I nearly jumped two feet in the air and then I felt suddenly real sick. I looked out across the field and Lester and Maude were looking at me. And I looked at them. I'm sure they were thinkin the same as me, and I felt real sick—because he told me he was going to do it and I said, 'go ahead then see if I care,' and you shouldn't tempt anyone like that. Then Lester starts fidgetin with that old hat of his, and for some reason I kept starin at that old hat. He and Maude kept looking to the woods. Then I kept saying, 'So then ya shot yourself—so then ya shot yourself.' And Ronnie started crying again—so I had to take him up there."

She stoped, her voice dropped off. The sound of the radio came from the upstairs.

"So maybe he did then," Maufat said stirring uneasily and looking toward Irene.

"No," she said, her voice a little angry. "Soon as I backed the car out I see him sneakin through the woods toward the back door. He couldn't even stay in the woods long enough to scare me, that bastard. So I ain't going home," she said. "I ain't going home."

"I suppose Lester and Maude have lots to talk about now," Irene said.

"Oh the hell with them—let them think what they want," Cathy said. "They're always saying stuff about people anyway and then Maude runnin to the priest every chance she gets."

"Shhh," Irene said.

Leah took the last sip from her glass, then set it down roughly on the table. She began to fidget with her hands; the fingernail polish that ran on her fingers, the few spots on her nails that she had missed. Under the light they all cast shadows faint and broken one within the other, so that all the shadows seemed to meet and splinter with the light. Her hair smooth and pinned back tight with that golden hair brooch she wore at times when she was going out. Her hair back that way made her face a little pointed. She wore it long before; before it had flipped under and lap upon her shoulders, and once when she was sliding with them her winter slacks and her hair like that dancing out as the toboggan went down—she looked beautiful then; then as the toboggan overturned and the snow powder came up about her, laughing as she lay there the snow powder landing lightly and resting on her good teeth and naked belly, laughing then as if it all were laughing with her. The clean cold blue air of winter.

"Let them say what they want," Leah said. "I suppose Annie, if she had her mind, poor old soul, could tell us lots about them."

"Yes, I suppose she could," Irene said.

Maufat stood and began to replace the empty bottles in the case. It was two now and still the sound of the radio from upstairs. They were silent again, only the sound of the radio and the sound of her father, his breathing a little heavy, shuffling back and forth.

Then Irene stood and began to clear the table. Maufat turned and went inside, stopping and turning at the door.

"Well, I'm going to see him tomorrow—that's what I'm going to do; I ain't going in to work tomorrow, I'm going up and see him before eleven, that's what I'm going to do."

"Now don't you go startin it all over again," Irene said.

"I ain't going to be startin anything *over* again!" Maufat said. "Anyone that does that—anyone that'd go and do that is crazy for sure."

"Well, it won't do any good anyway," Leah said.

"No, it won't," Irene said. "Cept start a big hullabaloo over it all again. If Leah can't do anything with him you're better off stayin out of his way."

"Someone has to get sense into his head," Maufat said. "Beatin up on a child like that is what I think." He stood standing, his hand running back and forth along the door, not looking their way, looking away to the dark inside where the child slept.

Then he turned instantaneously and was gone, the creaking of the stairway from the dark room.

"Well, I'll get those sheets and pull that couch out," Irene said.

Leah said nothing, still staring at the liquid. The youngness of her damp now like her eyes. Then she straightened all at once and put the bottle away, into her purse, and stood up rapidly. The liquor had made her look unhealthy. It was in her face as if it were all at once gone yellow and drawn. Then she straightened and drew in her breath and smiled rapidly.

"No, I think we'd better go."

"Leah," Irene said. "You stay here."

"No, we'd better go and see the old bastard, that's what we'd better do."

"It's after two now," Cathy said.

She moved out from her side of the table, stumbling a little, running her hands along her skirt as if to smooth it down, looking beyond her skirt at the dotted floor.

"No now, I'll go get those sheets down," Irene said. "You can't go driving across that bridge tonight anyhow."

"No," Cathy said. "Anyway Ronnie's asleep."

She looked at them. It was as if she wanted to talk to them all over again. It was as if she wanted to talk to them and then lie down. Her left hand clutched at the black purse tightly.

"Oh I don't care about him anyway—it just isn't fair for Ronnie."

"What?" Irene said.

"Everything—everything isn't fair for Ronnie. If it was just us— boy, that bastard; I'd be on a bus tomorrow—I'd be on a bus yesterday." She slumped a little in her stance as if the will that had been holding her straight and tight like that had given away to something else. She kept moving her purse against the left side of her skirt.

33

It was because everything was said and they couldn't say anymore. They stared at her. Cathy's eyes were tired—her head dizzy under the splintered light, the shadow of the fridge and stove reaching out almost to the centre of the floor. It made her more tired. Like swimming tonight with the beer; it was good, clean. It was as if she could swim forever—across to the island off the distant point. It was as if everything was clean, the brown dark water, the mud and seaweed dripping on her legs. Now it was the room, only it was Leah too. It made her tired suddenly, like the remembrance of some inside sickness growing with its roots from inside the head or guts. The casting of some dim uncertain shadow when she walked through the doorway.

"I'll get the sheets," Irene said. She moved out and was gone upstairs before any more was said.

Leah slumped past her, rubbing her right hand against her nose, smiling a moment from the side of her mouth. The warmth of her was still there, the smell of her perfume touching the air.

"And how are you making out?" she asked, then without waiting for a reply she went into the bathroom and shut the door.

But she wore her hair down then. That day she was bathing Ronald under the bridge. She was saying, "Swim now swim," and his little legs throttling the more she said it, because he wasn't afraid to get wet like some other children. "Ronnie's not afraid for sure—he isn't afraid I'll tell you that," Leah said, and Cathy came and sat under the bridge to watch them. Then Leah came out of the water with her brown legs shining with the moisture, holding him above her head and laughing, spinning him above her head, her hair long down about her shoulders. She said:

"How are you making out—where's everybody?"

And Cathy turned around on the rock to let her sit.

"I don't care where the heck they are," Cathy said.

"Now," she said. She took her hair up and ran her fingers through it, the wet of her fingers making it a little darker.

"Oh, they all went fiishin with Angela's father and last year they took me when they went and this year they didn't—and last night Angela said: 'We're going fishing tomorrow Cathy, ha ha—and Daddy's got a boat!' As if I'd care about a stupid old boat—I don't give a heck where they are, that's for sure."

"I remember you going fishin last year," Leah said. "I remember that—Irene helped you dig the worms; you got a fish, didn't you?"

"I got the biggest there," Cathy said. "Two minutes and I got the

34

biggest there."

"Well, that's why in hell they didn't take you," Leah said. She was watching Ronald crawl toward the low shoreline, her eyes straight ahead.

"That's for sure," Cathy said.

Leah went and picked Ronald up again and brought him back. "I remember Irene saying that," Leah said again. She took the cigarettes from her purse and lit one, blowing the smoke into the silence before them, the water almost stilled with thin white waves. Then without speaking, and with her mouth breaking out into a short smile, she handed it over. She didn't speak, but looked at the water, where every time a car passed over, pebbles and dust fell on it like spray. Even when Cathy took it she didn't speak, only her lips curled a little at the side of her mouth.

"You won't tell," Cathy said.

"Tell what?" Leah said.

"I used to smoke lots of times," Cathy said.

Leah looked at her, smiling. "Oh damn, he's goin toward that water again," Cathy said.

Then they started laughing. Cathy started laughing, every nerve inside her giddy. She kept blowing the smoke in front of her as Leah went to bring the child back.

"I smoke in the shed," Cathy said. "Behind Annie's there I have them hidden there sometimes."

Leah looked inside her purse.

"You want your nails painted?" she said.

"What?"

"You want me to paint—look like mine?" she said.

"Sure," she said. "Only I'm gonna go swimmin after."

"That don't matter," Leah said. She took Cathy's hand and rubbed her right hand along the fingers. "You have good nails," she said, her own hands warm and brown and quiet. "They'll look good when I paint them."

Ronald was going toward the water again.

"He isn't afraid of nothing, is he?" Leah said.

"That's for sure," Cathy said.

Leah stood again and went after him. When she came back she brought a beer with her that she had been cooling in the water. She sat on the rock and held the baby, opening the ale while she did so. Cathy was blowing the smoke before her in listless patterns. They were silent. The smell of the mill had come in, and the wind was growing a little from the east side of the bridge.

"What would Irene say if I gave you a drink?" Leah said, "S'pose nothin eh?"

"S'pose nothin," Cathy said, "I get drinks from Maufat lots a times."

Leah handed it to her and she took a drink, small and bitter in her mouth. Then Leah took the file and the polish and turned toward her.

"We'll go for a walk then," Leah said. "After I finish the nails we'll go for a walk down the shore if you want—to the store if you really want."

"Way down there?" Cathy said.

"Only if you want," Leah said.

She painted the nails silently, the bright red polish going on smooth and silent, and before she started each nail she filed it a little, rounding it out smooth and short.

"I wish I had long nails," Cathy said.

"All you have to do is stop biting them, that's all—let them grow out, just stop biting at them, and file them too every little bit and then they'll be real pretty."

But when her nails were done and dried they didn't look so good as Leah's, the polish seemed to crack on them, not like Leah's, and her nails weren't as long or as fine.

Then they went swimming and dried in the sun, the breeze from the east side of the bridge on their skin a little cool.

"Do you want to go to the store now?"

"Sure."

"Well wait—I have another beer in the water, just you wait until I finish that and then we'll go."

So they started out and walked down from the bridge to the point where the cove broke into open water, where the water was rougher and washed against them as they went round. Leah carried the baby asleep against her shoulder, her purse in her left hand swinging back and forth.

They walked down a long way almost without speaking, the sky above them blue and high and cloudless, but the clouds to the east would be blown in, the waves now swelling from that direction against the rocks, the rocks wet grey with the splashing of the waves, some jutting so that they had to be careful not to cut themselves when rounding. Then they came to the breakwater and climbed upon the shore road walking back up to it, the wind at their backs, her hair blowing about and against the baby's cheeks.

"He'll sleep anywhere," Leah said. "He's real good like that."

"That's for sure," Cathy said.

"I'll tell you what I don't like, swimming here on the shore—I used to all the time but I don't like to anymore."

"Why not?" Cathy said. They had turned and were walking up the short sideroad toward the store. Here it was silent, here the spruce and maples held them, the odd white pine rising up above the rest, solitary and sturdy so that the east wind, as yet, couldn't toss their highest branches. And here it was hotter—the smooth silence of a summer afternoon in among the woods away from the water.

"Well I'll tell you—do you swim there a lot?"

"Sure, sometimes," Cathy said. "I swim there at night sometimes because the waves are real big there at night."

"Well I used to swim there all the time too, until one night I was down there swimming with Mary—do you remember Mary?"

"I'm not sure."

"Well, she's a girl that used to live here, her mother is a real good friend of Irene's, and Annie's too, cept Mary is moved away now so you mightn't know her. We were real good friends."

"Oh."

"But we used to swim here at the shore lots of us all the time during the summer, cept one night Mary and I come down alone to swim, just before it got too dark and as we were walking around Old Face to the sand we looked down and we saw something in the water— Mary saw it first, it had come in with the tide and was washed up just where sometimes when the tide's low we build the fire—but the tide was high and it was washed up—guess what it was?"

"Somebody," Cathy said.

"No—sorta," Leah said. "Sorta, it was a dog drowned, a real nice purebred dog drowned in the water, and some of the fur was all off it and you could see its bones." Leah turned to her, "So I never swim there now."

"Would the water be poison?" Cathy said.

"Oh not *now*," Leah said rapidly. "Oh no, not now—you can swim there now; the water's probably real clean, you could swim there."

"Whose dog was it?"

"I don't know—but we ran and got Cecil and Shelby." She turned toward Cathy again. "And they came and got it and threw it in the dump but I don't know whose dog it was."

"Oh," Cathy said, "I know a boy who smashed an eel on a rock and then put it on a stick and kept twirling it around so he'd frighten Karen and me, but only Angela was frightened, cause she's frightened of everything."

"An old eel wouldn't frighten you," Leah said laughing.

They went into the store and Leah spent money on her.

Irene said: "Now I don't want you bummin off Leah; she don't have money for you to go bummin off her." "I never do—I never do anyway," she said. But Leah bought her things and they left the store and began to walk toward the highway. The highway was hot and silent, the air seeming to press up from it, the shadows of the spruce casting faint on its dark heat. She could see her house in the distance, and behind that, off behind the field, the house of her grandmother.

"How's Annie now?" Leah asked.

"Mom says she isn't too strong anymore."

"I'll have to visit her soon then," Leah said.

Ronald woke and shifted his arms on her shoulder and raised his head, looking from side to side. After a minute Leah said:

"I'm tired of carrying him—could you for a while?"

"Sure," Cathy said. "If he don't fall."

"Oh he won't fall," Leah laughed. She turned and went to hand Ronald over and then she stopped suddenly and turned to look behind her. A car had been following them slowly all this time, its right wheels on the shoulder of the road. They hadn't even noticed. As soon as they turned the horn started honking loudly. There were four men.

The car then pulled sharply out beside them and stopped. They kept staring at Leah who held the baby silently in front of her.

"What's this—what's this, you got a kid now?"

Leah didn't speak.

"You don't remember me?" the man said.

She kept staring at them; Cathy kept staring but she didn't speak. Only one of the men was speaking, the one on the far side of the back seat leaning over.

"So you got a kid now eh, and you don't remember me—are you married?" The men laughed. The horn started honking. The highway was silent.

Then they were all silent. Leah kept staring, unflinching, holding Ronald a little in front of her. A smell of heat and gas from it, its engine running.

"No, ser—seriously now, you don't know me, Niles—remember

me?" She glanced down at Cathy, her face blank as if something was there behind the blankness. Something there as she looked down so that she glanced to the man in the car again, quickly saying:

"No not really—I don't think. . ." Her voice was dry, not like it had been before when they were alone along the shore, when they were talking, when she was painting Cathy's nails. Not like that, so that Cathy kept staring at Ronald, his little face wide and reddish.

"Christ now—I come home, home now, here I am after being away for four years, four years I come home and you, I pick you out anywhere, anywhere and you don't even remember my name."

"Okay, okay," another man said.

"I'd pick her ass out anywhere," he said.

"Okay, okay let's go," another man said. Cathy kept staring at Ronald.

"Ya bitch my name is Niles," he said. "An yours is Leah—horny little Leah."

She brought Ronald up against her. Cathy looked up at her blank face. Then she nudged Cathy and they began to move away, walking along the side of the road rapidly.

"Home after four years—after four years, eh," the man shouted.

They kept walking. "Well, are ya married ya slut—or is that the one I give ya?" They kept walking. Then the car started again to follow behind them. Cathy was staring at a thousand pebbles, each different, she was staring and walking quickly because Leah was walking quickly. Then the car started honking again, it started honking behind them. The highway silent heat. Then the car sped out around them, the dust coming up against their faces, its wheels tearing at the pavement. They said nothing as they walked; the car was gone now out of sight as it roared across the bridge. Leah seemed to be staring after it for a long time. Cathy kept glancing at the baby, at her and then at the ground. As they neared the house Cathy laughed quickly.

"They musta been drunk, eh?"

"They musta been," Leah said.

"That's for sure," Cathy said.

There were ways in which she slept that seemed so soundless and undisturbed. Her hair was shorter now and streaked a little but as she slept curled beside Ronald she looked almost a child herself, and she fell into this sleep immediately after Irene had brought down the sheets. They went into the kitchen as soon as she had.

"I may as well get into these dishes now and get them over," Irene said.

"Not tonight?" Cathy said.

"Yes, I may as well get them done."

"How's Annie?"

"I don't know—the same I guess as always—it probably should be any time."

"It should be," Cathy said. Irene began to run the water, the blackness of the night against the kitchen window. It was two-thirty. "She should leave him and go away somewhere," she said slowly.

Irene didn't answer, as if she hadn't heard. Cathy turned and went to bed. There were sounds of the radio low from his room so as she passed it she stopped, listened. It was as if he were asleep.

"Orville."

No answer.

"Orville—you hear me, you don't run that on the batteries, you hear me—I'm takin it back tomorrow, you hear me?"

3

He woke from his pacing back and forth and back and forth, through the two small rooms adjoining one another. He had been doing that for how long? Hours? Muttering and cursing. Cursing and muttering. And then when he looked down at his scarred hand and saw the shotgun with the clip still in it, the safety undone—ready to undo him— he woke from his rambling and cursing, threw the shotgun off to the side of the couch and returned abrutly to the kitchen. "Ah yes, ah yes, ah yes," he kept repeating without realizing what he was saying. "She don't know nothing, nothin—not a thing that goddamn slut she don't know nothin nothin bout me and she never has cause why, cause she's a bitch that's why cause why cause she's nothin but a goddamn bitch cause why cause her only thing is herself cause why cause she's too stupid that's why." He returned to the kitchen and leaned against the stove. The tub remained back end against the corner, the water over the floor, the sheets strewn atop the counter. He looked at his watch— it had stopped again, it just wouldn't go for him. He had given it to Shelby and Shelby said: "Works fine on my wrist so maybe it's your wrist."

"If a watch is going to work it's going to work," he said. "And if it ain't—it ain't, so don't talk so goddamn foolish will ya."

"Well it works fine on me—listen, ha, hear it tickin."

"Well, give it back then, ya bastard ya."

"What?"

"I said give it back ya bastard."

But it was not going now—he held it to his ear. Nothing. It was supposed to be waterproof and shockproof and nothing. He took it off his wrist and shook it and then put it against his ear; still nothing. "Goddamn," he muttered. "Damn," he muttered. He threw it upon the counter.

It was still light out but the light was fading so it was nearing nine —yes it must be nine; and where was she the bitch—didn't care about his supper, didn't care if he starved or not. His stomach was burning that way again. He threw the child just to throw him, just to make sure she knew he would throw him, because it was her, it was, and the child went right over that way, almost as if it had it planned. It didn't cry at first, not until she started on him and then of course it started. A little cut and it started bellowing like a sick cow just to make him feel bad because it was her, it was. "Cause why," he kept saying—"cause she's a bitch that's why—and after what I done for her, went and almost sacrificed my life for her—oh she goes sittin in the car that way and me havin to go in there—*oh I forgot the stove you go get the stove.*"

He went over to the sink and spit in it and ran the water. His eyes were narrow and tight, sunken in his brooding face. "So she's the one that drove me to it—she is, and if I hada done it (I shoulda, I shoulda, I shoulda) and if I hada can I imagine makin her look some bad. *Oh how did poor Cecil die? Shot hisself. Shot himself? Yes. Now why would Cecil have to do a thing like that?* He spit into the sink again and shut the tap off. Then he began to turn the sheets over and over. There was nothing under them. Then he looked into the breadbox. Nothing. His watch had fallen from the counter and lay in the water on the floor. Nothing in the house to eat except perhaps stale pastry. He looked inside the jar and grabbed three molasses cookies, stepping back over the water and going outside.

It was warm still and smooth and calm. He walked out the gate and up along the highway, the cars already with their lights on passing him and he turning to watch the light now and then, his mouth full, his stomach still brooding and burning. But it was night now and the flies were out—they came at him around his head swarming as he walked. Lester's upstairs light burned—the downstairs and the yard shut out and blackened, the long grass of the field that he had walked through calm once more, and silent once more except for the night sounds that increased the silence. The good smell of the freshness of it. The flies came at his face scars. The taste of the asphalt of the road.

"Get outa here, go on ya black son of a whore!" He kept slapping at them and scratching as he walked. They were on his hands and face as he ate the cookies. "Sure I'll check the stove, ya bitch—ya hear that ya bitch? Sure I'll check the stove. And it the coldest son-of-a-whore a winter and me going in there and she waitin in the car so warm that I hada warmed for her. Sure, check the stove—check the fuckin stove. No man in his right mind stay with her—no man in his right mind put up with it—I'll slap ya, ya bitch I'll slap ya—I shoulda done it I shoulda I shoulda. I shoulda stayed in the woods longer, made her come and get me—make her find out herself. If Lester and that old bitch hadn'ta been pokin their fuckin faces in another people's business that woulda been it! That woulda been it!"

He muttered and cursed as he went. "Seven jesless years," he kept saying. "Seven jesless years." When he came to the crossroads he turned back toward the settlement and walked about a mile. There were no streetlights along the road. It was black tar, the smell of it and the night all around and the trees right out in clumps along the road, the flies still swarming as he walked. His walking slowed. Now and then he stared at the sky spotted with stars and the moon up high.

"All I need now to make my day is to meet a skunk or somethin."

"All I need now to make my day is to meet a fuckin skunk."

When he came to the hill he began to run—he hadn't run in a long time and so when he reached the bottom he stopped abruptly, breathing heavily and already sweating, an intense pain in his side. He waited for a moment and then he walked the path to the gate and up to the door. He pounded on it heavily, venting his rage upon it. No answer. He knocked again just as hard.

"Cecil?"

"I come to get a cigarette and a beer and not for your face."

"I ain't got no beer."

"Well, I come for a cigarette then."

"Where's the *one*."

"Don't know—don't care."

Shelby let him in and led him to the kitchen. The dishes undone piled in the sink. Shelby was smaller—came to his shoulder, the smell of him through the place. He threw a package of cigarettes on the table.

"So then, where are all the women you always say you *always* have here?"

"None here tonight."

"None ever here either ya bastard."

"Don't believe me if you don't want to," Shelby said. He was looking about for an ashtray.

"Oh cept squaws—I'd believe you'd stoop to squaws."

"Don't believe me if ya don't want to."

"Shit."

"Don't believe me."

"I don't."

"Don't."

There was almost a ringing from the outside still with him, its air still with him, the fly-bites everywhere and reddish on the reddish scars along his thick and almost callous arms.

"So ya didn't tell her then did ya, or did ya then?" Shelby said.

"A course I told her—she started her bitchin."

"Ya didn't tell her right," Shelby said.

"No what are you, some sorta goddamn woman expert or something —how ya supposed to tell her, you ain't married to the fucker so how do you know bout it, so don't tell me about it."

"Ya shoulda said, 'Leah, we ain't been gettin along too good lately' "

"I know what I shoulda said—and what I didn't say, and it don't have nothin to do with none of that shit."

Shelby handed him the ashtray. Cecil kept scratching at his scars, making the redness white then red again.

"Well, I'm leavin right soon as the exhibition is over—so you comin or not?"

"We'll see, we'll see—I'm in no big rush to decide about it one way or the other."

"The exhibition is next week."

They were silent again.

"What time is it now?" Cecil said.

"Ten o'clock—it's right there on the wall."

"I'm not blind," Cecil said.

"Where's your watch?"

"I left it home."

"Well, you didn't handle it right is what I think."

"I don't give a sweet Christ what you think. Oh Cecil, you should come up some night—oh yes, women up here every night just wantin it, just *cravin* it."

"I don't care if you don't believe me."

"I don't."

"Well don't."

"You got anything to eat?" he said quickly staring across to the dishes, to the cupboards half opened, to the clock above the cupboards, its second hand monotonous and silent, red and continuously moving.

"Make yourself a sandwich if you want."

"No never mind."

"So you don't know if you're coming or not?"

"I said what I said, that I haven't decided."

"Well, you should say 'Leah, I'm going out west until the end of the summer and then I'm comin back in the fall and we can start the store again.'"

"I ain't startin no Jesus old store again—you can see where it got me last time; almost blew up, that's where it got me."

"No, no but you could tell her that."

"Ain't tellin her nothin."

"Suit yourself."

Shelby rose and plugged in the kettle, and stood there with his arms folded watching the steam rise, the steam rising and whitening against his short blunt face.

"Well, I come up here for somethin," Cecil said.

"What then?" Shelby turned back toward him.

"I come to see if you were still selling that bicycle."

"I'll sell it if you'll buy it."

"How much?"

"$15."

"Well, I wouldn't·be able to pay you right yet."

"When then?"

"Well, before you leave—or when we both leave, whatever I decide."

"In a week then."

"Ya, when you leave you'll have the money."

Shelby stared at him momentarily and then pulled the kettle plug. He came back to the table to take a cigarette.

"It's out here in the back," he said.

Cecil rose and followed him to the shed.

"It's got good tires and a good frame on it," Shelby said.

"Oh I ain't so sure of that," he said.

"Well, if you ain't sure of that you ain't sure of nothin."

"$15."

"Not a penny less," Shelby said. "Not a penny less."

"Suits me anyway," Cecil said. He picked the thing up and carried it through the shed door. Shelby followed him, his hands in his pockets. The moon was up and all the stars were out high and spotted in the black. Cecil lit a cigarette he had in his hand, putting another one in his shirt pocket. He got on the thing.

"You're too big for that," Shelby said.

He didn't answer. He spit into the dirt and looked around. The woods were so close and black now, the sound of frogs. Years before he had stolen his cousin's bicycle and coming down across the turn it had lost its chain and he had lost control of it. Smashed the front end and twisted the handle-bars—years before. Before Leah, years before Ronnie, years before. He stayed on the thing.

"Are you going to talk to the *one* again then?" Shelby said.

"Oh I will, I will—I'll let you know."

"You're sittin on fifteen bucks," Shelby said.

"You'll be sittin on your arse," he said. He spit again. Then he began to pedal, slow at first, uncertain. Shelby walked behind him to the gate, hands in his pockets, the cigarette butt glowing in front of his short blunt face.

When he got out on the roadway he got off to walk it up the hill. Shelby had stopped and was staring at him from the gate.

"Are you going to talk to her again?"

"Say goodbye to all the women in there for me," Cecil said. He began to move slowly up the hill.

"Remember that fifteen bucks," Shelby said.

He turned. Shelby's face was gone, only the distant shadow and the cigarette flicking; its glow flicking back and forth to show where Shelby's hand was. He kept his cigarette in his mouth.

"Say goodbye to all the women in there, playboy."

"Don't believe me then."

"I don't."

"Don't then."

He turned and kept walking until he reached the top of the hill. He dropped his cigarette and spit into the dirt.

"Fifteen bucks," Shelby yelled. "And I don't care if you smash it on the way home, it's still fifteen bucks."

He didn't answer.

"Don't believe me then," Shelby yelled.

He got on the thing again and began to pedal. It came back to him
—he pedalled faster, the air cooling against his face, against the thickness of his scarred arms. "I'll say Ronnie, look what I bought you—
it's time you had one is what I'll say and how'll that make her look,
the slut won't even cook my supper, won't even *cook* it."

It was easy now; it was good to pedal. It was as if along the main
highway he could go forever, the night breaking and cooling against
him the way it was. All open—the dark fields to the water and the
lights on the opposite shoreline.

It was good pedalling until he came to his house again. He saw in
the distance there were no lights. He came closer, the car gone, the
dirt drive empty and soft brown. It was because they were gone—it
was because of that. It was no good anymore because he had wanted
to go in and say, "Ronnie, look what I got ya!"

He carried the bike into the kitchen and placed it against the stove.
He went over to the counter and dug out more cookies to eat, picking
his watch out of the water before he did so and putting it to his ear.
He wound it tight again and set it on the sheets. The tub remained
back end against the corner. He set it straight and then went to the
closet for the mop.

He began to mop the floor aimlessly, in aimless circles, the water
grasping within its substance the substance of the dirt, wringing the
mop dry and beginning again. Muttering half-heartedly in the dark:
"It's her, it's that damn Irene, I'm going ta phone her and let her know
my wife ain't gonna run all over hell just cause we had an argument—
I'll say 'Keep her down there then if ya hada raised her right she
wouldn't—' " He stopped short and threw the mop to the side, it standing aimlessly on its own for a second and then dropping with a thud
to the floor. He began to open the cupboards. Each one that he opened
he searched. He turned around and stared at the bicycle. He kept
scratching his arms.

"I don't want you going up there," Irene said.

"I'm gonna go now, I told ya all that last night," Maufat said.

He bent over to do his boots up. Leah came out of the bathroom
and stood by the door, her face tired. Ronnie was still at the table eating.

"I won't do no good cept start a big hullabaloo about it all over
again," Irene said.

"You don't have to come up," Leah said.

"I want to talk to him anyway myself."

Leah put on her sweater and smoothed her skirt. Still the warmth of her drawn flesh, in the air the scent of a young woman.

"Are you ready Ronnie?"

"Now don't rush the boy," Irene smiled.

Ronnie got up from the table. He was pale and white and tended to look like his mother, his hair almost blond white, his eyes grey and quiet. He didn't speak and came over to stand beside Leah.

"How are you this morning dear?" she said.

"Good," he said. He stood there with his hands in his pockets looking up at Maufat.

"Well, are you ready then?" Maufat said.

"Did you tell them at work?" Irene said.

"I'm going in this afternoon—I'm going in this afternoon. I'll say I missed my drive and there's little they can do about it. I've been there long enough not to care what they do," he added.

Leah and he and Ronald went outside. The car was still wet with dew. It sat at the side of the house where the sun hadn't been, the tires damp on the grass. It was a day; the sky clear and fresh, sharp bright features to the treeline and the houses, to the fields that lay between.

"I've gotta get a car," Maufat said.

Ronald wasn't talking; he said nothing on the way up, he moved not a muscle in the back seat, he did nothing save stare out the window, to the island beyond the cove as they crossed the bridge, to the old house that faced the shale incline on the point closest to the water. The water was bright and waveless.

Leah drove fast—she always did; there was always something that made her want or need to drive like that, swinging into the turns with her foot down on the accelerator. Maufat kept his hands against his lap, his face showing a grey-black beard starting.

She turned into her drive, the sound of the small tires hitting the dirt, the dirt loosening and scattering behind the wheels. The house looked dead, quiet, its white paint chipped and fading and the blinds and curtains drawn tight, shutting out the day and the view they had of who was in there.

So he let her lead the way with Ronnie between them. They went in through the small makeshift porch that Cecil had constructed but when she went to open the door she found it locked. She had to knock again and again.

"Call his name," Maufat said.

"He can hear me," she said.

47

"Cecil," he called.

"He'll come," Leah said.

He came to the door and unlocked it, turning away as soon as he did so and going back to the table. They went inside and stood in the semi-coolness of the shadowed room. He stared at them from the table, his chair tipped back, his head cocked a little, his hard grizzled face tight upon them. He kept scratching at the scar marks on his arms.

"I see ya brought up a friend," Cecil said.

"I come up myself," Maufat said. He glanced at Leah. She went over and drew the window curtains back, put the blind and the window up. Cecil gazed at all of them. He picked up a molasses cookie and began to eat it.

"What do ya think of a wife who don't come home to cook your supper?" Cecil said. He kept eyeing Ronnie but he was addressing Maufat.

"Depends," Maufat said.

"On what?"

"On why she don't come home to cook my supper."

Cecil kept his chair tipped. The mop leaned against the table. His face was brooding and quick.

"Say now, Irene went out galivantin and never come home to cook your supper."

"Depends," Maufat said. "Depends on why she went out galivantin."

"Only one reason *she'd* go," Cecil said, "And that's to get drunk—was she drunk down there?"

Maufat looked at the boy, silent and white, sitting with his hands folded on a stool beside the door, at Leah unconcerned, putting the sheets in the tub and running the tap.

"No, she wasn't, but the reason she come down last night—well, we know why she come down."

"She wasn't drinking my vodka last night?"

"I don't know, I don't know but I know I *woulda been* Cecil banging at a boy like that."

"How's your eye, Ronnie?" Cecil said. He glanced over at Leah, her back turned.

Ronnie didn't answer.

"How's your eye?" Cecil said.

"Good," Ronnie answered.

"If you can call stitches good," Leah said.

Cecil went over to the boy and crouching down peered at the closed gash above the eye: "It don't look too bad," he muttered. "It don't look too bad." Then he rose and stood, tall and heavy and thick-set.

"I can't understand why you did it that's all," Maufat said.

"Well, I had a bottle of vodka and it's gone now," Cecil said, "And I come home to talk to my wife about finding a new good job but she wouldn't listen—"

"For Christ's sake," Leah said.

"Now just a minute," Cecil said, his thick frame turning heavily on his feet. "Now justa goddamn minute, I come home to tell my wife that I want a better job and she won't listen, starts her screamin like that and I come home—it's my house I built the goddamn place and if I can't come home and talk to her without her screaming and gettin it all her way every time I try to do something, then I'm movin out and lettin her starve, and don't *you* kid yourself, MacDurmot, she'd starve."

"Then why did ya throw the boy that way if ya just wanted to talk?"

"Ronnie say that or she or what—goddamn Jesus yes, throw the boy, throw the boy, I never laid a hand on that boy in my life and it's no business of yours if I did. It's no business a yours, not a goddamn bit of it. But to get things straighter I never threw that boy no place, and if you were here you coulda seen that. She goes running and crying to Irene every time I get an idea about doing somethin, she goes runnin and crying—and lyin and fuckin lying bout what I did. I almost sacrificed my life for her but no more, no more, I'm not the kinda go look for trouble but the sweet Jesus don't you come up here and tell me what to do!"

"I ain't said nothing," Maufat said.

"Well don't," Cecil said. "Don't until you know who's lyin—don't come up here pickin sides."

"He ain't pickin no sides," Leah said. "Tell him how Ronnie got himself all cut then, tell him that if you're so big on the answers, ya bastard."

"Ya see ya see ya see," he said pacing back and forth, scratching at the scar marks on his arms, his face tight and heavy, his eyes quick. "Ya see what she's doin, don't ya—tryin to get Ronnie to hate me— ya see she's doin that, don't ya? I went to lift him out of the way—I went to lift him and he fell and hit the stove—I didn't want him havin to stand in the centre of the floor listenin to her go on. Yes fuck yes, I'm the bastard, the old prick, but whose vodka does she steal when she's goin out the door—whose vodka if it ain't mine?"

They were silent.

"No sir I didn't *throw* him against the stove."

He went over to her purse and took the bottle out. There was a little left, the transparent liquid, the label scratched by her hands as if a cat had dug into it. He took the top off and flung it past Maufat. It hit the side of the wall and shattered. Then he tipped the bottle and finished it and set it roughly on the table.

Leah walked past him and into the other room. Maufat said nothing. He didn't know, he didn't know what or how to say it. He had it planned but now he didn't know. The boy turned and went to go outside.

"Just a minute, Ronnie," Cecil said. "I got something for ya. I had it for ya yesterday afternoon when I come in here to talk some sense into your mother, to try and talk some sense into her, but I forgot all about it." His voice quieted. "I meant to give ya it then."

Ronnie stopped and turned toward him but said nothing. Cecil went out past him and into the yard. Leah came out with the shotgun in one hand and the clip in the other. She put it into the closet and shut the door.

He came back after a moment and brought it in through the door, his thin lips twitching at the corners where the scars hit. He said nothing and Ronnie said nothing. He brought it in and stared at them. Leah stood with her back against the closet, her head leaning against it and her eyes half closed.

"I got it for ya yesterday," he said. "It's a good bike, ain't it?"

The boy was still silent. He turned glancing to his mother, glancing to Maufat.

"It's time you had a bike—well time you did," Cecil said. "When I was your age I had three bikes—four bikes something like that." He laughed uncertainly. Maufat stood against the stove, his arms folded. Cecil picked up Ronnie and set him on it, his feet hitting the pedals, his hand on the handle grips. He stared ahead at Maufat. Cecil laughed again. "Well there," he said, "Well there—do ya know how to drive it, betcha don't do ya, betcha don't."

"Mom can teach me," Ronnie said.

"Christ I could teach ya—I could teach ya," Cecil said. "She don't know nothin bout it, nothin bout it at all," he laughed. "No she don't know nothin bout it for sure."

"How much did ya pay for it, Cecil," she asked.

"I got it from Shelby yesterday before I come home to talk to you," Cecil said quickly.

"How much did he charge ya?"

"$25 is all."

"Well, that's good then," Maufat said.

Leah went over to the stove and flicked the oil on and reached for the tea-kettle above the stove. The heat of the morning was pressing against the open window, the outside air burning and silent. Smelling the silence inside.

"You want tea," Leah said.

"No, no," Maufat said. "I guess I better start hikin along the road—I gotta be at work soon."

He hadn't said it, not said it at all. He turned and started out the door.

"You got a smoke I could have?" Cecil said.

"I got two in this package, here you take them then."

"Now I don't wanta take your Jesus last one," Cecil said.

"I got a fresh deck," Maufat answered.

He went out from the stale heat of the house into the bright of the day, the burning of it. "Shit," he kept thinking. "Shit." He went out the gate and began walking up the highway, the grasshoppers stiff and silent and deadened in the heat. He kept thumbing cars that passed him as he walked. "Shit," he kept thinking. "Shit."

4

They passed the elms that stood broad and hard, into the clover and then the burdocks and then the bog: cool even with the heat, cool and patched even with the sun like this on their half-brown backs, their tops loose against their shoulders.

The bog: wet even in the great heat, shaded from the heat by weeds damp and spineless with their growth. The sun splayed into it, setting off the patches to an even darker colour.

Here it was dark. It was cool. It rested outside the day as if it did not belong; set apart, melancholy in the solitude that she could sense stepping into it. The front of her top was down loose for the heat—Karen's half-red skin. The water was brown in the light; the muck balancing both extremities of the pool and their feet resting ankle-deep in the soft warm muck.

"I hate crossing just for berries; we shoulda saved some beer."

"We shoulda."

They laughed—then silence, the flies against their thighs they slapped at. Again and again the flies.

"Well let's move across or the flies'll eat us."

"Suppose?"

They crossed where the bog was driest, where the muck was cool half-clay in the shadows of the spineless trees. Nothing in here moved except the flies; water-spiders flicking in the ancient pool, the minute soundless ripples made by ancient forms. She came here at night during the first of autumn, it was good with the trees lit with the gold passing. Orville said: "Did you ever see a partridge in there?" "No." "Well, if you ever see one in there you come tell me where it is since you watch up at the trees anyhow—since you watch the stupid trees."

She crossed, Karen ahead, her feet making soft durable impressions in the clay. When they reached the opposite side they had a small hill to climb, through weeds leaning and drooling spit, through small briars that scratched at the bottom of her legs.

Then they were on the mound and the sun was brilliant hot again, the dust of the day and the shale-pit before them, the taste of pans and utensils rotting in the sun. She looked down at it: *when her mother was little she had a doll, when her mother was little the little doll was here in the pit with the utensils and pans. It would be winter and summer winter and summer winter again. Then they moved down from the field to where Annie lived now.*

But they didn't use the other dump, they never did. Irene said, "Maufat, load the trailer and take the garbage back." Others burned garbage, in the other dump at night they sometimes saw the inferno of it rising above the forest and resting on the sky. This was the dump that didn't burn, that sat and waited summer and winter and summer again. Now it was dry and shale-like in the heat, with a stench rising from it like a wave of heat itself, and beyond the pit the soft dry field and woodline.

There was no sound with the heat, there was nothing but the lack of sweat upon them. Karen's blouse-top tied around her belly and the buttons loosened, her half-red skin. They moved again, down the shale path carefully because of their feet, and walked across it, the shale rocks hot, passing the vacant barrel as hollow as the time it had been there. It was their dump; it was Maufat's barrel, or Annie's barrel, the ribs of it defaced and torn.

They came up the worn shorter path on the opposite side and then into the field with short sprouts of pine. Karen walked ahead again until she came to a small pine and dropped beneath it, leaning her head against it with her hand above her eyes as if not to admit the sun's glare. Irene said: "Would you come over today?" "No." "Why not?" "No—I wanta go pickin berries." The mole would be wrinkled red with the heat of the sun on the windows but it would be white when she was on the bed. Irene's face, white and sunless when her hands clasped the plastic spoon, and wiped with a napkin the mush from the corners of her wrinkled mouth. "Can'tcha get Laura?" "No." "Why can'tcha get Laura?" "Never mind then." "Or Betty—how bout Betty she never goes over." "Never mind—I'll go myself; I'll go myself!" She sat along the side of the tree staring down at her scratched legs browning to a darker brown, feeling the burn slant downward on her neck. Her short hair pinned back at the sides.

"You know Leah came over two nights ago?"

"Leah did?"

"And ya know what eh?"

"Cecil again like before?"

"Like before cept worse now," Cathy said. The needles under her were like blisters on her legs.

"How worse?"

"Real worse—" She stopped, laughed a little, because it came up from inside and she couldn't help it—not like she was supposed to help laughing at things that were that way. Like laughing at Annie in her senility almost. It was as if laughing at it would be laughing at Leah herself. "Real worse, ya know what he did eh; he took up Ronnie and smashed his head against the stove until Ronnie needed stitches from it, and then he threw water over the floor—" She stopped again. She would not go on. Karen handed her a cigarette and they smoked. Smoking in the heat made her dizzy; it made her close into something almost sad. They were silent for a while. Karen muttered, "It's too bad like that, it's too bad."

"And then guess what?"

"What?" Karen smashed the butt into the needles, the smoke sprouting and dying.

"I don't wantcha tellin no-one."

"What?"

"Don't tell no-one—he took up the shotgun and said he was gonna shoot himself."

"Oh, too bad he hadn'ta done it."

"Shhh," Cathy said.

"If I had a husband that acted the way he does I'd shoot him myself
—I wouldn't wait for him to shoot himself, cause I'd do it for him."

"Well, don't go tellin anyone."

"Oh, I wouldn't bother tellin anyone," Karen said.

"It's just that if it got around Leah wouldn't like it."

"Well, ya know," Karen began after another pause, "I don't even
like the look if him—I can't help it; he's just too scaly."

She turned to look at Cathy and then slid down upon her belly
facing her, lifting her reddish legs up, her reddish skin and the slightly
pointing face.

Cathy stirred slightly also, for a moment not knowing how to answer. *Leah said: everyone stares at another girl's boobs to see if theirs
are bigger.*

"He's not all scaly," she answered. "Just a little bit scaly but not all
scaly. He looked real good before the stove blew up that time; and
when he was married he looked real good. He just got like this after
the stove blew—oh, they fought a lot but not like now, not like after
the stove blew up. I remember Mom got real mad because Betty said,
'Oh they'll be fightin up the aisle and fightin back down again.' Irene
got mad at that—but he went a little strange after the stove blew up."

"He used to be real nice," Karen said. "Comin over and buyin us
ice cream on the beach and stuff like that."

"Oh, he's not so bad," Cathy answered. "Anyway Maufat went up
and straightened him out."

It was mid-afternoon with the sun hot upon them, the sweeping
branches of the small pine leading just down over them, affording
really no shade. They smoked and talked, smashing the butts in a small
circle into the faded needles spread around. She became dizzy and tired
and wished to swim.

"We should be in swimmin—ya know that," Karen said. "It's too
good a day to waste it."

They began to walk back down, crossing the field slowly.

"How long did your mom live back there?"

"Oh, till she was about sixteen or so—she used to have to walk out
the road in winter to school, it freezin—no plow'd get in this way ever.
They were the last ones that moved outa here."

The first shot startled them. There was no sound after the shot
sounded and faded. Karen kept in a twisted frozen position: "I hope
they're not aimin—" Then there was another one and she flinched
again.

54

"Well, let's go down—let's go down," Cathy said, moving out around her and leading the way, her feet moving quickly over the grass.

They came to the top of the pit, the gorged face of it sitting in the heat—and he, at the far end of it with the gun, poised solid on the rock.

"Oh shit, I thought Cecil had done it this time for sure," Karen said.

"I knew it wasn't a shotgun," Cathy answered. "I knew that."

He fired another time, unaware of them, the pan he was firing at resting on the shale slope to his right, the dirt and small rock spraying up around it as he fired, the sound of the echo in the still pit.

"I'm gonna sneak around on him," Cathy said. Karen said nothing; she stood watching, waiting where she was. Cathy moved downward into it, into its heat, into its open crooked face, stepping over the spoons and rusted things that splayed the ground, the rotted material of a skirt. The shale burned with the sun upon it the way it was; she moved, the shale burning at her feet. Quietly. He fired twice more, flicking the bolt back, the light shells dislodging and hitting the ground. Quietly. He fired again. She came up close behind him, the scorching of the powder as he fired.

"What are ya doin, Orv? What are ya doin, Orv?"

"I knew ya were there." He never looked, never moved.

"Sneakin Dad's gun out again, eh—sneakin Dad's gun."

"I knew ya were there."

Karen came down and stood beside them. Orville kept firing, his head straight, unleaning, and the black patch tied tight around his hair.

"Well, I don't think ya should be in the woods with it at this time a year—that's what Maufat says—so you'd better take it out."

He kept firing.

"He's gonna be mad if he finds out—if the police come they'll take it away, they'll take it away and you know that, you know that, Orv—so you'd better put it back."

He didn't answer.

"Orville," she said. "Orville."

There was a smell of powder lifting from the unoiled barrel of the gun. He undid the bolt quickly and stood walking away from them, in the direction of the bog. The pan remained dug into the side of the shale. They followed him. He moved quickly, his long legs moving up the slope. He disappeared over the mound.

"I was sure for a minute there that it was Cecil tryin it all over again," Karen said.

Cathy didn't answer. They were walking side by side and when they came to the slope she scrambled up it first to try and catch sight of him. But he was gone now out of sight behind the thick trees that enclosed the bog. They stood upon the mound for a moment. An anthill close to it built up over the years—the ants scurrying.

"I just don't want him to go nowhere else with it," she said.

He walked through the bog carrying the gun, darker now as the day spread; over their tracks that led in, back over the burdocks, parted and crumpled by their bodies and onto the road. He carried the gun barrel downward to the ground, his face straight, watching. It was a spotless quiet here; nothing moved in the mid-day.

After a time he could hear them coming out—their bodies moving in the burdocks.

"Orv," she called.

He kept looking straight ahead—straight to where the main road was, where the cars were passing. "They hada be back there, they hada be back there, they hada be."

He came out onto the main road—the dust the passing car made swirling up against his face. He turned round to them; they were far behind him now on the dirt road, their bodies tidy in the daylight, small in his eye. They walked side by side almost touching as they came toward him. *It was when he had his snowsuit on they carried him down over that hill running, seeing if they wouldn't fall because of the snow so deep, up to their middles that way. They carried him; he had one arm around Cathy and the other around her, on her red cap, the red hair flowing beneath it. And when they tripped and sprawled into it, the snow heavy-packed, he lost the patch. He wouldn't get up to face them. He lay face down breathing into it, searching to put his patch back on. He wouldn't lift himself. She said: "Orv, are you okay—are you good Orv, are you okay?" He kept searching for his patch and didn't get up. Until his hand found it wet and laced with snow. He put it back over because he didn't want her to see. Then he stood and left them, the snow in his neck cold and down the back of his snowsuit. "Orv." They ran after him. "Orv."*

They were walking toward him tidy and small in his one eye—their dim brown bellies fine and smooth.

He looked at their dim brown bellies and knotted shirts tied up high against the smoothness of their ribs slanting inward that way toward their low fine bellies in the heat. They were moving slowly past the trees and the trees were unmoving—and they too seemed unmoving on the soft dirt road. He stayed turned toward them and walked a few steps downward into the side drain. The cars still passing so he could feel the hot air off the asphalt of the road. They were talking to each other now, not looking.

"Well, I don't care if they do or not—I don't give a Jesus if they do or not."

He took the bolt out of the rifle and put it in his pocket with the shells. He turned and looked downward past his house. The car that had passed him no more than a distant spot, the kitchen window where, if Irene was home, she would be looking was blank and glaring. He couldn't tell if she was home. She was at Annie's for the feeding. He loosened his pants, undid them so that they fell down a little, his white skin in the white glare of the sun. "I don't give a Jesus if they see or not—they hada be there, both a them they just hada be."

The rifle rested in his hand, its barrel partially invisible in the dry weeds. He had to undo his pants farther. They weren't looking and a car on the bridge was moving across. A car on the bridge moving across. He twisted a little trying to watch both ways. He lifted the rifle, barrel down. The car was coming across the bridge and in an instant she saw; both saw. She yelled: "Orv—Orv what are you doing; you pull your pants up, what are you doing, Orv—Orville." Karen stopped still on the dirt road watching. He moved a little farther into the drain, trying to put the rifle in now so fast that the sight gouged at his thin right leg. "Oh fuck it fuck it I don't care." He put the rifle in and the rifle stock beneath his shirt. The car was coming alongside him and he was doing up his pants, his flesh thin and glaring like bone. It seemed he was bleeding on the leg. "Oh fuck it fuck it I don't care." He could only see the car at the corner of his eye. Cathy was running up, her woman body with the woman motion running. And he was trying to pull up his pants.

Then the car passed him, its horn blowing. Dust coming up in the heat. He cursed again. She was running, her belly as tight as the knot in her shirt, woman motion. He had his pants up when she came to him but it was as if the heat of the day was the warmth of the blood out of his gouged right leg. "Fuck it—I ruined the sight, that's what I done."

He turned out of the drain and began to make his way downward with the right leg paining.

"What in God's name are you doing?" She was walking behind him breathing, her chest, he thought, heaving with the sweat.

But he didn't answer. It was blood running down the right leg, the black unoiled barrel of the gun.

"What are you doing, Orville; what are you doing?"

He kept limping toward the house, she behind him. Then he turned abruptly to see her. Karen stood at the turn-off watching, her blouse buttons unloosened for the heat. *When they were in the bath he said: "I haveta pee." Irene said: "Karen and Cathy are takin a bath." "I have ta pee." "Go outside, it's dark." "No." "Well then wait." "I'll pee on the floor—I will." "Go outside, it's dark." "No." Then Irene said: "You two close the curtain cause Orville's comin in ta pee—ya got the curtains closed cause he's comin in ta pee?" He could smell them in the tub and they were splashing and playing in the tub and he could smell the steam and the soap, the steam rising off the pinkness of them in the tub. He tore the curtain back, the water soft grey in the light—he couldn't see and they screamed and screamed. Irene came in and he ran outside without his coat.*

Karen stood at the turn-off, her blue shorts in the daylight, the soft tightness of them—she was watching.

"What in God's name are you doing Orv?"

"I'm going home."

"What were you doing when you had your pants down—are you crazy—are you crazy?"

He looked at her face, brown and smooth, red where the flies had sucked above her forehead, red where she had scratched at the flies sucking into her forehead. Karen was walking down.

"For cops," he said.

"What?"

"For cops won't find the gun," he said. He was looking at her suddenly angry, for his insides moving him speechless, for his throat.

"Christ—right, holy Christ—right in the middle of everywhere ya take down your pants ta hide the gun."

Karen was up to them now. It was as if she was grinning, standing behind Cathy, a little taller. He turned from them and walked downward. Cars passed. He could hear them talking, coming behind him, Cathy talking. He walked as fast as the rifle would allow, painfully limping, the stock breaking into his ribs, making them sore. When inside he slipped the rifle out quickly and set it against the wall below his father's raincoat. There was blood on the barrel and pointed sight so he took some napkins from the kitchen drawer and began to clean it. Cathy and Karen came in and stood behind watching for a moment before going inside. He had his back turned and they couldn't see what he was doing.

When he went back into the kitchen they were gone to her room, quiet laughter that filled the house. He wet a facecloth and went upstairs also, along the small hallway, to his room above the back porch, with the window overlooking the dry path and heated field, the mustard weed, the scent of it in the night rising. He turned on the radio and undid his pants, running the wet cloth along the already-drying blood, exposing the gouge and the scar that ran like a short tail almost to the muscle of his knee.

His room was white and empty, the roof slanting above his bed, the dresser mirrorless and confused, the drawers opened crooked to the right and left. He finished with the cloth and threw it against the wall. He took off his patch and held it up, looking. It was alright, it was dry. He lay on the bed with his patch off staring, his patch in his left hand, the delicate soft woman voice of Karen.

"We're going swimming—you wanta come?" Cathy said. He started, the music from the radio. He clutched his patch, bringing his left hand quickly over his eye.

"You don't come in here."

"Well, we're going out swimming—you wanta come?"

"No—and don't you come in here." He moved the lace of the patch around his head, drawing it tight behind.

"I'm not comin in—I'm just askin a question—just askin a question."

"No."

"Don't then—don't then, but you tell Mom where I am if she starts askin."

He went out to the gateway after dark and was about to turn downward. There were three in the car, the girl was in the middle. They had slowly passed the house before when Irene said: "Do you know whose car that is?" He said: "What car?" Though he knew it had been passing. And now it stopped, heading upward, beside him just as he was going out. When the boy got out and stood beside him on the gravel, his hair black and his face lifting and rough.

"Where's Cathy?"

"Don't know."

"Are you her brother?"

He nodded.

"Is she swimmin?"

"Don't know."

The boy looked at him. They were even in height. He said nothing for a moment. Orville kept twisting at his swimsuit, his right hand

59

tight and twisting at the suit.

"She was swimmin before supper; do ya know if she's down there now?"

"Don't know."

"She's not in the house?"

Orville looked toward the house, the living-room lights shaded by the drawn curtains.

"No, she's gone out."

"Down to the beach then?"

"She went out with Karen and them after supper, I don't know."

The boy driving kept revving the engine, the girl looking. He stared at the girl and she tossed her head and turned away, the boy looking up from behind the wheel at him, at his friend standing beside him on the gravel.

"Then she might be down at the beach then?"

"Don't know."

"She might be down there; let's go down along the shore."

Orville walked behind the car and onto the road. The boy shouted:

"You want a lift down?"

"No," he said.

"Sure?" the driver said.

"No," he said. He kept on walking. The car turned and sped down past him, the night wind from it in his face.

When he went along the path in the darkness he began to run, hearing his own breathing, hearing the woods, hearing the car as it travelled the shore road. He clutched his red trunks in his right hand. Then he thought of his eye and stopped running. *Irene said: "You watch that eye," when he was playing with the knife on the lawn with Edmund. Irene said: "You watch that eye," when he was going fishing with Edmund and Jerard: Irene said: "You watch that eye; it's the only one you got, you know that now." Then she said: "Edmund, you be careful of Orville; will you be careful of Orville?" And Edmund said: "Yes" that way and he said: "I ain't goin fishin," and went back inside with Irene saying: "Why aren't you gonna go—go on, why aren't ya gonna go?" and Jerard and Edmund waiting just outside the door.* He stopped his running. The path was rutted in places, in places loose cuts and falls overlaid it. The sound of the night woods. He ran again, out until he reached the shore.

The water had a wildness to its swells, white and chopping and coming in lashing so that he had to wade around Old Face, the water dancing and mounting his pant-legs unevenly. Then he was on the sand walking toward the fire, his sneakers drenched with the feel of summer.

The fire was low and burning down, its low flames rising now and then and then sinking back into the coals.

Rance and Edmund came over the dunes carrying more wood. They came up to him, Edmund smoking.

"What are you doing here?"

"Where's Cathy?"

"Just left with those guys."

"What guys?"

"Guys from town—gonna go swimmin—hey, ya already been swimmin ya skinny little bastard."

Rance threw the wood on. Orville was shivering. The fire smouldered, had a thickness to it, grew.

"Have a smoke."

"Don't want a smoke."

"Have a smoke—that John guy left us with a half deck."

"Don't want a smoke—where's Karen?"

"She went home—have a smoke."

"Don't want a smoke, okay?"

He turned and went toward the rocks. Away from the fire it was colder.

"You goin in, ya bastard?" Rance said.

"Might," he said.

In the car it smelled like wax—something enclosed with the four of them. Julie wasn't speaking; her hair fair blond and long and the up-river on her. She stared straight—sat beside Andrew straight, never looking behind once, not even to say "Hello" when Cathy got inside, when she left Karen and Karen walked ahead of the car that way, waiting to be asked with the lights shining on her skin.

"Where we going?"

"I don't know—ya comin or not?"

"I might if I know where we're goin."

"Shit, I don't know—I don't know—go downriver maybe, to the restaurant, okay?"

"Okay—just a minute," she said. "I have to say goodbye."

Karen was walking ahead of the car almost waiting, the red hair down and frayed wet from swimming. They were both laughing—the water was deep tonight and rough upon them. And they went out a long way, the sand smooth on the hard floor of the water, the seaweed at moments as they went under. Then John came in the car. They were out of the water, sitting near the fire, the fire small, its coals a blue and red in the spotted darkness. She kept watching for Orville.

"I haveta say goodbye."

He kept pulling at her arm.

"I haveta say goodbye; I haveta say goodbye."

Karen was walking on the shore road in the lights, her body a smooth wet from the water and still the redness of the afternoon upon her. Cathy walked up behind her, the light making the dirt of the road glow in the stillness; in the stillness everything else black and worn into the night, into the sound of the water dashing against the rocks, making the fields and the road become the sound.

"Hey Karen—hey Karen."

Karen turned, her face empty and her eyes waiting.

"I'm gonna go for a drive, okay?"

"Okay, see ya tomorrow,' she turned and went onward out of the light so that she seemed streaked. The stillness and the sound of the waves.

"Hey Karen—hey Karen."

"What?" She turned in the semi-darkness.

"Well, I'll see ya tomorrow," she said. "Okay?"

"Ya," Karen turned and went onward—her body becoming a portion of the night, of the darkness and the sound of waves.

Cathy turned and went back to the car.

"Well, where are we goin, I wanta know." Leah said: *"Make sure, just don't tcha get in any ol car; you gotta make sure."*

"I don't know, shit, Andy; where are we gonna go?"

Andy looked up, his face broad and smooth and quiet. He didn't speak, shrugging his shoulders, looking and not looking—out past them: the coals a dying multicolour on the beach.

"Well, okay then for awhile," she said, silently. He tugged at her arm.

His eyes in the darkness stared at her narrowly, with his right arm over the seat. She bent ahead a little, listening to the sound of the car, the rough determined sound that broke the silence of no talking, that came to all of them, making them together and alone. Julie sitting straight and close to him, not speaking, and the smell of something so thick within it—body heat tempered with the scent of something, with the bottle Andy passed back.

"You want a drink?"

"No."

"Have a drink?"

"No."

"Have one."

"No."

Julie wasn't speaking. There was the upriver on her, on her smooth fine hair that caught in the light of oncoming cars, that broke and splintered with the light, the fine white portion of her neck showing the small golden chain.

"Have a drink," John said.

"No I said."

His eyes narrowed, looking at her as if inside him the motion and the sound of the car forced that anger to swell and abate with the motion itself, with the turns and hills they came to, fast in the night air. Rushing.

"Well, piss on it," he muttered, then laughed. She sat ahead a little, her shoulders slouched. He tipped the bottle and drank long, his hand slipping downward to her shoulders.

"You said we were going *down*river?"

"It's still young yet," he said.

"Well, where are we goin—up ta town?"

"Shit—ask Andy; it's still young yet."

She said nothing.

"We'll probably head down later," he said. "Why, you wanta go down?"

"Oh, it don't matter—I was just wonderin."

He pulled her back with his arm. She sat straight and stiffened in his grip. In the front they weren't talking, only the muscles of Andy's shoulders flexed with the wheel, and now and then in the darkness she caught his eyes in the mirror looking back.

But they weren't talking—as if she was an intrusion. He took from the bottle again before passing it up, Andy reaching for it.

"Well, he'd better watch that turn up here," Cathy said.

"What turn?" He looked at her, a smile hardly perceptible in the darkness—the rush of warm summer night coming in.

The car lurched into it, hitting the loose gravel, and then lurched back onto the asphalt. *Cecil would say: "Ya, well she got into it; she got into it, she got into the goddamn thing, her own goddamn fault with a bunch of fuckers from up town all liquored up—drivin—"*

"This turn."

He held her tighter and she went in against him because of the force. Then he was laughing, wild: like the wind tonight, silent unless brought to life by the force driven into it: the energy and the sound.

When they came to the crossroads there was no traffic, the houses dull and set together in the summer night, the rows of elms darkening the lawns with long quiet shadows. She sat back in his grip, opening and closing her hands upon her lap.

Then he sat up straight and looked out the window to the side lane they were passing, the rough engine throttling deliberate and steadfast.

"See her Andy—see her?"

"Who?"

"That one."

"Who?"

"That's the one—that squaw that Boyd took that time, remember?"

"Don't know."

"Don'tcha remember that time?"

In the front she tossed her head toward Andrew, her hair golden under the town light, the summer whiteness of the streetlamps shining in the lane. Yet he went unmoved behind the wheel, as if neither she nor John nor anyone could move him. Cathy was tight-lipped, her hands moving.

"Don't know."

"You haveta play cribbage with Dad," Julie said.

"Ya," he said.

He turned the car and headed back down, just as fast or faster into the turns. John settled his arm around her again. There was a part of her that remained immobile and stiff in his grip.

"We gonna go down to the wharf?" Andy said.

"I don't know. For awhile—pass the bottle back here—for awhile, Andy."

"Bottle's gone," Andy said.

"Shit."

Andy kept driving.

"I haveta go in now," she said.

"No, we're goin down to the wharf for awhile," he said. Andy kept driving—the lights of the house on.

It was downriver now, the night and the open bay. The bay swelling large, and the wharf smelling of the nets and traps pulled up on it, the distant blackness of water, and the smell of tar. *She walked upon the tar in the heat, Angela's father on ahead. "Oh I made a mistake," she said. He didn't turn around, his large lump of a body moving in khaki pants, the smell of his cigarettes and mint. "Oh I made a mistake," she said. She sat down upon the wharf trying to relieve the burning heat. Tar against the bottom of her feet. "Didn'tcha wear no shoes?" he said. "No," she said. He walked over to her, large and plump in his khaki pants. "Jees, ya didn't wear no shoes," he said. And it was anger in him for taking her. "I made a mistake," she said. She had set the worms crawling in the tin can on the tar, moistened in the earth. She stared at them crawling. "Well, ya shoulda—Irene shoulda given ya shoes— didn't she give ya no shoes?" "I forgot them in the porch," she said.*

It was blackness here. He turned the engine off and the car sat with no sound but the small ticking in it. It was the blackness of the water and night inseparable one from the other. The small wharf light flickering, the sound of the waves brutal over the slip. She could be with it, know it—the scraps of the herring rotting, the salt brindled into the mesh.

"You told Dad ya'd play cribbage," she said.

"Ya," he said.

"I haveta go anyway," Cathy said. He grabbed at her, his grip powerful as if she'd go down onto the seat. But she wouldn't.

"Let's go out for a walk," she said.

"Out for a walk," he laughed.

"Ya, out on the wharf," she said.

"Out to the wharf?" he laughed.

The wind came inward from the bay, lashed at them. Something showed anger in his high lifting face-bones when his hair lifted and twisted out of place. He walked slightly behind her, their pace slow. She walked to the tying pole and leaned against it. Water had saturated the knotted wood of the slip and tossed and heaved upwards against the iron rung of the ladder. She could feel the cold of saying nothing with the cold upon her skin. He said nothing.

The car horn. He said nothing.

"Ya comin?" Andy said. The car horn.

"How deep's the water here?"

"Oh, real deep."

"Think I can touch bottom here?"

"When it's low and quiet—in the morning just maybe."

"I'm gonna touch bottom," he said.

"Ya comin?" Andy said. She said nothing.

He stood upon the tying pole, barefooted.

"Are ya crazy?" she said. "Are ya crazy?"

"I'll touch her," he said.

"You're crazy—boy you're crazy." As if the water was busting forth in torment below the slip.

"I'll touch her," he said.

The car horn. The bay rapid and dark, so that if two miles out in it swimming there'd be two more miles of swelling. She stood aside looking.

"Yer crazy! Yer crazy."

"I'll touch her," he said.

As if it could lift him and carry him anywhere in the black. The car horn. But he had already gone between two waves lifting near the timbers.

"That water's real cold,' 'she yelled. "Yer crazier than hell," she yelled. Only the silent flick of his body entering and then he was lost. He was lost it seemed for minutes.

"Did that crazy bastard jump?" Andy yelled.

She didn't answer.

She was looking—far out past where he should come up. Andy got out and came beside her soundless. Then his head rose out of it far to the side of where he went under. Only the tiny bob of his head rising.

"Yer crazy." She turned to Andy. "Boy, he's real crazy." Then she couldn't see him.

"Where's the ladder?"

"This way," Andy yelled.

"Where's *this* way?" he yelled.

"Over here," she yelled. She couldn't see him. "Oh, yer crazy," she said. "Over this way." She couldn't hear him.

She couldn't hear him.

"Ya still there?" Andy yelled.

"La de da," he yelled.

"Where are ya?" Andy yelled. Then she saw his head again, the waves lifting his whole body back and forth like a toy.

"Right below ya—boo!" he said.

"Well, get outa there cause we haveta go," Andy said.

"Oh, I might swim a bit and get refreshed," he said.

But he was moving toward the ladder, his body looking almost powerless in the waves.

"La de da," he said. He reached the ladder and came up it, standing upon the wharf barefooted and drenched, his hair scrawled against his face.

"Look what I found," he said. He opened his hand and showed her the dirt. It was his whole face glistening. He rubbed it against his pants.

"You'll have to get somethin to sit on," Andy said.

"Ya," he said.

"Boy, you're crazier than hell," she said.

"Julie, let him sit on your jacket."

She looked, the fine chain on her smooth neck.

"Piss on it," John said.

"Let him sit on the fuckin thing—come on now," Andy said.

She handed the jacket back and then turned again.

They headed up, he shivering uncontrollably. Andy turned on the heat.

When they turned into the drive the lights were still on in the kitchen.

"Where'll ya be next week?" he said. He didn't get out of the car. She peered back at him, his wetness on the jacket.

"I haveta work the picnic."

"The picnic?"

"At the church," she said.

He laughed.

"I'll take ya to the exhibition," he said.

She looked at him.

"Oh I will; I'll be down," he said. "The picnic," he said.

She went inside. Orville was up alone in the kitchen, his legs thrust upon the table.

"Didja go swimmin?" she said.

"A bit," he said. He stared at her silently.

"You should go swimmin more," she said.

He stared at her. *Leah said: "Don'tcha ever let none of them touch none of ya on the first date—don't matter who he is."* And then he picked up his Coke and drank from it closing his eye.

5

When he came to that side of the trickle of water it was already noon, past noon; the drizzle low, slow now and then hitting at his face as if it were the spray from the swell of a wave. It was when it hit him (something foreign and outside himself) he was conscious of pleasure. He turned his face against it, watching the darkening sky over the low brooding trees, pressed down upon the land like the blood-full brooding of a mosquito's belly. The trickle behind him turned black with mist, revolving slowly in small indistinguishable ripples over the smooth black water, as if the ripples and the water were separated each from the other.

He walked inward along the brook shore carrying the axe blade-outward near his knee and the hammer through his belt. Every now and then as the mist came against him he lifted his left hand and touched the smooth felt of the patch. The water narrowed almost to nothing and split into two small trickles. He wore Maufat's raincoat and the steel-toed rubber boots, limp and clumsy upon his thinness.

When he came to the point where the water broke he followed the half-red mud bank on the left side, the boot marks sucking into it ankle-deep. Here he had the mist full, like some webbed curtain passing on his face. He was silent, hearing his boots sucking and sinking into the red layers. The water came to nothing. There was a wet field and then it started again with a little lake. He crossed the field, sinking almost to the top of his boots, the high grass limp and drenched yellow, the stink akin to the heat of rotting. Then it went over his boots and he could feel the brown spent water rise inside them, drenching the sweat of his feet.

He cursed and went onward, swinging the axe before him slowly and methodically yet without purpose, each swing hitting nothing save the drizzle and the grey summer air. The grey outline of trees at the far end of the field, and the grey mist of the outline behind him. Until he reached the wood again where it was dryer, calm and brown with no sun upon the path or the overhanging branches. The drizzle was cut off now almost completely.

"How much nails did you take?" Cathy said.

"A bunch."

"The whole bag of them?" she said.

"What was there."

"What was there—well that's the whole bag a them."

He didn't answer. She looked at him quietly her mouth turned in. The dim light of the outside shadowed the room, let her stand there with her mouth pensive, with her frame in the noon-hour, motionless —part of it, with her legs spread apart faintly and the skirt too low against her knees; with the brown colouring of her skin seeming tainted by the lack of heat. The shadow of her skull dim upon the fridge. And her eyes large, not faint like the eyes of his mother.

"What are you gonna do with them?"

"I'm gonna go out to the woods."

"What are ya gonna be doin with them?"

"I'm buildin a goddamn fort in the woods so as I won't haveta come back here again."

"Oh, well may be then big shot ya might be ableta build your fort with a bunch of nails of your own—stead a takin Dad's—and his hammer, and his axe, and wearin his coat—"

"Shut your mouth."

"And his boots."

"Shut your mouth."

"No."

"Shut yer mouth."

"No."

She moved closer to the fridge and put her left hand upon it. The shadow of her skull moved against the wall, elongated upon the wall.

"Where are ya buildin the fort?"

"Never mind." He turned away from her and went into the porch. There was the odour of the garbage clinging to the cool damp air, the curtain drawn down on the streaked window.

"Ya should tell Dad you're takin the stuff," she said. "That's all," she said.

The drizzle was cut off now but the branches that he had been gathering for some time were wet, the small place he was clearing stumpridden, the stumps reaching out sharply from the soft dirt. There was a row of alders and spruce cuts that shaded him from the pathway and behind him to the right the soft gurgling noise of the small brook moving to the lake. The lake was down farther, a hundred yards down farther along the path.

He began to work, clearing off the branches and falls that he had gathered at one side, the branches full green, a darker, thicker green now than at any time of their standing. Because they were full of the earth and the dirt and loose needles, the needles that had lain in the soft black soil throughout the summer. The black soil that had gathered and collected in this seclusion so thickly that when he walked with the hard-toed boots, the clots of it dug out and turned upward to face him.

Now the shrill peeping of a bird, only the once; only one. Silence.

Then after the silence he could hear nothing but his own quiet tramping in the still, grey light. Then the shrill peeping of it again. It would be in there, hidden by its grey colour in the grey day, so much alone in the summer foliage that it would be lost to everything but itself, that only its sound would be heard and measured by other things moving. Sap clotted the palms of his hands.

He began with the axe at the sharpened stumps, making them splinter and break as effectively as he could, making the dirt fly upwards near his eye so that he closed it now and then, being blinded when he swung. He didn't think of what he was doing, what purpose it would all be for—he didn't know that; he knew nothing save what he was doing at the present, that it had to be cleared in order to build, that he wanted a pocket of emptiness there before he began to use the hammer and nails. A pocket of emptiness surrounded by the still quiet, and the swilling sound of the brook.

He worked. The day grew darker, the drizzle came down upon him like mist again, full in his face when he looked upwards at the sky. No sound of the bird now as he worked, as he finished splintering all the stumps that might possibly deter something that he might do, as he took the boards and the plastic from the place where he had hidden them and began to measure the boards off in some random and senseless way for something that he might do. The rain came. It beat upon the plastic like it did upon the plastic covering the porch windows in the fall; it beat upon the black raincoat so that the stains of the tracks ground into it seemed to emerge and linger on its surface; so that he could taste a firm taste of soot upon it; so that the black soil clots dampened and disintegrated into the earth where he had torn them from; so that the splintered stumps went white in the pulp, lying exposed in the soundless dirt. So that he himself felt the water and the sweat and the dirt run off him. His hair dampened and hung down against his eye. It went darker with the rain, his thin sunless face against it.

"Bastard," he said. "Bastard." He kept at it. The hood didn't matter, he wouldn't use the hood, so that in time it too became as wet as all other things. The boards went a damp black in the rain and finally after measuring and thinking how they might go he threw the plastic covering over himself and sat upon the dry ground that it afforded, waiting. His face was white looking through it—hearing it beat upon him. "Bastard—bastard."

Nothing came with the wet but the hunger of all day, the look of the woods. *But he said: "I'm goin so as I won't be back," and Cathy said:*

"Big shot." So that if he had it built he would stay here all night, because Rance wouldn't build it with him, Rance said: "What—a fort, shit a fort," and he said, "Fuck ya then," and Rance said, "Fuck you." He began to walk away and Rance said: "A fort—fuck you MacDurmot." He kept walking. Rance said: "Fuck you one-eye." He didn't stop and then in a minute Rance walked beside him. He didn't stop and Rance kept walking beside him along the shore for a long time. Then he said: "Ya, well I'm sorry, okay?" Orville didn't stop. Rance said: "Ya, well I'm sorry, okay?"

But the shadows were lengthened and rain came spotting the plastic. His pensive thinness underneath it. It was the massive silence of the woods, a coat of darkness groping through and under the lower limbs and boughs. He brought the axe up against his knees and held it there.

What was behind him in the woods he didn't know, what was moving forward in the grey twilight upon the path he didn't know, and if it was something, almost *anything*, he would wish to move outward toward it, to see it before it trapped him, though he didn't know if it was at all; it wasn't at all!

And yet behind the spotted branches so that his heart was pumping, and behind him moving upwards against the slow trickle of the brook —no, it would be back where he started, back where his tracks would be found in the half-clotted earth where he crossed, where his tracks were only faded imprints almost washed away. It would be there sensing and moving, walking, smudged with the red grime of clay, its face not a face, its arms not arms, and it was moving nearer. It would stop —see that he had crossed the field, see that in the distant shelter beyond and behind the clump of trees he had gone, and now it was in the field moving, its body not a body. It was something grotesque on the path moving nearer, or behind him, moving silently, only breathing through the dark shelter of the woods.

It was in the shelter of the woods limping nearer, dragging a bloodied leg, its eyes—its eyes watching. His heart was pumping. He held the axe in his firm thin hands against his knees, watching, almost seeing in the darkened limp shadows, *it* that was moving nearer. It was upon the path in the twilight dragging a bloodied leg, an arm jammed in a logging drive, he heard Maufat say that *it* yelled.

Then Lorne—it could be him. Lorne went down to see him, it was Christmas so Lorne went down to see him there and he never moved from the fire so Lorne went in to touch him and he never moved from the fire and then Lorne went back out to bring in the turkey that the church had sent down because it was Christmas. It was cold but there was no snow, it was only cold and when Lorne came in again with the turkey it was black and cold inside and a wind was blowing on the inside as if all the windows were open and he was no longer beside the fire. He was no longer beside the fire and Lorne saw him and ran. "Where was he?" Maufat said. "He was in the fire," Lorne said. Because he was in the fire his arms that long and his face all twisted just like some animal, and though he wasn't looking he was seeing just where Lorne was. The fire coming up around him that way doing nothing to him and his face turning like an animal's. And when Lorne ran outside he saw the glow of it all lighting up the dark blackness of the inside. But it was cold on the outside and yet there was no snow and when Lorne backed the car down from the drive and went to turn he heard this strange yelling and he couldn't say what it was except he said it wasn't human and then just as he had turned his face away and turned it back again, no more than a second or two later, the man standing in front of him before the car, rigid and barefooted and it was cold, zero almost though there wasn't any snow. "How did you get away?" Maufat said. "He seemed to back outa my way," Lorne said. "Sorta except I didn't see him move—I never seen him move to the side until he was there at the side of me door and I don't remember drivin the car out past him because I remember I was starin out past where the water was turned to those ice-faces along the shore—a hundred yards or more gone ahead on the road and when I looked through me mirror, he was standin halfway on this side of the woods barefooted and it that cold, watchin. Then he was gone," Lorne said.

His pensive thinness underneath it. It was the massive silence. His heart pumping, so that it pumped like the rain pumping on the outside of the plastic, the black green branches staggering with the weight of the afternoon.

The weight of the afternoon staggering and spattering upon the plastic, the rich smell of the woods with rain, the woods clotted and heavy and silent with rain.

He turned his head from side to side watching the branches themselves. The shadows around him lengthened with the time and he began to shiver with the cold upon him, on his wetness, on his hair and skin. But nothing came, there was nothing behind him moving, nothing staggering forward on the bloodied path—nothing because nothing showed itself. Because it was nothing.

"Bastard," he said. "Bastard." Rance wouldn't come with him. "Bastard," he said. "Bastard." Because it was nothing, he thought. It was like thinking when he burned the candles in his room with no-one home in the evening, that someone was moving up the stairs slowly toward his room, toward his flat-shut door in the silence, walking that way step by step. The smell of church wax that curled with the smoking flame against the walls, the flame flickering and sputtering multicolour against the black, luminous as a shadow.

And he would lie on the bed within its light, within the orb of it, smelling the dry altar wax dripping and sputtering; go half to sleep there and then in an instant *start* because of hearing something. He would blow out the candles and hide them beneath his bed, open the window and wait; trembling almost. Yet nothing, nothing! As if when moving to open the window he was letting go his own fear with the smoke of the candles that drifted out. He would start again and listen. It would be gone, quiet, desolate save for him.

He was shivering and uncomfortable and yet he didn't move. He waited. It would be over and when it was over the twilight sun would be out against the sky, the bay so calm and warm that he would walk out to it and swim, the beach saturated by the storm. Yet now he was cold and hungry. He waited. "Bastard." It was in the dark shelter of the woods limping nearer dragging a bloodied leg its eyes—He was under the plastic watching, stinking now of the rank smell of the plastic.

It stopped slowly, mist forming as it did so. His limbs were stiffened from sitting; he moved out of the plastic and threw it to the side, glancing upwards again. It seemed to envelop the earth again, the drizzle; it seemed to cling to the trees like some fine and gigantic web. He gathered the undressed boards he was using and rolled them in the plastic. They had gone black. He listened. Everything was silent, only the large occasional drops falling through the mist. It had gone half-black here—late afternoon now, or later he didn't know—he had lost track of time. But it was late now. Late. He hid the things again and picked up the axe and held it blade-outward at his knee. He stared deeply into it, into the hidden branches, into the trees gnarled and twisted. And there was nothing—nothing but the bird again, one note shrill, only the once and that was all—nothing.

"Orville," she said.

She was behind him. He didn't turn; his face tightening at every muscle. Where was she? It was as if his boots were frozen into those upturned clots he was standing in, into the bareness of the dirt that he had turned up. "Orville," she said. He turned slowly, not answering.

"Orville," she said. She said it louder. She was on the path walking toward the lake; perhaps past where he was. "Orville," she said. "Mom's all worried—it's after supper. Orv?"

He moved out slowly following her voice. For moments he didn't see her. For moments there was no sound from her. He moved carefully so as not to make a noise. Then she turned on the path and started walking back and he saw where she was—his jacket on her and her hair wet. She began walking toward him on the path. "Orv—Orville —Mom's all worried, she thinks ya might have fell on yer eye, she thinks ya might be blinded out here, Orville." She was walking past him on the path now. He was no more than a foot away standing in the alders so she coundn't see him. The drizzle greyed her brown face as it whitened his. He reached out his hand.

When she screamed it was soft as if she was frightened of herself screaming; she grabbed his hand in her own, the pulse of it beating. When he reached out it was the jacket collar near her throat that he had managed to touch. And now her hand was holding his and her eyes were wide with fright. He stepped out of the alders and even when she recognized who it was her eyes still remained wide in some childish fear.

"So," he said. "Followin me."

"No," she said. "Not followin ya at all—Orville, do you know what time it is? What in hell are ya doin out here this late, Mom's worried stiff."

"What time is it?" he said.

"Nearly seven and Mom don't know where ya are or nothing."

"Nearly seven," he said. She looked up at him with her eyes still a little frightened, with the lips quivering in the grey drizzle that was clouding the woods more and more as it got later. "So," he said.

"So—come on home to eat," she said. "And I hope ya didn't use all Dad's nails cause I didn't mention them to him but you better mention them to him if yer gonna use them."

She began to walk ahead of him on the path. He saw the smallness of her dim in his one eye, the streaked jacket of his low against her thighs. He walked behind her until they came to the field. Then she turned and began walking around on the fringe.

"That'll take forever," he said. She kept walking.

"Well, I'm not crossing it," she said.

He watched her walking. Then he started crossing it, sinking below the yellow grass. She was walking around on the fringe, her body moving slow and dark, close to the alders.

"Ya know what?" he yelled. He was standing in the middle of the field and the black flies were about him, at his hands. He swung the axe around his head. She was moving out around some bushes, her back toward him, his jacket limp below her thighs. "What?" she said.

"Guess who I saw comin up here?"

"Who?" She was out around them now, moving easier but she would have to move around more; she would have to walk a long way around. She flicked her face toward him. He kept swinging the axe. "Who?" she said.

"Mallory," he said. She kept walking. "Who?" she said. "Mallory," he said. "You know the one Lorne went to see." She flicked her face and then she stopped, turned completely toward him, dim and half-buried in the branches that stuck out around her in the loose twilight.

He began to move across the field knowing she was watching him. He began to run, sinking into it above his knee so that in his boots he carried the mud and brown water of the stinking field. He was swinging the axe, each swing cutting nothing but the drizzle, the air. "Mallory," he said. "His face is all burnt and he's walking around here someplace—I saw him this afternoon." She was far away now moving around lonely on the fringe.

"Orville!" she laughed. "Stop that!" She laughed.

"Truth!" he said. He started to move up the path. So that she couldn't see him, so that he stood hidden watching her. "Orville," she said. "You wait up--Orville!"

When she couldn't see him any more because he moved onto the path she stopped still against the chokecherry bush; leaning into it because of its foliage. The field was rank with yellow grass.

"Orville," she yelled, "You wait up—" There was silence about her, from all sides of the woods a silence and a dimness the evening drizzle made. Her boot toes sunk into the corner of the field, the wet underneath sucking at them. Here in the winter, before it crusted over, it froze on the underneath, the yellow stalks brittle in the fresh wind, the ice that supported the yellowed stalks purple under the coldness of the sun. "Orv, wait for me on that side," she yelled. Nothing moved after her yelling; a signal that all the woods was emptied save her. She didn't think of it: he was on the other side waiting. She didn't think of it.

"Orville," she yelled. "I walked in here alone lots a times so don't think yer so damn smart."

She began to move again out around it. But it was as if something was moving with her now when she moved; as if what he said was moving with her out around the things she was passing; as if in the darkness what he said was following her. She looked behind her. It was silence. In there the brook was still running to the lake, the lake still mirrored and the trees rising around it. Nothing else. Nothing else. She had moved through here before, the quiet insides on an afternoon, the fresh mud and good damp clotted earth. "Orville," she yelled. There was nothing.

It was as if when Lorne saw him black smoke or something came from his mouth—as if he was standing by the fire and after Lorne went out and came back inside there was a wind blowing and all the windows were up, and Mallory was in the fire, his eyes red and following Lorne: wherever he went the eyes went and his face was just like a wolf's. His arms and his face were twisted about him and the fire came around him and soot all about the floor. Lorne ran to his car and Mallory was standing before the car burnt and barefooted, it cold and where he stood that icy.

"Orv," she yelled. "Orv—you wait."

There was nothing but a fine film of drizzle on her face in the darkness, and the smell of the drizzle with the high grass and the night. She moved out into the field because near the trees, moving around on the fringe, it was as if something could reach out—though it was nothing, it was lies: it was nothing.

The water soaked her legs as she moved. She couldn't move fast and yet she was moving across it, soaking herself, the rank water and yellow weed against her legs.

It was the fear that had started her and he that had started the fear. The fear like a flood, something heavy that washed against her. And when he ran across the field and onto the path, it left her upon the fringe alone. The branches were dark; she couldn't see inside and there was something inside perhaps, near the brook—*Mallory near the brook Mallory near the brook.*

She was alone now running across the field, her fine legs blackened, her eyes wide, staring for him on the path, wanting to see Orville standing on the path. It was the way he ran from her, she was in here before alone, it was quiet and in the winter the white starkness of it. Yet she was running. It was stupid! It was stupid.

"Orville," she said. "You wait up."

She came to the path. Here the trees were larger. She was on the red clay, the mud swung and slid beneath her feet with more resistance now. It was cooling, the night air killing the drizzle that had for so long been against her face. The short pinned hair wet with the mist. He was nowhere. The path swung slowly to the right where the trickle would be and following the trickle the brook. Her eyes were watching. He was nowhere. Behind her, perhaps behind her. "Orville," she called lowly. It was stupid.

She would not look behind. She kept following the path, the trickle growing out larger to her left. There was no sound except the mud that swung under her; no sound until the hand and she screamed.

It was his whole body coming out of the air and the hand reaching for her. She saw it all as shadow and screamed. She grabbed at him because it was fear and he had started the fear. When he swung out of the air she knew it was him; as if instinct told her before fear who it was. Yet it was as if something went blind inside her and she had to grab at him and start screaming. She was crying. It was stupid. Then he tried to grab her hands. She was punching, it was panic—her face was panic. She knew it was him—she knew, and she was trying to scratch him for fear.

Then he stopped still and tried to grab her hands.

"You're stupid," he kept saying. "You're stupid."

She was crying now so that she couldn't speak, only her throat and her eyes burned with the pain of crying. She was trying to punch him.

"You leave me alone," she said. "You leave me alone; I'm tellin Mom ya slob ya slob."

"Yer stupider than hell."

She was punching him against the side of his neck.

He backed away from her and picked up the axe from the tree where he had stuck it. Then he moved backward along the path watching her.

"I was just goddamn kiddin with ya," he said.

She made no move toward him and he turned and followed the path, his boots coated with mud. She followed close behind crying and unable to stop. She kept her eyes on him, his longness set into the distance, the twilight and the sound of the frail drizzle in the trees. It was the fear that had started her and he that had started the fear. It was stupid.

"I was just goddamn kiddin with ya," he said. It was nothing. It was lies and it was nothing.

6

If his appearance bore any resemblance to her mother's—to Irene's, she didn't see it. She had been out, the day so brilliantly clean, clean the way it always was after a fall of rain because the rain drained the dust and grime off the flowers and the sun dried the rain and left everything calm.

She came back because she had to work at the picnic. She came back over the dry, hot field. When the barn was there years ago it was the largeness of it, the slanting moss-eaten roof before they tore it down, the slanted sides of it in the winter, the snow high and crimson white in a cold, almost purple sun; and they climbed against its sides, standing on the tilted fence-post and then upon the maple, the branches slipping with that fine sliver of ice, their mittens soaked, their fingers purple. When they were upon it they stood bravely against the night air, their shadows silhouetted and suspended one against the other; Leah laughing.

Laughing they would jump off it into the snow, the snow in their mouths and faces and eyes and up against the underneath of what they wore. Leah would jump and then Cathy behind her, so that Cathy was frightened of landing on her, frightened that when she was in the air she wouldn't be able to help it—falling, she wouldn't be able to stop. Her free motion against the air.

Now there was nothing but the remainder of the roof, and the grass that grew about it greener than the rest. The roof looking smaller than it had when they climbed upon it. Lorne saying: "You get yourselves off that roof—Leah!" Leah saying: "It ain't your roof, smart arse." Lorne saying: "I'll tell Irene, I'll tell Irene." Leah saying: "Go shit yerself." Cathy laughing; Lorne walking through the snow toward Irene's and stumbling, Cathy laughing and Leah saying, "Go shit yerself, smart arse."

The barn was down, it had taken them no time at all, its sides crumbled and the eggs of the swallows, and the swallows darting and diving at the men and each of the men seemed to pay them no mind; except Orville throwing stones that broke against the air and hit nothing, out past the barn and the swallows darting.

"Where were you?" Irene said.

"Back the field."

"Back the field; well, ya shoulda stayed in ta help me."

"I'll help ya now."

"I gotta be down there now—I can't wait till all the people start comin in and you should be down there—what stand ya workin in; did ya find it out?"

Lorne sat at the table with Maufat playing cribbage. He looked at her as she entered, then nodded as his eyes went back to the cards. He picked up the beer and drank from it. The window behind the table was open wide yet the smell of the bread she had baked was strong—the turkey still cooking in the oven, the glare of sweat on her white forehead. The long-legged thinness of Lorne, his legs reaching far under the table, the bones of his shoulders jutting up against his shirt: "Where Orville came from," as Maufat said. He picked up the crib and counted it, pegging fourteen, which edged him slightly ahead. Then he finished the beer.

"Nother beer?" Maufat said.

"Good," Lorne said.

"Cathy, get Lorne another beer," Maufat said.

She took one from the fridge and opened it, handing it to him and stepping back.

"I gotta work down there in the cane stand," she said.

Irene took the turkey from the oven and set the pot on holders near the sink. Irene looked tired—the grey whiteness of the sweat upon her brow, because she had been up last night cooking and this morning Orville had said he wasn't going, and she didn't know where he was again: "I ain't going to any stupid picnic."

"You're getting dressed and coming."

"I'm savin my money for the exhibition."

"You come—or ya won't get to the exhibition," Maufat said.

"I ain't goin I ain't goin I ain't goin," Orville said. Cathy looked at him and he caught her in his one eye and looked away saying nothing. Then he was out the door.

"You get back here," Maufat said. "Jesus Jesus," Maufat said.

The game was over, Lorne winning. He sat up straighter and drank the beer and Maufat stood placing the board back in the cupboard.

"Are ya ready—I magine Lorne has things to do," Maufat said.

"If I hada help I'd be ready."

Lorne drank his beer as if he hadn't heard the comment. As if he was good, Cathy thought, as if he was good. And then Maufat said: "Well, I'm getting a car soon as next winter." Lorne said nothing and Cathy turned to help her mother.

"You know I don't know why they bother with those damn picnics any more," Lorne said.

"Why?" Irene said. Cathy batted the cake icing against the side of the bowl.

"Well, who goes to them for all the fuss?"

"All down and up above the bridge, and the cottagers and the people from town," Irene said.

"I wouldn't give a cent to them," Lorne said.

"Oh, we all know that," Cathy said. She batted the brown icing against the side of the bowl. Irene looked at her, the grey eyes sharpening. Lorne didn't hear. He moved his chair out and stood.

"Any priest sayin that," Lorne said.

"He's real old now, Lorne," Irene said.

"We need a new priest—any priest sayin that. 'There are those that will help at the picnic and there are those that never helped.' And then he called out the names like that. 'It's just like the good thief and the bad thief up there on the cross next ta Christ and he knows who's helping at the picnic.' "

"He knows," Cathy said.

"What?" Lorne said.

"I said he's old," she said.

"And then saying that we'd burn in hell if we didn't help at the picnic—burn in hell, he'll burn in hell goin out to bingo every night and spending every cent in the damn collection—Betty's too sick to go around baking pies and cakes and running down there all day and waiting on people—what does he expect, that she had nothing ta do but spend her money and time on a picnic so he can spend all the money on bingo—and goin to those shows?"

"What shows?" Irene said.

"Those shows there runnin up there in town with the girls in them half naked—all naked. I know. I know. A guy told me he's always there. So I won't let Betty go down—picnic."

"Oh, I don't think that's right," Irene said.

"Well, it is, it is, I know it is," Lorne said. "I know it is."

Cathy moved her legs tighter. She stared out the window.

"It's just that he believes like the church 50 years ago—and he's too old so when he says that ya just don't haveta mind him."

"Trying to scare us into helping at the picnic. Sure he's too old, sure he is—but who gets the good priests around here? Not us—the Indians, the Indians and the French. The Indians down there on the reservation and we pay taxes ta keep them alive and mosta them never even go to church mosta them don't believe in God or nothin—Indians and French get the goddamn good churches and the priests. Look at any French town ya go to, look at it ya'll see churches higher and better than the one up town—ya don't even see the roads paved around here unless an election."

"Well, that's not his fault," Irene said.

"I ain't sayin it is, I ain't sayin it is, all as I'm sayin is that when he says I'm gonna burn in hell for not helpin at the picnic then I ain't gonna help at no picnic."

"Oh well," Irene said. "Ya just gotta remember he's old—he must be over 70—he married every one of us around here; he must be over 70."

"Close to 80," Maufat said.

"Well, no-one is going to tell me I'm gonna burn in hell," Lorne said.

He backed to the side of the stove and stood there as if contemplating all that he had said while Maufat opened him another beer. Cathy scooped the icing out of the bowl and onto the cake saying nothing, her lips tight together.

"Ya need any more done," she said.

Irene shook her head.

"Well, I'm gonna change then."

"You comin down with Lorne—we're leavin in five minutes."

"I don't needta be down there yet."

"It'll save ya from walkin."

"I don't needta be down there yet," she said once more. She turned and went past them, into the room and up the stairs, and she was halfway up when Irene yelled:

"You see Orville out around? You know where he is?"

"No."

"Well, if he comes in you get him to come."

"I'll try," she said. "I'll try."

She went into her room and slammed the door. Still she could hear Lorne again as she changed; unsnapping the tight snap that marked her belly, the red traces of her shorts against the soft brownness of her skin. The early afternoon light came from the window that showed the road. It was a shadowed heat in here; a shadowed quiet.

"Indians and French," he said. "Under the bridge ya can see any time ya wanta go under the bridge that it's all fallin down, it won't last no winter like everyone is sayin, but no matter how much ya give ta taxes—-taxes Christ every Indian down there is livin off me and Maufat—"

"Well, that's not his fault," Irene said. "He's just old now."

"I don't give a damn how old he is, no-one is gonna say I'm gonna burn in hell."

There was a silence again; there was a shadow and in the shadow her naked skin.

"He gets terrible coughin fits," Irene said. "Laura was tellin me when she goes down he's fine one minute and she starts waxin the floor and then the next minute he comes out and he's walkin over the floor just as if he don't have any idea what at all she's doin, or that she's there at all and starts coughin up and flickin his ashes each and every way—so he's old now, he don't even know half the time what he's sayin up there on that pulpit."

She was in her dress smoothing it down against her legs, the musk of the dry sunlight hitting the window, glancing into the dry room.

"Well, if he's old then tell me this—that he goes up ta those shows and that he goes ta play bingo—carryin on worse than Cecil, yet we all yell at Cecil, which is half Leah's fault, ya know yerself I ain't sayin nothin new."

"I don't know what they have to do with this," Irene said, her voice tired, sharpened.

"Nothin, nothin—all as I'm sayin is that we need a new priest—"

"We'll get one soon—he won't be around much longer," Maufat said.

"No cept it's a shame that the picnics'll be dying out as soon as he goes."

"I know—I know," Lorne said. "I ain't got nothin against the picnics—and I'd send Betty down there ta help if it weren't for him."

She sat on her bed cross-legged and listened. Then she heard the movement and the door, and then the complete silence after the car backed away.

The ticking of the small clock upon her night-table, the unsteady sound of it in the slanted room. She lay upon the bed smoothing her stockings down. The distant sound of his car on the distant road and then the halting sound of it as it turned off toward the church. "Goddamn Orville," she thought. Just to hurt them he wouldn't go—just to hurt them he'd rather be out there at his fort, the summer leaches in the yellow field and then along the damp path—

82

When her skirt was that way on her she looked older and knew she looked older. She went out of the house leaving it open so that if Orville came back he would be able to enter, and walked the shoulder of the highway. Within her was the goodness of feeling the sun and the unconscious feeling of herself being older. The pure simple cleanness that came with the heat of the afternoon.

She was late. Yet she moved in the afternoon no faster than she usually did. The hushed sound of the pine on the opposite side, the hushed flit of the sparrow passing along the wire as she moved. She heard the Volkswagen behind, yet kept moving. In her legs there was strength: the strength was the feeling of maturity that she seemed to possess. Allison stopped.

"You going down?"

"Yes."

He opened the door for her and they drove on.

The church, white, stood high upon the shale bank and beyond the shale banks the shore and water, calm blue now; the pines high with their roots dug under the very soil they used for graves. The church stood with the cross pointing into the sky and nothing. The stands had been set up and only the workers were here yet, moving about not entirely sure what they were to do. The tables being set up.

She got out of the car and moved along the newly painted gate, the gravestones on the far side looking blank and smooth in the afternoon. She glanced their way—the flowers that grew up upon the edges of the yard, and moved in the slight breeze, the grass over the grave mounds green.

"Where are you in?" Karen said.

Karen moved in the sun, her reddish hair fresh washed and shoulder-length, the ground giving way to her inch-high shoes. "Where are you in?" she said again. Angela was behind her, the plumpness of her white dry arms in the sleeveless dress.

"Canes," she said.

"I'm with ya," Angela said.

They went into the centre of the ground, where most of the people were. The sun was glinting upon the church, making it glare white, making the dark stained-glass windows shine in an unintelligible pattern in their eyes. They said the foundation was hard stone and it took a year to dig under it deep enough to lay it out, where the charred bones of Indians were found, that the workers threw up with the stone and dirt and shale, the bone no more a part of anything but of the dirt itself, no more than the shale itself. Sometimes a bursted skull that the workers found. And the priest then, which was a hundred years ago or more, blessed the workers as they dug yet blessed nothing of the bone because the bone was more shale and dirt that they threw with their picks and shovels than anything else in existence. "Yet it was their sorta church before it was our church," Leah said.

And the boy was sixteen, only sixteen. He began working in May that year, which was one year after he came. He was the first in the graveyard, nearest the water—*Josiah Murphy 1852*, it said. It said: *Leaves his wife and seven beloved children*. "As if a boy a sixteen could have seven children," Leah said. "He musta had one dancin cock," Cecil said. "Maybe he wasn't sixteen—maybe he was twenty-six," Cathy said. "It says right on it sixteen," Leah said. It was the cracked tombstone nearest the water, water on the autumn shore. "He musta had one dancin cock," Cecil said. "Will you shut your Jesus mouth?" Leah said. Cathy said nothing.

"Well, how did you make out the other night with him?" Karen said.

"I made out good," Cathy said.

"Gonna go out with him again?" Angela said.

"Don't have any idea."

Angela laughed short and nervous, her head twisted a little and her teeth to the sun.

"Well, I don't," Cathy said.

They were near the centre of the yard, Irene and Leah in the distance setting the tables about. The cars were arriving already and already those that were working were in their stands. "I tell ya how he died, he fell from way up there a hundred years ago from right up there, they had a sorta frame around it and they were liftin the bell from the inside but he was on the outside and he fell all the way, right against the steps where we go ta church, over a hundred years ago," Leah said.

"I heard he got a pick in the head," Cecil *said*.

"I don't care what you heard—" Leah said.

"A pick in the head cause he was fuckin about and wouldn't pay attention."

"Oh yes," Leah said. "Oh yes." There was still the brown spot on her knee where she had kneeled on the ground beside the grave, it saying: *Dwight Everett 1874–1949 / Annie Dunstan Everett 1879–*.

"What do you say?" Cecil said turning back to her. "A pick in the head?" She looked at Leah, Leah said nothing. "I don't know," she said.

Leah said nothing.

They stayed in the cane stand all afternoon and people gathered without them noticing. At first only a few cars and a few people wandering aimlessly from stand to stand, taking a turn throwing ringers on the canes or at the horseshoe lane; the women's perfume on the air that way, neither stale nor sharp, just resting upon the air, unmixed with it. So that when they passed you could smell it from their hair, bodied high and held with spray; and the men silent. The heat on them both. The women gathered in groups, their heels digging into the soft brown dirt, their legs gently white in the sun. The children running.

The wall of the bay behind them spread out blue. She was working and the sounds grew, children running from stand to stand. And she would say: "Ya haveta ring it all three times, ya get three shots at it for a quarter." The women would flick the rings weakly, the men too hard, driving out against the side of the backing and landing useless in the dirt. Then she said: "Ya haveta ring it just twice—ya have three tries." Angela looked at her giggling, the soft white flab of her arms. The women flicked the rings weakly as if they would tear their suits when they threw, and then would look away smiling clumsily. The men too hard. When the women threw, the smell of the perfume was there in the stand with the heat of the afternoon that she stood under. They would be bent forward just slightly.

But then she had no time to notice the crowd. She kept watching for Orville. Young girls threw too awkwardly, the rings veering off or never reaching or hitting Angela who stood at the backside to pick them up again. "Goddammit," she thought. "He's back at that fort; he's back at that fort."

The smell of Noxzema on the slightly dried faces. The red sun patches on the cheek. The upriver accent and the accent of the bay, of downriver, the nets and the water.

"Well, where didja go?" Angela said.

"We didn't go nowhere—down to the wharf."

"Parkin eh?"

"No, he went swimmin."

"Oh," Angela said. "Gonna see him again?"

"Don't know; don't care."

"Sure."

"I don't."

"Sure."

In summer the church wood had the scent of age because it had stood longer than any other building there, and the scent of its age closed about you in the silence inside; the candles, the wooden doors that opened inward and the wooden Christ, his hands dripping blood on his half-darkened wrists. His feet clubbed inward and held together by a spike. In the opening by the rear doors the night came in fresh with flowers and pine, the wind gentle from the water. The confession box that she stared at each time she opened the inside door. *"Is Leah in here yet?" Irene said. Cecil was standing by the altar, Shelby a little behind him looking back. "She ain't here yet," Cathy said. Upstairs the sound of the organist pumping her feet on the pedals, the dry night light coming in so that the pines stood statue-still in the heat and the short twilight distance. The faint worn handmarks on the warped pews. When Annie used to come they rented their pews; Annie had the pew closest on the left. The candles sputtering in shadow below the Virgin, her cracked face and her hands uplifted with a choir of small childlike angels about her. The silence, the organist pumping her feet on the pedals. Maufat kept twisting. Then Leah came in, the dress yellowish-white and long, her face reddened with the flush from the makeup and the heat. "This damn thing doesn't do me one jeesless bita good," she said. It was in her face, happiness and pain, that she kept turning to the people—to Cathy and Maufat and Irene with her eyes. "You look real nice," Irene said. "Yes," Maufat said.*

The grounds began to clear, people standing in a line at the tables. A few youngsters still throwing balls.

"You gonna go eat first, or me?" Angela said.

"You go on."

"I'll be back as soon as possible," she said.

"That's alright."

Angela slipped out from under the stand. Cathy was alone leaning against the backside by the canes. The dampness hanging on her back. And from the corn boiling in the pots the steam rising silently. *Shelby kept looking back as she walked up the aisle; then came Maufat, and Leah on Maufat's arm behind her not four paces and the sound of the organ loud and hollow in the dim church; the passions etched on each window in red and blue—the clouds red and the mountains blue-purple and clean so she often thought how good it would be to live there. Even when He was spiked to the cross and raised, the mountains raised behind Him in the same unchanging colours, the beautiful gown of the Virgin weeping at His feet. Shelby nudged Cecil; Cecil unmoved.*

When she saw him he was standing there watching. He was with

86

Rance and she did not know how long he had been there. She waved and came forward; Rance staring downward at her.

"You gonna try?" she said. Orville said nothing.

"Will ya try to talk some sense into your brother—will ya?" Rance said. "One day of the year and ya know what—he wouldn't even have a drink—he wouldn't; well, Jesus he wouldn't even have a drink so will ya talk some sense into yer brother?"

Orville kept watching her.

"Ya see Irene?"

"No," he said.

"Well, ya beter show her that yer here—she's worried about ya not comin," she said. "Ya gonna try?" she said.

"Try," Rance said. "Try—he wouldn't try nothin."

"Maufat's over there eating now, so you better show them you're here," she said. He looked at her; Rance staggering in the dry heat and the church behind them, its tall ancient cross pointing into nothing.

"I'll try," he said. "How much—quarter?"

She nodded and handed him the rings.

He stood sideways when he threw, glancing from the corner of his right eye. He took his time aiming but pretended he didn't, pretended it didn't matter; as he pretended always when he fired the gun, Maufat saying: "Ya haveta learn ta cock your head into the sight—ya haveta learn that or ya won't hit a barn door." The first one glanced off the cane. "Only two and ya win," she said. Rance kept staggering. He aimed again, his feet moving outward solid in the dirt. He threw again and it landed on the cane; and then he threw the third time and it went sailing over and hit the backdrop. She went and picked the rings up.

"Can't ya do nothin?" Rance said. "Can'tcha do nothin?"

She came back to them.

"You try it then, Rance, you try," she said. He was staggering.

"A Jesus quarter for that," he said.

"Well, try," she said.

He spit up and took the rings from her. Then he laughed:

"Now ya gotta give me some room," he said.

"Go on," she said. Orville stood heavy-legged in the dirt. Rance didn't take his time, didn't aim as if when he missed he would take it as nothing. Yet he didn't miss—the first two landed on a cane.

"What'll I do with this?" he said, holding the last ring in his fist.

"Throw it," she said. "Throw it," she said laughing. "Those were only luck," she said. He sneered and threw the last one purposely against the backdrop.

"You can keep the stupid cane," he said.

"No, take it," she said.

"No, ya can keep the stupid cane."

Rance walked away in the direction of the tables.

"Ya wanta try again?" she said. Orville leaned against the front rope. He shook his head.

"For nothin," she said.

"So this is what ya call a picnic."

She turned sharply. John stood on the other side.

"Oh hello," she said.

"So this is what ya call a picnic."

Orville began to move away, kicking the dirt, the dust of the dirt lying against the flat blackness of his shoes.

"Orv, ya wanta try again, Orv?" He didn't turn around. "Yes, this is a picnic," she said.

"Well, I went to your house but ya weren't there so I figured ya'd be down here."

"Ya wanta try the rings?" she said.

He shook his head, staring at her, his rising cheekbones.

"No, I just wanted ta know if yer comin with me to the exhibition tomorrow night."

"Ya, I'll come—what time?"

"I'll be down," he said. She looked at him, said nothing.

He looked off to the side. "Okay," he said, "I'll be down—I gotta guy waiting for me now." He moved away into the crowd. She watched him. "I thought ya'd be selling kisses," he said. She felt tight in the belly.

"No," she said.

"Well, I'll be down," he said.

It was an hour before Angela arrived.

"I thought ya weren't going out with him, I saw him, I thought ya weren't, I saw him."

She kept glancing for Orville.

"Shut up."

"Ah ha, I thought ya weren't."

"Shut up," she said.

88

7

Irene said nothing about it to her until it was almost time; until she had changed into her new slacks and was sitting near the window in the room. She was watching the cars as they passed along the road; the yellowed grass blew constantly in the ditch behind them, and above the thin branches of pine the clouds were forming grey.

"I hope it's not spoiled for you by rain—it was so hot yesterday and today I knew it was going to have to rain."

Along the horizon the sky was still open, settled with the milk-white mist that settles above the water after a day of heat and sulphur. Irene stood beside the banister watching her, and it was in her watching. She knew what the question was before it was asked and yet it didn't matter. It still gave her some feeling, an unaccountable heaviness upon her.

"I don't care; it's only a stupid exhibition anyway," she said.

"Well you don't think John would care if he goes?"

"I don't know—I don't think he'd care."

"Well, all you have to do is just keep an eye on him a bit, and see he gets home alright. I mean just know where he is and let him come home with you—John wouldn't mind that, would he?"

She shook her head.

"Well, I don't like to ask anything like this but he's been saving up for it and I don't want him to go alone, that's all—and he has no-one to go with, that's all," she said.

"It's alright," Cathy said. "Where is he—it's alright."

"He's out to the store—he'll be back soon probably," Irene said.

She sat in the chair until he came in and then went into the kitchen. The smell of the hot iron and her mother at the board, the sound of water and each stroke of her mother's hand an effortless perfection.

He was heavy with the sweat of running, his face flushed and a dampness to his shirt. The rim below his eye was beaded with perspiration. He threw the package of tea-bags on the counter and stood there the heat pulsing along his arms and head so that he appeared swelled for the moment.

"Hello," Irene said. "You wanta go to the exhibition with Cathy and them?"

For an instant there was no response. His arms fell inward and he moved back against the counter, thrusting himself up against it and turning his head. She didn't understand; he said nothing. He folded his arms together. The dampness of his shirt.

"Well," Cathy said. "Ya wanta come—get on the tilt-a-whirl with ya and watch ya get sick."

"Ya better get changed if yer going—I've got a fresh shirt for ya here—ya don't want to go all sweaty."

"No, I want to go alone," he said.

"I don't want you going up there alone," Irene said. "And how will you get home here if you go up there alone?"

"Hike."

"I don't like you hiking alone," Irene said.

Cathy set the tea-bags in the cupboard and turned to him.

"It doesn't matter to me," she said. "Just ask John; he won't care cause it doesn't matter to me."

They were all silent for a moment and he looked at them steadily, his arms folded that some day would be thick and strong, his body still heaving that some day would be broad and strong. His blond hair dangled along his forehead in the heat.

"I'm not tagging around; I want to go alone," he said, his voice calm. "I want to go alone, not tagging around with them."

"And what's wrong with that?" Irene said. "Lotsa boys go to the circus with their sisters—lotsa boys do."

"I'm not tagging along with them," he said. He walked to the door and into the room. "I'm going alone tomorrow night."

"Well, you're not going up there, you're just thirteen and you're not going up there alone all hours of the night over my dead body. Now you go with them or stay home."

"I'm not going with them," he shouted. "I'm not going with them."

"And I don't want you runnin like ya were doing tonight any more," Irene said.

"He could go with Rance," Cathy said after he had climbed the stairs.

"I don't like him going up there and wandering around by himself, without anyone to keep an eye on him."

"Well, if there was a bunch of them went up nothing could happen."

"Yes, and if there were a bunch of them went up a lot could happen; a lot could happen."

Her mother turned back to her ironing; her shoulders hunched inward as she moved the iron. In another minute the car was in the yard. She threw the light jacket over herself and went into the porch to meet him.

"Hello—ya ready?"

"Listen, can Orville come with us?" she said. It only took a moment to see his face that way; the skin drawing tighter and whiter around the jaws.

"I mean just get a drive up and back is all."

"I don't mind, except we'll be hikin back cause they aren't comin."

"Oh."

"They want to go later in the week; they say it's no good the first night."

"Oh."

"But shit, he can come."

"Well, come on in; I'll ask him."

"No, I'll wait here."

"Oh come on in."

"No, no I'll wait here." He was eyeing past her into the kitchen where her mother ironed with her head down.

She went to the foot of the stairs.

"Orville," she called. "You ready—you coming?" She waited a moment, "Orville—you ready?" Another moment. "Orville."

"I guess he isn't coming," she said going back out.

There was only Andy in the car so she sat in the middle between them. And then the wind and the taste of rain bloating the heavens, the dark clouds making the twilight sink into the night. An ore-boat in channel water. As they approached the town they could see the long sweep of the ferris wheel revolving.

"So you don't think it's going to be too good tonight?"

"Oh, it'll be good," Andy said. "We're just waiting till later in the week."

"Oh," she said.

When they neared the place the streets were lined with people and cars, the parking-lot full and the large white building lit up and decorated. He took them as far as he could along the street and then backed into a yard. Even from this far down the sound of music, the sound of loudspeakers and the roar and scream of the people on the rides. The smell of animals about—of dung half-warm and hay and upturned mud.

"You want to sneak up this field and over the wire?" he said as soon as Andy had turned out into the street.

"No," she said. "Why, do you?"

"It'd be worth a try," he said. "They aren't going to have nothin here but horse-hauling so there shouldn't be anyone around—oh the guy that looks after the strippers' tent but that's all—so just follow along out of sight of the floodlights when ya get close and then just jump over the wire."

"How high is it?"

"I'll help ya over," he said and started moving across the field slowly with his hand back ready for her to take.

"Maybe we'll get caught."

"Shit," he said. She couldn't stop her nervous giddiness as they walked. Every few feet she said, "Now I'm not gonna be able to get over that fence." "I'll throw ya over." "I'll break my neck." "It isn't the Empire State Building ya know." "I'll break my neck—they'll think I'm tryin to sneak into the strip show or somethin."

They reached the fence and crouched along it. It was too high for her, the wire sticking out like nettle from a plant. Here the sounds were loud, the people loud, the rides and the heat generated from the machines. John was ahead. The twilight had turned to dark so that only his darkness was there and when he moved he moved like a shadow, except when his frame was caught by the light.

Behind the tent the barbed wire ended and a wooden siding began. He turned to her and stood. They were out of the light now, yet they could see the hundreds moving in circles, the girls when they screamed upon the rides, suspended for that second before the machine twisted them around again: their legs and their arms, their mouths.

"It gets lower down farther—I'll help you over first and then jump over."

"You said a man would be around here."

"Well, if we stand here talkin about it all night he will be."

Music came from a loudspeaker above the strip tent. To her it was coarse music, something that set them apart as much as the inside tarp where they did their act, as much as the powder so thick as to make them seem yellow or blotched. Their eyes so damaged and remote as not to be affixed to any time or place. And yet *there*, the smell of the sawdust, the tent, their half-covered loins and tinted hair. It was something coarse and comic, with the shouts of the children, the taste of candy and the rides.

Something so ever-present—that what they were doing upon the stage, comic in its lack of decency, was within her, within the men who stood watching. It was what she felt; that it reduced them all to something below what they were, what *it* should be for, what they should be. And yet she, before, had watched them gyrate and twist under the floodlight as they were being introduced, Karen saying: "You could do better than that, MacDurmot—that nigger there looks pregnant."

John had his hands around her waist ready to lift her, his strong thin fingers just below her ribs. "Now grab hold, grab hold," he said and she felt herself lifted, her arms reaching the top of the siding and John moving his shoulders under for her knees. She balanced one leg over the siding and felt it sway beneath her. The tent was so close that she was brushing it with her arm and was frightened of falling against it. "Don't let me go; don't let me go." "I got ya; I got ya," he said.

Then she swung over and felt herself drop, hitting against a tent peg and falling sideways. It was black. For an instant she heard no music and then the music came again. Far above her the gleam of the floodlight and to her right and left the sound of motion, confused tramping. John on the other side. Just before he came over she caught the sight of his face and then he landed beside her, laughing.

"We'll go around this way," he said pointing to the right.

They walked cautiously, stepping over rope, he in back of her with his right arm steady at her side. When they came to the end of the tent he stepped in front of her and moved out quickly, taking her hand. They were into the crowd in an instant—he was laughing.

"Dammit, my slacks got mud all over them from that damn fence," she said, trying to brush it away.

"It's not much—don't worry about it."

It streaked along the inside of her legs. When she had put her legs over it must have come off the siding. She tried to scrape it away—mud or something else she didn't know.

"It don't smell very good."

"It's alright—ya can't even see it."

They were far beyond the tent walking with the crowd, half of it coming toward them in a zigzagging fashion, brushing against them, lotion and perfume and the nauseous sweet heat from the rides. When she looked up there were only lights—the ferris wheel and the bullet above them and the sky a dull black.

"It isn't much this year, is it?" he said.

"It gets smaller and smaller all the time—even the ferris wheel don't look as big as it used to."

"That's because you're bigger," he laughed.

Once men rode a bicycle on a wire a hundred feet from the ground with no net beneath them, and there were clowns that year, and three elephants they paraded around the ring each in all directions, making them stand on their hind legs, and sit, and roll over, bathing themselves in the dust. That year Irene took her and Leah—they went on all the rides, Leah holding Cathy tight and screaming, though she herself never needed to scream, and when they were in the bullet Leah said she was going to get sick but she didn't. That was her favourite circus, because then the rides were more than rides and the clowns more than clowns. When Irene went to play bingo in the open tent she and Leah went in through the horror-house, Leah had her by the hand saying: "Don't be scared Cathy—don't be scared." But she wasn't scared. Then they went in to see the alligator-man and the two-legged dog. The lights were brighter; there were more lights, the kind that revolved in the air, and more stands with dolls the brightest she ever saw dressed yellow and red. They went in to see the two-legged dog. The tent was dark with only a spotlight over the pit where they kept it, and it lying prone in the sawdust, and the woman going into it saying: "Up, up," and it rising on its two legs for a moment and then falling again. Leah said: "They cut the darn old legs off that old dog." And the woman turned to her with lines almost green in her face, almost purple under her eyes and her kerchief blue over the thick solid hair. Then Leah turned to Cathy and said it again, said: "They musta cut the legs off that old dog."

The woman said: "Come in here young girl and see for yourself."

"I'm not going in," Leah said.

"Come in and feel if they were cut off or not," the woman said.

Leah looked at Cathy and then looked at the woman. The tent was dark except for the light that shone on the dog and the woman in the pit, urine and sawdust and sour milk. Then Leah walked in quickly and stood by the woman. They were almost the same size except the woman was different, looked like Old Face, the rock lines upon her, in her skin, purple the colour of veins.

"Up, up," the woman said. Leah looked back and smiled. "Up, up," the woman said. The dog hopped upon its hind legs, its tongue lying flat out the side of its mouth.

"Up, up," the woman said, "You feel there, put your hand there and run it across and see if the legs were chopped off. Up, up, stay, up boy," she said. Leah looked back quickly and smiled. She took her right hand and rubbed into the white fur, stained with flecks of sawdust chips and urine and sour milk.

"Up, up," the woman said.

"No, I guess not," Leah said.

"They weren't chopped off, were they?"

"I guess not," Leah said. She walked out of the pit and went up to Cathy.

"You know where that dog came from?" the woman yelled to them as they were leaving.

"Where?" Leah said.

"It came from Ohio—you know where that is?"

"Yes," Leah said.

"Well, that's where it came from," the woman said.

They moved out into the bright lights of dolls dressed the colour of red and yellow, of the warm night air.

"They were chopped off—but I didn't want to say nothing."

"Why?"

"Cause they're just as liable to kidnap ya as anything and keep ya in the circus and make ya become strippers or something—and that dog didn't come from Ohio either."

"Oh," Cathy said.

The exhibition this year had the horror-house but no two-legged dog, no main tent where men ran on bicycles above the crowd. Still there were the rides—and the chance stands where you could win a doll, and the lights and the smell and heat. The men in the stands yelling out to them as they went by, the whirring of the great motors that ran the machines. The candy—she would bring some home for him, she would say: "Here Orville, I got ya some cotton candy." Just like Maufat once bringing it home for her, drinking, and Irene saying nothing for a day.

They went around four times. There was no-one that she knew—she kept watching for Karen and Angela yet she knew they wouldn't be coming. John stopped now and then, holding onto her hand to talk to someone. She stood looking into the distance as he talked.

She watched the people on the rides, how they would be lifted and set back again and turned and twisted, swung into motion by some gigantic force in which they put their faith. Screaming with fright or pleasure. She never screamed—it was silly to scream when she was on them; when she herself decided that she would be strapped in, frozen into place by the weight of the air. Her lips went tight when she was on them, her face solid and her hands clutching at the bar.

John tugged at her hand and they moved around again. They said little to each other, and she kept looking at the ground while they walked, watching the feet stepping around about her, the discarded refuse.

"Well then, who was that guy?"

"What?"

"Who was that guy—you were just talkin to?"

"Kevin Dulse—lives about eight miles up from ya."

"I never saw him around before."

"He never is around very much," he said.

"Why?"

"That's just him—he never is around very much; ya have to half beg him to do anything."

They were silent for a while.

"Well, ya wanta go on the rides?"

"Sure, which one first?"

"It don't matter to me."

They turned and moved through the crowd toward the ferris wheel. When they got on their chair was moved along until all the seats were filled. They were almost at the top before it started; she looking out over the town, the river dark between the two sides, the small string of houses underneath, the two mills a thunderous mass of redness and smoke. At the cove the large bleak chimney that she could just discern rising in the warm night.

The last person being clamped in they began to move. Going up there was a surge, a lifting, a feeling of energy. With her head tilted she faced the dark sky and seemed to be shooting into it, leaving earth to meet it, meeting the clouds that pressed upon them, bursting through the clouds into some other sphere. Her eyes were opened—her lips pressed tight. Her eyes were opened like they were opened when she was looking at a snowfall, with her head tilted and her mouth opened to catch the flakes. Her eyes were opened that way now, as long as they were shooting upwards; and then going down everything left her, went out of her, hung inside her gut like emptiness and her head went forward, her eyes closed. They were shooting downward into the dirt, into the face of the man who ran the machine.

Then John was talking to her; they were going down again. He said: "Scared?"

"No."

"You're not?"

"This is my favourite ride," she said.

"Well, it's no fun until you're scared," he said. He began to rock the chair back and forth. They were going up again. The sky was lost: he was rocking it back and forth.

"John," she said. He started laughing. She tried not to look at him, to look only at the sky. They were going down again. The sick loss within her, her legs pressed together at the knees. "It's dangerous enough without you foolin around."

"I thought this was your favourite ride."

The sky was lost. She kept her eyes closed now.

"It is unless you don't stop fooling around."

He kept laughing because she was scared, because he knew he was making her frightened. It was something inside him like the night he jumped from the wharf into the water. The chair was moving violently to his motion, and they were going down again for the last time. The wheel was slowing up. She kept her hands on the bar, her eyes closed.

And when they came to a full halt and the man pulled the lever to let them out she was still sticking to the bar as if it was her only safety; her only device.

When they came off the ride he was exuberant, happy. He grabbed her by the wrist and carried her along swiftly. She felt all the muscles within her tighten at his grip. She stared ahead vacantly into the oncoming crowd not wanting to look at him, to see the ones she passed. Yet strangely enough she saw them very clearly, their quick and half-unnoticed movement, the fast and subtle looks. The look of the man in the orange hat, tilted backwards on his broad black head, the texture of his summer-light jacket. And she thought: *Now what if it begins to rain on that jacket he'll be drenched for sure!* The woman eating fries from a cardboard plate; her mouth moving like something rough and mechanical yet not mechanical at all; and the little one that clutched to the back end of her slacks toddling along behind her, her own plate half-turned, the food half-dripping into the dirt.

They passed along. There were others too—crowds at the stands leaning over, aiming through stationary guns at objects small and coloured and distant. Images of animals revolving on a wheel, disappearing and reappearing, only to be shot at and missed or hit as the case may be. The laughter and the ring of tin when they toppled. He moved her to another crowd, a crowd waiting in line for a ride. She felt nervous now because he only wanted it to be dangerous—he only wanted it *unsafe*. But they were going onto the tilt-a-whirl and he could do nothing on it—there was no unsafe measure he could take, nothing more dangerous than the spinning of the large iron chair about in an endless wind.

"What are ya going to do this time—push me out?" she asked when they were sitting, walled in on three sides by iron and iron mesh, with her legs firmly braced even though the thing had not as yet started.

"You weren't really scared, were ya?"

"No— you're just a little crazy, that's all—what if the chair broke or something?"

"If the chair was going to break that would have little to do with it."

"It just ruins the fun," she said.

"It's what makes the fun," he answered.

It spun on a circular floor. For all the sound there was only wind and screaming. It would jilt them one way as if they were heading forever in that direction, as if nothing could ever stop them, the wind upon her face so fierce and her eyes clamped tight. Then it would be suspended in less than an instant and she would open her eyes. They would be torn the other way, everything pressing upon them from the other side, the pressure through the twisted mesh of the iron seat. And the screaming from the others. He was laughing again, like a child, excited over each new current of air; each successive shock or jolt would make him laugh in wild amazement. She clutched onto his large right hand. The black night revolving, spinning as if in space, as if outside of space, as if somewhere there was no control. She with her lips pressed tight and the circus. The man leaning on the stands firing into ornaments that dropped and reappeared, and the legs of those upon the ferris wheel. Her eyes shut. The greedy swelling in her stomach. The wind, the music. Then the lights when she opened her eyes again.

Walking was strange. There wasn't dizziness in her, but some turbulence that made her step awkward and confused; unable to get her balance and sight the ground, as if it was moving: rolling dirt mounds and humps, the cakes of grass. The smells were stronger now also— every smell came to her and into her nostrils with more poignancy— the food, the oil and grease, the night, the half-wet tarps and the men. The men and women themselves took on an odour in this turbulence. Their faces and eyes dusted with sweat or perfume or both. The stickiness of the heat in a night awaiting rain. The red drunken-looking patches upon their foreheads or mouths. A woman carrying a child cranky and half-asleep.

"Well, did I scare you there?" he asked.

"You didn't have to—you don't want to go into the building and see the displays, do you?"

"Not really—if you do though?"

"No, it don't matter," she said.

"Do you want to go on the bullet—since I didn't scare you last time, maybe I can get up to it now," he laughed.

They continued to walk. The turbulence was going, the ground more stable. The music was so implanted in her by this time that she didn't really hear it, unles they passed the strip tent where it came as something almost violent upon her. She felt heightened and lowered by it: heightened because those on the stage in their frayed silk costumes were contorted with such grossness that she felt better than they were. She hated them. Lowered because what they were doing was showing *her* to the world, debasing themselves with something that she could feel deep in; as if it inflicted upon her soul the same crudity and confusion, the same hollow death. She hated herself for watching them. "Come in and watch," he said over the loudspeaker. "Come in and watch the hole—the whole show," he said. "She gonna twitch it and twatch it any way ya wanta watch it," he said. "She gonna shake it loose like a bucketa juice on a cool and frosty morning," he said. "This is the show, the one and only show—for the big boys put on by the little ladies right inside." Contorted with such grossness that she had to laugh, laughing because she had a feeling in herself that was almost vile, that she couldn't explain, laughing because it was a wanting to hide, a hatred and an unknown kind of glee.

They walked some more, in and about the tents and stands and rides, watching the people and talking.

"Tell me about Julie," she said at last. She was getting hungry now.

"What do ya mean?" he answered. There was no expression. He stared into the crowd vacantly and twisted about his hand as it clutched hers.

"She's awful quiet, that's all."

"She doesn't know ya or she'd be talkin."

"No, I mean it doesn't seem she wants to talk to me—I feel sorta stupid."

"Why in hell do you feel stupid?"

"I don't know—I just feel she don't want to talk to me."

"Maybe," he said.

They were silent again for a long time. He clutched her hand, pressing his large one over it, on the summer brownness of it. Then Kevin came along again and John talked with him. They talked about going to the island to dig clams, bring beer along; lie in the sun. Again he never looked at her while he was speaking. She clung onto his hand as something foreign, divorced from him as if she wasn't there at all. She began to watch the crowds again. *To go out in the boat, the green water—and then the sand of the island was so white and hot, and rested against the incoming tide with a clean and burning intensity; and the woods sprang up greener behind it, and at the other end a shelf of rocks strangely formed and beautiful—and the sea for miles of a distance, gently swelling.* The boy moved around them and was gone.

"I thought ya said ya could never get him to go nowhere."

"Sometimes when he's in the mood for it,sometimes—you hungry?"

"Ya."

They went to a stand and ate and then onto more of the rides, the octopus and the bullet, both making that turbulence rise in her again, both making her feel the sweet dropping inside her. The bullet swung them round and round in a violent upending, their feet one moment facing the ground and the next, by the revolution of the giant tube, swinging them out into space far faster, far more viciously than the wheel could ever do.

He was quiet after this; they walked along for a moment, the sweet threat of rain still impending.

"I used to go with Julie a while back," he said.

"Oh," she said.

"Ya—I took her out once or twice a while back," he said. She didn't answer because she didn't know how.

It was foolish to worry over something that didn't matter—someone that she didn't know. She didn't care—it didn't matter. The screams from the whirling machine, the rain was starting, sweet and good and warm. *The man with the light summer jacket, with the orange hat far back on his black head.*

"How long's Andy been going with her now?" she asked.

"Oh a while." He cut short. "A while," he said again.

They had passed the place a dozen times during the night but this time it was raining. She tugged at him.

"You want to go in and have your fortune told—have ya ever had it told before?"

He stopped and held her back, the rain streaks along his white high cheekbones and black hair. He smiled lightly though not the way he usually did—the smile was sad.

"You don't believe in that stuff?"

"Sure—why not, it's fun."

"I suppose you believe the crap they teach ya in church," he said.

She looked at him; his face was unmoving.

"Yes," she said. "Of course, why?"

"You never even thought that it was all bullshit—like this is."

In her it was different. *This* she thought of witches. *That* spoke of God.

"It's different."

"It's not different—it's all the same."

In her it was different; it was one side and the other, one was fun, one was true.

They were silent. The rain hitting her face, on the mud streaks along her thighs. The dirt also was becoming muddy, the litter, the cartons and the tents. Those on the rides, their legs and arms. They were still moving, screaming. The water came down along the sides of his black hair and ran the length of his cheeks.

"Well, are ya coming in or not—I'll pay for it if you don't think it's worth it."

"I'll pay for it, come on," he said.

"You don't have to pay for everything," she said. He took her hand again and led her to the tent.

"I know I don't but I'm going to," he said.

The tent's inside was very small and narrow. The woman sat just outside the door and beckoned them through the narrow opening. There was a dank smell though the dirt on the inside was dry, the place warm and darkened, the only light being an electric lantern hanging on the side of the tarp, its cord hidden by piled boxes. The woman herself was old and grey, had a shawl wrapped about her. Her eyes looked as if they weren't seeing you but passed beyond you, into you, and her skin was leathery, the deep gorged vulgar brown wrinkles seeming to thicken and stretch it. She motioned them to sit down and sat beside them. They sat on crates with wool blankets draped around them. The light of the lantern hit her face, made her all the older for it, her nose hooked upwards a little and her mouth sunken into the wrinkles that ran crossways along the sides of her jaw.

She motioned to Cathy first and taking her right hand turned it palm upwards, running her own coarse fingers over it as she spoke. She moved her jaws as if she were chewing and spoke so quickly and quietly as to be almost inaudible to them. Cathy bent forward to hear her moving mouth, seeing the whisker traces black and grey above her lip. She said:

"You are young girl—you have many friends I see and they like you very much where you are with them at school and sometimes you work with them, you have many friends I see and they like you very much where you are with them at school and sometimes you work with them, you have many friends but sometimes you are afraid I see to trust them with your feelings but you shouldn't be afraid, and you will go on a trip, your line is long it shows a good life but there is trouble in your life there will also be joy, over this young man and another young man —you will have money in your life and be happy with your children, you will have three children and be married twice in your life—you like this young man very much. (Here she was rocking on the crate and her voice was no more than a whisper.) And you wonder if it will be him you marry and he likes you very much but you are young girl and there is much time to decide, though you will go on a trip after and you will have money in your life and right now you're young and it's early to decide. (Here she broke and shifted her position, the light of her eyes gazing blankly at the hand and then up at Cathy's eyes.) You are young girl and your family loves you very much and you love them and there is much happiness and pain and you love sister and brother very much and they love you though sometimes you fight but it doesn't matter the fights and when you go you will send presents and you will be married twice in your life and have money and friends." (Here she sat up completely. Her rocking ceased and she let go of the hand.)

She turned in her seat to face him. Cathy settled back and watched, the things that were said pulsating inside her though some of it she had hardly heard at all. But there was being married twice, there was *that*.

The rain was falling heavily against the tarp, the area outside full of running voices. The woman held his large right palm in her hand, her coarse fingers breathing lightly over it, and as she spoke she began to rock side to side trance-like. She said:

"You do not know some things you would like to know, they bother you—you would not come in here tonight unless this young girl brought you, this young girl you like very much but you do not know —there is the line on this hand broken and you have to decide many things in your life for there are two ways in your life always and you will take only one way in your life so then there are things in your life that you have to decide. (Here she looked up at him quickly.) There is joy in your life with your friends and family and this young girl but you have to decide because you will travel in your life and you will have money sometimes and then sometimes you will not have money but mostly you will have enough money and friends though you will be sad in your life also, depending on the road you will live long or not long but there are things you have to know and decide and one road you will be married and have children and one road you will not marry though you are young now and uncertain and have to decide." (Here she stopped moving again, sat up and let go of his hand.)

There was complete silence save the sound of rain hitting on the tarp. They stood and John paid her and they left, moving out into the crowd again. The crowd was lessening and moving faster, though the rides and stands were still operating and under a large tarp bingo was being played.

"Waste a money, wasn't it?" he said.

"I liked it," she said. "Why, don't you think she told the truth?"

"Everything she said was easy to say," he said after a moment. "It could come true or it couldn't and it doesn't matter a hell of a lot whether it does or not."

"Oh, it's still fun," she said.

They were moving into the building now and just when they were coming to the side entrance she saw Cecil moving a few feet in front of them. She didn't know whether or not to speak; he was here, he could be drunk.

She called his name and he turned around. They were inside the entrance now and Cecil came back to them, Shelby behind him. People moved around them in all directions.

"When did you get up?" she asked.

"Shelby and I were going back down now—we've been up for a while—why, ya want a drive down?" He spoke quietly his huge massiveness over her; though she could smell liquor she knew he wasn't drunk, that drunkenness in him meant more—meant meanness and physical energy.

"We wanted to look around a few more minutes," she said. "So we'll hike down after."

"Yer crazy, it ain't gonna stop raining, ya know."

"Well, we want to go around again anyway—for another fifteen minutes anyway."

"Well, we'll wait for ya out in the car," he said.

She looked at John. He was standing back looking at them all, saying nothing.

"Oh, you don't have to," she said.

"Irene'd have a shit fit if I didn't either," he said.

"No, she wouldn't," she said.

"Go round again, we'll be out in the car waitin."

They moved off—Shelby almost dwarf-like beside him, into the crowd, where his huge shoulders and head stood above the rest.

John took her by the hand once more and they visited the exhibits on the inside. The building was crowded because of the rain and people were continually moving into it at the various entrances, bumping and jostling and moving slowly.

"If there were a fire in here we'd all be crushed," she said.

"Fire'd haveta work some Jesus hard to start in here," he said.

They moved about the displays—a few live deer they had penned at the far side, the machinery on the centre floor and the painting exhibit and the gift centres upstairs. They moved around in a complete circle before speaking again.

"Well, you'd better go out if you want to catch your drive," he said. "It'll save me from having to hike back up in this rain."

"You wait here then," she said. "I have to run out to get some cotton candy."

"Cotton candy?"

"For Orv," she said.

The circus grounds were dismal, the loud rain hitting and sputtering off the machines. They were also naked grounds—save the bingo; the stands were closing, curtains and boards being drawn over them, the games deserted. She caught the candy stand just as the lights were being shut off. They put a thin paper over it for her and she covered it also with the arm of her jacket running back. Running back the mud splashed up about her, the rain soaked to her skin and the cardboard litter everywhere turning to something sickly under the mud.

By the time she was inside again she was soaking. She stood by the entrance door where she had left him and watched. There were people everywhere though she could not see him.

"Hell," she said. "Hell."

She moved toward the parking-lot exit at the other end still with her eyes to the balcony overhead. "Hell," she said. "Hell." Then she thought of Julie sitting in the car and never turning around, and his large half-red hand closing over hers that night in the back seat. She was angry now; she hated *her*. It was when they were on the bullet he didn't laugh, his eyes in the rotating turbulence were not laughing, his voice not laughing or teasing, not wild but bearing the brunt of the movement with the thought of *her*. As if by mentioning her name she had set something inside him to lock or freeze. "Hell," she said. "Hell with them!"

She was at the exit, moving through the turnstile. Cars were jamming the two lanes of the parking-lot, their glaring lights showing the uncontrolled pattern of the storm. She went to the steps and searched for the car, and then stepped down and began to move along the lines.

"Hello," he said. "Where the Jesus did you go to?" He came down behind her and grabbed her arm, the pressure of his hand closing upon it. His hair was soaked and lay wet and lank along his face.

"I couldn't find you—I couldn't find you," she was shouting.

"Well Christ, what were you going to do, fuck off or something?"

"No, no I waited—I couldn't find you."

"Oh," he said.

"I waited and I couldn't find you."

"Oh," he said. "Do you know where the car is?"

"Help me look for it," she said. She tugged at his arm and they walked down along the lines, the smell of exhaust, the clots of wet earth forming puddles.

"Well, anyway," he said. "I was up at that surprise-package stand and got this for ya." He handed the small gift-wrapped parcel to her. "And then I went out looking on the grounds for ya." She held it to her ear and shook it. "I don't even imagine it's worth anything; ya always get screwed on these deals." She put it in her jacket pocket. "Then I came back to the entrance and waited so I thought ya musta fucked off."

"I was at the entrance waiting," she said.

He shrugged and said nothing more.

"Do you want me to open it now?" she said.

"No, no it don't matter; it ain't worth nothin."

"It is so; it's worth a lot it's—"

Her voice was broken off by shouts from men around the car. A group of them had made a semi-circle near the hood and Cecil's largeness rose in the middle above them. He was shouting but what he was saying wasn't clear, only his large blackness in the black night, in the rain and the confusion, was clear. When they came nearer they saw a boy in the dirt, his hair in the dirt and his right arm rubbing the dirt and blood off his face. She shrank back immediately; something nauseating welled up in her gut and she couldn't speak. She grabbed tighter onto John's arm, her fingers almost claw-like on his hard muscle and bone. It was revulsion from seeing dirt and blood and matted hair, something that was human and yet savagely brutal when the younger one stood, his eyes animal and his face contorted with vicious cursing.

He came at Cecil with his boots and Cecil stepped sideways in an instant and hit him hard with his left fist on the side of the head. The boy was carried reeling into the dirt near the edge of those that made the circle. Blood from above his eye, from his mouth and nose, and the car lights shone on his naked face, on the white the rain had illuminated like a sickness, on the streaked dirt that ran the length of his jaw, on the blood that oozed out from it. He brought himself back in an instant—out of the dirt and into the night air. He went back again swinging wildly. He hit Cecil with two punches before the man sent him to the dirt again, and again he was up standing.

"Now fly the fuck outa here," Cecil said. "Fly the fuck outa here or I'll kill ya."

Yet he came back, the light and the blood and the rain. Something almost desperate in his screaming—his screams charged with something that made her sink farther into herself. He was hit hard again, and again. He was swung into the dirt and kicked in the face. Blood showed from behind his ear. Then Cecil threw him against the hood and hit him into it so that the sound resounded in the lot. Yet he had his hand up and was clawing at the big man's eyes in some last and hopeless animal attempt. He was thrown into the dirt again.

"Now fly the fuck outa here."

The boy stood again—blood and dirt in his hair.

"Come on, Dane—come on fore the cops get here," John said.

"I'll get you," he said. "I'll get every fuckin one of ya—I know ya all, I'll get every fuckin one a ya."

"Come on Dane now," John said.

"You get him the fuck outa here," Cecil said.

He moved through the crowd and walked slowly along the lane hitting the hoods of cars with his fist.

"I'll get you—every fuckin one of ya."

"I'd better go with him," John said.

"You know him?"

"Ya—I better go with him." He bent over and gave her a slight kiss; she was trembling and couldn't stop, the sight of the blood and the face being punched, it wouldn't stop. He kissed her. "I'll give ya a call," he said. He started moving after the boy.

"I had a good time," she called after him.

He turned back for a second and waved.

"Young fucker," Cecil said when they were in the car. She sat in the middle, Cecil rubbing at his face where the boy had dug into it.

"Guy's crazy," Shelby said.

They were silent. Once out of town Cecil took a pint of rum from under the seat and began to drink, passing it every now and then to Shelby.

"How did it happen?" Cathy asked.

"If I knew I'd tell ya," Cecil said.

"It weren't Cecil's fault at all," Shelby said. They were silent for a moment.

"Remember that fight you had with Niles—that was the best fight I ever saw."

"That was a good fight," Cecil said. "He's another bastard." He took another gulp from the bottle and passed it back.

"Ya musta stood ten minutes fuckin punchin," Shelby said.

Cecil said nothing. The rain was still hitting the windshield viciously. the road black with the rain, and on the inside a warm smell of pine. They were silent for a long while, moving downriver slowly. She felt warm inside now, and tired; the feeling of coldness and fear had left her. Yet still there was the face—the white sick skin.

"She shake it loose like a bucket of juice," Shelby said. "She twitch it and twatch it," he said.

"Are you going out west or not?" Cecil asked.

"I still want my money," Shelby said.

"Then you're not going."

"No-one to go with."

"Yer gutless," Cecil said.

"No-one to go with."

"Gutless."

"Suit yourself."

"Gutless."

"Suit yourself—I still want my money."

"You're gutless." Cecil laughed.

"I still want my money," Shelby said as if not hearing.

They passed Leah's; the lights still on. He shifted uncomfortably and had another drink and then passed it to Shelby once more.

"She twitch it and twatch it," Shelby said.

Cecil looked out toward the bay.

"You musta almost killed that bastard," Shelby said.

February 1968

It was as cold inside the shed as out. The snow crept through the door and penetrated the floor, and the air had the glazed stillness of ice, especially near the window where it seemed to settle, and beyond that the naked twists of trees and the thin crust of the field. There was no shelter in here—simply a closing off of the outside. He stamped back and forth, moving his thin arms for warmth. It was windless outside; the rawness setting upon your mouth and jaw freezing it as you walked, your steps frozen and empty and irregular.

They were as frozen in here. Still though amongst the things—the dust and torn lampshades—there was a subtle remembrance and warmth. They sat here winter and summer again; the hot thick stench or the silent void and cold. He snapped on the light and leaned against the door to close it shut. The rabbits looped over a beam that ran above the window, hung grotesque and stiff, their cold forms leaving blood traces on the pane.

"50¢, $1.00, $2.00, $2.50," he said, feeling their solidness with his hand, his breath coming white before his eye. "$2.50," he said again. The rabbits looped and stiff, the hard blood clotted against their mangled necks where the fur was torn, exposing a thin purple bite around the throat. He grabbed the two strings and hauled them from the beam, putting them over his shoulders. In here the musk tempered by the freezing, the long length of shadow the naked light made, of him, of them. He left and went into the night again.

It was nine o'clock. When he came back over the field Annie's bedroom light was on. Irene was up there now. He moved quickly by the old house toward their own, the black pressing upon him on the crust, the crust in places giving way. When he was on the highway it was even colder, the stilled and twisted hides moving slightly with his movement.

"They look like cats—I can't; you sell them," Irene said.

"Just cook one," he said. "Just one," he said.

"Oh Orville, I can't—you sell them."

"Well don't then—I'll throw them away."

"Maybe Cathy will," Irene said.

"I'm not touching them," Cathy said.

"Ya think we're too good ta eat rabbit," he said.

His right hand smoothed the hardened fur. Still on the fur there lingered traces of summer brown. He walked along the road half a mile, the exposed stones like stubble, the exposed blood hardened on strangled throats. The rawness was at him again; out of the black hardness, out of the motionless woods, the long bare movement of the road. He was alone on it, the sound of his boots.

"Ya think we're too good ta eat rabbit," he said.

She looked at Cathy and they started laughing, and it was the laughing. Cathy sat with her legs up across the table, with her skirt that way and her legs up across the table, and he could hit her, he could punch her, because she thought: her hair at her neck and her blouse tucked that way because she thought: that John came down here only when he was drunk and she didn't know, that he'd come down here and stand in the doorway with the door open letting in all the cold air and say "Oh hello, Orville," and she'd smile as if it was real nice and then go out into the yard with him and lean in the muddy snow against the back of the porch with him and then he'd say "Oh good-bye, Orville," and he could hit her, he could punch her.

The exposed blood hardened to winter, to the flecks and wisps of snow that moved and scouted through the cracks in the road. It was the blood that made them run, that was warm and clean inside them making them run; and now clotted and hardened to the flecks and wisps of snow, their limbs twisted, slightly moving with his movement, breathing with his breathing. In their eyes a vague winter stillness, like under a branch the ice melting down in mid-afternoon, their eyes like that, like a thaw of ice, or impure clouded water.

He came to the lane and leaned against the pole, the light on him, on the dark bare highway. The cold had moved against his legs so that he couldn't feel them any more, so that they were numb now, and against his face. The rawness came through his coat as he moved his arms, the lane to the shore road solid and black, the trees that grew on either side.

"I'm not touching them," Cathy said.

"No," he said.

"I'm not touching them," Cathy said.

"No, fuck," he said.

109

"*Orville*," Irene said. Cathy was laughing.

"It's only a stupid old rabbit," she said.

"I'll throw them away," he said. "I'll throw them the *fuck* away."

He moved backwards into the porch watching.

"Orville!" Irene said.

There was one caught by a snare that wasn't dead. The rest had strangled themselves in trying to escape, the bite of the snare tight on their throats. There was one in a snare that hadn't moved, that had waited in the cold, motionless, its nose moving, sensing out the air when he walked to it, the day quiet with the freezing.

He circled it, went round by a small hedge of alders. "Hello," he said. "Hello." The rabbit's ears went back tight, a trace of summer brown still around its muzzle, the alders an inch thicker with the glazed ice over them, the sky sharp blue. "Hello," he said, and the rabbit's ears went up and it turned sideways to him, shivering—the woods calmed and still as sharp needles in the fine blue air. When he looked past the rabbit the shapes of ice were hanging on the boughs and limbs, making white the inside trees.

He moved around the alders, taking out his knife, and when he hunched on his snowshoes there was pain pulling at his thighs. He felt heated from walking, the cool air now entering at his neck. He sat hunched watching it, the knife extended. The knife could cut through the knot of the snare just behind the neck, and then it could run. "Hello rabbit," he said.

The rabbit shivered, unmoved, its left front paw crooked in the air, and the fine smooth features of its fur and face, and the bright glistening instinct in its eyes. The quiet of the day and he was saying: "I'll let *you* go, rabbit—I'll let *you* go." He watched it for a long time, it unmoved—the day quiet. Only its ears would flick a little this way or that —only its ears and the soft unnoticed twitching of its nose. It had waited out the night and hadn't moved, padding out a small circle in trying to stay warm. Then suddenly he grabbed up its ears and held it; it kicking out, before he cut through its throat, the clear dark blood spurting and receding. "Hello rabbit," he said. "Hello."

There was something in this darkness as he ran along the lane, the sky and the earth and the sound of his boots. It was like the blood hardened and the blood running, the exposed slits along the throat and the pulse and vein. There were only forms now making movement with his running, and yet when the rabbit moved he thought: "I'll let it go," and when he was holding it up, it kicking, he thought "I'll let it go." It was watching, and when the knife shoved in its throat as if through no movement of his own, not the power of his own hands, it was still watching.

The lane led to the shore and the shore to the blackness beyond. The road was lighted at intervals between the houses, but most of them being used only in the summer were boarded and shuttered and locked. He moved to his left, staring out over the ice, the buoys in the distant channel water. The taste of smoke lingering on the night, the burning of oil or wood in stoves.

He came to another lane and moved up it, the crust hardened to support his weight, the house and the small white heat of the lights.

"Orville got rabbits," the little girl said after letting him in. He stood in the small kitchen. Allison came from inside the room and leaned near the stove.

"How many, Orv?"

"Five."

"$2.50."

"Guess so."

Allison took out his wallet, his long smudged fingernails going through it, and handed him the bill and the change. He gave the rabbits to the girl before turning to go.

"What's Maufat doin?"

"Eh—don't know."

"Tell him I'll be up one of these nights to see him."

"Ya."

"Ya wanta stay in ta get warm."

"It's okay."

"Tell him I'll be up ta see him."

"Ya."

He was out in the dark once more, colder now because he had been inside. He shivered, feeling the night press upon him as if it was something else, as if it was more than the dark. The immense desolate expanse of bay, and if he were out there now, in it how far out? Where would he be? He spit and waited. It would be easier to cut across the two fields if the crust was hard and find his way to the main road instead of going around. If the crust was hard he could do it because he knew his way. But he stood there waiting, spitting, watching the blackness. If out in it how far out, where would he be? It was the blood hardened and the blood running.

It was his teacher. Then he was looking outside and there was snow falling into the lot and the other building huge with its cement blocks, the green shutters drawn down in the light of afternoon, the grey sky and smell of chalk. He was staring at the other building. It was as if time had stopped it, as if it could be now or before, as if Maufat could be sitting behind those drawn blinds, as if Cecil could be sitting there, and the snow would still be falling, large and wet into the grey lot below, the empty traces of tires and running children. It was as if behind those closed windows the figures that moved were the figures of people who were not there but of others long before, or those who would come after; of those who had died or those who were not yet born. He shuddered in his seat—the linoleum floor, the quietness of the place, the afternoon, the ticking of the heat. The snow reminded him of supper—the taste of going home.

Outside was dismal but he could not look away, the street and the trees heavy, and now and then the glimpse of a pulp truck or a car, a woman walking. He shuddered. It was the building dark under a brooding sky. He sat for how long not knowing what he was thinking, not knowing how long. He wanted to go home it seemed, to have the taste in his mouth of the snow falling; yet he didn't know how long or what he was thinking. The shadows moving in the afternoon behind the blinds. Then his teacher went to the board. "This is infinity," his teacher said. "A man wants a motel room and there is one with an infinite number of rooms but every room is filled. The manager says: 'I'll put you in room one and put the person in room one in room two and the person in room two in room three, and the person in three in four and so on and so on—so that everyone gets a room.' " His teacher smiled. "Yet all the rooms are filled."

He shuddered and spit. The weight of the rabbits off him. Even they seemed to have a warmth about them, the solid heaviness of their forms. It was later—he knew it was later. He turned and started on the crust across the field.

The crust was solid and firm and he walked easily, moving with the shape of the field in and about the growth of spruce. There was still smoke in the air and the fine freezing on his jaw, his hands within his gloves turning to numbness so that he moved them together and apart. His long spindly legs moving as quickly as they could, his rapid breathing.

He left the main field and entered another smaller one, and another after that with the crust becoming softer, and he was sinking, breaking the soft shell of it with his weight and stopping now and then to rest.

112

In this darkness he couldn't tell where he had been or where he had come from, the blotted space behind showing no signs or traces; seeing nothing of the ground save what was at his feet. He turned and walked faster in the direction of the road—where he thought it was, where it should be. "Christ," he muttered; her laughing was there again, "Christ," her legs that way on the table, and her hair. *It was because she didn't know that he'd come down only when he was drunk, and say, "Oh hello, Orville," and he wouldn't say "hello" and say, "Oh good-bye Orville," and he wouldn't say "good-bye." It was that—she didn't know and it was her laughing.*

He felt cold because of it, more than the freezing he felt cold from knowing and her not knowing—from her laughing as if everything was good. He stopped for a minute to look about him again—and if the road was *there* he would cut through the spruce and if *there* he'd keep in the field. He spit out again. There was no road—there was nothing.

This far into the woods the smoke from the houses was gone. The night air sharp and the stars sharp. Nothing was here. Nothing. He could turn and retrace the three fields, each field broadening, and then he would be safe upon the shore road again. If he did that it would take how long? His ears and his face; he was frightened for his ears and his face, the continual stab through everything he wore.

He would continue on. It would be no more than five minutes before the fields closed off to the spruce. When in the spruce there would be sounds of the highway—cars passing. And he knew it; he knew it all, the trees—the trees and the fields and the road.

He stared about him again. Once in the summer he had teased Cathy in the woods. "I'm only goddamn kiddin with ya," he said. She looked at him so white and trembling that it wasn't herself, it was fear and not herself. He backed away from her with his axe and it was in him for an instant to hold her—to stop her from shaking, but then he hated her for shaking and had to turn away. She followed him all the way home crying and trembling, and he walked so that she wouldn't lose sight of him in the alders. He spit again. The road was farther across the field. But there wasn't a sound. If only a sound. He didn't know.

He began again very slowly, his direction changed somewhat, thinking that if he didn't meet the road he would meet the lane. One joined the other—he would meet one. And yet he was sinking in the crust, practically each step he took, the broken shell running hard against his legs, the undersnow within his boots. He began to run. Yet the

113

giving way of the crust stabbed at his knees, and he fell. He moved the fingers, numb within his gloves.

He stopped when he fell the fourth time and waited in the snow. Where was he? Only his breath short and painful and hard. If he had worn a scarf he would muffle it around his face. He breathed into the top of his coat, the warm breath along his chin and neck, his hands covering his ears. Listening to the pulse and rhythm of his heart.

Partridge in the winter bury themselves in the snow, to be warm, and at times when a crust forms they are lost underneath, and stab with their beaks at the crust from underneath. He stayed sitting a moment longer: "No, this is the field so the road is fuckin that way." He waited. Or maybe in the darkness he was turned around and the road was *that* way. It couldn't be. He didn't know. "Christ," he muttered. The road was that way, to the upper right. He knew it. *And when they stab at the crust from the underneath sometimes they are freed and sometimes they aren't freed and sometimes the fox trotting across sees them.* He stood once more brushing the snow from him. Inside there was hotness at his throat, a hotness and burning at his temples. He wouldn't cry. *And when the fox trotted across them they were still, petrified as fossils are petrified. They waited. If the fox saw them it would begin scratching, and if it began scratching they would wait, motionless, their feet tucked into the feathers of their belly.* He wouldn't cry. He could start back now but he didn't know how to start back. He could move to the upper right now but he didn't know if that was the way, and his knees were paining from the stabbing of the crust when he went through. *When the fox stabbed through the crust with its claws the bird might be quick enough to fly out of its reach, or its wings might be caught within the crust itself and then there was nothing.*

His right knee seemed bleeding, and there was a growing discomfort behind his patch. He raised his left hand and smoothed over the felt, rubbed his fingers over the skull-bone where the pain mounted. Where the pain mounted so that his right eye watered. He wouldn't cry. It was *that* way, to the upper right, and then through the spruce he would listen and hear the cars passing and be safe.

He moved to the upper right. He would be safe there, the long black highway under the streetlamps, the smoke again. And his bed, in his bed with the warmth of the quilt Annie made when she was how old, and he would lie under it. It had an age of its own—the bright pattern faded. He began to laugh. She had made round circles and little men in it. He began to laugh, shouted—shouted again. There were small stars in the sky, distant: How far distant? His teacher said, "This is infinity, a man wants a motel room—" He shouted again to listen for his echo, yet there was none, or if there was he didn't hear. He didn't want to cry—he didn't want to cry. Maufat said: "Any man who got sense can walk outa any woods in this here province in a day—so any man gets lost and freezes in this woods is his own fault."

He shouldn't have breathed into his chin that way for now the breath had turned to ice, and the whole of his chest was more chilled than before. He was shivering very badly. It was that you shivered, became numb and then shivered again—then numb again and then almost warm. Maufat said: "Those Indians I don't care it was their own fuckin fault." "Oh Daddy it wasn't," Cathy said. "It was their own fault, weren't it Cecil?" Cecil drank and nodded. "One-eyed jacks wild," he said. "No deuces," Maufat said, looking to Orville. Orville held his cards back. "It wasn't the Indians' fault," Cathy said. "Talk or play cards," Maufat said. "Talk or play cards."

Even now the trees still retained warmth. When he moved into them he found the snow deeper. He walked in a way, but heard nothing. Where was he?

It was so black inside that being in a few yards the field was lost to view, and in front no more than spruce, no more than that. No sound. He didn't want to, yet in his throat he felt it swell so violently—the fear so voilently within his throat. He didn't want to. If he had taken the shore road he'd be out on the highway now, he'd be under his quilt and the soft warmth of the room with the freezing no more than something jagged on his window, on the outside ledge, on the porch that ran slanted beneath it. And Cathy would be reading and her light would be on and it—"Christ," he yelled, "Christ you Christ," he yelled. Cathy would be reading. Cathy would be reading. It was late and his mother was waiting and he had to go home; he had to go home. "Chirst you Christ—hate you hate you," he yelled.

His legs were weak, trembling. Then almost quietly the upper parts of the taller spruce began to sway. He leaned against a small tree and waited and when he put his hand down to rub his knee he found the right pant-leg torn. Perhaps the trees were always swaying that way. If it was daytime he would follow the swaying and find the highway. He would stare upwards and follow the sky. But he couldn't tell if there was blood running or blood hardened on his knee. He rubbed his fingers over the skull-bone where the pain lingered behind the patch. "Christ—I hate you, Christ; I hate you Christ," he yelled. "I hate you

Christ," he yelled. "You think you're so fuckin good," he yelled.

He wouldn't cry. He would go back over the fields to the shore road but he wouldn't cry. He would walk straight out because the bay was out in that direction. Yes, the bay was out in that direction. He began to laugh again, taking off his glove and feeling the blood hardened upon his knee, the slit in his jeans a hand-length long, his fingers too numb to move.

She would be home reading, Irene waiting. The pain lingered behind the patch so that his right eye was sore behind the temple. Once in the summer she came to the stairs: "Orville." He didn't answer. "Orville." He was silent.

He was on the bed, his patch on the dresser. He said: "Don't you come in here," and she was opening the door: "I got ya something." "Don't you come in." "Cotton candy." There was rain on the tin porch beating just benath his window. He stood and she was opening the door, yet he stood waiting. Her hand appeared holding the candy, only her hand and the candy. "Don't you come in here," he said: "I'm not," she said. "Here." "I said don't fucking well come in," he said: "Shutup in there," Maufat said: "I'm not comin in—here," she said. "Do you want it here?" He ran to the door. "Don't you fuckin ever come in." "Here Orv here," she said. He slammed it on her hand. "Understand," he yelled. "Understand."

She began crying pitifully, her hand caught in the door, as if it was broken, as if he had shattered every bone without even knowing why. He took the candy and threw it. "Understand," he yelled again; crying because she was crying, because Irene was out of bed, saying: "What did you do Orville—what did you do?" And he couldn't answer because he didn't know why.

The trees were blowing. It had changed to a freezing wind, at first only wisping and now a force that made him sheltered within the trees. But he must move to the fields again—find his way to the bay—go home. He must go home.

He rubbed his hand occasionally over the patch. There was nothing to do now but start back; find the bay, and the shore road and home.

He started across the field again. When he looked down he could see how he had come across, the wind like long snapping branches at his face and ears. "Oh deary deary," he sang, laughing again, his eye blurred by the freezing, his head down following the tracks his boots had made. He had forgotten about his feet in the woods, now out here every step he took was heavy and painful. The snow and crust inside his boots rubbed against his socks and lining, making his body colder.

There was silence no longer; instead a mournful winter gale twisting and grating the trees on either side of the smaller field, his ears sharp to it, listening to every sound as it rose and fell through the wood. Maufat said: "So you only got yer one eye—ya got good ears."

He walked this way for some time, lifting his head now and then to look behind. The woods a distant invisible blackness. *Mallory stood naked in the snow, his arms not arms his face not a face.* He ran a little but it did no good, the crust so slight beneath him that he fell more than once, the powder beneath the crust entering his sleeves. If they had cooked one rabbit, if *one* because he wanted them to.

He walked a long way from the trees before realizing he was no longer following his track. That he was to its right or left he didn't know, yet there was only the smooth undisturbed crust beneath, his weight penetrating it again. A dog barked far to his right. It was the trees in the wind not the dog. He was crying. His mother home. Cathy reading beside the quiet yellow light upon her bed, and the warmth and the smell of dust underneath where the magazines were piled. *She handed him the candy and he jammed her hand. He didn't mean to, his arms went up and shut the door and her hand jammed, her little little hand. "Give me my radio—jesus just give me my radio." "What's going on in there?" Maufat said.*

He rubbed his hand over the patch. He was crying and it was like the wind or something, like the isolation of where he was. Where? To the right or left? If he found the path again he would be under the quilt which Annie made; the quilt that was part of the old house, of the musk of his room with the rain outside.

He did not know. They said you must sit down and rest. They said if you are lost you must sit down and rest and not to panic, and if you are panicky you must take your jacket off, turn it inside out, wear it for a while, take it off and turn it right again. Then you'll be calm. If you are lost at night you must wait until morning, until the sun shows the trees for what the trees are and the snow for what the snow is, and that you must not panic.

He was crying; couldn't stop. Even though he tried it seemed to be there in his throat, in his eye burning with the cold and the pain behind his temple. "Oh ya think yer so fuckin smart—Christ! Christ!" he yelled. He yelled it again. A dog barked to his right in the trees.

But he would not wait till morning. They said dig the snow out and sit in it and if you have matches dig the snow out and use boughs and

117

kindling to start a fire. They said a fire would calm you, for you to sit with the wind at your back. But he would not wait until morning.

He moved to his right thinking that this field must entre the next in that direction, that in that direction he must finally reach the bay. And then he could stop at Allison's and be warm. Be warm. "Oh deary deary me," he said. "Oh deary deary me." He walked slowly, at a pace that allowed him to test the crust before putting his full weight upon it. In the distance a dog barked. "It is not the trees—it is not the trees," he thought. He stopped abruptly and listened. There was no sound for many moments. "I'm close to the highway—I am, I'm near the good old goddamn old highway." He began laughing, the wind biting at his lips and teeth. He waited, laughing. There was no longer any feeling of the blood on his knee, of the cold stabbing at it; only the wind biting when he was laughing. Yet there—it was to the right—upwards. The dog did not bark again. It would not bark again. "Oh Christ make him bark, make him bark." It did not bark again.

He turned upwards and began to run. If this was *the* woods then it was only a little from the highway, and the highway a little from his home: so that he could feel the sun through his window on a May night when he watched Maufat painting the shutters; so that he could see the long delicate sweep of the brush in the hands of his father, and the long evening; and Karen after riding on Reginald's horse coming to see Cathy; and he could smell that too, the horse sweat between her legs where she had straddled it, and her brow sweating, showing the freckles almost golden. He wanted to go home. He would not wait. *Build a fire so that the smoke is away from your face and sit—if it's night don't move!*

He was in the woods. If it was *one* woods he would be going to the lane, if *one* woods to the highway. And if he was turned around in the dark? He was crying, the branches twisting and whipping at his face and in here even darker though the wind was cut off. Only the sound of it more horrible. *There was one in the snare not dead that had waited out the night and the cold not dead. He said: "Hello rabbit" and the blood spurted but he didn't mean to; with one flick of his knife to cut the knot and let it go. "Oh Christ please Christ oh Christ please Christ."*

He never stopped, never looked behind him. When he slowed it was because of the branches whipping about his eye. *Irene said: "I don't want ya runnin, fine thing runnin and ya only got one eye."* The snow was even deeper in here, the hard naked trees. There was a pine, nettles gone and yet the cones still clinging. He walked past it into a small clearing. It wasn't the highway or the lane. It was a clearing that led to a small path lined with alders. His legs were weak and trembling and his gut felt hot, more than it should be; hot as fever and sickness.

He moved between the row of alders, the snow above his knees entering where his right pant-leg was slit. Above his right eye was burning where the branch had slashed it. He was crying again, walking unsteadily in his weakness and not knowing he was entering a yard.

He did not know it. The wind was still at him but there was smoke again. There was a swing buried above its seat, and a long shed adjoining the house. He did not know it. Then a light snapped on in the porch.

Above the chimney the soot and small flecks of cinder in the smoke that drifted in the air. The swing was buried in the snow. And the night black as it was had the goodness of the shed and house. "Christ," he said. "Christ."

He knew where he was now—down at least a mile from the lane. It was the wrong one—the wrong field he had circled to. He was laughing now, running along the highway, the night and smoke and the vicious wind shouting at him, and him laughing and it shouting at him. "Christ," he said. "Christ."

2

It was Cathy who answered the call. The woman's voice was trembling, almost crying, and it was hard at first to tell who she was.

"Betty?" Cathy said.

"Is Irene there?"

"No, she's still with Annie—she should be back though, soon enough." She glanced at the clock above the sink: "This you Betty?"

"I'm comin up—she'll be home? I'm comin up."

It was just after 10.30. The wind was beginning to rattle the panes, deflate the plastic covering about them. Maufat had his beer with him sitting at the kitchen table, and the cards with him, flipping them over again and again. She went into the kitchen, putting the brush through her hair, watching the clock.

"Who was it?"

"Betty—she's comin up."

"Game of crib?"

She shook her head, then ran the brush across her hair again. He turned back to the cards with a grunt.

"You always win anyway," she said.

She had waited all night for John to phone but he hadn't, and all last night, but he hadn't. The wind. It seemed so strange that the night had turned so vicious now. All afternoon there had been that quiet freezing in the air, that sharp intangible freezing that contracted the earth and sky. When Orville had come in from checking his snares, his face, his expression was part of it. And he had gone out into it again.

The last time he said he'd phone he hadn't, and the time before that. She tried to put it out of her mind by counting the strokes of the brush. She threw the brush across the counter and went inside again, sat by the phone.

It was going on eleven. She wasn't going to wait all night. She picked up the receiver and began to dial and then slammed it down again.

"What in hell's eatin you?" Maufat said.

"Nothin."

"Don't make so much noise," he said.

She didn't answer. Another minute and she climbed the stairs to her room and undressed, staring out at the empty highway—the black solid trees moaning in the woodlot on the opposite side. She picked up a magazine and began to read, her school-books lying untouched on the dresser, where they had been since Friday afternoon. In the summer it would be over—she would go away. Some city because it was easier in a city. She and Karen had talked—how they would travel, where they would go. "We have the whole world," Karen said. "Anywhere in the damn world we can go—like *Europe* or somewhere. But if we're gonna go together then ya haveta wait a year for me—ya don't mind that do you?—you don't mind waitin one year?"

"And what'll I do for that year—sit around here?" Karen would begin imagining things for her to do—work, she could work in town, take a secretarial course at night school—

But it was easier in a city. And maybe she'd wait for Karen because it would be lonely to go alone. Now that she thought of it upon her bed, in her room among her things, the bottles on the dresser, the ever-present hardly noticed scent of powder. Everything was *safe* here, and where it was *safe* she knew it was easy enough. So then she would wait for Karen. They would go together to some city, an apartment or something.

She had waited for him all night and the night before to phone, and he hadn't. The chill was replaced by a burning, a heated flush rising on her face. She rolled on her back and closed her eyes. She wasn't tired. He hadn't phoned. Only if Karen were graduating with her, then in four months she could go to him—walk to him and say: "I'm leavin tomorrow." Then look at his face.

"For a trip?" he'd say.

"No, for good," she'd say. Then look at his face, and see what he felt when she told him that.

She sat up and listened. It was as if the phone had rung—but it hadn't. Sometimes she dreamed of it ringing and her running to answer it, and he was on the other end laughing at her; and then sometimes she dreamed of being at school and all his friends would be there laughing. She would walk away and he would grab onto her, holding her, holding her and all his friends would be laughing. She didn't know why. She stood and looked out the window.

"For a trip," he'd say.

"No, for good," she'd say, then look at him.

What she was thinking left in her a sensation of fullness, of sickness. Because she wanted him to *know*. It was very strange—she wanted to leave them all, and yet she wanted him to *know* that, and in knowing it ask her to stay. If she just left it would do nothing because then she wouldn't know what he was thinking, how he was thinking—and she *couldn't* go. "For a trip?" he'd say. "No, for good," she'd say and in saying that his mouth would turn white and sour, his eyes glare. "I wanted to marry you," he'd say. "Too bad," she'd say. It would swell in her: the ripping apart—the knowing that it was in her hands alone, and that now she didn't care—that she didn't care! "But I wanted to," he'd say. "I had it planned." "Marry Julie," she'd say, "if ya think so much about her." Her voice would be calm. "Christ," she said because she couldn't release it, the torment and the pain of wanting it to work her way. "Oh *she* thinks *she's* so goddamn good."

She went into the hallway—soundless except for the wind in the eaves of the house. "I won't phone him—I won't ever phone him, and I don't care if he phones me up again cause I won't go to the phone if he does." Black except for the small yellow light filtering through the crack of her bedroom door, her naked feet on the cold floor, the wind against the plastic and in the eaves of the house.

The night like it was and Orville would go out; just for rabbits. Just to worry Irene, and cursing and swearing. If she was to touch them she'd feel sick so she said: "I'm not touching them," "No fuck," he said glaring at her. When they were stripped they were like cats and she'd feel sick stripping them, but he didn't understand. She went into his room and pulled the quilt from the bed, wrapping it around her. Here it was colder, being above the porch, the air with ice in it, and the blackness and the outside. She huddled in the quilt bringing her feet up under her. It was a quilt Annie had made a long time ago, ages ago. She sat on a corner of his bed listening. How many people had buried themselves inside of it, how many ages ago?

If he came down again she wouldn't go outside. He would stand in the porch and then he'd turn and walk out to the road again yet she wouldn't call him back. Even if it was like tonight with the wind and the freezing she wouldn't call him back. The quilt around her and the air cool in this room, like that October when her grandfather stood for the picture, and the woman inside the window just catching the light in her face, staring out when the picture was being taken. It was cool in the room like that, yet under the warmth of the quilt it didn't matter. The patchwork fraying and coming apart, the circles in it splitting out, because she had made it how long ago? Irene said: "It ain't gonna last forever, Orville, the few dollars ya get off them rabbits I'd save—ya spend it now it'll be gone before ya know it."

If he came down again his face would turn white about the lips and hateful, and he'd look at her and if he started cursing she'd close the door because he wasn't going to curse at her any longer, and she'd go back inside and watch as he went out to the road again, in the freezing, trying to hike up—and she'd never once call to him, and if he called tonight or any night she wouldn't answer. But he'd be on the road hiking up—and it wouldn't matter to her. It wouldn't.

When she woke there was Betty downstairs, talking to Maufat. She stood quickly, with the quilt still about her, her bare feet hitting the cold floor, and looked through the window. The wind was vicious now and it was dark black. There was no light at Annie's, which meant that Irene must be coming home.

She could only have slept five minutes or so, no longer. She went down the stairs into the kitchen with the quilt still about her. Betty was sitting, her auburn hair, her face lined, and Maufat was standing by the fridge smoking. He turned back to her as she came through.

"I thought ya went ta bed."

"I was just up there." She stopped, looked at him. "Why, did someone phone for me?"

"No."

"Hello, Betty," she said.

Betty looked up and nodded, a slight smile, the fingers of her right hand lightly rimming the teacup before her, the steam of it rising into her hair and the lines in her face. The wind again.

"I wonder where the hell Orville is," she said.

Maufat grunted and looked at his watch.

She was growing heavier on the legs, Cathy thought. Now only her face had that lined thinness to it as the steam from the cup touched against it that way, making it white and moist. Though even Irene's legs had grown heavy now. Because both of them were older, and the way she remembered them together was that day at the beach with their swimsuits on, their legs and faces and shoulders white. Though that day was at least seven years ago and they had come to the beach with her and Angela and Orville, and she remembered on the underside of Irene's leg the long thin bluish vein when she lay that way to get some sun. And Angela out in the water saying: "Come on in, Orville." "No," he said, and the water lapping against her fat brown belly, against her bathing-suit that covered it, blue with yellow flowers. "Come on in, Orville—ya afraid ta get yer patch wet?" "No," he said: "You shutup—you shutup!" Cathy said.

Seven years ago at least.

"How you makin out up there this year—it's your last year eh?" Betty said.

"Oh ya. Okay I guess."

"What ya gonna be doin next year?"

Cathy shrugged. She picked up the brush near the sink and began to stroke her hair, the warmth of the kitchen on her bared right arm. Then Irene was knocking at the back door and Maufat went to let her in.

"What the hell you have it locked for?"

"The wind; what in Christ ya think?" he said.

Irene stepped inside taking her boots off, her face red and the sore that had developed on her mouth the last little while still there. Her slacks wet and snow-covered where she had fallen coming across. She didn't notice Betty.

"Yes, and I coulda used yer help over there too," she said once inside the door.

"I suppose," Cathy said, throwing the brush to the sink once again. "But I have work ta do; it's my last year, ya know that?"

"I know that—I know that, but that don't mean—" She turned and broke off in an instant, as soon as she saw Betty; the woman sitting there patiently over her cup of tea, which she had not taken from, and the steam still rising about the lines in her face, still mixing with the whiteness of her face and with the air, a transparent moistness to it all. The wind outside battering at the plastic.

"How is Annie?" Betty said, "I'll haveta get over some time too—"

"Oh, she's about as good as could be," Irene said, her voice softer. Maufat went to the fridge and took another beer, opened it and stood beside Cathy near the counter.

There was that look on him, of *it*, of what he worked in, the track and the cinder, something of the smell of the tracks leading away into the distance. One day when she was in town with Irene they went to meet him, and he was angered, and stood there in his overalls and rain-jacket—there was a soft drizzle in the afternoon sky and the reddish buildings looked damp and dismal and the reddish cars were shunting. She did not notice him at first because there were three or four of them, standing with their overalls and jackets on just where the cars were shunting, and a few more walking the length of the track. But he turned to them and was surprised. They stood farther down watching, beside the door of the freight building. Then he walked over to them, and he looked part of it, and his face was grey—the grey that was in the sky or in the track leading away, a grey with a dampness in it—an almost softness, beaten down.

"What the hell ya doin here?" he said to them, smiling a little, and looking around to the other men watching him. He was trying to smile a little but he was angry. There was mud dripping off the back. She had never before seen the expression on him, or such a grey face. It was the only time she had gone there, the first time she saw the men and where he worked. "We came up ta town this afternoon—for Cathy ta get some stuff ta go back to school," Irene said. "Oh," Maufat said. "I thought for a minute something might have happened to Orville." He looked around again. The men had turned and were moving down the track farther. "Yer lucky ya caught me here—I'm usually not on the track at all; I'm usually in the warehouse." The men were moving away. "Well," Irene said, "how ya getting home tonight? We were thinking we could wait and get a drive." He looked back at the men. "No, I likely'll be hikin home—ya can wait and hike down with me."

"No, it's too many to hike with three," Cathy said. He smiled and turned to watch the men again. Such a greyness to the tracks and the day, the smell of early autumn in the drizzle, the taste of September—

124

and on his skin the look of it.

He drank his beer, slowly watching Betty and Irene as they talked. Now and then the wind mixing with the voices in the room. Cathy stood beside him, waiting.

"So how is Lorne likin his new car?" Irene said.

"Good," Betty said. "He likes it good."

There was silence. Irene stood and poured herself a cup of tea, brought the pot back to the table.

"Ya want some more?" she said.

"No," Betty said. "I still got some."

"Well," Irene said. "She don't know anybody anymore—I don't think she's gonna ever recognize anyone like that—but I don't think she's in pain or anything—I keep her fed on the medicine and the pablum, and that seems ta be good enough. Though I don't even think she'd want food unless ya wanted to give it to her."

"I should try to get over more and help ya out—it isn't fair you doin it all," Betty said. Cathy looked down at her. She was staring into the cup, the tea lukewarm, so that the steam no longer rose from it, so that her eyes looked dull and lukewarm staring into it.

"Well, I have Cathy here to help out," Irene said. "I have Cathy here, so it isn't that much of a trouble at all—and I don't have three school-age kids either, like you have, to chase around all hours—so I don't mind," she said, her voice that way: kind.

"I'm pregnant," Betty said. "I'm pregnant again."

Irene stopped speaking and looked to Cathy. Maufat went to the fridge again, and opening a beer left, going into the other room. Cathy heard him in a moment on the stairs.

"What?" Irene was saying. "What?"

"It's been my second month," Betty said. "I'm 44," she said, "and I don't want to start all again." She started crying and Cathy felt nervous, because she didn't know how she felt about it, how she was supposed to feel, or what to say.

"Well, are ya sure—are ya sure?" Irene said.

"I know I am—it's been my second month and I know I am."

There was silence. Betty was trembling, crying softly, but that was all, and the wind on the plastic outside. Over the fields the rabbits running and if they came through on the path where he set the snares they would strangle; there would be nothing for them but the coldness of the wind and the wire on their throats presing like that—like she saw before when she went with him to his lines. He said: "This one's yours!" holding the rabbit. "I don't want it," she said. "It's yours," he said. "I set this snare for you." "I dont want it," she said. Because it was cold enough for them without that, without the cold thin wire on their throats, the thin copper biting into their flesh. Betty was trembling, crying softly, but that was all.

"When do ya go to the doctor?" Irene said.

"I'm gonna go up Monday—Lorne's gonna drive me in when he goes to town."

"Well, ya know it could be change of life," Irene said. Betty said, "No." "Well, it could be," Irene said. Betty kept shaking her head.

"Ya know how old I am?" Betty said.

"I know—but that don't mean nothin."

"That's why," Betty said. "It's like starting all over."

"But that don't mean nothing," Irene said.

Betty said nothing. Irene glanced up and then back at her cup, taking a drink from it, looked again to the clock above the window.

Cathy went to bed, putting the quilt in Orville's room before she did so—the fine scent from it, the feel of age. She was tired now and it didn't matter.

Yet when she lay down she couldn't sleep. She waited a long time in the dark, hearing the mutterings of the voices from the kitchen with the sound of the wind. Then she heard Orville and Irene was yelling at him.

"What happened?" she was yelling. "Where the hell were you?" She was yelling.

"Out selling rabbits—out sellin rabbits."

"It's damn near twelve o'clock," she was saying. "What happened to you?"

3

In the evening the sky was slate, coming down to touch the earth, the snow in the fields. He sat in front of the window, watching nothingness, with the chair tilted on two legs and his feet against the small paint-chipped ledge, with his cigarettes and whisky beside him—watching nothingness. She had gone out again—Irene's probably, with Ronnie: "And I won't be home tonight," she said. "Fuck ya," he said.

It was not cold anymore—not like with the wind the day before, yet there was a chill in the house always there—always. It came in from

126

the windows, up from the cellar underneath. He drank from the pint. If she wanted to leave he'd certainly let her—if she wanted to leave and take the kid he'd certainly let her.

Now and then a car on the highway. "I'd certainly let ya, ya goddamn bitch, ya goddamn bitch," he said under his breath, then laughed. "As if it'd bother me, as if it would, as if her goin away would bother me—fuck bother me, here's the ticket, get on the Jesus train and go—and I suppose—"

He stopped short—there was nothing in the house save his voice or the lack of it in the air, the tilted clock silent on the wall above the sink, the clock he bought her for Christmas: "That I got ya for fuckin Christmas," he said again, then laughed again, drank again.

It was no good—he couldn't understand why. She would sit all day like that and never move sometimes, and be dressed, her makeup on, her eyes flashing, and crying for no reason sometimes: "Because yer not workin," she said. "Get a job," she said: "Get yer own fuckin job." "All right I will—I'll go away and take Ronnie and me and Ronnie we'll go, and then I'll get a job." "Well, go then," he said.

But it was more than that and it made him uneasy to see her sitting there, sometimes dressed like that, and then crying besides. She took the car and went down again, he thought, Goddammit, he thought. "Goddamn bitch," he said. "Goddamn bitch."

But he stopped saying it—there was no more use in saying it anymore. The quiet. He put his hand through his hair down the back of his neck feeling the scald mark on the back of his neck, the thick disordered flesh. When he was a child: there was wind, and in the summer you felt it coming at you through the long grass in the fields when you lay there—the breeze off the water, and blueberries budding in the hot blueness and the sun dancing and glinting, and trees all of a colour in the distance like fine good smoke. Like fine good smoke rising with the dust created on the road and the slight wet smell of his shorts—and when he first saw Leah that time, her standing, the water smooth around her smoothness, the sand a fine brown hotness on his feet and she looked over at him, and then started talking to Mary—and he went to the edge of the beach, the breeze on the salt and on the charred log at the beach's edge. She kept talking to Mary—then she'd look over. He took a beer and sat on the log watching them in the water, knowing that in her head each time she went under, the good full shape of her in the waves, that she was thinking, Is he watching? Her youngness.

It was the good total youngness that she still had even now, even in

127

the musk smell on the half-soiled bed, the sweat along her back at times mounting. Yes, even now sometimes in the shape of her legs when she moved, in the laughing. Yes, that day in the field with the breeze on her almost slight nakedness, and he over her and he had waited and waited:

"I love ya—I guess," he said.

"What?" she said.

"Ya—I guess." Then pain and stupidity hit him for saying it all, then the pain and stupidity left him and he felt better, he felt out of him rise a necessity to say it all, and he looked at her, her face expressionless because of what he said. "Ya I do, I guess," he said. But he felt he didn't want her to say it back, that he didn't want her to speak. When she did he became angry, not knowing why. He held her mouth so that she couldn't speak, laughing so that she wouldn't know why he didn't want her to say it, because it was not in him to have her say it—to ever have her say it; the day bright, the sun burning on his back. When she said it he laughed louder, stupidly:

"Sure ya do," he said.

"I do."

"Sure ya do."

"If you love me why can't I love you?"

"Sure ya do."

He picked up the bottle and drank from it. There was silence. He wasn't cursing her any more, in his mind the past—that day with her when she told him, something cold came over him. He cursed at it— at that feeling he had, at the day itself—and then at her again; leaving tonight to run down there; every goddamn chance she got to run down there.

Sometimes when he looked at her he felt that if he held her at that moment, at that precise moment, he would hold her forever, but then it would pass because she would turn and speak, or without even speaking ruin how she was at that precise moment—when he saw her in all the same substance of the gentle nakedness of that day—and then something cold would fill him, something bad in his taste and he wouldn't want to look at her. He'd look out and stare along the roadway. She'd say: "Cecil," and he wouldn't be able to answer, because of the badness that had replaced the moment itself: "Cecil!" she'd say: He wouldn't answer: "For Christ's sake—Cecil, will ya listen?"

"What the fuck ya want now?" he'd say, and it would be over, lost; the feeling and the badness both.

He rose and stood before it now, watching the same roadway, high-way, he had watched for years. All the seasoned things in the air he knew, the bright golden weather filled with the touch of pollen, as if it rose, formed from the swollen grass; and then in the autumn, the ditch clay formed and hardened, the rock—sunken into the earth itself; earth into earth like some resemblance of a blotched face—his; and then in winter, *now*, at times the sky slate, coming down to touch the snow in the frozen fields, sometimes almost brilliant with the scent and the sense of cold. Darkness with the brilliant sense of cold. Between the distances of yellow light that fell from the road lamps, the darkness. He drank from the bottle again.

He could stand there for hours—it didn't matter; what mattered was the sense at times of being completely alone, standing or sitting, staring into something, into nothing. It gave him that freedom which he could not understand or explain, a feeling which issued from within him. He would think of her when they were younger; her body never the same body, her smell never the same smell, and he would think always of holding her at that precise moment (sometimes it was Mary, in the water, sometimes he thought of her), yet what he thought of really was no one thing at all but timeless things—days when he lived on the settlement, when he knew her only as a young girl that lived below the bridge.

He had watched so many times from this position that he could, if he acknowledged it to himself, know every trace of sunlight and dampness that hit the road, and tell the season, day and hour just by that—just by the wind blowing the leaves and the way the sun spoke of them, just by the cloted dooryard mud in April, the way the heels of her shoes were scuffed by the mud or the film of dust they collected in June when she would walk up to Ronald's closing. The minute healing and bursting of the pavement and the blots of tar.

What was it? They were gone down again both of them, she leading him out of the house by the hand, saying, "And I won't be home to-night." "Fuck ya," he said. "Little Mommy's boy—little Mommy's boy," he said. "You leave him alone," she said. Ronnie said nothing. Then he said: "Well, that's what the Christ you're makin him—makin him think I'm the old scar-faced bastard, making him think I'm the bastard."

"Feel sorry for yerself," she said.

"Fuck ya—fuck ya," he said.

At first it was just themselves, knowing what he had said and what she had repeated, it made him behave as if it could never be unsaid. He didn't know. It was as if because he had spoken *that*, the breeze on her almost slight nakedness, his large hand stroking along her shoulder, that all things followed. It was as if he was into it without even knowing or understanding. He cursed, the whisky burning at his insides every time he swallowed. Under the distant roadlamp a figure appeared walking toward him, then disappearing. "Christ—all I need," he thought. "All I goddamn well need."

They hiked to the dances and then home again. At first it was just themselves. It was her. And then it was what people said: "Oh Leah and Cecil, they'll be fightin to the altar—but they'll get to the altar" —and what people thought, and then it was the people's thoughts becoming their own thoughts without him knowing why. He didn't know.

He turned from the window and went to the kitchen sink. Maybe he wouldn't let the bastard in. It wasn't because when he said it he didn't mean it—it wasn't that; and her looking at him and him holding her mouth so she wouldn't say it back. It was because he could never say it again—never. She said: "Ya didn't ever love me." He never spoke. It was raining and they were standing against the rear door of the post office, and she was crying but he didn't answer her. He looked out to the rain, and the side-street littered, and in the air the full smell of oil and town vapour, the clinging of it to the buildings all along the side street, to her wet thin summer skirt and blouse, and the dark brassière underneath. "Well, I don't care," she said. "I don't care," and in her eyes was the waiting for him to say it. The smell of oil and vapour with the rain. He watched it again—the town so quiet. "We better start hiking anyway," he said. The black thin strap of her undergarment showing, as if above the thin drenched material the breath heaving inward and outward in short quiet sobs. He started walking —looked back twice before she followed.

Shelby didn't knock. As he came under the kitchen window he saw Cecil, waved and then came in through the back porch without knocking. Cecil didn't turn to him when he entered, drank again from the bottle staring out to the road and field, the ice-slate sky and reeling quiet of the darkness outside.

"What the hell ya doin in here with all the lights out?"

He didn't answer. There was a time that summer when he walked across the field, soaking from the after-rain and the field-wet, with the shotgun. It was to scare her—to know himself that he could go out into that woods with the gun, and do it if he *wanted* to, with her or anyone else not being able to stop him. That he could, to let her know that, to say to her: "If ya don't stop bitchin cause ya haveta stop yer bitchin." Yet he knew, and she knew. When he threw the child he didn't mean to throw him, and when he grabbed the gun, went into the dooryard, the sun so bright his eyes squinted, so bright his scars burned with it, they both knew. She watching him from the window at the side.

Shelby snapped on the kitchen light. The presence of the small man behind him made that oneness and quietness go—that goodness within him of being motionless in his own home; the lights out, the road, the winter. Shelby was talking to him but he didn't answer. He turned round, drank and handed the bottle over.

"Oh, ya got some," Shelby said. "What the hell ya doin in here with the lights out?"

"Thinkin," Cecil said, taking the bottle back.

"Yer thinking, are ya?" Shelby said.

They sat at the kitchen table. It was as if Shelby brought into the room, not the sky, nor the snow—but the place where he lived, something of the smoke at the back of his shed that lingered there with the undried pulp, the clinging of bad manure and soot and particles of cinder in the ice. It reminded him of once, walking the road to school and back and tasting it coming from the houses and the air.

For a long time they were silent. He couldn't bring himself to talk, to answer; the answers made by the passing of the bottle back and forth.

For a long time they were silent, Shelby fidgeting. His hands were skeletel, unclean, the bones protruding against the black-and-reddish skin, the nails long. He moved them across the white table-top in the cold room, reaching every now and then for the bottle, Cecil watching them when he did so—the hands of a small man moving that way. Then he took the bottle himself and finished it.

"So yer thinking, are ya—what are ya thinkin about?"

The dim light, the sound of the small fridge, and inside her clothes tossed across the bed.

Shelby unzipped his coat and leaned back.

"I brought some wine."

Cecil didn't answer.

"Well, what in hell are ya thinkin about?"

"Nothin."

"Nothin—nothin, ya bin sittin here for twenty minutes not speakin, thinkin a nothin."

Cecil took the wine and drank from it. Then he passed it over and stood, going back to the window again. It was the white; hands that were drawn reddish over the white. He didn't want to look, didn't want to speak to him. She wouldn't be home, he'd keep the door locked not to let her in, but she wouldn't be home. Going down there, always the same, Ronnie tugged along by her hand—her face tonight, the mascara dripping.

He went into the room, up behind her, just after supper. There was that damp warm heat from the stew that they had had, and her light neck felt warm when he put his large hand over it, and the skirt that she was zipping up the side, her naked thigh balanced in the thin twilight. "Leave me alone now," she said, "Come on," he said, trying to smile that way, his large hands on her. "Screw you," she said. The sun was low over the fields, glancing purple—the long winter emptiness on the road and the houses to the left, as if sleet had cut at their windows because of the reflection, because of the black cold glare the windows made. She straightened her stockings and he felt inside him, an emptiness running through him. He moved his hands along her shoulders downward. "Screw off now, I'm going ta bingo now." He wanted to come into the room after supper with her, wanted to have her lay in his arms, the softness of her heaving in his arms. He didn't know.

"Well, if ya ain't gonna talk to a man I may as well fuck off," Shelby said. He turned around and grunted. The wine was gone. In the room her clothes tossed on the bed, the yellowed walls, the white blind half-drawn to the outside night. Shelby lifted himself and went to the door, stood there, fidgeting, his tired small eyes staring.

"What the fuck ya starin at?"

"What the fuck were ya standin here in the dark for?"

"Nothin."

"For nothin?"

"Yes, for nothin."

"Well, yer fuckin crazy is what I say."

"You'll get a good swift kick is what I say."

Shelby opened the door and stood in it. He threw his fist out, yet Cecil did nothing—so he started cursing again. Cecil looked at him.

"And any time ya get around ta it ya owe me some money."

Cecil said nothing.

"Fuck-face."

"What did you call me?"

"You heard me."

Cecil started toward the door.

"You heard me," Shelby said, slamming it. Then he was out in the yard, throwing snow at the window, "And ya owe me money," he was saying. "And I'll get it from Leah."

He locked the door, turned the light off and went into the bedroom.

The bedroom was warm, silent. In here even the cars passing sounded distant. Or was it him, tonight? It didn't matter. He lay on the bed, a long time motionless. When a car did pass he could catch the walls, as they moved in shadow, the light glancing through the half-closed blind, the small light fixture over the bulb. She wouldn't be home—not tonight, he tagging behind her that way, not looking at him—never looking. "As if I m the old scar-faced bastard," he said: "Feel sorry for yerself," she said.

What was it? It was Shelby. Because if a man ever said that to him he wouldn't take it—he'd lash out at the man, and yet Shelby tonight stood in the doorway cursing and he said nothing—he stood there watching and said nothing.

Because of that time, her warmth coming through her skirt when she ran into the water; the water to her waist and in the smoke on the shore the sand-gnats circling; the fire hot and red on his bared arms, the light of the fire in the darkened air. He sat listening to her voice out in it, the small happy voice echoing over the waves, and then her coming from the water and the skirt twisted to her legs, inward, her legs a fine shadow underneath.

"Good ass there," Niles said.

"What?" he said.

The water running from her legs into the dirt, the bared blouse soaked and her breath heaving.

"Good arse there," Niles said.

"What?" he said. The sand-gnats circling against her as she moved, her form uncovered to the smoke on the shore wind, to water on the shore wind—the fine thin undergarments that she wore.

Niles looked at him, then at her again, the steam rising from her clothes, the burned embers of the fire and the heated dying coals.

"Nothin," he said.

"What?" he said. The red coals of the fire glowing on her legs.

"I said *nothin*," Niles said.

"Fuck off," he said.

"Don't think yer the only one that's ever been inta that," Niles said.

"What?" he said.

"Inta that bitch," Niles said.

They faced each other. It seemed that all strength left him and then when they started at each other all strength came back, and then when all strength returned, as if it rushed along his veins, he was swinging. As if swinging out at something, someone was the only outlet to the strength and anger that went through him. He couldn't see. Niles hit him four times and he went back, not seeing, the smoke and the sand-gnats circling in it, the darkness circling and Leah and Mary shouting. But he did not go down. Niles hit him four times without him ever once connecting and yet he didn't go down. Then he found himself, began to block away the punches. The sand wet and sinking, the smell of shore water on the shore night and the taste in the confusion of the fists against his head. Leah holding him, her drenched softness clinging to his left arm, so that Niles hit him again with him helpless, unable to swing out.

"Cecil!"

"You fuck off me now."

Because she was holding him, he couldn't swing. He kept blocking with his right, Niles swinging with his right so that it was hard to block and she on his arm that way.

"Yer gonna get hurt," he said.

"Cecil!"

"Yer gonna get hurt—take her off me, Shelby, take her off me."

"Cecil!" Her wetness pinned against his arm. Shelby did nothing, the smoke in his wizened face.

"Take her off me, for fuck sake, Shelby."

"Cecil."

"Yer gonna get hurt." He could see nothing; Shelby only a form, the smoke against him and the black flecks of sand-gnats above her head and her screaming. He threw out with his left and she went reeling. He didn't know if she was hurt. Then he began swinging, connecting with both right and left. It seemed as if Niles' face crumbled when he hit, he didn't know. He didn't know if she was hurt. Then when he thought Niles would go down, he didn't, and when he thought he had won he hadn't. He felt nothing of the blood running from the corner of his mouth, over his eye—saw or knew nothing of the blood on Niles' mouth or face.

"Cecil!"

He pushed her hard out of the way, swinging her in the direction of the water. Then he grabbed Niles around the neck and put him down. It was sheer weight that brought him down into the sand, wet and sinking, both of them, their hair and clothes mud-ridden, the stale smell of smoke and river.

"Cecil!"

He felt nothing inside. When she came back he felt nothing of her, heard nothing. He kept swinging, Niles' face bloody, his mouth opening and closing and he kept swinging.

Then Niles threw him off and stood. They faced each other again for a long time, his face stinging. He felt the blood now, saw the blood on Niles' face and mouth, an almost soundless ringing in his ear.

"Yer both crazy," Leah said. "Yer both crazy."

She walked along the shoreline to the bridge. In a moment Cecil followed, the streaks of blood from his mouth already hardening against his chin, and over his eye a blotched, oozing disquiet, a burning pain.

"Yer crazy."

"Next time you latch onto me in a fight you'll get a good swift kick in the arse."

"Ya well, I don't like fights," she said crying. "I don't like people fighting."

He lay back in the bed, his eyes open, her clothes scattered under him—the loose bed-garments on the floor. "Let her go," he thought. "Let her and him and anyone that wants ta go with them go—cause if it was up ta me they'd go."

There was silence in the house again, only the unquiet of his mind. He laughed again and cursed and then was silent, all this only half-realizing that he was speaking into nothing, only half-realizing that they were gone down there again for the night and that she wasn't in the room to hear what he was saying—to understand what it was that he was shouting. As if she was in the room with her hair down; with the mascara like it was this evening.

He continued talking for a long time, stopping at intervals to realize the silence itself. His arms were trembling without him knowing it, and he was cold now. It was as if she was in the room and he was saying everything and she was listening without saying a word; not able to say a word because everything that he said was true. "Sure ya do," he said. "Sure ya have everyone on this river thinking I'm the bastard that no-one could live with—cause I'm so mean, and I beat the kid—*feel sorry for yerself, feel sorry for yerself*, yer the only bitch that does any feeling sorry for yerself around here—so ya can pack up and fuck off, pack up and fuck off any time ya like—ya know that, ya know that—then why the fuck do ya stay?"

He wished he'd taken more of Shelby's wine. Because there was nothing left now and a pain seemed to come over him while he was speaking, so that he stopped short and listened. Over his head when the cars passed the light reflected against the ceiling and the walls, against the mirror tilted on the dresser and the dresser drawers left open after she had changed again. Then her face came back—the way it looked—and he shut his eyes.

It was that she didn't even try to stop him, she just took no part. "I'm going to bingo now," she said. It was after supper—the wet warmth of the stew that they had eaten. In the room when he closed the door the thin cold winter light through the venetian blind drawing faint against the yellow walls. She didn't stop him, she took no part, lay motionless and removed upon the bed—her face looking up at him that way, her mouth twisted, a hollowness about it somehow that he had never seen before. It was because he had wanted her to lay soft and warm in his arms, because she looked at supper as she had looked before—the good total youngness of her movement and her form. "Christ Jesus," he said.

He brought a blanket around him and rolled on his side. It was that she took no part.

"For Christ sake woman," he said.

She looked at him, motionless and unmoving, her legs together almost rigid. Then he began to curse and she said nothing, and he felt inside all hatred and rage; something that he was powerless to control, powerless to stop himself from hurting her as if hurting her was the answer to what she was doing—as if hurting her that way was the answer to the way she looked, to the way her legs went rigid under his hands.

And it was his hands. All the time he was doing it he saw the scars; the stove again like that night when he went toward it, and then the black redness of not knowing once the stove blew, of being reeled backwards and feeling it, the endless desperate energy and heat—that when he fell that night he could feel through every second of his unconsciousness the blind dark redness of the heat.

She said nothing. Not once did she speak—not once did he think of anything but the stove and the flame, of finding himself being dragged from it. Only the knowledge that he was hurting her and cursing her and that he couldn't stop.

He was trembling under the blanket, a pain that went through him every time he thought of it, of her standing afterwards and going to the dresser to change, her fine legs almost sickly by the light through the blinds. She didn't cry—not even that. It was as if an emptiness came into the room and touched them and they couldn't speak. Then she turned and went to the door. She went outside and called Ronnie and when he came in she said:

"We're going down to see Irene."

Cecil came from the bedroom.

"Sure fly the hell down there," he said. "Great place ta go—and make sure ya tell them everything," he said.

"And we won't be home tonight," she said.

"Sure I'm the old scar-faced bastard—I'm the bastard, ya got him believin that so's he won't even come near me."

"Feel sorry for yerself," she said.

"Fuck ya, fuck ya," he said.

4

Out of the back door in the yard he stood bareheaded, in the field where the wind hit at him tossing his hair. Cathy stood behind the back door watching his slow movement, his head down. Whenever he stopped to look behind him he became a grey stiff form in the grey day. And even in his movement there was something unclear; as if in the cold field he was at once upright and slumped, as if the field was at once flat and potted, and he moved with the ruts and furrows of the ice and snow. He stopped again, looking about him, then he moved again—brought his hand up over his ear. He was coming back.

"Maufat's coming back," she said.

Irene stood and went to the window. Orville didn't answer. February and the wind was raw, glazed ice over the fields and the torn shoots exposed purple in the morning.

"Maybe he's sick," Cathy said.

"He didn't say nothin ta me," Irene said.

When he opened the door she could hear the wind catching at it with a slight cracking of the wood, catching her skirt and legs so that she stepped backwards. His raw face and tight grey eyes.

"I have to get up with the bus this morning."

"Yer not sick?" Irene said.

"No, he left and went up early," Maufat said. "Bastard," he said.

Cathy didn't speak. In the porch there was a winter's hardness and when the gusts hit the plastic of the window she felt it over her; the panelled wall held it tight—the tightness of freezing. Outside the fields were ice, the barns remaining solitary and black, lingering untouched and gutted in the light.

"So did Laura say why?" Irene said.

"Laura didn't say nothin," he said. "I'm just gonna get my own car."

Cathy said nothing. He moved past her into the kitchen where he went to the fridge and took a beer.

"Now yer not drinking that," Irene said.

He looked at her, his fine eyes silhouetted by the unfresh shadows, closed in as if the walk back and forth across the ice and hard snow had drawn his skin to the temperature of the outside. He opened it without speaking and finished it in two swallows.

She felt something dull along her back, felt it start inside her. *Karen said: "Do you get sick—I get sick, for three days I'm sick, do you get sick?" "No, I don't," Cathy said. "I never get sick."*

"It'll ruin yer stomach," Irene said.

"Its my stomach," he said.

In the room Leah and Ronnie slept on the outpulled cot, the darkness of the drawn blind on them. It was because they had come down last night away from *him* again and Leah was crying and when Leah began crying Ronnie began crying. It was that every week now she would come down and she would say, "He don't think I'm goin—he don't think I am but I am—he thinks he can run me but he isn't gonna run me, and me and Ronnie we're goin just as soon as I've the money." It was because when she slept she slept like a child looking like Ronnie's sister more than his mother, looking even with the makeup and her tinted hair as if she were a child, with her hands that way closed into small white fists and her legs curled inward one beneath the other. That when the shadows of the room hit on her closed face she looked *little*, Cathy thought—she looked *little*.

Outside even above the wind the sound of saws in the woodlot, the sound of a sharp grinding emptiness. To work in there it would be cold, you would stand to your knees in the frozen snow, the limbs and boughs sharp and rigid, ice and the hunger of morning. With the wind you would feel nothing toward midday, only the ache of working. She

138

shivered.

"Karen's here—I'm gonna go out now," she said.

"Ramsey won't mind ya going up with the bus," Irene said.

"That ain't what I mean," Maufat answered. "That ain't what I mean."

He went up with them this morning on the bus, waiting with them in the freezing, his face hard and dry, his fine grey eyes staring at the opposite woodlot. When the bus turned from the shore road he watched it, stepping behind Cathy when it slowed. In the wind the faint unnoticed scent of winter, the scent of no-growth and the moaning of twisted limbs.

"Ya got yer lessons all done?" he asked.

"I don't have none ta do," she said.

It seemed that speaking opened into her warmth, the solitary warmth of her middle, exposed her to it, to the freezing of dry dawn air and the taste of ice. She clamped her mouth again. Along the road the sound of the bus stopping and starting. The wind again.

It wasn't her face so much she minded—it was her legs, the skirt blown up about her thighs and her legs freezing, patching them white and then red through her stockings. It was the road with an inch of ice on it and the branches twisted. Orville stood beside Karen, his head straight and the wind at him, at his bared wet head and naked ears.

"Ya shouldn'ta combed yer hair with water," she said.

Karen looked up at him. He didn't answer. In the woodlot the shadows cold, the bare sound of the saws.

"Ya shouldn't have," she said. "Yer gonna get pneumonia."

"Ya should cover your ears," Karen said.

"I'm not cold—you should cover yer legs," he said. He turned away from them and spit out, his warmth gone into the cold graded snow, the crusted emptiness. When the bus stopped Maufat stood back until the rest of them were on.

"Mind if I come up with ya, Ramsey?" he said.

He didn't take a seat; he stood just above the door, his hand on the bar. Cathy and Karen went to the back, Orville following them. There was the scent of oil and tin along the dark aisle and among the students in the rows of seats, the half-bitter jesting of early morning.

"I'm gonna haveta get myself a car," Maufat said.

He lurched unsteadily with the bus, with the grating of gears and the sluggish movement, his large tight fist on the bar. When others entered he'd move closer to it. "Excuse me," he'd say. "Excuse me." He could have taken a seat if he'd wanted, yet he stood, once in a while almost falling when the bus lurched forward again, his lunch bucket placed at the top of the steps, it too tilting. "Ya got yer lessons done?" he'd say and then look to Ramsey and wink.

"I'll haveta get myself a car," he said.

Ramsey didn't answer.

Through the flecks of frost she could see the river, the ice clean and naked, its ruptured middle showing the current of black water, the blank opposite shoreline and the wood. Something liquid that churned beneath the underbelly of the ice, alive beneath the flows, rising out black and the gulls above it. The sky was white now, the wind blowing hard into the trees. Every time the bus stopped Maufat would try to remain standing and when it started again he would go backwards to the railing and laugh a little, his laugh empty—and then he would speak to Ramsey again and Ramsey would answer him. Yet it seemed it was only his voice in here, mixing with the movement and the smell of oil and tin, with the cold flat air of the inside. That it was only his voice out of place with the dry coarse mutterings from the other seats.

"Orville must have a girl friend," Karen said. "Slickin up his hair."

He sat alone in front of them, his thin hair wet and the yellow string of the black patch tight against it.

"Shhh," Cathy said.

"Well, he must have, don't you think?" Karen said. He didn't answer. The swaying and sluggishnes of the bus, the dry cold air entering against her face.

"Shhh," she said.

"Who is it, Orv—Orv, who is it?" Karen said.

Everything had whiteness and she couldn't stand the lingering over the britle fields and roadways, the staying always too long. Standing there you would be empty against it, like the barns were empty. There would be no fullness, no scent of growth or decay as there was in the summer when she emptied Annie's garbage, the rotting of the bottles and cans together with the lilac and maple, the brown warmth from the crust of the branches, the brown life. She didn't know. It was when she stood in the fields and the weed-spit wetted her legs and the sun hot on her she was *there*, and when in the winter she emptied the garbage the brown bags frozen to her arms, the rawness of the drifted snow she was not *there*.

In the fall they played in the long grass, it tinted yellow, and everything a ripeness or an after-ripeness. The barns had the look and taste of *fullness against the dry cool boards. She would hide there, the after-noon casting a faint orange glow on the place where she hid, on the turning colour of her face and skin. "Caught ya," Leah said. "Ohhh," she said. "Caught ya," Leah said.*

"I don't know how I'm gonna make it this year," Karen said.

They were entering the town—now, in early morning, the lower bridge spanned the flat river naked, the sun glinting against it. The smoke from the two mills white on the white sky, scentless. In the bus the cold air coming in on her face, and through the frosted window the dark contracted look of convent and school. Leah went to the convent, she never had. The dark drawn windows facing the road.

"You're luckier than hell bein in yer last year," Karen said. "But you better not go ta anywhere without me."

Cathy didn't answer.

"Ya better not," Karen said.

Cathy shrugged and remained silent. It seemed too early for speak-ing, too cold. With the pain sharpening along her back she leaned her head and closed her eyes, not opening them until the bus stopped be-fore the doorway of the school. Maufat picked up his lunch-bucket and opened the door, looked to them for an instant. In the lot he moved stiffly and silently in the frozen air, the blackened boots he wore step-ping regular and strong across the hardened ground. After a time the one free hand against his ear.

There were three buildings, the brick of them red and black. Be-tween them the wind cut violently, the ice stood high and broken against the walls. When she left the bus she knew she was coming to something she didn't want, that in the evening leaving it she was re-turning from something that she didn't want. It was more in her *feel-ing*—that the shadows cutting in the afternoon were softer than the shadows cutting the building sides at morning. In this space in the afternoon the wind would be quieted, the half-darkness of twilight would make the outside softer. The trees less bright raw against the raw white sky.

"I don't know nothing of what we have to do for today," Karen said.

"I never do," Cathy said.

The sound was hardly audible inside the classroom. Perhaps the jani-tor's broom in the corridor, the sharp sound of chalk against the board. Then there would be stillness and silence again. If he came at noon she wouldn't go. They would say: "John's here, Cathy," yet she wouldn't move. She would not go outside with him when he said: "Come on outside." She would turn her head. In this room it was too hot, a smell of dampness—of sweat and people almost sweetened inside her, the smell of paste. There was sound again. She looked up.

Across the long field she could see where her father worked; when a train watered she would watch for a time until a sound inside the class made her stop watching—she would wonder what *he* was doing, or what *they both* were doing. She didn't know. She would not go with him. *He never phones, he thinks he can never phone and then come to get me at school—cause he's crazy if he thinks that anyway.*

The school was large—each of the rooms the same. When they moved through the corridors while changing class she avoided speaking. A damp faint odour clung to her, clung to all of them inside here —the voices boisterous and loud in the hallways. It was as if they were let loose from something and wished to run, to be wild for an instant, to shout and scream, push each other, only to be running to it again, only to be returned—to sit locked in by the short small desks in rooms no larger than any of the rest. The boys jumping at each other, rushing each other against the walls. Through the large back window of the corridor the sun was strong, the dust unsettled in the air.

She avoided speaking very much. It was that she was too tired to speak this morning; the flow angry and uncertain inside her, damp and sweetened like the odours of the air, the smell of chalk in the unsettled dust. She did not know if it was her, only her—if what she was sensing was her moistness, the clinging of her warmth and blood. She became frightened that it was. That when boys passed her they knew instinctively by the scent of her what was happening. "That's not true," she thought. "That's not true—because they can't."

In this room the sun hot through the white windows. It was nearing midday. If she arched her neck slightly she could see between the two buildings, see the sideroad beyond the cement wall and the trees cold-hard grate-naked, or to the other side, the jail yard and the church, its large iron cross standing high against it. Beyond that the tracks again and the wood.

"I don't feel good," she thought. "I don't feel good." She lifted her head and looked at the class, feeling suddenly weightless, her head weightless—the white cold metal of the window sides reflecting the sun and outside in the yard the small children let out, their blackened forms against the harsh iron of the ice. It was that she had come in this morning and now she didn't feel good. Karen said: "For three days

142

I'm sick—for three days because it's real bad for that time and I just drag around for it, and in the morning I hate gettin up at all." "No I don't," Cathy said. "I never get sick."

Because there was something in here that made her feel it more, that came with the breath and the sweat of the people behind the too-small desks, along the white tiled floor, like paste or the smell of soft lunches in soft paper bags. Her head was spinning. It seemed that if she kept it down she could concentrate more—that if she lifted it she would become dizzy—the plaid skirt of the girl next to her, the yellow blouse.

She would not go to the sick room—she would go home, because you had to lie down, and the teacher would ask questions about it and then he would give you aspirin and make you lie down. He'd stand in the hallways and look back. The door would be open so that all the noise came in, all the noise and the smell of the janitor-polish in the hallway. He'd look at you to make sure you were lying down, that you were really sick. And when the students passed changing class, or at noon hour they'd look in, they'd say: "What's wrong now—eh, eh, what's wrong now?" She would go home—if she was sick she'd go home!

"I don't feel good," she thought. "I don't feel good." The morning was almost over, the younger children walking home for noon hour, their small black coats sharp against the day, the outside light stronger on the inside than before. She felt cold now and empty, that damp heat once on her no longer a heat, the force inside her no longer a warmth. She felt her face whitening. She looked down at the stiff pencil forms on her paper, the greyness blending with the white. "If ya can do as good as Cathy in school then ya'll be doin somethin," Irene said. "So she might like school cause I don't like school," Orville said. "Well ya could do good too," Irene said: "I don't like school," Cathy said. "I useta like it when I was yer age but I don't like school any more." "Well ya do good," Maufat said. "Ya didn't fail a year—ya never failed—Orville's gonna fail." "He's not gonna fail—now put that into his head that he's gonna fail, all ya need ta do is put that into his head that he's gonna fail!"

If she looked to the teacher she could see the red mark just above the chin that ran from his chin to the edge of his lower lip. She stared at it. He had his eyes lowered, his head down correcting papers. When she had first come here he had scared her. It seemed he liked scaring people; it seemed he liked that. He was well over six feet tall and his arms were long and huge and his head was large, larger than anyone else's head that she had ever seen, his eyes deep in his tight protruding skull.

He bent his head lower to the page so that the scar disappeared, his red hair combed back over a bald spot. She stared at the spot, the light that entered through the thin windows reflecting on it, a patch of dull white skull with the red hair combed back over it.

It was that she was very frightened of him—very frightened, because when she first came to the school she knew nobody, knew nothing of how to act. And so when he stood there in the middle of the classroom with the warm almost sad air of autumn on him, with a suit that he wore every day all year long, grey with faint strips on it, with the spots of fresh chalk-dust on it, she was frightened. Because his voice would be calm one moment and he would be joking and when he was joking the class would relax. Then suddenly he would stop joking. He would become angry and begin to yell and she'd be frightened, his huge massive frame, his great long swaying arms. And he would walk up and down the aisles checking their work, one by one. "Let's see your scribbler—for yesterday—I don't want to see the work you're doing now—yesterday."

He'd pull the scribbler up and examine it with the person waiting. Waiting. Her stomach would go tight. It was because she was in grade ten then and had just come here, knew nobody, knew nothing of how to act. Many times he'd grab her scribbler and look through her work entirely—question by question, page by page—as if he was happy frightening her, as if to see her sit there frightened made him happy.

Now she looked at him. Her head was aching but she no longer felt dizzy. Out in the yard shouts, and the second bell from the elementary school, its dark black stones in the frozen air. He couldn't frighten her —not the way he had. Without knowing it she could sense almost without error what he was going to do—when he was going to tell a joke, or be angry, or run to the back of the classroom and stand over someone, making threatening gestures. Now it was more comic than frightening. She looked at his head bent lower, the thick red skin of his shaven face.

When he raised his head the mark on his chin showed again. She raised her hand and asked to be excused. He looked at her a moment before grunting his approval.

She went out into the corridor and walked to the washroom. "I don't feel good," she thought. "I don't feel good." It was as if the place smelled of cooking, of lunch. Through the far back window of the corridor the midday light settled in the dust, made a warmth of the dust that lightly touched her skin, the winter-drawn features of her face and her lengthening hair. In the washroom the large side window was open, the freezing mixing with the stale warm air of the inside, the soap- and toilet-smell that made her stomach weaker. She stayed five minutes.

The sky was raw blue, and the noises of the outside. Across the field-path children made their way to lunch and she could hear the flat sound of their boots, their flat cries in an air that carried with it the taste of the town—of the small houses near the track, and the track itself: "Where is he now—where is *he*—if *he* comes I'm not gonna go. *He's* gonna say *come on Cathy*, but I'm not gonna go."

She leaned against the window and put her head outside. There was still wind, but not nearly so strong, that blew against her face and hair; the cool freshness of it. She felt good again, and inside her she felt strong again, watching the children. She breathed deep into it four or five times, and it was against her face and in her hair. When she looked down the ice chunks that lined the wall were clear and good, the sun glinting on them, the echoes of the children on them. She didn't want to take her head inside, and after a time the slight wind began to freeze her face—she remained there, remained. Began to hum.

Irene said: "Leah is smart enough and there's more to Leah than you think cause she's smart enough when she wants to be but she just didn't like school and ya couldn't keep her in it." She continued to hum. From this position she could see the freight house. It was that she didn't care if he got a car—it was that she didn't care. The noise of freights shunting and then quiet. Orville said: "Ya always say yer gettin a car and ya never get one." "I'll get one," Maufat said. "Ya always say ya will," Orville said. "Even Cecil's got a car." "You leave Cecil be," Irene said. "Ya always are braggin that ya are," Orville said. "I'm not always braggin," Maufat said. "Don't say I'm always braggin."

Now the ice and snow held something good, the fresh blueness of the sky and the currents of air. She started to sing, shifting the weight on her legs, and then pulled her head inside and turned around.

Julie was watching from the far end, by the sinks.

It was something like horror that grabbed her. It was something tight like in the classroom, like fear. Julie was watching her.

"Hello," she said.

"Hello," Cathy said. Her face was cold, red from the outside, cold along her arms and neck. She was singing and all the time she was singing Julie was watching her. Her long narrow dress as if she'd never show her legs, Cathy thought, as if she was afraid to show her legs.

"How are you?" Julie said.

"Good," Cathy said.

She moved past her into the corridor. The same faint light, the same heat, the same uncoiling. Julie was watching her—all that time. She felt something; as if she was stupid, as if Julie would think now that she was stupid; a cold sweat along her that she couldn't understand. "It don't matter—it don't matter I'll sing when I want to, it don't matter."

She went back to her room, the door opened part way and the sounds within. As she came to her seat the bell rang ending the morning. There was no scribbler on her desk but she didn't notice that—she noticed nothing, only the quiet eyes of Julie from the far end of the sink caught in the half-brown air that wrapped the room, the smell of toilet and soap. The eyes staring at her when she turned around as if they had been watching her all the while.

People began to get up from their desks and move about the aisles, laughing with one another. She sat back down and stared vacantly ahead, at the seats in front of her, at the long blackboard scrawled with numbers and signs. It was that all this time she had said: "Julie is stupid, just like a little kid, a little kid." It was because all this time she had said to Karen: "I can't even think why he'd think of her."

"Did she useta go with John?" Karen said. "Is that the one that useta go with John?"

There were times when she actually felt better for saying that, as if when Karen believed what she said that was all that mattered, it was true then. Now she felt different. She stared ahead, the class retreating into the corridor. She had been hungry but now she wasn't. It was something like shame, the force of which had started in a certain kind of horror as soon as she had turned about.

She stood and looked down, noticing her scribbler missing. She began searching the floor.

"There's no need to look, Cathy, I have it with me," he said.

She looked up. He stood at the front of the room with it in his hand, the students moving around him slowly. The red mark from his lower lip to his chin and his red hair combed back over the white balding of his crown.

She said nothing.

"You decided to go running about this morning—I was just wondering if your work was done."

She said nothing.

"Maybe you'd like staying in after class and doing it—if it costs you so much trouble doing it while you're here with us?" He was tall, over six feet, and his huge long arms swung to and fro as he spoke, and his large head bobbed a little. The class stopped moving around him and stood to watch her. Some of those that had already gone into the corridor waited there to listen. "Alright, get out, get out," he said to them, his voice raised, loud as if he had been waiting for a chance to make it loud. He stamped his foot, "Out." The students moved again, most of them laughing. "You only have four problems done," he said. "What were you doing, sleeping? You're not coming into my class acting like a block of wood." The students that had moved through to the corridor still waited. They waited because his voice was constantly rising, because he was stamping his foot, and his arms high in the air and then by his side, and then in the air again.

"Five," Cathy began.

"Five," he said. "Five—do you call this the fifth problem, 'If x equals a to the fifth power?' " He tried to imitate her voice when he said this, holding her scribbler in his large right hand before him, his lips puckered, a spot of dust above them. Outside the window the sky was blue now; she could hear the shouts of children. She looked about her, the sweet thickness of paste and desks. " If x equals a to the fifth power,' " he said again. "Is that what you call the fifth problem? Is that what you call the fifth problem?"

"No, but I didn't feel good," she said quickly.

"Most mornings I don't feel good either—most mornings I have to come in here and look at people the likes of you," he said. "But I get my work done—it would be too bad for me if I didn't." He looked about him, saw those in the corridor still watching him.

She felt something solid in her throat and her lower lip began to tremble. She had no control over it. And then the feeling of dull heat inside her throat and her eyes watered, a burning sensation along the bridge of her nose. He was trying to make her cry. He was. She knew he was, that it didn't matter—nothing of what he said really mattered —he was just trying to make her cry. Yet knowing this did no good. She looked down at the floor, and the floor—it was as if the tile was moving beneath her. "I don't feel good," she thought. "I don't feel good."

"Well, fine, keep it up—keep it up. You won't graduate but keep it up, be like your *sister* before you—" He stopped short. She looked up at him, her lip trembling, and her eyes—the water in them. "Or your aunt, or whatever she is," he said quickly. He stopped short again, then turned to the people in the corridor. "I said move along so move along!" He shouted, his face getting more red, his eyes in his thick dark skull. He turned back to her, "Well, you can do what you want," he said.

She said nothing. It was as if he wanted to leave the room now.

"I used to travel on the bus with Leah," he said. "She was the smartest person on the bus too," he said. His voice was softer, as if talking to himself—as if trying to find words to say: "But she didn't study—did she?—she could have been *anything*, but she didn't study—and you're, you're as smart or smarter than she is—so I want you to study."

She said nothing. He was trying to talk nice to her and it was because he was trying to talk nice to her!

"Don't worry—I know everyone down in that area," he said.

She began to cry. It was because he was trying to be nice to her.

"I don't feel good," she said.

"Well, don't cry," he said, his voice kind and soft, his large thick head. "Go along to your room," he said.

"I don't feel good," she said.

"Don't cry," he said.

She cried in broken sobs, trying to catch it in her throat and control what was inside. He went to her and handed the scribbler back and she took it without looking at him at all, looking downward, seeing his shoes, his pants, grey, the chalk and the winter and the sunlight on them. Her tears didn't run, they simply watered and burned her eyes, blurred them so that all she saw was the colour of his pants and the room.

She took the scribbler in her hands and pretended to look through its pages as if it would be alright if she looked through its pages. It was because she wanted him to see her looking through the scribbler, to have him know that she was sick. She had her feet so close together that she stumbled backwards and looked up, a lock of her hair falling across and becoming damp from the dampness of her eye. He moved to the door.

When he moved he didn't walk like other men, like Maufat or Alton walked when they were downriver, when they were home. They walked lamely, shunting their feet deliberately in the cold earth, they had more power. He walked without power, without the expression or mood of power that gave the men she knew something of a possession of what they were walking on, of the ground, snow or earth—of the cold between the naked boards, and the heat against the upstairs bedrooms and the hall.

He walked to the door and turned around. It was as if he couldn't leave the room with her knowing that he had been stupid, with her knowing that he had said something wrong. She looked at him knowing that—sensing it as she sensed the softness between the buildings in the twilight air, the softness of going home.

"So I don't want you to turn out like Leah," he said, his face twisting into a peculiar expression of pain, the red mark from his chin to his lower lip becoming almost invisible the way he spoke, his parted ugly teeth. "Not that there's anything wrong with Leah or anybody else," he said. "But I want you to graduate—and I know Leah," he broke off, looked at her. "So I want you to catch up," he said, leaving the room.

She went back to her own room feeling weak and hot. When she sat at the desk she became cold, and shivered, and bit into her lunch without caring. When someone told a joke or laughed she smiled weakly. Her arms began to shiver. It was that everyone in the classroom was now making jokes about the teacher, hating him, asking her questions. It was that she felt stupid, and when she had walked the corridor back to her own room—she felt as if they were all watching her, from every room; felt as if when she wiped the dampness from her eyes they would think of her as being something different from what she thought of herself as being. All the time she was walking she pictured someone else walking.

"He's an old bastard—the hell with em," Leonard said.

"I know that," she said.

"Anybody that'd make a girl cry is a bastard," Leonard said.

She felt sour, said nothing. She felt sour; "girl," she thought, "girl." She didn't remember. It was as if someone else was in the class crying and she had been watching, hating the teacher yet hating that person crying.

"If I were you, Cathy, I'd take it to the school board—talking about your parents. He's not allowed to talk about your parents, anybody that talks about your parents I'd bring to the school board."

Hating that person crying even more than *hating* the teacher, even more than that. Then it became Julie watching from the corridor, her eyes caught in the dust moved by the sunlight through the back window—looking and *hating* Cathy in the room crying. It became Julie knowing Cathy in the room crying, looking and hating every movement, every sob and then not hating the teacher at all, only hating Cathy in the room with her stupid wide eyes wet and the sobs thick in her throat. *"Oh I don't feel good—oh I don't feel good."*

She felt herself no longer, felt a certain sense of shame overpower her. For a long time she sat in the chair trying to overcome that feeling, but it was impossible to overcome anything. It was impossible to stop feeling sorry for the teacher, his wide-gapped ugly mouth and the chalk dust on his faded suit, and the red scar that ran beneath his lower lip. "He's only trying to teach—he's right because he's only trying to teach," she thought.

Most of the people went outside after they had eaten. She sat alone in the far corner of the room, watching the people outside moving slowly in the snow, and across the long field the sound of the station, the quiet of noon hour. It was not that she didn't have a right to cry—it was that she had been singing with the breeze on her. She had been singing and then turning around it was Julie watching.

Now that she was alone in the class room she began to wait. It was something that she had tried to hide—this waiting for him, wanting him to come. All morning she had been sure that he would be standing by the door of her room when she came back to it at noon hour, and then when noon hour came she had forgotten it, thinking only of her own crying—the eyes watching her from every room. "I don't feel good, I don't feel good." And then it had started first as a small growth —a glancing out into the hallway every time someone passed, pretending even to herself that she wasn't caring, that she wasn't glancing out. Now it was something different. It was a desperation building inside her—a fear that he wouldn't show at all—that he wouldn't come. "He thinks he can come here at noon without even ever phoning me, he thinks he can just come and say: *Oh Cath—let's go out Cath* and I'm gonna hop from my seat right up and go out with him smilin, cause he's crazy if he thinks that anyway he's crazy."

A longing for him to come so she wouldn't look at him when he did, a longing for him to know that she didn't care whether he came or not. That she would stare out the window when he came and she wouldn't look, she wouldn't—and then he'd come into the class, his long black hair and the whiteness of his face drawn tight over the bones, the tightnes of freezing. And he would come to her desk and put

150

his hand on her shoulder, soft, the cold largeness of it over the small-ness of her shoulder.

He would say *Oh Cathy, let's go out Cath,* and she'd say, *I don't feel like it today, ya can go out by yerself* and he'd say *But ya haveta come out* and his lips would be white and tense over his tense face, the eyes small and black, and she'd look up at him so very calm that her heart would be calm, not even beating, and she'd say: *Take Julie—since you're always bringin her name up, take Julie for a walk.* He'd look at her and she'd turn her head away, slow, and look out to the station again, so that he'd see nothing but the back of her long hair caught good by the winter sunlight on it, and then he'd take his hand away, stand there for a minute. And all the time he'd stand there she wouldn't look, she wouldn't say a word. *Well good,* he'd say. *Yes good,* she'd say, *Julie works in the office down the hall.*

But she couldn't think that now, she could think nothing but that he wasn't coming, he wasn't coming. There was nothing inside her now but the fear that blocked away all other things. "That goddamn teacher," she thought. "That goddamn teacher."

Inside this building, at this time, there was no sound—the sound of no sound in her ears when she tried to listen. What had happened, what was happening made her feel the weight of something clinging inside; the touch of coldness on her skin. Her legs began to shiver so that she couldn't control them, and again her eyes watered. She looked about her—the room, the school was empty: "Oh he thinks he's so damn smart."

She wiped the water away. Her eyes looked awful—if he saw her, her eyes would look—squinty—yes squinty like Angela's eyes looked, like that time when Angela—"Christ, he thinks he can just walk around and make people shake just cause he's the teacher he can make people shake, and yell at them and yell about their family and yell about Leah."

Leah her fists closed white and little with the shadow on them of the drawn blind when Cathy ran downstairs in the morning because she had come down from him again like she always did—

She began to cry again. "I don't feel good—I don't feel good." There was no-one in the room now, no-one anywhere yet when she cried she tried not to cry—she tried to let the clinging stay in her throat and not come out, tried to stop the shaking in her legs and shoulders.

Then she stood and became calm. Outside the flat surface and the station. She took her lunch to the front of the room and threw it in the basket, and went to the washroom again. "It don't matter," she thought, washing her eyes, the burning from her face, the coldness of the water refreshing. "It doesn't matter—it don't matter."

Because now it was afternoon and then she would be home. She would go upstairs and lie down and pull the quilt over her and lie down, smelling the dark odour of the quilt and under it the safe clean odour of herself.

But when she came into the hallway John was leaning against the door of her room. He watched her coming toward him. She kept looking past him and then down at the floor. She would walk past him she thought, she would walk by and go down the stairs. He watched her coming. It was that she pretended not to see him, all the time watching his face, the expression of it, calm like stone; all the time wanting him to come toward her, wanting him to wave and come toward her—knowing that he wouldn't. Then because she couldn't help it, she began to smile.

She didn't want to smile, she didn't wish it. She wished more than anything else the breaking apart of it all, her feeling the breaking apart and knowing that she was the one, to feel it tearing inside her, knowing while she did so that she was the only one who could prevent it. Yet now because she was smiling she raised her hand and waved, could see her hand rising in front of her face almost as if to hide her smile.

"Hello," she said. He watched her coming and then pushed himself from the door and moved a little toward her, all the while his eyes on her. He didn't smile, only nodded. In the dark light of the hallway his skin looked brown, winter brown and the jutting cheekbones made his face look cruel. He nodded again.

"What are you up to?"

"Nothin," she said.

He looked at her and shrugged as if he was cold. They were silent for a moment.

"Ya were s'posed to phone me the other night," she said.

"Ya," he said. "Forgot."

"No ya didn't," she said laughing.

"I did," he said.

"Well, it doesn't matter anyway," she said, swinging her hair back and shaking her head. He looked at her. She moved to the door. "Ya wanta go for a walk?" she said.

They were outside. In the early afternoon the grounds were empty, the weak sun on the white snow made her squint her eyes, coming from inside the way she did. And it was cold also, her face and jaw frozen and her knitted white mitts no protection, so that she shoved her hands into the pockets of her coat.

The chalk mark above his upper lip. When she thought of him again she cringed, closed her eyes to make it go away—he in the classroom, his arms that long and the large and awful mouth.

"Will ya wait up?" she said.

"Oh," he said.

He turned around and watched her come up to him, then he turned again and kept walking—just as fast as ever, the hard leather boots he wore squeaking in the snow and sounding awful, the heels digging into something that was cold and freshly graded. She couldn't open her eyes very far because of the cold white blueness of it all—the sharpness. She rushed to keep up.

"Do you know where we're goin?" she said.

"Ya," he said. "I know where I'm goin."

She didn't answer. Once on the street they turned up toward the station—at the tracks the red warning lights flashing. She thought of Maufat. She thought of Maufat, and then Leah—and then back again to the teacher.

"I had a hell of a time this morning," she said panting.

"Oh ya—why's that?" he said.

"Oh its this teacher—he picks on everybody—and this morning he picked on me—as if he thought I'd be frightened because he was pickin in on me—Jesus in Grade 10 I useta be frightened of him—Mr. Holt —do you know him—Mr. Holt, he's a great big guy—bigger than anyone I ever met before—bigger than anyone—do you know him?"

He nodded. It was as if he wasn't interested in anything she had to say, and yet she kept speaking, more now because she had begun and didn't know where or how to stop. Only his face and the sound his boots made, and the scrape of a beard against his chin. They passed the church, the front steps unshoveled, the crusted snow formed in tiers all down the steps. She felt that she wanted to stop speaking, but somewhere inside herself she was afraid to stop, afraid to stop because he wouldn't care. She kept taking breaths between sentences and trying to keep up.

They came to the tracks and turned along the lane.

"Yer goin home," she said. "Yer going home." She stopped and looked behind her—the long street, a man crossing it just below the school. He turned around and faced her.

"No-one's home," he said. "No-one's home all afternoon—why don't ya jig school this afternoon?" he said.

"I'll get in trouble," she said. She looked at him; the air now with a peculiar sense of burning, of cinder. If it came from the tracks she didn't know, or if it came from somewhere else. It came from beyond the tracks maybe.

He looked past her and laughed. Behind her the graveyard, and the large white crucifixion where Jesus hung.

"Ya must be really afraid of that teacher," he said. "Old Holt," he said.

"But I'll get inta trouble," she said.

"Didn't ya tell them ya were sick?" He looked at her, straight at her. He turned and kept on walking.

"Didn't ya tell old Holt ya were sick?" he said.

He kept on walking. It was that she had never done it—only that once. "If Maufat sees me I'll get skinned," she thought. "If Maufat sees me I'll get skinned."

Only that once in the summer—it was raining. They had gone for a walk out along the beach, and crossed the field below Allison's, the sharp grass cutting at her legs. And then they had gone to the light-house and it smelled damp and old and she said, "I ain't goin in there," and he said, "Come on—come on." And when they went in it was dark and old, the beams smelling ancient in the darkness and he said, "Come on, come on." She clung to his arm. Then it was that she felt good—like in the stomach sometimes she felt good and she said, "I ain't going in there." But she was already in and she was laughing. When he turned to her she was laughing and then he kissed her and she stopped laughing, and she thought of Orville because Orville didn't like him—Orville never liked him, and she couldn't stop feeling good. Then where they were there was no light and his hand, and the rain and inside the smell of timbers in the rain. Then when she stopped laughing he kissed her and she couldn't stop feeling good.

It was that she had never done it—never—only the once. She followed him behind to the house, hiding behind him from the freight building and the tracks. "If Maufat sees me I'll get skinned." She wasn't cold now yet she wanted to go back. In the school she would be safe, the desks warm, the faint soft ticking of afternoon and the smell of chalk-dust and paste. When he came to the house, the darkness of the verandah grey in the light, he turned to watch her approaching. She came to him and stopped, looked up at him, then at the house, the small upstairs window with the curtain closed.

"It's my period, ya know that?" she said.

He didn't answer.

5

When he opened his eye the thought came immediately that he would have to get up now, dress in the cold dark air that surrounded his bed, and go immediately into the cold dark air outside. He looked about him—the small clock on the night-table ticked luminous, the minute-hand coming now almost exactly to 6.30. So that in an hour it would be through, over. In an hour the light outside would be hazel on the snow.

He moaned and rolled over, pretending even for a second that he didn't have to hurry. Yes sleep! Yes sleep! No-one was awake, no-one. That they could sleep regardless of his having to do it, made him angry. He lay with his fists clutched tightly under the quilt, listening. There was nothing, not even wind. It was that they didn't care.

He pulled the blankets from him and stood quickly, the air dry and cold, making him shiver into himself as he dressed. Outside was pitch blackness and not a sound, and they slept—none of them knowing that in this moment of their sleeping he was up and ready to go out. If only a few more minutes sleep, he thought—a few more hours. He cursed.

In an hour it would be over; it didn't seem time enough. He left his room and went into the hallway. The air here was warmer, Cathy's door ajar, and if he could stand in this warm air he'd be asleep in seconds. It gave him such a comfortable feeling—one of being unwilling to move from it. He could slump in the corner by the stairs with the darkness and the warmness on him and be asleep. He cursed and went downstairs.

Except for Leah and Ronnie gone, everything was as it was the morning before. The curtains drawn closed and the blinds down, a small chill and an emptiness in the kitchen—the feeling of something left over and undone from the night before, a feeling of disorder, as if they had all leapt up at once and went to bed too soon. And what was it? It was that six hours ago he was sitting in the large chair watching television—not tired at all. And when he went to bed he lay there, motionless, not able to sleep. "Ya'd better get upstairs now," Irene said. "Why?" he said. "Cause ya haveta serve Mass in the morning. "So," he said. "So Mass comes early," Cathy said laughing. "So," he said, "I'm not tired. "Ya will be," Cathy said. "So what?" he said. "Ah ha," Cathy said, "ya will be—ya will be." "Shut yer mouth," he said.

He turned on the kitchen light and noticed the time, grabbed his jacket and pulled on his boots. He would have to run. He didn't even want to go—he wanted to be off the altar: "I'm quittin the altar anyway," he said. "Sure, be a quitter," Irene said. "Quit the altar—and then quit school, and then work the boats," she said. Leah said nothing. "Sure," he said, "I will—I'm gonna quit." "Sure," Irene said. "Don't be a quitter," Leah said, and then she smiled at him. "It's stupid bein on the altar anyway," he said.

Yet now he would have to run—run to what he didn't want to run to just to do something he didn't want to do. He felt sour in the mouth and bad. He went into the bathroom and turned on the light, looked at himself quickly in the mirror. Then he straightened and paused, for a moment unable to think. "Jesus Jesus," he said. He had forgotten his patch.

When he was outside the air was far warmer than he thought it would be—at this month, at this time and hour. It made his face waken, his pulse quicker. It made him feel happier. He ran along the road, slowly at first because of the night-sleep on him and then faster —feeling the fresh wet air of a February thaw, the dull patched uncertainty of the road. And though it was still very dark, more dark perhaps than when he went to bed it was as if with his eye he could see the snow, sallow with the damp air on it, the trees saturated, with the heavy limbs, and the limp slush forming in the soft air along the drains. And all this made him feel very happy. Because he was awake now and no-one else was awake and he was running and no-one else was running.

When he came to the church the white structure looked black, and he could see from the base of it, where the snow covered the small foundation windows, to the tip of the large cross—the solidness rising into the air. He was panting, out of breath. But running all this distance had made him feel alive and good. He went around to the side door and opened it—looking up at the steeple again. Across the flat parking lot the priest-house, with the kitchen light on, reflecting outside to the shimmering wetness of the thawing snow. He went inside and snapped the light on.

The warmth and smell of wood and closeted space, a certain perfection of stillness that he experienced only here. Above him on the vestry wall the clock, its second-hand moving remotely and silently. It was already five to seven. He took off his jacket and boots and put his altar sneakers on, opened the small ancient walnut cupboard for his surplice and soutane. Garments worn before him by people who now had gone.

It was so strange. Even to himself he couldn't admit that at one time he had wanted to be on the altar. That being on the altar seemed to him the greatest possible thing—and every Sunday he would go into the vestry after Mass. First he would kneel by the altar railing and say, "Hail Mary full of grace, the Lord be with Thee." Then he would genuflect, light a candle below the statue of Mary and Joseph with the little Christ. He would be hoping the priest would be watching—and then he would climb the stairs to the vestry, the stairs and the vestry smelling older than any other place, filled of the taste of the brown wood. The altar boys themselves towered over him—and it seemed to him at that time that being one of them was the greatest thing in the world, as if nothing else was better—as if being one of them (the way they took off their sneakers and threw them in the wooden sneaker boxes, and pushed each other about, and undid their surplices and soutanes and hung them lazily)—that being one of them was the most important thing he could do. Because Irene said, when they wore the red garments, "Don't they look good!"

He would go into the vestry and stand just near the exit. The boys would be putting the wine away, and the large red book, with all the long silk markers in it. He would stand there watching, and when the priest came up to him, old even then, with his withered mouth and hands—it was at that moment a priest he wanted to be, because being a priest seemed the best possible thing, being a priest you could touch the Host when no-one else could touch it, and you could speak in Latin when no-one else (only the altar-boys themselves perhaps) could speak it. And there was no way a priest couldn't go to heaven he thought, because God had picked that priest to be a priest and go to heaven. Yes, to be a priest you would go to heaven without even worrying if you were bad because you weren't *bad ever*, you were always *good ever*. You were filled with grace all the time—you were white all the time like snow.

"Yes, little man," the priest said smiling. His mouth so withered even at that time that it looked like when the balloon burst in the trees and hung there limp, and then the wind blew it down.

"I want to be on the altar," Orville said, his eye looking up.

"Yes, yes," the priest said. "Well, when you're in Grade 4—are you in Grade 4 now?"

"No—3," Orville said. And the priest smiled and patted his head.

"Well when you're in Grade 4," he said.

There was the sense of something other in the vestry, behind the walls; perhaps the softness of flowers that even now in this month seemed to permeate, or the reluctant wisp of incense and candles. It was that when his mouth opened something came into it that came into it at no other place. He was reminded of somewhere where he had never quite been, or somewhere where the fullness of a June night was upon his flesh and skin like it never really had been.

He was drowsy again, yet not with sleep—he had no need or desire to sleep—only the longing. It was strange. Each time he served Mass the same longing came over him—he didn't know where from, or what exactly it was.

He went out onto the altar, bowed instead of genuflected. It was dead. Here, the candles unlit, high in their iron holders, the gold cross, the gold covering stained and spotted, which he removed and folded in his hands. Instead of what was inside—in the vestry, in the quiet of some enclosed dark wooded room, here was something barefaced and open. If the altar smelled like the room and the room like the altar it would be alright—it would be the way it *was to be*, and now it was the way it *wasn't to be*. He lit the candles. It was seven o'clock.

When the old man came in and began to put his vestments on Orville stood to the right of him with his hands folded, staring at the wall, at the small vestry cross, and then at the closed brown door beside him. The priest grunted and coughed, took a handkerchief from his sleeve and spit into it. His face was yellowed and wrinkled and tired. He mumbled something to Orville but Orville didn't hear him. Then he mumbled again.

"What?" Orville said.

"I said—after the next storm, you'd think someone would come down here and shovel out my walk—instead of me having to wade up to my knees to get over here."

Orville said nothing. He bowed to the cross when the priest was ready and they went out to the altar. In the high arch of the windows the light began to streak, setting off the painted things within a dim brown colour—the seats and cold winter statues. The priest bowed at the altar and kissed it and began to say the mass. He said it very quickly in the morning.

With his hands folded and kneeling and standing and kneeling again it went all very much the way it always went; it was at the same time this morning as the other mornings he became tired of kneeling and his knees sore, and at the same time this morning as the other mornings he became tired of standing and his feet sore—and the grunting, mumbling of Latin from the bent back of the withered priest and the mubling of his own answers that he didn't hear; and then the priest stopping and spitting into the spot-stained handkerchief that he pulled from his sleeve, and then crumpled it again and shoved it back so that his sleeve went back, and when his sleeve went back, the white hairless underside of his hairless arm.

The white was outside now casting white on the inside, into the air. Orville thought of the white, and the priest lifted the host, white in his age-stained hands. It was that God couldn't come into the host—because there was no God. He shivered. *Cecil and he were walking along the river; Cecil said: "I'll take him Irene, cause I'm goin so I'll take him,"* and then he felt bad and didn't want to go with Cecil. But it was that if he was in this church and God was looking at him then he was all *black* and the priest was all *white* (though when he spit snot into the yellow handkerchief from his yellow face and buried his yellow face in it—then he was not white either—and mixed with the dirt in his mouth and things; though there was no *Host*). He shivered. *God could strike you dead, God could strike you dead. And when Cecil and he were out in the river his line got tangled and Cecil said: "Spend half my day fuckin around with yer line,"* and then he didn't want to *fish any more and the water was grey-black and rough where they were and he was scared and he said: "Oh God help me, oh Mom help me,"* to himself so Cecil couldn't hear.

He rang the bell. The priest broke the Host over the chalice and began to chew on it—his old mouth chewing on something white, and trying to stop from choking. And he couldn't take the Host because if God was in the Host he was *black* because the last time he was to confession was six months ago. *Father forgive me for I have sinned, the last time I was to confession was six months ago.* Then the priest would know that he was black—because yesterday he had said, "I ate and I couldn't receive," and the priest said, "Well, don't eat until after Mass." But there was no God in the Host or anywhere. The priest coughed and then drank from the chalice. *Cecil and he were walking*

159

*along the river and the bear came down from the bushes and stood by
the river and Cecil said: "Come on, ya black son of a whore, ya black
son of a whore." Because he thought the bear would run, but the bear
didn't run, it grunted and sniffed the air. Because Maufat said, "Bears
usually run—ya can walk through the woods any time and never get
close enough ta see a bear." So when the bear came down Cecil must
of thought it was going to run.*

The priest gave him the Host. He opened his mouth and took it,
leaving it flat against his tongue, feeling it dissolve into the water, into
the nothing. He felt as if he was going to shiver—as if he couldn't
control himself and he was going to shiver—and if he shivered the
priest would know—that he was black inside like rotting. *God could
strike you dead, God could strike you dead.*

*It was Sunday and the bear stood black against the white sky and
rough water. He sniffed the air and grunted. Cecil said: "I'll rock ya,
ya son of a whore, ya son of a whore," and Orville picked up a rock.
He was scared and picked up a rock. Cecil said: "Fuck now, put that
down, put that down," and he dropped it into the water. The bear
walked away a few feet and snapped off a small tree at the side of the
alders. He looked back and grunted. "I'll rock ya, ya son of a whore,
ya son of a whore," Cecil said. Then the bear crossed at the low part
of the water and walked into the woods. "Indians think they're the
devil," Cecil said. "Fuck," Orville said. "Fuck," he said. Cecil laughed.*

The priest took the remainder of the wine, washed the chalice with
it so the bits of crumbled Host would not be lost, washed around the
chalice rim with his small yellow finger and then drank it down. Orville looked at the cross, the small blood markings on His hands and
feet. It didn't matter—because there was no grace, there was no God
—it didn't matter. Yet inside he felt uncomfortable and sick, because
when the devil is inside you God couldn't come inside you and when
God is inside you the devil couldn't come inside you. He shivered. The
priest bowed and kissed the altar-front, the candles flickering red paths
across his yellow face.

They turned and faced the pews. There was no-one in the church.

When they were in the vestry again it was quite light. The priest
said nothing for a few moments while he was taking off his vestments,
and then sitting on a wooden chair by the side of the door he coughed,
lit a cigarette and looked at the time. It was 7.30 now. Orville kept
his surplice and soutane on until he had snuffed the candles, laid the
gold cloth over the altar-front and taken in the book and wine-jars.

The old man sat looking at him from the chair.

It was almost that he was part of that chair—part and parcel of the brown, with his brown old shoes, and stooping over to put his low black rubbers on the handkerchief fell out from his sleeve, the cigarette smoking in front of his eyes. Orville washed out the wine-jars and put them in the cabinet. When he opened it the richness of the wood left unbreathing. He placed the large red book in the cupboard above. He took his sneakers off and stood there sock-footed.

The priest said:

"Ya can tell them the whole place was empty this morning." He rose and walked slowly to the sink to run water on his cigarette, and standing there with his back turned kept talking. "I don't know what they think will save their souls—I don't know what they think—do they think?" He kept talking with the low stooping blackness of his back in the brown vestry room and quiet air, with the priest cupboard left unhinged and his vestments so long that they reached over the closet siding and onto the vestry floor.

Orville had no thought yet of anything. It was that he had done it before and now they were burned and now when he wanted to burn some he had no more. He needed only one—that was all, and yet he didn't think of it with the priest there. It was 7.35 and the priest was talking: "Or if they think they can lay there in bed all morning and then get into heaven—deathbed Christians, well—well deathbed Christians if they want to be." He turned back around. Orville was hanging up his surplice and soutane. "But if they're the thief on the right hand of God or the thief on the left hand of God—come judgment they'll find out."

He stopped and lit another cigarette and Orville hauled on his shoes and boots. "Not one in the church today," he muttered. "Not one in the church—don't they realize that they couldn't even breathe, let out a snore without Him wanting them to? Let out a snore," he said again, and chuckled angrily—at them, at Orville. Orville put his jacket on and waited. He knew what he was waiting for but he didn't know why —it was impossible. With the priest there it was impossible, and yet such a strong urge, so that tonight when he came home and it was dark and Cathy was upstairs and Irene was with Annie he could take her radio—he could take her radio and go into his room and shut the door, and the fine thick scent of church wax as he lay upon the quilt.

"I'll tell you a story about deathbed Christians," he said. "Deathbed Christians oftentimes don't make it to the deathbed. There once was a young man—oh long ago, as old as Maufat is now," he said. "Or would have been."

Orville looked at him, yet the old man wasn't looking at Orville. He was staring into the blank vestry with blank, withered, red, waterless eyes. He dragged on his cigarette again. "Well, he would have been—he was in my parish all his life and served the altar for me—and went to Mass every day, and took communion every day—every day mind you—every day. And then one Sunday he didn't. Why?" He looked at Orville, Orville stared above him. "Why? Because he wanted to go duck-hunting—in a boat with a friend of his, and on a Sunday—a Sunday, the one day that Christ Himself set aside for observance of the Mass—the holy Mass, and he went duck-hunting—with a friend. And that friend is alive today, and you know him so I won't tell you who he is." The priest stopped, and with an almost cold, stupid look stared straight at him. "No, I won't tell you who he is—but you know him." The priest stopped again and turned around, ran the water over his cigarette. He stood there mumbling to himself. Orville moved to the cupboard where the large red book was placed, the inside smell of wax and unbreathing wood. He kept his eye on the priest—the old man mumbling to himself. "Not one of them at Mass—most of them never put more than a quarter in the collection, but they wonder why we're the poorest parish in the world, they wonder that—" Orville lifted the cupboard latch and the door swung silently, which was good, and he had his coat on, which was good. Then he stepped away from the cupboard. The priest was talking, he would have to go meet the bus and the priest was talking and why didn't he stop talking, why didn't he leave like he left yesterday morning? Orville stepped away from the cupboard. He wasn't listening. In his mind now: the good smoke filtering in the long dark above his bed and the silent orange flame glowing and sometimes sputtering; and one of Maufat's beers that he was drinking, alone with the radio playing.

"Asleep in their stinking bed," the old man said. And then as if to forgive himself: "but Christ pity them, and I'll pray for them, and little do they know that Christ does pity them." He was too old to be a priest, Orville thought. Lorne said, "We need someone else—a younger priest if he wants me down there listenin ta that," and Irene said, "it's just that he's old now and has the old ways and is old now," and Lorne said, "well, too bad about him, isn't it now?"

He opened the cabinet door wider, his long arm reaching out but as yet not moving any closer.

"Well, I'm gonna go home and have breakfast," the priest said. "And you have to catch your bus," he said. "So I'll tell ya what happened."

"What?" Orville said.

He moved closer to the cabinet. The candles there on the lower shelf white and wrapped in plastic. The priest turned round and went over to his cabinet for his coat, a bright blue winter coat that looked absurd upon him, and tucking the bottom of his vestments up into the cabinet closed the door. He hadn't noticed Orville at all—hadn't looked at him. And now Orville put his long thin hand into the shelf, reaching for the candles, smelling the wood, frightened and not taking his eye from the priest, who wasn't watching him.

The priest grunted and coughed as if something swollen were in his throat, as if the Host had been caught there and wouldn't go down. And Orville was trembling. He didn't know—why didn't he take his hand away and then it would be alright, because if he took his hand away it would be alright. He wouldn't steal them today—he would tomorrow, why was it that he was stealing them today? It was stupid. Above the ridge of his forehead he was sweating—and sweating on his back. He clutched the plastic but there were three inside it and he only needed one. Cathy wrote in her diary but she didn't keep her diary any more. She wrote: *Orville takes candles, Orville takes candles,* but she didn't tell.

"And that one Sunday he didn't go to Mass—and all the other days and months he went to Mass and took communion—and that one Sunday, Orville, he drowned, on the day God ordered for Mass." He paused. Orville froze, his hand unravelling the plastic bag. He froze: *Oh God don't let him turn around, don't let him turn around.* The priest bent to buckle his black leather boots. "Drowned, well God have mercy on his soul, on Sunday when he should have been at Mass." He stood and turned around. "That's what happens to deathbed Christians —that's what happens." He grunted as he stood and turned around. Orville was staring at him unable to move, unable to bring his hand away, unable to step from the cabinet, unable to move.

"What's that?" the priest said. "What are you doing now?"

Orville froze. He said nothing, his lips tight together watching the priest, his face so that the blood left it, everything left it and he was alone, immobile with nothing inside him but the weight of a bloodless fear. "What are you looking for?" the priest said. The old man with his face so withered that it looked like when the balloon burst in the trees and hung there limp and then the wind blew it down. He said nothing. Then the old man's face became very strong, as if something like iron passed over it, as if he knew already all that was going on. He said nothing more, he simply walked up to Orville and stared at him silently; but in that silence his face was iron, his face was all the years of the church and the large cross and blood at the hands and feet; it was a white sheet of something hard and rigid, his thin pointed nose breathing the quiet vestry air.

"Orville," he said. Orville's hand trying to unravel itself from the plastic without Orville moving. "Orville," and in his voice was calm understanding and pleading, as if he had been disturbed by it so suddenly that he didn't know. He didn't know. It was as if the priest had wanted it to happen all this time and all this time was waiting for it to happen just to bear the burden of the cross of it happening. "Just so he could say," Orville thought, "just so he could say and tell the story, as if he was always goddamn right," Orville thought. Because the old man looked like that now, *always goddamn right*, with his face and large lucid red eyes that were coming out when he stared, and the immaculate cross down from his withered neck on the immaculate chain that his grey scarf partially hid. When he spoke there was the scent of Host and church wine on his breath in the quiet vestry air.

"What are you taking Orville—what are you stealing from here?" When he said stealing his voice changed expression, high and forced and hating. Orville took his hand from the plastic and removed it without him moving. He stared at the cross and the chain, and the grey scarf around the neck. He said nothing. "The immaculate heart of Jesus," he was thinking. "The immaculate heart of Mary."

He turned away from the priest and went to the door, but when he was about to open it the old man caught him by the coat sleeve, with all the strength in his old arms, and swung him around. Orville did not know what was happening; he did not know what strength there was in old arms or that they were swinging him around. For an instant the door and the outside with its soft wet air all became not there. And when the priest swung him around and struck him hard on the face, so that the patch went askew on his face the priest was not there. There was a sharp burning pain on his face. He lifted his hand and put the patch right, and then he saw the small unconscious drool of saliva on the priest's lips. The clock said quarter to eight and the bus would be turning from the shore road. And Karen would be standing by the gate-post watching the bus turning from the shore road, with her legs and the good softness of her. After the priest hit him, he stepped back and took his Kleenex from his sleeve and blew into it and wiped his mouth with it. His hands had the folds of old skin about the knuckles; leathered yellowed skin. He wiped his face and lips and nose and put the thing back. "Don't you know God could strike you dead—God could strike you dead," he said. "Go out of my church," he said. "Go on —go out of my church—ya'd think Irene and Maufat would teach you not to steal."

"What are ya speakin a my parents for?" Orville said suddenly, surprised at himself. "Yer stupid," he said. "Yer stupid—I wasn't touchin nothing."

The priest looked at him, his eyes narrowed.

"I wasn't speaking of your parents," he said.

"Ya were so, ya were speaking of Irene and don'tcha ever speak about her again and don'tcha ever hit me again," he roared, "don'tcha ever hit me again."

"Go on out of my church," the priest said. "Go on—you're crazy. Maufat will hear of this, go on out of my church." He put his old hands on Orville's coat and tried to shove him back. They were strong and the bones almost bursting out of them. They were strong so that Orville couldn't move them even when he tried to move them, and the priest was snorting, his nose like sweat, and his eyes closed pushing Orville back.

"Go on out of my church—ya could go to hell and God could strike you dead."

"The devil thinks God's a bear—cause there is no God, and the devil thinks God's a bear," Orville said, crying, swinging his coat free and turning around, and the priest pushing him at the back now.

"You're crazy—go on out of my church now—you're crazy."

"And yer old and stupid, and blow your nose," he shouted crying. "And blow your goddamn stupid nose," he shouted crying.

Such strong hands that were like iron of the cross, he thought. He walked up the church road, and everything was fresh wet. His legs were so weak and his stomach so weak that he hated to move. The bus passed the church lane without him even to the end of it, and then he thought that an hour ago everything was fine and good, and when he ran, he ran strong in the darkness and the priest liked him. But now the bus passed the church lane without him even to the end of it. He was scared now—he would have to go home.

He turned around and saw the church in daylight, the snow melting over the foundation windows. *When they were putting up the bell on the steeple a man fell, and he was only seventeen—in 1852, only seventeen. And he fell from the outside of the steeple to where the steps are now.*

But when he fell he stood and looked about him. They said he stood where his own blood was and looked about him. And all the workers were looking at him and he was in his own blood. He said: "Christ, I'm alright," and all the workers knew he was dead but were looking at him, in his own blood that kept flowing from him, his face shattered in. "Christ, I'm alright." Yet everyone knew he was dead.

Maufat was unloading all afternoon. In the quiet sky there was a feeling of spring wetness that made the lower bone of his left arm ache, because every change in weather did this, and wet weather especially. He was unloading freight-cars that sat quiet and without an engine on the third track. Above that track the gully ran upwards, the snow slush brown now, into a small field fenced with rusted wire and dirt brown houses to the left. Far below the station, when he looked he could see the school.

Out of the school came children and when they came up past the station into those brown houses they smelled like the brown houses did—of sulphur and silt-brown water. He tried to see Cathy come out of the school but he couldn't, and then he tried to see Orville come out of the school but couldn't. "Maufat," Alton said, "Maufat," and he grabbed hold of the wheeler and went over again.

Every time he lifted down a crate it hurt his arm. He said: "Hand me down two now," and Alton said: "I can't hand ya down no two." "What are ya, weak?" Maufat said. "Ya need the fork lift," Maufat said. "I don't need no goddamn fork lift for this," Alton said. Then both of them laughed.

Both of them laughed and he leaned against the red-brown of the car and watched the children in the silence plodding along the street in the weak afternoon. It was that they had bleak, tired, stone faces when they moved and went up the gully path to the houses. And when he saw them everyday he said: *At least I take care of my own,* and then he would turn and look. But today he couldn't see Cathy coming out of the school; he didn't see Orville. They went up through the gully path, little—like bleak stone in the twilight.

Vickers came out and Vickers said: "Get off these goddamn tracks —get out of this yard—you'll get run down." Then he turned and

166

before going back into the freight-shed he turned back. "MacDurmot, see that they don't start playing on these tracks."

Maufat looked after him and grunted, saw him swing his big shape into the door again, and then the shape and form of him behind the window-glass. His hair was always combed so neat and not a trace of sweat in it, and he always sat all afternoon taking the slips from the crates and looking at them, marking them for pickup or delivery, and using the phone. Maufat swung the wheeler around.

"Get out of that," he said. "Ya'll get run down."

The children moved like twilight stone when the slush is over it, at darkness when the wind is calm and smooth on the face. They moved up the gully path to the silt-brown houses on the left. Then they were there, then they were gone—little in the half darkness, and he thought: *At least I take care of my own.*

When he swung the wheeler about it leaned on his left side and the topmost crate slid sideways a little, and in his arm it was like bone splinter. It hurt like that. Alton was in the car moving crates to the door. He moved along the platform to the shed, saw on the sky the shade of evening drawing in. Vickers said: "One more wheel load is all, Maufat."

"One more wheel load," he said going back.

"I have two back up against the door," Alton said. "Now I moved two out here," he said.

"It ain't me," Maufat said.

"It's son of a whore," Alton said. "Don't make no difference," he said, "ta me," he said, lifting a crate down. It strained both Maufat's arms, and tore at the rough skin on the palms of his hands.

"Ya chase those young fuckers off the tracks?" he said.

"Told them," Maufat said. "Told them—Jesus now, hold'er hold 'er."

"Why don'tcha wear gloves?" Alton said.

He leaned against the red-brown of the car. There were no more children coming across the track. When he looked down the school-yard was deserted except for one bus, and an emptiness rested there, a drawing-in of shadows on the building's sides. And then the small coarse hum of the bus as it started away.

But he didn't see Cathy coming out; he couldn't see Orville. Alton said: "Come on, let's get this in." Then he said:

"Saw that big doe again."

"This morning?" Maufat asked.

167

"Just comin across the field," Alton said.

It was autumn at darkness and the wind was smooth on his face. He had crossed the road and gone into the bog, seeing once inside only the half hundred feet or so before him—the gnarled trees and the smell of wetness. He carried the rifle pointed at the ground, and when he came into the bog he stopped. Below him the leaves had the look of things going back into the earth.

"Might just *jack it*," Alton said.

"No ya ain't," Maufat said, swinging another crate down. It was growing dark, so the town smelled of night, and the steady light from cars on the long uphill.

"Why—ain't hurtin no-one if I get it now stead of someone else gettin it in the fall," Alton said.

"Leave her be—it's no time to shoot her now," Maufat said.

"Why?"

"It's just no time to shoot her now," he said.

And when he stood inside, not a hundred yards, he had the smell of its musk and excrement on the wetness and the knowledge it was in there. He had put the clip in at the start of the road, and now the clip in and the safety off he brought the rifle up and rested the barrel across his left arm. The wind was smooth on his face so that it couldn't smell him coming in. "It's here," he thought. "It's here." The wood was silent—the autumn hunger in his mouth, the taste of its musk on the wetness of the leaves. An excitement, like younger when naked he had moved through the woods on a day with Irene, and she was skipping ahead of him to hide her nakedness from him, from herself. The pressure of the air all about him, on him, on her slight thighs in the naked forest. An excitement like younger.

"Move her around and take her in," Alton said.

Alton handed him the last crate as he said this, and Maufat grabbing it felt an unbearable pinching beneath his elbow as if someone had shoved a needle into it all at once. All at once. He tried to manage the crate but couldn't and it fell into the warm trodden slush beneath his boots. "Christ," he said. He bent and picked it up again, still with the pain, and lifted it onto the wheeler. "Must be gettin old."

"Must be," Alton said. Then he laughed. Maufat laughed. Yet when he twisted the wheeler around it was in his arm like bone splinter. It hurt like that.

Yet that night he saw, heard nothing. His breath rose pale before his eyes and when it became very dark he unloaded the clip and went.

Once out on the road he saw where they (a doe, a fawn) had crossed. "They crossed the road when I was in there for them," he thought. "Christ—right here they were crossing while I was in there for them."

They had tricked him—moved around and out onto the road, the last place he expected them to be, and he was saying to himself, "Ya tricked me, old girl, ya tricked me," and he was laughing inside and happy; happy that they had done that, because he had expected them inside among the dull branches and not on the road. He looked back into the bog, its shadows solid now. And then into the wood where they had crossed, and then at the sky, seeing a murky darkness, a fullness in the smell of it.

Irene was pregnant with Orville. When he came in and put the gun away she said: "Didn'tcha get it?" "Didn'tcha get it?" Cathy said, trying to sound in tone like her mother.

"No," he said. Then in an instant he was angry with himself for not having gotten it, for feeling happy that the doe had taken the chance to lead her fawn across the road. "I'm goin out tomorrow," he said. "So wake me at five—and I'll go out before work," he said. "She's out there," he said.

Irene said nothing more. Even now at eight months no more than something small and rounded in her belly, a small mounded bulge in her blue print dress. "It should come out easy," Lorne had said. "Whatever it is," he laughed.

He didn't get out until after six, and the dawn just breaking into morning was silent. Ice had formed on the mud and water, gave it a clean sensation to step upon, and there was a clearness in the air. He put his clip in as soon as he entered the road, and took the saftey off, hobbling, he was trying to walk that softly. The morning cold on his hands where he held the rifle and he was thinking a hundred thoughts, all rapidly, all running into each other so that none of them made any clear sense at all. "I wonder why Annie's frightened of me—every time she's playing with Cathy and I come in she looks as if I'm about to bite her, and they crossed the road here," he thought. "Now I'll wait a while here—as if she thinks cause Leah's someone else's I'm mad at her all the time or something—that goddamn bastard," he thought, saying bastard to himself about a man he had never seen, that had entered her two years before he had known her and then it had taken him two years after he had known her, and it had taken him to say, "Well, ya think I'm gonna head out if I knock ya the fuck up," for her to let him and when he did it he was scared—even though he was old *enough not to be scared he was guilty, and he thought of himself time and again running away if it ever did happen. "And then where would she be?" he thought to himself, looking down at the ice crystals in the mud.*

He turned and followed a small path into the bog. He didn't know. Perhaps he should stay on the road because they would cross on the road and trick him again. "Christ, I can only be in one place," he thought. He walked a few paces and turned, waited. Then when he turned to walk again something startled and ran into the alders. He didn't see it. "Christ, I can only be in one place," he thought. And then without seeing it he could hear it running very close to him. It ran by him in the alders, its small hooves on the frigid leaves. It was the fawn.

When the fawn crossed by him all thought lapsed into nothing and he was trembling. He tried to see it clearly but couldn't, and he heard the crack of dead things under it, or fallen branches. Because it was frightened. He knew it was going to run to the other side of the road, and shivering with cold and excitement he rushed to follow, saying to himself: "Don't rush yourself—ya can only be in one place." Thinking that if he called in sick he would have the whole morning. And when he was thinking this the doe stepped out before him in the ditch beside the road. The fawn was on the other side, into the alders, and the doe stood, undecided. He couldn't see her but her front legs were trembling because she stood so straight. Because she had come out on him like that she was gripped in a fear that left her nowhere to run. The fawn had crossed and gone into the alders. He couldn't see her because there was the sick agitation of having her there; and she stood so big in front of him no more than ten yards away, her front legs trembling she was standing that straight. When he fired she jumped up and then sprawled in the ditch, kicked her hind legs high out and was dead. "I can only be in one place—I can only be in one place," he was thinking. There was no blood, only the smell of the shot-hole in her flesh.

When he twisted the wheeler around Alton jumped from the box-car, shut and padlocked the door. Then he moved alongside of Maufat to the shed. Staring at him. He was growing old because he was afraid he was going to drop the wheeler now that Alton was looking. He moved it into the shed. But when he left it there he couldn't straighten his left arm because there was too much pain.

"Ya know Betty's pregnant again."

"She is?" Alton said.

170

"Guess so—and she's too old now for that."

"How old is she?"

"She's in her forties now," Maufat said.

Alton looked at him. The wind was warm on their faces in the fine twilight, the slush waterish purple beneath their boots.

"Yup—too old for that," he said again quietly. They moved across the lot and up on the sideroad where Alton's car was parked. He took his black rain-jacket off and threw it over the seat. He rubbed his elbow in the quiet dusk.

"I know where there's a good second-hand car," Alton said.

"Where?" he said. Then he said: "Never mind anyway—I wanta get a new one, ya get a second-hand, yer gettin someone else's problems."

When they closed the doors there was no wind, the slush purplish under the lights would be turning to ice again, the thin outline of the brown-silt houses, decaying brown. *There was a boy he chased in there one afternoon. It was hot and a stench rose from inside the doors. When he came into the house where the boy went the boy was standing with his back to the thin curtainless window, looking at him with large sick eyes.*

He said: "Ya stole them flares—give them back now—or ya could be arrested." The boy looked at him with large sick eyes, and his body was thin and unhealthy. And then Maufat didn't know what to do. There was a small girl on the floor, and when she looked at him she began to cry.

"Jeanne, go tell Dad," the boy said, and then he began to cry. Outside the grass grew up to the window, and it was yellow, and the small girl on the floor with her dirt-yellow legs so that Maufat didn't know what to do.

He said: "Come on—give them flares back and it'll be alright." There was a jar of jam, and in the heat it smelled very sweet, and the house was so thick it was without air, and flies buzzing and crawling on the jar.

The boy said: "Jeanne, go tell Dad," but the little girl was crying so loud and the tears were red on her face.

"Goddamn Vickers ya know," Maufat said.

"Never mind him," Alton said.

"He'll chase those kids off the track—now ya'd think he'd have somethin better ta do with his time."

"None of them bastards have anything better ta do with their time."

171

The flares smelt of powder and heat, and he could see the boy clutching them in his hand, and the house was so thick it was without air."

"Them are dangerous—ya'll get blown up," Maufat said. Then he turned and went out the door, the air and sky thick with a lifting stench, and he thought, "Jesus, I hada go chase him—I hada go chase him."

But it was because when he came down across the tracks he could smell the child and see the brown of the house, the inside brown, and the yellow grass and stingers in the grass, and large watering eyes in an unhealthy head. Along the track he saw the waste from the flush of the trains and grasshoppers ticking and jumping from tie to tie and he began to think: "That boy, he has to grow up here and it ain't his fault he has to grow up here," and all of a sudden it was the heat hitting him on the head, burning into him and the blue sky with the stench from the yellow grass and he was afraid in his stomach and lonely. "Goddamn me I hada go and chase him," he thought.

He was staring at the ice forming again from the water and not saying a word. From time to time Alton said something and he an-swered. And then Alton said:

"Tired?"

"Oh, a little," he said.

"How's yer arm?"

"My arm—oh it's good, why?"

"Just wonderin," Alton said. "So you're figurin on gettin a new car."

"I'm gettin somethin," he answered. "Soon too," he said. "I figure if Vickers can get a new goddamn car every year I can get at least one." Then for a long time they said nothing more.

When Alton let him out and he walked across the field Irene came from the house to meet him. He didn't know by the way she looked what had happened because he hadn't looked at her. He was looking down at the slush forming into ice and his boots sinking into it. All the time he was thinking that Alton would jack the doe and that he shouldn't, and that he would tell him he shouldn't again tomorrow. Then he thought that if Alton did shoot it, he would give half the meat away, and half of the half to him, and then he tried not to think about it any more. Because Alton was right. Because if you didn't get it now someone would get it in the fall. Because that always happened— someone always got it before you did in the fall.

Irene came out to him with a coat wrapped around her. It was still warm enough in the darkness to feel good when the wind hit his face, and looking and seeing her walking toward him, the dim outline of the bulky coat, made him feel good. She stopped and waited for him to come up.

"Father Lacey phoned," she said.

He eyed her, said nothing.

"He said Orville's off the altar for good," she said. "He said Orville's been stealing stuff from him all the time—from the altar, candles and stuff."

There was pain again in his left arm and the wind came at him in the darkness. When he saw her he saw an old grey coat of his, with the lining torn at the bottom. He looked up at the darkness and the wind was cool on his neck.

"When did he phone ya?"

"Just there now—just there now because he thought you'd be in."

He walked past her into the shed, and turned and waited for her to come up behind him, and then he went into the kitchen. When Cathy said, "Hello," he said "Hello," and ran the tap for water.

"Where is he?" he said.

"Upstairs," Irene said.

There was no light on in the boy's room and he wondered if he was asleep; he wondered if he should knock or something. He rubbed at his left arm and he didn't know why he was upstairs. If the boy was asleep he would knock, and if the boy wasn't asleep then there should be a light on.

When he called his name the door opened. Orville looked at him and then went downstairs into the kitchen.

"What were you doing in that church?" Irene said.

"Nothin."

"Well, ya were doin something—stealing from the church; why were you stealing—why were you stealing?"

"I wasn't stealing anything," Orville said. "He's as blind as a bat and stupid and I wasn't stealing nothin."

Maufat followed him downstairs, and when he was walking downstairs he realized that he didn't know what to do—what was he to do? Because perhaps Orville wasn't stealing and perhaps it was nothing but a mistake—perhaps there was no truth to it at all and it was nothing but a mistake. The priest would phone again and say it was a mistake.

He came into the room and stood beside the fridge and listened. He listened for a long time, once in a while looking to Cathy who remained silent behind the table. Irene was talking and Orville was talking and then Irene was yelling, and Orville was yelling. He kept rubing at his left arm because it was like a bone splinter now—it hurt like that.

"I wasn't stealing nothin," Orville said. "I wasn't stealing a goddamn thing from that altar."

"Then the priest was lying," Irene said. "Father Lacey is lying and you're not lying."

Orville turned around and his eye looked about him and he was scared. It was all in his face that he was yelling because he was scared. He kept moving his hands when he talked and clutching his fists when he talked.

"Where's my jacket?" he said. "Where's my jacket because I'm leavin—I'm not sittin around here getting called a liar because I'm leavin."

"Yer not leavin anywhere," Irene said. "I'll phone Father Lacey back then," she said.

"You phone him back—you phone him back, and I'll talk to him, I'll do the talkin," Orville said.

When Irene went to the phone and dialed the number Maufat could see her arm shaking and her face rigid. He wanted to do something—but he didn't know what to do, and when he looked at Cathy it seemed that she didn't know what to do. *Orville is lying*, he kept thinking, *Orville stole them.*

Then when she had dialed the number she held the phone for Orville to take, but he wouldn't take it. Instead he folded his arms and leaned against the sink staring at the floor.

"Take it," she whispered. "Here, take it." But he kept staring at the floor.

"He don't need ta take it—I will," Maufat said. Orville looked up —said nothing.

When Father Lacey answered he said:

"I hear Orville's in some kind of trouble."

"I've told Irene what he's done—what he's been doing," the old man said. "He's off the altar for good—he's been stealing candles from the vestry, and I don't know for how long—but this morning I caught him red-handed."

There was a pause.

"I had a feeling it was either he or Rance and this morning I caught him red-handed."

"Well, maybe it's Rance too," Maufat said.

"Yes, maybe it is," the old man said. "But I can't say—I just know I can't have him around my altar; I mean you're the parents and you should discipline him but I can't have him around my altar."

"Well, then he won't be around yer altar," Maufat said, not knowing who he was angry at but angry all at once. "No, he won't be around yer altar," he said again, his voice changing into somebody else's—not his own. "But that don't matter," he said suddenly. "I just wanta get at the truth of the situation and try to figure out the situation."

"Yes, well you'll have to get a confession from Orville—now if he wants to see me and apologize then everything will work out, the whole thing will be forgotten."

"Well, we'll see, but I have to get at the truth of the situation, and then I'll phone you back."

"Good good," the old man said. "God bless," he said.

When Maufat put the phone down and turned Orville was still staring at the floor. "I work all goddamn day and I come home to this," he said. "I haven't even had my goddamn supper yet."

Orville looked up and Maufat went over to him.

"Did ya steal them goddamn candles?" he said.

Orville didn't answer.

"Did ya steal them goddamn candles?" he said again.

"I took a few old candles," Orville said.

"Ya stole them," Irene said.

"That's like stealin from God—ya know that it's like stealin from God," Maufat said.

Orville started to walk away.

"Don'tcha walk away from me now," Maufat said, grabbing onto his neck and swinging him around. "Don'tcha walk away from me or I'll kick yer arse."

"Ya will not do that," Irene said

"He better not walk away from me," Maufat said, swinging his arm and lightly hitting the boy's chin. "He better not walk away from me."

"I'll walk away from you—ya think God's got wings or somethin?" Orville roared. "Ya think angels got wings and fly around?" he roared.

"No I don't," Maufat said. "I don't."

"Ya do so—ya think angels got wings or somethin—because yer all stupid," he said, turning and walking into the room and then running upstairs.

"Yer the one that's stupid," Maufat said. "Stealing from God."

He turned around and ran the tap for water. His left arm was still paining and his face was hot and red, because he felt stupid—he felt he had been stupid.

"Are ya gonna phone him back?" Irene said.

"No, I'm not going to phone him back—I wanta get my supper; are ya gonna get my supper?"

"Yes," she said.

In the left field was where the doe would cross in the morning. He turned around and leaned against the sink and Cathy was staring at him.

6

With this winter Shelby had begun to see a change in himself. When the hairs came out on his face they came out grey instead of brown, and little by little they came out grey upon his head, and on the knuckles of his hands.

When he woke it was in the evening. He lay upon the mattress for a long time, and then feeling colder and colder he got up, threw his pants and shirt on and went into the kitchen, put the kettle on and sat in a chair. He whistled to himself while the water boiled. It was five to seven and he had done nothing all day but sleep. Nothing all day but sleep, he thought.

It was that he didn't feel like doing anything. If he went into the room to turn on the television he would turn it off again. Like he did the day before, he would go back into the bedroom and lay upon the mattress, light a cigarette and think. Then he would wish he could go to sleep again. His back was sore from sleeping all day and he was tired from sleeping all day. Right now, at this moment he felt like sleeping again.

He rose from the chair and made tea and went to the window. Outside the road to the settlement was bleak and empty. There hadn't been a snowfall in days, and everything seemed dirty—the woodlots themselves naked and dirty. Yesterday it had been very warm but today it was cold again—freezing, and the streetlamp that lighted the roadway just above his house had something of a small frigid halo around the lamp.

He drank his tea black and stared out the window. A little girl passed the house with her arms folded into her coat. He watched her until she disappeared and then went back to the table, picked up the cards and began to play solitaire, every once in a while looking through the deck for the card he needed.

He turned up, little by little, all the cards he needed and then put his aces up, and then all the cards until he had the four matched suits. Then he shuffled them again, sat back silently in his chair and stared.

It was that when he came down the road that day the afternoon sun was bright on the mud and the mud was infested with small flies, with the smell of their freshness. While he walked he thought of nothing, and saw nothing, only the sun, only the mud rising over his naked feet. Then he walked into the water for a time—and the water was so warm it was sick warm because it had been cut off at low tide and remained stagnant and low in the mud. After a while he climbed up the bank and lay in the grass and watched the boats passing in the channel, and the tide rising over the slow water that he had walked in.

Then it was supper hour and he was hungry; a little wind coming in blowing the sweat from him. The day was still bright warm and a haze settled over the water as far out as the first buoy. If he thought at all he thought of eating something cold and good tasting. But he lay there staring at the full blueness of the sky and wondered where the blue led to—if the blue went on and on, and when the blue turned to black. He knew that black surrounded the blue, that the blue surrounded the earth and the black surrounded everything else. That the black was always there, and the stars were always there. Though he had thought when he was younger that the stars went to bed in the morning. Now he knew that it was just the sun that made the blue and made the stars go to bed. After a time the sun moved and began to hurt his eyes. And he knew also that the sun didn't move but that the earth moved, though he couldn't feel it moving. He knew that the earth moved so fast, being pulled in a circle around the sun, that if he wasn't held down by some great force, the force of the earth and the sun, and the earth moving, he would be hurled miles and miles into the void and the black.

He thought of this as he lay there and then forgot it again and then thought of something sweet and cold to eat—the smell of strawberries in a glass dish with cream.

When he heard the laughing of people far down the shore he rose from the grass and followed the bank path down. As he was going down the path he saw a girl walking in the water. She was tiny and small and about fourteen and she held in her right hand a reed she

177

was making waves with. She had a skirt and blouse on and the skirt was tucked up above her thighs and the blouse was thin yellow, her small white arms dangling from it. She was about fourteen or fifteen and she was singing; and she was thinking she was alone. When he looked at her legs he saw her skirt done up across the back of her thighs, and he stopped and watched her in the water playing with the reed. He knew she was very pretty though he could hardly see her face; but her blond hair was short and she was pretty, because when he looked at her ears her ears were so small and well shaped.

He stood on the path and looked out over the bay, and then down at the girl, and then at a ship coming in—a distant speck on the water. If he could get on a ship he would go all around the world and settle nowhere—and be a sailor and go all around the world. Because when those ships passed in the channel he always thought of that. He stared at the ship and then at the girl who was thinking that her reed was a ship. Yes, she was thinking that her reed was a ship and she didn't know while she was singing that he was standing above her on the path.

"You can't sing," he said.

The girl dropped the stick and turned around frightened. At first she didn't see him, and turned back around looking in the direction of the bay.

"No—you can't sing," he said.

This time the girl turned and walked from the water. Her legs were white and shining wet. When she came from the water she straightened her skirt and looked about her. Then she looked up on the path. She had a very small pretty face.

"I can so," she said.

"I don't think so," he said.

"Do I care?" she said.

He followed the path to the beach and walked toward her. The sand was warm and dry and shifted beneath his feet.

"Don't run away—I ain't gonna bite ya," he said.

"I'm not runnin away—I'm goin down ta see Leah," she said.

"Leah who?"

"Just Leah."

"Well, I'm going down there too," he said.

She shrugged and laughed and walked away from him, and he laughed and told her she couldn't sing. Then he walked beside her and she was so small, the naked whiteness of her legs.

And then for three years he went down to that beach and those houses below the bridge, and waited for her to come from the bus after school. And when she talked to anyone else he got angry and wouldn't talk to her. He went with Cecil at night to meet them under the bridge and when he wanted to be alone with her she never wanted to be alone; so they followed Cecil and Leah wherever they went. He found that he couldn't speak to her and that everything she said made him angry. And when he talked to her she didn't seem to be interested but was always listening to what Cecil was saying—or what Leah was saying and wasn't listening to him. Whenever he tried to kiss her she would kiss him but whenever he put his hand *there* or *there* she would take his hand away. Then he would look down at her feet. They sat on the stringers beneath the bridge and on spring nights the water was high and black and there was the smell of tar. And whenever he put his hand *there* or *there* she'd take his hand away. She'd say:

"Oh look how the water's rising—it's gonna be up and flood the ditches." Then she'd laugh. And he'd hear from the other side of the bridge Cecil and Leah murmuring to each other and that seemed so much better. "As old Lester would say—look how that water's rising —it's gonna flood them ditches." Then she'd laugh again but he wouldn't laugh. Then she'd toss her head and shrug because he wasn't laughing, and look across the river water and the bay water. The spring would be so fresh with the wind, and so silent sometimes that they could hear the last ice cracking in the channel.

"You know if we fell from here we'd drown for sure," she said.

And across the water there were lights from the houses with people married and settled—people who had their own homes and were together, under dark blankets at night. They sat here under the bridge and along the sidings people had scratched their names and the dates. He wanted her to be with him under those blankets at night, and something filled him so much: the longing for it, the impossibility of it because of her laughter.

"I wanta drown sometimes anyway," he said.

"What?"

"I said I wanta drown sometimes anyway." And the tone in which he said it made it clear to her what he was saying. She swung herself about and stood on the stringer balancing one leg before the other. She didn't look at him. Then all at once he hated himself—hated her and for an instant wanted to push her into the water. On the other side of the bridge he could hear Leah and Cecil, and they were talking to each other and Leah was laughing.

"I hate yer guts," he said.

"Good then," she said. She didn't look. And he wanted to push her into the water.

The night was black and the water swift. They could hear the water beneath them, and she was balanced on the stringer, with a heavy coat and large boots, so that if she ever fell the heaviness of her clothes would take her under, and the current would carry her. He thought this and became terrified. Why had they ever come out here? Why did they walk up and down the stringer every night?

"Listen—we better go in," he said.

"Okay," she said.

He swung himself around and stood and held out his hand for her. But she wouldn't take his hand, even though she was looking at him now. He was going to speak but she said:

"I can make it."

"No, ya can't—ya can't make it—yer gonna fall into that water, Mary, yer gonna fall inta that water—now take my hand."

She shook her head. Then he tried to grab her hand but she pulled it away. When she did that he could see her right foot slip a little and he thought she was going to fall. But she didn't. He made no other attempt to grab her and turned, walking off the bridge.

"Hey," she said. "Hey—ya gonna wait up for me?"

"No," he said, "I ain't."

He walked off the stringer and onto the cement structure. Leah had taken shoe polish and had written one night: *Leah loves Cecil and he loves me too.* Now he was standing where she had written the words, and looking back he could see Mary moving slowly in the darkness. He could see her high white spring boots inching sideways on the stringer and his heart was pounding. In his ears there was a ringing noise.

"Are ya gonna fall?"

"No!" she said, as if telling him to be quiet. But he couldn't—he kept asking her if she was going to fall and he was afraid. He thought: *Now if she goes under it's gonna be my fault—oh God if she goes under; poor little Mary if she goes under.* He could see that for moments at a time she wasn't moving—then her feet would inch slowly, and then she'd stop again. And when she was five yards away he could see the outline of her face, and the mud on her boots. He stared at the mud, and for some reason he loved her now more than he ever did—

because he loved her; because he thought: *I love her—Christ I love her.*

A car came over the bridge and the stringers began to tremble and pebbles fell from the underside into the water. She had nothing to hang on to.

"Shelby," she said. "Shelby."

"Christ," he thought. "She's gonna fall, she's gonna fall. Christ," he said.

He moved out onto the stringer again. When he got close enough to take her hand he could see that she was crying. Her eyes were looking at the water. So he said:

"If ya ever fell the current would take ya right inta shore anyway," and he laughed. But she kept crying, so he said: "Oh look how that water's risin—it's gonna flood them ditches." Then her crying broke into frightened laughter and he took her hand, leading her onto the cement. It was that she was crying and he knew how young she was—how little she was.

They walked to the top of the bridge and he let go of her hand, but she grabbed it again and tucked it with hers inside her coat.

The next morning he went into town. He kept repeating, "Yer crazy, yer crazy," over and over to himself. But he had thought of it the night before while walking her home, and then lying in bed it had kept him awake most of the night—knowing that it wouldn't work, and yet that it might. Because it was final—it was one way or the other. It excited him because he knew he was frightened.

"But it's one way or the other," he thought. "Today we'll find out." He went into town, hiking, and all the way in he was frightened. But the night before she had cried, and had taken his hand. Then he thought she would be mad at him, never speak to him again. "Fuck it," he thought. "It's one way or the other!" All the way into town he tried to keep everything out of his mind. He kept repeating, "Fuck it, it's one way or the other."

When he went into the jewelry store and asked for the ring, the woman showed him the whole display. She told him that most men brought their fiancées in and talked it over. When she said this he felt stupid, and guilty of something. He didn't know whether to leave or go through with it. "Yer crazy, yer crazy," he kept thinking.

He stared at the rings so as not to look at the woman, and felt himself sweating. "Fuck it," he thought. "It's one way or the other." Then he turned to the woman again and asked for the one he had in mind.

"Now can I pay down on this now and the rest later?" he said.

"Of course," she said. "If I have your name and address and where you work."

"Well, I'm cuttin pulp on my own lot right now," he said.

"That's fine," the woman said.

She wrapped it for him in a small blue box and he left. He wandered about the street for a while and then went to the tavern and had a beer. Only now did the whole thing seem impossible to him. While he drank his beer a sudden thought, a sudden feeling came over him—that she would laugh in his face and spit on the ring. He took it out of his pocket and tapped the box gently on the table. Yes, it was because Cecil and Leah laughed and could do anything and he was always frightened of putting his hand *there* or *there* and when he did, it was always so clumsily and she always took his hand away. And why did she take it away? Because if she loved him she wouldn't take it away. And Cecil always said: "Are ya gettin inta the little one's pants yet?" And he'd be angry. Yet he'd pretend he was because he knew Cecil was with Leah. And again at night he would try and again she would stop him. It was a feeling of wanting to joke with her and talk with her the way Cecil did with Leah—to have her laugh because of what he did or said—to be able to pick her up and throw her into the sand or snow the way Cecil did with Leah. He always felt he mustn't do that with her—that he mustn't do that.

He finished the beer and left, walking in the streets for a while, clutching the box in his hand. "The hell with it—if she says no she says no—if she says no she says no." He kept thinking *no* because he didn't want to start thinking *yes*. "If she says no she says no—if she says no she says no."

It took him a long while to get downriver. When he did he sat under the bridge until after 3.30. It was a cool spring day and he was hungry and cold but he sat under the bridge all afternoon so as to be close to her house. When he rose his legs were stiff. He walked to the top of the bridge and waited another hour there, and was almost asleep when he heard the bus.

When he heard the bus he was confused and felt stupid. The bus passed him before he began to walk. "Yer crazy, yer crazy," he kept thinking. His legs were trembling and his arms were trembling, and he felt sick inside—the closer he got the more frightened and sick he became.

When she left the bus he was still up the road from her, and when she saw him he lifted his hand. She stopped for a moment, waving,

182

and then went into the house. "Christ," he kept saying to himself. "Christ, yer crazy."

He kept walking, never taking his eyes off the back porch door. "Now she's just gone in there with them books, and she'll be out— she'll be out."

He couldn't keep his arms or legs from trembling and he no longer held the blue box. The roadway was turning stiff with an April wind, and they had thought the river would flood because the warmth had come that early. But today it was cold and there was a cold stiff sky, grey—far down a dog crossed on the grey road. "I wonder how their feet don't fall off in the winter." He kept staring at the back porch door, and when he was nearing her drive she opened it and came out.

"I haveta go to the store," she said. "Ya wanta come?"

He grunted and walked beside her.

"Boy, what a day—I'll be glad when this year's over," she said.

He kept silent. When they were on the shore road he put his arm around her but he felt it shaking.

"What are ya shakin for?" she said.

"I'm cold," he said.

"Yer cold," she laughed.

"I was out around all day," he said, taking his arm away.

"Did ya see Leah today?" she said.

He didn't answer.

"Eh?" she said.

"No, no—I haven't seen her since last night." He glanced down at her white boots scuffed by the mud and dirt-brown snow, and they were cold looking, and he couldn't think of them the way he had the night before when they inched their way along the stringer in the dark.

They reached the store and went inside.

They were walking up the shore road now, he carrying her parcel under his arm. He could see in the distance the main highway, and the streetlight.

He thought: "Before that."

Then they were no more than a hundred yards from the streetlight and he thought: "Before that."

They came to the main road and turned up it and his legs were trembling and his arms were trembling. She walked beside him small and silent and pretty—the only sound between them the rustling of her parcel under his arm.

He clutched the blue box in his hand.

"Are ya coming across to the island with us if Cecil fixes up that old boat of his?"

"Might," he said.

Then it was as if he were in a daze, because when he swung her around he was holding to her so tightly that it hurt her arms and she tried to wrench them away and he kept staring at her thighs under her jacket and dress. When he looked at her face it was white and she turned it away from him.

"I got somethin for ya," he said. "I got somethin for ya here." He was trying to talk calmly, and he knew he wasn't talking calmly. "Yes, yes," he said, "I got something for ya here—I went up today and got it." As he said this his lips began to sputter and he felt saliva coming over his chin and he was frightened. He went to take it out of his pocket and she said:

"No Shelby—I'm goin away as soon as the summer."

"No yer not," he said. "No, yer just talkin—ya ain't goin away now." He took the box out of his pocket, talking all the time without realizing what he was saying. He brushed his chin with the back of his arm to take the saliva away.

She took the box and opened it and took out the ring and looked at it. It was as if for a moment she wanted to try it on, and she was silent. He stared at her, his legs shaking so badly and his teeth chattering against each other and his eyes on her. She felt it with the fingers of her hands.

"It's a nice ring," she said.

"It's a good ring," he said.

"Shelby, I'm just eighteen and I ain't getting married—now I know you were thinkin about this, but I'm gonna go away as soon as the summer," she put it in the box and handed it back.

"No yer not gonna go away," he said. "But I knew ya never loved me—ya never," he said, the words coming out funny and a tightness in his throat.

"I do as a friend," she said.

"As a friend—as a friend," he roared. "I couldn't even touch ya— I couldn't even get close ta ya."

She grabbed her parcel from under his arm and walked away.

"Yes and take this too," he roared, throwing the ring into the water in the ditch.

"Don't you throw that away," she said.

"I will goddamn throw it away," he said. "I will goddamn throw it away," feeling terror and stupidity and clumsiness.

"I liked ya as a friend," she said. "I liked ya as a friend—don'tcha throw that away."

She turned from him and walked on, and he could hear her crying. But she wouldn't turn around and when he called "Mary" she wouldn't turn around.

"I will goddamn throw it away—I will goddamn throw it away," he kept saying—and she was walking away from him, and he was crying.

He lit the fire in the oil stove and drew back in his chair. The tea was cold. He cursed and set it on the table, picked up the cards again and then threw them back.

"I will goddamn throw it away," he said. Then he got up and walked into the room, looked at the television and without turning it on walked out of the room, picked up his coat and went outside.

The air was sharp—it made his breath stick inside him, and the sky was black with a few stars. Perhaps if that girl hadn't walked under the light, perhaps then he wouldn't have thought—but that girl. Perhaps she was like Mary with the reed, swinging it in the water. "Jesus —Jesus I will goddamn throw it away." He walked along the road, the sound of his rubbers squeaking in the snow. He didn't know at all where he was going, and he remembered that he had lighted the oil stove and had left it burning. Now and then he put his hands up to warm his ears.

The roadway was scraped by graders until it showed purple in the dark, and off to either side the snow mounds, rigid and silent. When he came in sight of the main road he thought, "I'll go get my money— I'll go get my money."

He turned onto the main road and walked quickly, staring out at the lights across the bay, and then at the fields, naked and dark, their twisted fences half covered and slanted by snow, and then at the houses. As he came up to the house he thought of Leah and from Leah he thought of her. Because she was married now and had two children. But he wouldn't speak; last time she was home with her husband and the children he didn't speak. He'd walk right by her—and she was different now, older looking.

He spit and went around to the back door. There was only the bedroom light on and he knocked again and again, and then Leah came.

"Hello, Cecil here?"

"No, I think he's uptown, Shelby—at least that's where he headed for."

Leah came to the door. She was dressing and he smelled the warmth of perfume on the cold when she asked him in, and he stood inside the door, his hands to his ears, and looked at her. When he looked at her, he saw the zipper of her slacks was undone, and he couldn't stop looking at the white lace and the white thigh.

Then she said:

"I have to go to a party—so if ya wanta sit here until Cecil gets home, but I don't know—he got a drive inta town with old Lester, so I haven't a clue when he'll be home." Then she pulled the zipper of her slacks tight, and her small hand moved and flickered and made a shadow on the kitchen wall—and the smell of the house was like the smell of her, yet it was mixed with the heat of the oil stove burning and the shades drawn in the room.

He said:

"Well, I just come down for my money—Cecil said he might be able to give it ta me tonight."

She looked at him as if she didn't understand.

"The money for the bicycle that time," he said.

"You mean he hasn't paid ya that yet?" she said. She shook her head and muttered and then took a small can from the ledge behind the stove.

"It's $25, ain't it?"

"No-no, it's $15," he said.

"Ain't it $25?"

"No-no, $15 is all," he said.

She took the top lid off the can, and then another lid that had flour in it.

"$15?" she said.

"Yep," he said.

She handed him the money and then placed the two lids carefully on the can, not spilling the flour. Then she took the can and went into the room with it. When she came out he said:

"I just might wait here for a while, ta get warmed—what party ya goin to?"

"Cathy's eighteen," she said. "So Ronnie and I are gonna go down."

"Cathy MacDurmot—eighteen," he said. "Well, I think I might stay here and see if he comes back."

"Shut the stove out when ya leave," she said.

"Ya, I'll probably wait an hour anyway," he said. He looked at her. He felt he had nowhere else to go.

"Well, I tell ya right now that he's got somethin sneaky about him— his face or somethin is sneaky," Leah said, leaning forward on her chair, her elbows on the table.

"I only see him once in a blue moon—I mean when he sometimes comes in with Cecil or somethin ta pick you up," Irene said, dealing out the cards to each of them separately. Then she added: "But I know what ya mean—he looks sneaky."

"I kinda feel sorry for him," Cathy said.

"If I didn't feel sorry for him he wouldn't be sittin in my kitchen— the only friend he has is Cecil, and I don't know why Cecil puts up with him." Then she stopped talking, picked up her cards and looked at them, winked at Betty, who was her partner.

It was almost nine. She had picked up her guitar and left the house with Shelby sitting in the kitchen. Ronnie came from behind the hen-house when she came outdoors, the wind frozen on him.

"What were ya doin out here? Ya'll die."

He smiled and got into the car, the red hat pulled down over his ears and the back of his head, his legs snow-ridden where he had walked in the drifts.

"Ya'll die," she said again. "Boys, it's cold ain't it?"

Once in a while as she drove she stared at him. He was looking at the road as if seeing something beyond the lights. When they crossed the bridge she said:

"You're getting bigger every day—you'll soon be as big as Cecil."

"Bigger," he said. "I'm gonna be bigger."

"And stronger?" she laughed.

"I'm gointa be bigger," he said.

It was the cold that made his cheeks fresh looking, and the snowsuit that made his body strong looking, so that when she stared at him crossing over the bridge, with him looking at the flat darkness of the ice beneath, she felt warmth, and then sadness in her throat.

"Yes," she said. "Yer gonna be the biggest man around here."

"No, Orville is," he said, looking at her, his tiny face under the hat and his lips pressed together.

"Orville?" she said.

"Yes, Orville's gointa be the biggerest man," he said.

They were sitting around the kitchen table. Cathy was back in the corner with her chair against the wall, her head resting back against it, listening to the talking. She had a beer settled in her hand that Maufat had given her, and she drank from it slowly. At first they were talking and she was listening and then they were talking and she wasn't listening. She lifted the bottle and sipped from it, watching the cards being played out, trying to remember what was played and what was still held. When Leah's jack came out she sat up and laughed, played the five on it and took the trick.

"Yer down—yer down."

"Son of a bitch," Leah whispered, then she said: "Betty, why didn't you have the five."

"You should've known I didn't have it—the second hand woulda went to me now if I had it."

"Yer down, yer down," Cathy laughed, drinking from her beer and then marking the score. "We should play this for money Irene."

"Just because yer eighteen—just because yer eighteen," Leah said. "We'll beat ya yet—what are ya, what is it?"

"95 ta 35."

"We'll beat ya yet," Leah said.

Maufat and Lorne came from the room where they had been since seven o'clock. When they saw the card game they stood by the fridge and watched for a moment, now and then glancing at the cards held. Then they took the last of the beer and opened it.

"We need more beer," Maufat said.

"Now we have enough beer," Irene said.

"There ain't any left."

"I still got my first one goin," Cathy said.

He looked at her for a second, turned away from the fridge to the sink. She could see the back of his head bent and the redness of the skin over the muscles of his neck. "But who heard of a birthday party without beer?" she said.

"Listen—ya may as well have a beer now or then in here," he said, turning back to her. "In here as out there and down the road. But don't let me catch ya drinking with no fellas," he added. "Yer not that old that ya can go out drinkin with fellas." He rubbed at the elbow of his arm and looked at the floor.

Irene said: "Now she isn't doing that."

"I know, I know," he said. "I know—I'm just sayin."

Cathy took a drink and stared at her cards.

"I'm just sayin is all," he said, looking to her. She was staring at her

188

cards.

Then he said: "Lorne and I are goin down for some."

Lorne stood by the fridge. When he finished his pint he set it on the table, looked at Cathy and winked: "Eighteen, eh?" he said: "And no boyfriend yet." She didn't answer, turned to Irene: "25," she said. "25," Irene said. "Don't worry, don't worry—I got the hand."

"Oh, she's got some fella somewhere or other—but he's too scared ta come in the house," Maufat said. "She's been seeing him and seeing him and he ain't yet been in the house."

Lorne took his coat from the back of Betty's chair. She hadn't spoken all evening, sat there gazing at her cards. When she looked to Lorne she said nothing, and he said: "We'll be right back up." She turned to her cards again and played a saver on a no-trump lead.

"Why the hell did ya do that?" Leah said.

"Do what?" she said.

"Ya played yer nine out—ya shouldn't of played yer nine out."

"Oh—well, I didn't mean to."

"We'll be right up," Maufat said. "And make sure he doesn't sneak out of the house."

"Who?" Leah said.

"Orville's not allowed out of the house," Cathy said. "Except ta go ta school."

"Oh-hoo," Leah said. She glanced to Maufat, then to Irene. "I see," she said. "I see."

Outside the coldness on his face after the beer and the wine drank in the room where he and Lorne had sat without lights, hearing sometimes Ronnie's voice and the sound of the radio from the bedroom upstairs. It was good to have the coldness on his face and there were stars in the sky, and coldness in the snow and ice. Then they were inside, they had talked and talked and Lorne said: "Ya know she's pregnant again," and Maufat listened.

Now they were in the car and driving downriver. The farther down they went the fewer lights there were, the deeper the blackness, as if it were the blackness of the bay swallowing the land. When they were in the house Lorne had said, almost whispering, "I'm afraid she's too old eh—ya know—I'm afraid she's too old," and Maufat listened. Then Maufat said: "Ya, I know—it's bad, I know. But she'll make out good."

Now they were going down beyond the lower river, down beyond the lights and familiar houses. In the house whatever Lorne said he listened to, and he said nothing. But out in the car it looked like burnt-out winter—it looked as if the land was roots and frozen grass and not snow, though they could see little in the dark, little from the lights of the car. Because Lorne had talked in the house Maufat talked now.

"Ya heard about Orville ain't ya?" They were crossing Oyster Bridge and Lorne shifted down.

"Oh I heard somethin," Lorne answered.

The pavement was bare on the other side and the dark trees still. He made Maufat want to talk. Maufat said:

"Met a moose over there on the low ground last time I come down with Alton."

"Didja—cow?" Lorne said.

"Young cow—young cow." The pavement was bare, and in the air it was the blackness he had seen on nights like this for years, and he remembered. He remembered the pavement and walking.

"Young cow—so did I tell ya bout Orville, did I?" Maufat said.

"Nope—I just heard somethin."

"Well, he was caught stealin candles and stuff from the church."

Lorne said nothing, but he shifted again and the car eased. For minutes there was a silence.

"Ya, why would he do that?" Lorne said.

"He just did it, I don't know—he just did it is all; how da ya know what kids are gonna do?"

"I hoped ya kicked his arse for it," Lorne said.

"Oh, I was gonna—don't ya worry, I slapped him and I was gonna but Irene stopped me from doing it—she's always stoppin me from somethin," Maufat laughed.

He looked over and Lorne's lips were closed one upon the other. The pavement was black winter and twisted and he was thinking of Annie's house—that night when in the middle of a conversation Irene had said—so quickly that he hadn't caught it at first—"Leah is my child, I thought ya'd better know that cause she's my child and she ain't Annie's child." And when she had said it Lorne lifted himself from the chair in the room and went upstairs. *And it was as if he was now lifting himself from the chair in the room and going upstairs.*

"So well, he did it and it's over," Maufat said.

"How much do ya want?" Lorne said.

"What?"

"What do ya think we should get?"

Maufat looked over for a moment and saw in the ashtray the flicker of light from his burning cigarette, and stared at the radio dial and the heater.

"How much—couple of cases—quart of wine for the girls—get them on the wine," he laughed.

He kept staring at the burning cigarette in the ashtray, and the sound of the car and the warm heat on his face.

"We going to Ramsey's?" Lorne said. "Or Denot's?"

"Ramsey's eh," Maufat said. Then he said: "It's over anyway."

Lorne picked up a cigarette and put it in his mouth and lighting it off the butt he said:

"Well, I don't have too much cash."

"How much do ya have?" Maufat said. He felt tight in the chest and he stretched in the seat.

"Not too much," Lorne said.

When they turned into Ramsey's Maufat said:

"Don't matter, I'll get it—ya can pay me back some time."

He went out into the snow and walked around to the back. In the back the bus was parked, and when he went into the house he felt angry and wanted to say: "Ya buy yer own goddamn beer," but when he went in the back door and Ramsey said: "I got some rye here tonight," he left and went back to the car.

"Ya want some good rye?" he said.

Lorne looked at him and shrugged.

"It don't matter if you can buy it, Maufat," he said. And Maufat said:

"Ya, let's really get goin—let's really get goin—Betty's pregnant and Orville's a thief, let's really get goin." The cold made him move his feet in the snow. Lorne shrugged and said: "If you can buy it, Maufat," and Maufat went inside again. He bought rye and wine and beer and came out.

All the way up he stared at the road with the rye open in his hands. Lorne had a beer in his hands. When he took the rye it was as if for a second he couldn't swallow and then he swallowed, passing the bottle over and Lorne passing him the beer. Then Lorne would take the rye and pass it back. When they came to Oyster Bridge Maufat said: "Tramp her," but Lorne geared down.

"I hope it's gonna be easy on her."

"I hope it is too—I hope it is too—I hope she'll make it alright, and she will make it alright, ya don't haveta worry about that."

"But it's late," Lorne said.

"Oh that isn't gonna matter," Maufat said. "Look, I got a kid fourteen who's stealin from God."

He didn't know why he was saying that.

"What d'ya think I should do to him?" Maufat said.

"Shit, I don't know—kick his arse."

"I hope he don't start stealin all the time—and breakin inta places and gettin inta trouble—maybe it's because he's only got one eye."

"I don't know," Lorne said.

"Maybe it is."

"I don't know," Lorne said. He swallowed a mouthful of beer and shifted again.

"We haveta get our house fixed up with another kid comin."

"Ya that's right," Maufat said. "Ya'll have a bunch of them—well, everything in that old house of Annie's is yours."

"We'll have to do somethin."

"Well, it won't be too hard—I mean ya got the furniture, and ya can lay down another room in that place of yours, no problem—I'll help ya lay it down, no problem."

Lorne said nothing. Clasping his hands on the wheel that way he looked as if he had just lifted himself and gone upstairs. *And when he went upstairs that night Maufat said: "Don't make no difference ta me, Irene." Then when he went home he felt happy. Everything looked calm, and it was starry and there were furrows of snow in the ruts of the road. He kept thinking of Irene and feeling happy—happy that she had had Leah, happy that she had told him, that she had her plaid skirt on with the frills on her blue blouse. Everything.*

When they turned into the gate Maufat said quickly:

"So you don't know what I should do with him."

"I don't know—no," Lorne said, then he added after a moment: "Kids are gonna be kids anyway."

Then Maufat shut up. He shut up because he had asked and had gotten no answer, with Lorne gearing down and then shifting into high gear all the time, as if Lorne was saying, "Let's not talk about Orville stealing cause if you can't bring him up right like I bring my kids up right then I don't wanta hear about him stealing from God."

And so when they were going up the steps to the back porch, the steps creaking under the weight of their boots and the cold, Maufat said:

"Ya think she'll take some wine tonight?"

"Betty?" Lorne asked.

"Ya, maybe a little wine would make her feel good," Maufat said. "I hope it makes her feel good—I mean I bought it to make her feel good."

Then they closed the top on the rye bottle and went inside. Inside the back porch they could hear the guitar strumming and Leah's voice, Cathy's voice breaking in every now and then. They had been playing cards but now the cards were scattered on the table, and there were four empty beer bottles on the table. In the far corner Cathy was sitting, smoking a cigarette from Leah's package and Leah was playing the guitar and singing.

Every time Cathy joined her both of them started laughing, and they had to stop. Then Leah would begin playing again. She was playing, and the music was full and loud. When she sang Irene would hum, her head moving a little and her fingers tapping the table in time. Leah said:

"Sing Irene."

"I don't know the words."

"I'll sing," Cathy said. And then Leah started laughing again and had to stop.

"What are ya laughing at—I can sing," Cathy said.

"Yep," Leah said.

"I can," Cathy said. *"Have you seen my blue-eyed son, killed him a man with a sawed-off gun*—now that's singing," she said.

"Yep," Leah said.

"Yep, it is," Cathy said.

Maufat came in and stood by the sink, and looked tired. Every now and then Cathy would break from her singing and her laughter to look at him—and when she looked at him she knew he was tired, and old faced and grey—and that the rye he carried in his hand was the rye he had bought for them to drink—and that the beer he put in the fridge was the beer he had bought for them to drink. She looked at him and noticed that his face was smaller. That when she was little his face was a big face and his arms were big arms and when he carried her along the river his hands were large hands that felt rough and warm. Now his face was worn, with an untidy grey on it—a small thing with small narrow eyes. He stood there a moment and then poured a rye for him and Lorne, and with his back to them ran the water.

He said:

"He didn't sneak out, did he?"

And Irene said:

"No, now Ronnie's up there with him and they're playin music."

"Good—as long as I know that," he said.

Have you seen my blue-eyed son, killed him a man with a sawed-off gun.

"I don't know the words or the music to that," Leah said.

"Get somethin else—get something else," Irene said.

"Play *Little Rosa*."

"It's too sad," Leah said.

After Maufat handed Lorne the rye he poured a glass of wine and walked to the table, setting it down in front of Betty without a word.

"What's this?" she said. "Now Maufat, yer not trying ta make me drunk."

"This stuff won't make ya drunk," he said. "Want some, Irene?"

"I'll have some, I guess," Irene said. "But just a little," holding her finger up to indicate how much.

Maufat went back to pour another glass, and then taking two more glasses and measuring them all at the same level—three-quarters full —brought them over for Irene, Cathy and Leah.

"Get me drunk enough and I'll sing anything," Leah said.

"Well sing *Little Rosa*, cause I like *Little Rosa*," Lorne said.

"I'm not drunk enough yet," she laughed, and shifted herself and began with the guitar again:

We got married in a fever
Hotter than a peppered trout
We been talkin bout Jackson
Ever since the fire went out
And I'm goin ta Jackson
Let loose a my coat

And as she sang Cathy listened, wanting to join in but afraid to ruin the rhythm of the voice and the music; hitting her hand against the table as Leah went along. *Yes, hotter than a peppered trout and we been talkin bout ol Jackson ever since the damn fire went out.* Because she couldn't sing—not like Leah could sing, not with the words coming out that way. And the guitar and Leah's voice with the guitar all made her think of fire burning and two people burning and then ash, and the cold greyness of early-dawn coals when the fire has burned to

194

nothing on a beach. And then she thought: "He told me he'd be comin down, he promised he'd be comin down, but I betcha he won't be comin down."

When the song was over Leah's face looked red. She took her wine and drank half of it, and there was sweat on her forehead that made her look better, healthy. And she laughed when Cathy started clapping.

"I haven't even warmed up yet," she said. "I'll get goin."

"Sing *Ring of Fire*," Cathy said. She was still thinking of the ash and of him, and of the burning—and now Leah with her flushed face looked like what she was singing. "Sing *Ring of Fire*," Cathy said, again beginning to sing it herself but unsure of the words. *"I went down down down and the flames shot higher and it burns burns burns"*

And then Leah joined her with the guitar. *"Oh down down down in the burnin ring of fire."* And while they were all singing Maufat and Lorne looked on from the sink, saying nothing to each other. From upstairs there was no more sound, the radio drowned by the guitar.

Maufat and Lorne took their rye and went inside. They sat in chairs opposite each other, looking at their glasses. Then the sound of laughter, the sound of Leah and Cathy and Irene, and then Leah singing:

Goodbye Papa, please pray for me
I was the black sheep of the family
You tried to teach me right from wrong
Too much wine and too much song
Wonder how I got along.

"Ya know, she's a good singer," Maufat said.

"Yep," Lorne said.

"No, now she's the best singer around here, and plays that guitar just like it was talkin too." And then he added in a whisper: "It'll be good for Betty ta hear it, ya know."

Lorne looked at him with the glass held to his mouth, and it was as if he didn't want to hear of it any more. He finished the rye and Maufat finished his, and then Maufat went to get more. When he came back Lorne said:

"I suppose I told ya about Mallory that time at Christmas."

"Oh ya," Maufat said. "He musta been some sort of witch or somethin like that."

"I don't know," Lorne said.

"Well, there are people like that, witches like that—and Father

Lacey told me—"

"Ya, well I don't know whatever he was," Lorne said. "But I went down and it was real freezing and they wanted to give him a turkey. I hadn't seen him before, ya know—never out of doors, Christ ya'd never see him eh?"

"No, I never seen him—only that time when he passed us in his canoe on the little river and he was real weird lookin—like his face was havin a stroke."

"Who passed him?"

"Allison and I the time we run the river."

"Couldn't a been him."

"It was, it was," Maufat said.

Lorne shook his head.

"It was now, he was taller than you and ugly—his face was all twisted up and he went by us without even looking—and we were in the water with the boat behind, keepin our riggin in the boat behind, and coming down in the water."

"Couldn'ta been," Lorne said.

"Now it was," Maufat said. "I was casting and I hada quit casting cause he come right by me without looking and I didn't even see him till he was right there and Allison didn't see him till he was gone past, he was that quiet eh?"

Lorne stopped looking at Maufat. Then he put his head down and stared at his boots, and then took another drink. When the music stopped there was music from upstairs—and they could hear Ronnie's voice, and then the music of the guitar and Leah.

"Well, I don't know," Lorne said. "Coulda been him I suppose—mighta been."

"But I didn't ever go inside his house or nothin like that—like you did," Maufat said. "So what happened when ya went inside that house —I mean I heard so many stories about it."

Lorne took a drink, and then taking a cigarette lit it and leaned his head on the back of the chair. Maufat stared at him, at his tallness stretched out that way, and for a second he felt that if he had said, "Buy yer own goddamn beer," it would have been better—it would have been right.

"It was that he was standing in the fire," Lorne said. "That's all—when I come through his door it was dark inside and I couldn't see him and I turned and he stood there in the fire with his arms as long as my legs and all twisted about him."

"Ya, that's what I heard," Maufat said.

"Yet no-one's seen him go—but he's gone, and he ain't dead, and he ain't in his house no more—he's gone somewheres."

"I heard that he moved that drifter into the bay all by himself—right from his back field."

"I heard that," Lorne said. "But I don't know—I don't know."

Then they were both silent and Maufat stood and stretched and went to get them another drink. When he was out in the kitchen Cathy looked at him, at his face grown flushed. She said:

"Alton coming over tonight?"

"Don't know," he said. He turned his back to them and poured the water, and again she saw the hard muscle along his neck, and again she felt some strange sadness. Leah had put her guitar aside and they were talking. He turned and said:

"Aren't ya gonna play any more music?"

"I will later. What'd ya wanta hear, Maufat?"

"I don't know," he laughed. "Somethin—whatever ya wanta play suits me and Lorne."

He went inside with the drinks and saw the lights of the truck and Lorne's face flushed in the light and the shade transparent because of it. He gave Lorne his rye and sat down again. The truck throttled quietly in the yard and there was no sound of doors or of shutting down. He waited and drank, and Lorne said:

"Yep, no-one's been that close to a witch in a fire."

"I thought ya said he weren't a witch."

"I didn't say he wasn't a witch—I said I didn't know—but I figure he is one—and if you'd saw him you'd think the same."

"I told ya me and Allison saw him when we run the river," Maufat said. "He was just like some sort of ghost or somethin on the water."

Lorne said nothing and Maufat drank. He wished he had of seen him in the fire with his legs and arms that long and then Lorne running out and backing his car, and then Mallory standing beside him with his feet in the snow, and it was freezing twilight.

"He chased ya out of the house, didn't he?"

"I left the goddamn house—he was just like a wolf or somethin and I left the goddamn house."

"Well, he didn't chase ya out?"

"No, he was standin on the road when I backed my car down, and I was watchin in the rear-view mirror and then I remember scannin the bay and when I looked up there he was—there he was in his bare feet and it was zero."

The truck was still throttling in the yard. Maufat went to the shade and drew it, seeing the lights glaring on the hard snow.

"Cathy, there's someone out there for ya."

"I know," she said.

"Well, are ya goin out or is he comin in?"

"Might," she said.

He could hear Leah laugh, then Irene said:

"I don't know why he don't ever come in—is he scared of us?"

"Don't know," Cathy said sharply. "Don't know."

Leah laughed again. Then he heard Cathy get up and go outside.

When Cathy went outside it was freezing cold and she had put no coat on. The steps where she stood sounded with the slightest shifting of her feet, and she could see nothing for the glare of the lights, only the snow and the frigid small spruce and the end of the field. She didn't go down the steps. She stood there and waited yet no-one came from the truck and she folded her arms tightly into her breasts for warmth and kept stamping slowly. There was something inside her like fear, yet not fear—she was afraid to have him come in the house and she was afraid he wouldn't want to. It was more like the dreams she had had of him and them laughing and her running and falling and then their laughter. And in those dreams she felt frightened and yet not frightened. She looked at the truck and then the lights went out and the motor shut off.

"John," she said.

There was no answer for a moment and then the passenger door opened and John got out. Immediately she could tell that he was drinking, so she came from the steps to meet him. Walking with just her shoes on she was afraid of falling.

He said:

"So I made it, little woman." He carried a wine bottle in his hand and she said:

"Drinking."

"I thought there was a party—I made Kevin drive me down here because I thought there was a party."

"Is that Kevin?" she said, looking up at the truck window again.

He didn't answer and then he took the bottle from under his coat.

"Here," he said. Again she felt frightened. In the house she was drinking and singing, and the music was a force in her that made her happy, and the drinking was happy. Out here it wasn't happy.

She took the bottle from him and put it to her lips. It was chilled by the night and when she looked up she saw stars and then she closed her eyes and swallowed.

"Come on for a drive."

"No," she said.

"Christ, come on for a drive."

"No," she said.

There was silence.

"Why don't you come for a walk inside the house, sit down and get some beer or something?"

He shook his head and spit and looked at her and then tipped the bottle again. The truck started again—the loud throb of its engine.

"Is that his?"

"His old man's," he said.

She was shivering, her legs hitting one another in the dark, so that she wanted to go inside.

"Well, I may as well go back up with him—is yer old man in there?"

"Yes."

"And that big bastard that beat up on Dane?"

"No—his wife is—Leah is, she's real nice."

He laughed.

"Dane's looking for him with a pick-axe," he said.

"He'd better not," she said.

He turned away, walked a few paces and leaned against the house.

"Come here," he said.

"No, I'm freezin and I'm gonna go in—ya both can come in."

"Shit."

"Well, I don't see why ya don't ever come in—I go inta yer house with Dad workin right at the station I still go in."

"Shit," he said, then laughed again. In the air was nothing, his voice.

"Come on in for a moment," she said. "See Mom."

He shook his head.

"I'm gonna go up—you goin ta winter carnival?"

"If yer gonna take me I'll go," she said laughing.

"I'll take ya if ya can get up."

"I'll get up with Karen," she said. "We can hike—so I'll meet ya, eh?"

"Ya," he said. He stepped from the side of the house and came up to her, the truck and Kevin behind the wheel.

Then he took a present from his pocket.

"What's this?"

"Somethin—it's yer goddamn birthday, isn't it?"

"Yes."

"Well, it's somethin," he said. "See ya later." He walked back to the truck.

"John," she said. She felt good and the coldness wasn't there. "Ya want a kiss for this?" she laughed.

He waved and got into the truck, swung himself up into it as if he had been wanting her to see the way he swung himself up into it and she knew when he waved that he was pretending that he didn't want to kiss her. She was happy. She said:

"John."

"I'll see ya later."

When she went back into the house and opened the present it was a charm bracelet.

"Boys, those things are expensive," Leah said. Irene said nothing. "Boys, if a man give me one of those," Leah said nudging her, "I'd latch onta him."

"You shut up," Cathy said.

"I'd latch onto a fella like that," Leah said.

Cathy went to the fridge. It was so warm in here and comfortable with them talking, and now she wanted John inside talking with them.

"I wish he wasn't so queer and come in ta see ya," she said to Irene. She opened a beer at the sink and stood there smiling—unable to stop herself from smiling so that Leah looking at her became giddy with laughter.

"Some day I'll go out there and drag him in," Irene said. "That musta cost him," she said.

In the room when Maufat heard the truck start up the road he felt comfortable again. When Cathy was outside he listened for their talk and couldn't hear it and every time Lorne said something he was startled out of listening and had to answer. But he wanted to hear the boy's voice and how he talked and what he said. When Cathy was outside he didn't want her there because he thought: "If he can't come in here he must be some scared of somethin," and this made him angry— that she would go out there, and he wanted to hear the boy.

But when they started talking in the kitchen about the present and how nice it was he became uneasy again. He didn't want the boy giving her things, he didn't want that. He looked at Lorne while Leah was talking and Lorne with the last glass of rye in his hand wasn't speaking any more. Maufat got up and left the room, took a beer from the fridge.

"Now I don't want ya drinking too many of those," he said to her.

"I'm not drinking too many," she said.

"Yer only 18—yer not 21," he said.

"I'm not drinking too many," she said. Her face looked as if she didn't understand, a little scared when she looked at him. So he said nothing more, and then Irene said:

"Oh Maufat, it's her birthday."

"I just don't wanta carry her ta bed," he laughed.

"The way you two have been at it we'll haveta carry you ta bed," Betty said.

"It wouldn't be the first time," Irene said.

Maufat said nothing. He turned and went to go into the room when the door opened and Alton came in. His pants and hands were covered with blood and there was blood on his jaw.

Maufat turned to him:

"I got er," Alton said. "I got er."

"That doe?"

"I got er."

"When?"

"Just at dark—little after six—I got her—she's already hoisted."

"Shame on you," Irene said.

"Someone would get it before him in the fall," Maufat said. Alton stood there smiling, not even closing the door, streaks of blood on his jaw.

"She's gutted and hoisted," Alton said, his eyes large and happy. "Come on and pick yerself out a quarter, ya ol bastard—ya know, Irene, the old boy's gettin too slow ta work—ya must be hard on him at night." And he laughed. Then they all laughed.

"Ya got er, did ya?" Maufat said. "Ya went and got er."

Alton stood there happy—as if he was picturing to himself again and again the doe and the clapping sound and the doe down, the trickle of blood in the snow from the naked wound.

"Come on in and have a beer first, ya bastard," Maufat said. "And I'll take her hind if you don't mind."

"Shit," Alton said, thinking of her hoisted.

He stood there happy.

For John all things were true in dreams—all things ordinary and unnatural became one, and remained one. It was the fish flicking in the water and a great fire raged on both banks of the river. He *knew* then, as soon as the flicking fin turned to human form, that it was *the great fire.* Then as he witnessed it from atop the bank, all the people running and screaming turned to reptiles and slithered into the water, which was boiling now because of the heat of the fire. And all this was natural and not strange as he watched it. Then he was also a reptile in the water and the dogs that came down from the small shack houses beside the edge of the wharf tried to bite him as he went under.

There was a smoke choke-black when he surfaced and came out and walked toward the shack-houses, burning—and red-skinned people came out of the burning houses crying and writhing in the flame. Yet he was walking on the same side of the river he had left and looking out and down he saw Chinese junks trying to save the screaming reptiles in the water; and though he was frightened it was natural that those junks should attempt to save those thousands upon thousands of reptiles in the water with their screams pitiful and their heads in human form. And then there was a lady with a hat-box who walked beside him in the hot mud, and this lady had a fine velvet dress, and when he looked at her a bear came over the hill and began to dance with her. Then he remembered that all animals are friends when there is a fire and the bear dancing with this woman, with the flames shooting in the sky behind him, was a friend.

He had had this dream a few months before and now during the evening of the winter carnival he had another dream.

He said: "You wake me—I have to meet Cathy down at the school so you wake me."

When he went upstairs it was just that time when the dusk formed cold shadows in his room. Outside the station was loud and the patches of snow lay broken on the road—the houses above the station dark and unlit.

He was in an igloo and it was Christmas. He could tell it was Christmas because of all the hundreds of brilliant lights upon the igloos that lit the dark sky, and because of the chimneys and candy. He was with his father in an igloo and outside the sky was murky and inside it was cold.

His father said: "We have to find a tree," and they went out and drove on motorcycles down a long dark road that went down and down and became muddy and never seemed to end. And above them on both sides of the road there were spruce trees walled together and high— so high that when he looked at them he didn't want to see the tops. And they drove and drove. His father was ahead and became smaller and smaller in the distance. And the distance was so far, and the road wound down and down and never seemed to end so that John was afraid of getting lost.

Then he couldn't see his father any more and he was alone. The night sky was murky and dark and he tried to speed the motorcycle but couldn't. It wouldn't go for him. He kept thinking: "He has the axe—he has the axe," thinking that he must find his father to get the tree.

He met his father again because the road led to a town and in this town people were everywhere, scurrying with trees—and the trees had ice glistening on them, hanging from their boughs. His father was in the middle of the street watching the people, the axe in his left hand, and a great jacket on that John had never seen before. When his father saw him he pulled from his pocket a large watch, saying:

"Yer an hour late."

And because of this watch John knew exactly where they were— what town it was—and he said:

"My trolley-car broke down—so I had to skate."

Then he looked across and there was a great blue lake covered with ice, and he pointed to a speck on the far side that was his trolley-car.

When he looked again his father was moving ahead of him in the crowd, and the crowd was jostling and pushing, each of them with a tree of his own and each of the trees glistening with the ice hanging from their boughs. He followed his father and they walked away from the town, the people so numerous that they had a hard time moving, and he had a hard time keeping up with his father.

When they got to the outside of the town there was a forest with blue smoke rising and rising—and the sky was as clear and as ice-blue as the lake, and then John knew that this was where the Christmas trees were and that all this time they had been travelling to this place —*knowing* all this time exactly where they were going. They went down a small path with tiny houses on either side, the houses smaller than the trees, smaller than John, so that John wanted to stop and speak to the people in them. But when he stopped he heard his father's chainsaw (for it was a chainsaw now and not an axe) and he knew he must help carry the tree.

As soon as he knew he must help carry the tree he became very weak. The tree was as high as the spruce trees on the muddy road—larger than any of those the people carried in the town, yet it hadn't an icicle on it. His father moved around to the front, and John picked it up and there was dirt and a thousand roots hanging from it.

They began to move again, but at once he knew they wouldn't go back through the town—that they would head up the lonely sideroad that was pitch dark and had the smell of rotting stumps, and as they moved up this road the tree became larger and larger, and the road wound upwards and there was a dark veil covering it. Then John knew that he must take off his skates—because he hadn't done this yet, and the tree was very heavy. He called for his father to stop and took them off, and moved again in sock feet up the incline.

But as they moved the snow became deeper and deeper—so that it was waist high. He was level with his father now and they no longer had the tree but were moving over a field of waist-high snow. When they came to the edge of the field John began to run, sinking into it and then bounding up—and when he looked behind his father had fallen and was lying in a snow mound, almost covered, his hands swollen large and the tree across his face.

"I'll get help," John yelled. "I'll get help," and he ran down a hill and into a parking-lot. At the far end of the lot was a large building and John knew that this building would be there. It was lighted and all its doors were open and people were bringing their trees into it to be registered. He felt very cold and slowed down, and then suddenly he found himself crawling through the door—so cold that his legs and feet were numb and he could no longer walk.

Yet there was no-one in the building any more—and though he screamed and screamed no-one came. He screamed: "My father's hurt; my father's hurt," and no-one came. Then at the side door a woman entered. He couldn't see her face. He said: "My father's lost in the snow."

And she said: "Again?"

"Yes," he said and then he laughed. "The old lad's lost again—so come on with me and we'll haul him out."

The woman never moved and he couldn't see her face. Her hair was long and covered her back and she wouldn't turn around. When he asked her for help again she didn't turn around, and then the room became very red, and he could see her dancing behind the bar and drinking from a glass. When she raised the glass her hands were small.

He said: "Come on, I'll show you where the tree is," yet she didn't answer him and he ran to hit her but he was moving so slowly that he couldn't at all.

"Did you lose your trolley?" she said.

"Yes," he said.

She moved away from him and out the door and he began to follow her. Her back was to him and he couldn't see her face. Then they were on the snow-mounds searching for the trolley-car—and there were thousands of snow mounds, each of them the same, and she kept moving on ahead all the time, never turning to wait for him, nor ever speaking. He began to explain something of importance but forgot what it was, and then he was cold again and crying. When he began to cry he saw the tree and his father under it—the tree across his father's face.

He rushed up to it and called to her. She was to the left of him now moving away.

"Here he is," he shouted. "Help me take the tree off—here he is." Yet she kept moving away. He tried to take the tree off the face himself but couldn't and then he unbuttoned the shirt to give the chest air, and when he did that he saw the heart pounding. Pounding. It was dark blue and the veins surrounding it were blue and it was like ice—the whole chest was this colour and heaving, so that he knew if he didn't lift the tree off the man would suffocate. He kept yelling and screaming and clawing at the tree, and yet the woman stood with her back to him—not watching him. Then there was no more tree—it was gone, and yet the snow was so high that he couldn't lift the man out and the man was screaming, ice forming on the heaving blue chest and the veins in the heart. He kept trying to lift his father out—trying to lift him, but every time he moved he was afraid his father's arm would break. And then when he loked at the face it wasn't his father at all—it was *himself*. It was himself in the snow mound that he was trying to lift—and the lips and chin were dark *grey*.

He looked up and there were thousands of snow mounds and he was crying and screaming because the woman wouldn't help. He said: "Help me, God, help me," and when he said this she turned around and in the greyness and the whiteness he could see the face staring at him and laughing and it wasn't a woman at all, it was *himself*.

He stared straight above to the ceiling. It was total darkness now and cold, yet he was sweating, his clothes sticking to him. For a moment he lay there, feeling heavy and exhausted, and then he lifted himself and sat on the edge of the bed, staring at the night-table. There was no sound from the station now, no sound in his room or in the house—but his heart was beating, the pulse in his ears. He sat for a long time feeling exhausted, feeling the pulse in his ears, and then he moved and went to the window. When he did so he saw Jeanne hauling her baby on a sled along the road and he thought: "How old is she—fifteen—fourteen when she was knocked up?" The window was frosted and she disappeared. Then he turned and walked back to the bed, trying to think who it was—what his dream was, and then of Jeanne again and he laughed. He turned on the light—it was 7.30. 7.30 and there was no wind and he had to go down there now.

"Jesus Christ," he thought. Because he didn't want to go down there —with her, standing there in line with her. Why had he asked her down there and why had he spent so much on the present? "Fuck," he said. "Fuck." He lit a cigarette and lay down again, stared at the ceiling again. He tried to picture her—she would be dressed and want to dance and her hair would be done, and her hands small and brown and sweating and her face brown—and her eyes, and she'd hold hands with him and want to dance. Why? Because he didn't want to give her the present and yet he gave her the present. When he thought of it he hated it, yet he had given her the present.

It was her face and then her eyes would be done and she'd be thinking she was pretty, and she'd be thinking that he wanted her eyes done and her face pretty and her hair lifted. "Jesus," he thought. Because he didn't want her thinking that.

And she said: "Oh cause every time yer drunk all's ya talk about is when ya went with Julie, ya know that's all ya talk about is what a great time ya had with Julie."

And he said: "Yer full of shit, now shut up."

They were standing behind the back porch of her house and Bruce was waiting. She started crying and Orville's light flicked off—and in her tears there was something that he hated. He grabbed her shoulders and they were shaking, and yet he didn't care if they were shaking— he didn't care at all. He began to laugh.

"Yer full of shit—I don't even care as much about that arsehole as I do for you—which isn't very much."

"I *know* it ain't very much," she said.

"No, it *ain't* very much," he said, mimicking her words. He laughed but there was nothing in it. Orville had shut off his lights. It was in the fall and he could smell the leaves rotting, and smell her back porch, the smell of garbage, and he said:

"Why don't yer old man clean this place up?"

"Don't ya talk about Maufat," she said. "Or my house either—we can't all live in a fancy house," she said.

And it was the word *fancy* and the way she said it that made him laugh. "Oh I know," she said. "Ever since the exhibition ya'd wanta go out with Julie—ya'd wanta go out with her again. *She's a secretary at the school, ya know Cathy—ya'll see her cause she's a secretary at the school.* Big Jesus deal what she is, eh?"

"Shut up or I'll kick yer arse," he said. Bruce honked his horn and he could smell in the trees the wind of fall. "I don't wantcha talking about her ta me," he said. "Or I'll kick yer arse," he said.

"No you won't," she said. "Ya won't do nothin." She looked up at him and her eyes were grey and full, and he didn't know why he didn't walk away, and he started laughing again. When he laughed she turned away from him, and he thought, "Well, it was five months anyway—so I'll just walk to the car—get in the fuckin car and go." Yet when she walked away from him he saw in the shadows of the fall darkness the fall rotting, her form small and handsome in the night. He grabbed her arm and when he did so she straightened and turned toward him. She said: "Just don't ya talk about her no more—John, just if yer goin out with me I don't wantcha talking about her."

He didn't say anything but he kissed her and her mouth opened and she went back against the wall, and his hands were there and then he broke out laughing. He didn't know why he didn't walk away, and then he didn't know why he was laughing. She became scared. He said:

"I wasn't laughing at you."

"Then who were ya laughing at—who were ya laughing at then, John, if it wasn't me?"

"It's not you," he said.

Perhaps the way she had moved that night in the darkness forced him to call her back. He didn't know. He knew that when he laughed at her that night there was nothing in it but a strange coldness—to stand back and laugh and watch her hurt and crying and to still laugh. Then what had happened?

When he was drunk he thought of Julie—he thought of driving on the back of Andrew's bike and Andrew spinning out in the yard when he stood with her by the porch door and then Julie said:

"Who does Andy go with?"

And he said: "I don't know, he's got some slut somewheres." Because then he knew it was *Andrew* and not him—then he knew it was not him.

He left his room and went downstairs. In the kitchen the sound of the fridge and the calendar over the fridge. He pulled on his boots and coat and went outside—the air sharp against his face, the porch creaking. From this direction anywhere he wished to look it was snow and station—the street quiet and deadened and the station lights fixed and permanent and unsheltered. And suddenly he felt he had come out a thousand times and a thousand times before that and a thousand times again onto the same patch of porch, the same unsheltered boards creaking, and those station lights reflecting strongly on the snow—a bitter drying and freezing to his face because of the cold.

He went off the porch and into the night. All the way down the street he kept his hands in his pockets—kept gazing at the silent white cross over the graveyard. What would he say? Because he would stand by her and she would be with *Andy*—because when he spoke he could never speak to her again—never and the softness of her would be there—

There was a path that broke through the snow beside the jail and he followed it, and when a dog barked it sounded savage so that he jumped and cursed at the same time, and turned about him. There were three dim lights behind the cell windows and the snow had piled and piled there all winter, the crust and ice forming hard and dirty to the walls. The dog barked again and he said: "Go on, bark, ya cocksucker, son of a slut-fucker." Then he turned and walked over to the small bank and onto the school lot, and the windows were all lighted, the snow sculptures gleaming.

When he came to the people standing in line he couldn't see Cathy. He couldn't see anyone he knew. People were talking and laughing and passing concealed bottles back and forth, and girls huddled together and stamped their feet against the cement steps and shouted: "We want in; we want in." And he felt that he didn't want in—that he would rather go downtown, go to the tavern. He looked up and the sky was black, raw, without a star, and every time the wind hit at his face he felt the scalding pain of cold. He was sheltered somewhat because of the people who had gathered to the side and behind him. He kept staring at the sky, at the lighted windows of the large red building. "We want in—we want in," they shouted. He didn't bother shouting. He didn't do that. He waited and looked about him for someone he knew; and when he saw Andy and Julie coming from the lot he turned away, looked in the opposite direction. They came up and stood beside him and Andy said:

"The little one here tonight?"

"Not yet," he said, staring in front of him.

"Any booze?" Andy said.

"No—you?"

"In the car—you want a drive downriver after?"

"If she ever gets here," John said.

People were yelling and screaming, "We want in; we want in," yet the doors remained closed and the people crowded together for warmth, and when they crowded together Andy put Julie between them so she wouldn't be crushed and put his arm over her and held onto John's shoulder so she'd be safe. Yet the crowd pushing and shoving made her fall one way and then the other, and whenever she fell against him, he'd look straight ahead. She said:

"How are you?"

"Good," he said.

And then she didn't speak to him anymore, but he could feel her against him every time she fell.

"John—John," Karen yelled. They were far back in the crowd that had gathered almost to the other school and were shoving forward. "There he is—he's way ahead," Karen yelled. He turned and saw Cathy's face, small under the fur hat pulled over her head.

"I'll be inside," he shouted. "I'll be inside if they ever open these goddamn doors," he said again.

"Open the doors," he shouted, and then all the crowd began shouting with him. And when he shouted he didn't know why he had started but now that he had started he couldn't stop, and the crowd was pushing and shoving so that people were yelling, "We can't breathe, open the doors—open the doors," and Julie kept falling against him, and he felt her against him.

When the doors did open they were all pushed backwards, crowded even more together, and the student police kept shouting, "Stand back —ya can only come in through two doors." So they were pushed closer and closer together and it was harder and harder to breathe. He didn't feel the cold now, he only felt the need to remove himself from the crowd that was yelling and laughing and then yelling again—to walk away and sit down and breathe. Yet Julie kept falling against him and when they were pushed back to let the first people in she slipped and he reached out his hand to support her back. Andy and he kept her from falling and he took his hand away and stared ahead.

"John," Cathy yelled.

"I'll," he said, "I'll see ya inside." He looked back, seeing only the top of her fur hat, the little bob of it on the top of her head and he wanted to go and sit down and breathe.

They were on the top step now and he could feel the warm air from the doors. Still they were so crowded that no-one could move—the people at the back shoving to get inside.

"John," Cathy yelled. He didn't answer her. Then he and Julie and Andy were let inside the door and he looked back and saw her on the steps, her eyes on his when he turned around.

"I'll wait for ya here," he said. "I'll buy your ticket and wait here."

"John," she yelled. "Karen's gonna faint—she's gonna faint."

"What d'ya mean?" he said.

"She's gonna faint—John, she's gonna faint—help her get in."

Then Cathy yelled:

"She fell down, John, she fell down."

They brought her through the crowd and set her on the inside steps. She didn't speak. Her face was white and the makeup on the under side of her eyes was wet with tears. Cathy unzipped her coat and stood over her.

"Are ya alright?" she said. "Karen, are ya alright?"

"Yes," she said.

"Do ya wanta go home?"

"No, it's okay," she said.

They stood beside her. He stared at Karen and at Cathy bending over her, with her hat pulled down over her head.

"Are ya sure, cause we can go back down?"

"No." Then one of the girls selling the tickets came down and gave Karen water and as she drank he could see the under side of her chin and the whiteish freckles. He wanted to walk away and not be with them. Andy and Julie had lost their place in the line so they moved away and when they did John felt that he had been left with Cathy still bending over Karen and the smell of the hot air in the school and the crowd of people, he felt he had been left. He cursed and Cathy said:

"What are ya mad at?"

"This goddamn school for not letting us in," he said. Julie and Andy moved away in the line.

"I know, we coulda been squashed to death out there," Cathy said.

Karen drank from the water again.

"I'll get the tickets," he said.

"Ya got the money?" she said. She stood and he could see the brace-let on her bare dark arm just below the sleeve of the coat. "Christ," he thought, "Christ."

He nodded and went into the line.

It was that he felt afraid, standing beside them, that he would have to be with them. He didn't want that. Watching Karen swallow the water with her eyes still wet, and Cathy standing over her saying: "How are you? How are you?" and the crowd of people moving around and watching. It was as if he were one of them—as if he had followed them here and was a part of the screaming, a part of the fainting. He cursed again; that Cathy thought that he was part of them. Yet he didn't know why he felt that way. When he bought the tickets he stood and waited for them inside, did not go back to where they were.

Karen stood after a few minutes and came up the steps behind Cathy. And every few minutes Cathy would say: "Do ya feel better now—are ya better now?" And Karen would say: "I feel alright now."

John said nothing. They stood at the entrance to the auditorium—and though Andrew and Julie were on the far side, near the stage, he didn't go over to them. There were girls from Karen's class around her saying:

"What happened? What happened."

"We coulda all been squashed to death for this stupid dance," Cathy said.

"Did ya faint?" one of the girls said.

"I don't remember—I think so; I was dizzy and everything and I fell down," Karen said.

Just below the stage people had gathered to wait for the band—most of the crowd went in that direction as soon as they came in, yet John stood by the door watching them pass him, watching the girls talking, and said nothing. And when he looked across he saw Julie holding onto Andrew's arm, and then laughing. She did not look at him—yet she was laughing; like that night at the movie when he came out and followed her in the snow and the snow was powdered and she was laughing when he pushed her down. Like that night with him when she was laughing—and he was singing, and he said:

"I can play the mouth organ! I play it backwards." She was laughing.

He looked away. Under the lights the freckles on Karen's face showed reddish. When Cathy came over to him she said:

"Ya musta paid an awful price for this." She held up her arm to show him she had it on. He looked in the other direction quickly.

"Not too much," he said.

"I'm gonna go over and see Teresa," Karen said.

"Yep," Cathy said.

"Are ya getting a drive down later, Cathy?" Karen said.

John looked at her.

"I'll find ya a way—Andy or somebody." Then he turned to Cathy: "Not too much—it's your birthday, isn't it?"

"So? I didn't getcha anything for yer birthday," she said. "I didn't getcha nothin—I don't even know when it is."

"It's around."

"When is it?"

"It's around."

She laughed and grabbed his hand and when she grabbed it he felt a soft moisture and warmth and she said:

"If ya don't tell me when your birthday is I'll give the bracelet back —I'll give the bracelet back."

He looked at her—said nothing.

"Ya want it back?" she said. She was laughing.

"January," he said.

"January?"

"Yes."

She held his hand and they walked to the centre of the floor.

It was different from the music of Leah. She *felt* it differently. When they began to play it was loud, and soon the floor was filled with people—so that the auditorium became hot and she forgot about the cold outside, the ice outside.

She had taken her coat and hat off and when she danced her arms were free and her legs were free—and her arms were high in the air and then by her side and then high in the air again. And when her arms went high in the air the silver bracelet slid back on her arm and when she noticed it sliding back on her arm she thought: "He bought it for me—he bought it for me," and she became happy. It was music that made her happy—that when the sound of it came to her she was happy.

And her arms were high in the air, and looking out beyond her arms the whole auditorium was raging with arms and faces and people moving and the music swelled in those people moving, so that she became happy and twirled around and clapped her arms in mid-air. Twirling around she saw only the brown and the white and the colour of different faces and different expressions and yet all these expressions were somehow like her expression.

She looked over the heads of those that were shorter and into the backs of those that were larger, and now the music was making her lift her feet and now the music was making her clap her hands, and then the music was making her arms shoot outward into the air that was filled with the heat of sound and people. So that she thought: "He bought it for me—he bought it for me." It wasn't Leah's music. And the lights came down upon people's heads and made the heads brighter, the hair brighter and she thought: "I hope my hair—"

Then the music stopped and everyone stood motionless again.

John stood beside her and she felt the sweat on her and her face heated.

"You know this is the first time I've been to a dance with ya," she said.

He looked beyond her into the crowd of people.

"I don't like to dance much," he said.

"Why? I do—ya danced that time down home," she laughed.

"When?" he said.

But the music started again and she forgot what she was saying. She forgot John and the way he was moving and only felt the need for the way she was moving—because the music made her move that way. When it was low and soft—and the singer soft—the dancers moved their arms and legs, but it wasn't the same. She felt it wasn't the same as when the guitars and the drummer and the singer became loud and rasping so that you couldn't discern the heads and faces of the crowd, because you were concentrating only on the music.

And she felt it was strange that the music acted that way—that the music could make you do what it did, that for every sound there was a sound in you that was the same, so that when the sound of the band was heard the sound in you was heard, and when all the sounds of all the instruments were heard a thousand sounds were heard at the exact same time within you and you would lift and sing with it and *become it* on the sliding floor—on the floor that slid under her so well because she felt it all so well, she felt all the sounds inside her, all at once, so well.

When she looked about at the people she thought: "No-one's dancing as good as me," and inside at that very moment she felt none were; because their legs weren't as strong and their thighs didn't catch the rhythm like she knew her thighs did, because when she looked down at the floor and saw her own feet, her own breasts, her own thighs, she knew that it was her that was moving. "No-one's dancing as good as me," and when she looked at John, he was watching her, and she knew he was watching her thighs and her rhythm, and others behind her were. And when she was at a dance downriver when she was thirteen and Leah said:

"Yer a damn good dancer," and she said: "No, I'm not," and felt stupid and stopped dancing because Irene had said, *I don't know why they haveta go around shakin themselves like that*; and Maufat had said, *It's just stupid is all*. So she stopped and felt funny and her breath was heaving. Then Leah said: "No, yer a damn better dancer than I am," and smiled and Cathy laughed. "I'm better than Angela and Karen anyway for sure," she said, and Leah laughed. "Don't ya think she's a good dancer, Cecil, don't ya think?" she said. And Cecil said, "S'pose."

Now she forgot about everything but what the music did and she was happy; she was happy like the days when they jumped from the barn and Lorne said: "You get off that barn," and Leah said: "Go shit yerself, smart arse," because she felt in her arms and thighs and stomach that same exhaustion and power that was transmitted through the air and beyond the air. And she thought: "John gave me the bracelet," and then she laughed and said:

"Thanks for the bracelet."

"What?" he said.

"I said thanks for the bracelet."

"What?" he said

When John moved he moved always slow, the same pattern to his feet and legs and arms, the same expression of looking past her in his face and eyes. When he moved his shoulders were hunched, and his head tilted, as if he might punch out at something or grab somebody —as if he was Cecil grabbing onto that boy at the exhibition. When the music became faster only his arms moved faster—not his legs or his head. And what he watched behind her in the crowd she didn't know, and then sometimes he would watch her—when she lifted herself round quickly and her dress lifted, he would glance at her form moving.

When the music stopped she said:

"I said thanks for the bracelet."

"Are ya gonna thank me for that all night?" he said.

She said nothing. The way he said it made her feel empty. She said nothing and looked about her—to the far side where Julie and Andy were, Julie's white face and small tidy body. She looked away:

"So are you and Andy still tearin round as much as ever?" she said.

He nodded his head, then he said:

"I never danced at yer place."

She laughed.

"Shit," he said.

"That night when ya were drunk, the night ya tried ta walk up the side of my house," she said. He looked at her.

"Ya were dancin all over the yard," she said.

"Shit."

They danced again and then sat down. For moments at a time they would stare at the dancers and say nothing, and each time she stared at the dancers she stared at Julie and watched her, and it seemed feeble and out of place and wrong the way Julie's body moved under the lights, upon the sliding floor—as if it wasn't right for the music.

"Then why don't ya like dances?" she said.

"Because everyone's an asshole at a dance," he said quickly.

She said nothing.

"I go to the rinks sometimes when I'm pissed enough, just ta watch the women."

"Oh," she said. "So that's where ya are when yer sposeta phone me up."

"When am I sposeta phone ya up?" he said, as if forgetting something. He looked at her.

"Sometimes when ya say ya will," she said and then looked at the people dancing. For moments Leah's music had come back harsh and sad.

"Well, I like ta dance anyway," she said.

For a long time he said nothing and she stared at Julie moving awkwardly and clumsily on the floor. And he said:

"Well, you're good at it."

"What?"

"You heard me."

"No, I didn't."

"Shit—I said ya can dance."

"Oh," she said and laughed. "I try to."

When the music stopped at intermission he got up and went with Andy outside. "Where ya goin?" she said. "Gonna get some wine," he said. "John." "I'm gonna get some wine, okay?" he said.

She sat alone in a corner chair and looked into the crowd, trying to see Karen. But when she saw her she was standing with girls from her class and they were talking to Mr. Holt. She didn't move. "Goddamn Holt," she thought. "Goddamn Holt—pig," she thought again. She didn't move. "Though he thinks he can come ta the dance and dance with all the girls and everyone's gonna like him—pig."

She got up from her chair and went into the corridor where it was cooler and walked back and forth, drinking a Coke. Then she went to the front entrance to see if John had come in, and then she went back and sat down. All the music had died away in her—like vapour disappearing—and she wanted the music to play again, and the people to dance. Then she thought: "If John starts drinkin he'll start dancin," and she laughed.

She looked at the two charms on her bracelet—one of a small schooner, one of the Eiffel Tower—she looked at them a long time, delicately fastened to the small bracelet on her wrist, and at her nails carefully polished and rounded and smooth, and then at the necklace that lay soft between her breasts. When her breathing moved her breasts like that her face was pretty, a quietness to her whole body that she had noticed before the mirror in her room. At dusk before the mirror in her room she could feel the soft quietness of herself, the fresh nail-polish and the scent of perfume that Karen had given her for her birthday, with her breasts moving against the clean new blouse.

The music started again and still John didn't come back. When Lawrence asked her to dance she looked toward the entrance and saw he wasn't coming. She said: "Good enough," and they went onto the floor and she danced. When she came back Julie was sitting in the chair beside hers.

"Hello."

"Hello," Cathy said. She sat down and watched the crowd, clapping her hands together softly.

"Do you think they'll be coming back?" Julie asked.

"Hope so," Cathy said, still clapping, still watching the crowd. Ten minutes passed, and because of the dancing and the sound and confusion they said nothing more.

"You people getting a drive downriver with Andy and I?"

"If you don't mind," Cathy said.

"I don't mind," she smiled. Then she said: "What do you plan to do after graduation?"

Cathy shrugged and looked at her.

"Well, I'm sick of my job already."

"It looks like a good job to me," Cathy said.

"Yes, but I just left school—and here I'm stuck in it again—I'd rather do something else—maybe university," she said.

"Well, I'm not doin that—twelve years is enough on me," Cathy said, still clapping her hands rapidly to the music, not even knowing any more that she was.

There was a silence and the music stopped.

"Karen and I'll probably go away."

"Where?"

"Away—Ontario or someplace else—Europe maybe."

Julie looked at her.

"Europe!"

Cathy sat back in her chair and picked up the warm unfinished Coke. When she drank she closed her eyes.

"Maybe," she said. "Just ta see some places or something like that."

"But not to live there," Julie said.

"I wouldn't live there—Karen might; she said she'd love to live there." She held the Coke in her hands and chipped at the glass with her nails. "I'd like to see the Eiffel Tower anyway."

"What?"

"When John was getting me this bracelet I asked him to put the Eiffel Tower on it."

"Oh, let's see," Julie said and Cathy held it out and drank from her too-warm Coke and closed her eyes.

Karen moved along the fringe of the crowd and came toward them. She waved and Cathy waved.

"Let's sneak a smoke in the washroom," Cathy said.

"John and Andy are kicked outa the dance," Karen said.

"What?"

"They're kicked out—they started knocking down the snow sculptures and Mr. Holt went out at them—sayin he'd call in the cops—"

"Who started knockin down the snow sculptures?" Julie said.

"Both of them were at it."

Cathy said nothing. Then Julie said:

"Well, let's go."

"Can I get a drive down too?" Karen asked. Cathy looked at her and said nothing.

"Well, let's go," Julie said again, standing and walking away from them—as if she thought it was John and not Andy—that it was only

John.

"Come on," Cathy said.

"Well, if ya don't want me I won't come," Karen said.

"Come on," Cathy said.

They went outside, Karen followed slowly, Cathy turning and saying: "Come on." Yet she followed no faster. When they were outside a wind had come and it was freezing, and John and Andy were standing in the lot passing the wine and John was saying: "Drink 'er Turcotte, ya son of a whore." Then he'd make a lunge at a statue and bounce away from it, some of it crumbling onto the lot.

"A-woo," he yelled and bounced at one again. "A-woo."

"John," Cathy yelled.

"A-woo," he laughed.

"Stop that, John—let's go home," Cathy yelled.

"A-woo," he yelled.

"Yer crazy as hell," Cathy yelled. Andy laughed. "Beat it John—beat it," he said.

"A-woo," John yelled.

Julie said nothing.

All the way in the car Julie said nothing. When Andy drove he drove too fast, and the road icy. Cathy was scared because the road was so icy, and Andy passed another bottle of wine for John to open.

"Jesus, don'tcha think Cathy's a nice little—" John said. There was no reply and he put his arm around her—she went stiff and took it away, and he said: "Andy, what d'ya say—isn't Cathy a nice little da da da da," and he laughed and then opened the wine.

"Sure she is," Andy said. Julie said nothing. Karen stared at the road.

"A-woo," John yelled.

"A-woo yerself," Cathy said, taking his arm away. "Last dance I'll go ta with you; you lads don't go to that school no more but I do."

Karen stared at the road.

"Now don'tcha think she is?" John said again.

Cathy felt heavy in her throat. Karen stared at the road.

Then he said:

"I'm just kiddin with ya," and he put his arm along her open coat, but she took it away. Then he was silent and drank, and passed the bottle to the front seat and Andy reached back and the car went skidding but he held it to the road. Then Andy laughed. "Fuckin statues, eh John?"

"How many bottles is that y've had?" Cathy said.

"How many bottles is that y've had," John laughed.

"Fuckin statues, eh John?" Andy said, tipping the bottle with one hand on the wheel. Karen stared to the side of the ditch.

"Will you both just be quiet?" Julie said.

"Yes—just be quiet," Cathy said.

They took Karen down first and then came back to her house. When they were in the yard John got out and went with her to the door, the lights shining on them and the lights from inside. John smelled of too much wine, and cold air. He took her to the door.

"Don'tcha ever do that again," she said.

"What?" he said.

"Make fun of me like that," she said.

"I wasn't makin fun of you, and Karen didn't faint, and yer an arsehole," he said. She stared at him.

"Karen didn't faint."

"She did so."

"No, she didn't—she wanted atten—attention," he said, staggering off the porch steps.

"She didn't."

"And all's you want is attention, ya stupid bitch," he said, looking at her, his eyes narrow.

"I'm gonna go in—find somebody else ya can make fun of."

"I wasn't making fun of ya," he said his voice loud and heavy with wine.

"Shhh."

"I wasn't makin goddamn fun of ya, ya arsehole, ya stupid arsehole."

"I'm goin in."

He walked away from the porch and then jumped in front of the lights and landed on the hood. Then he went around to the passenger side and got into the back seat, and the car moved out of the drive and up the road.

She went into the house. When she came inside she was thinking: "Goddamn make fun of me," and her coat was opened and the necklace dangled loosely on her breast. And when she came in Irene was sitting there, her eyes wide. She was staring at Cathy and Maufat was in the corner by the fridge. She was staring at Cathy. She said:

"Annie's dead."

Maufat went into the room. She said:

"Annie's dead."

October 1969

It was that now, after these years, the load and burden of it was presented to her as some inescapable kind of thing—of belonging to this house where the autumn rain could be felt in dampness that came from the cellar, and where every movement of his created a fear and an anxiety within her that at any moment he would stop, come into the room, and when in the room he would say:

"Come on."

And she would reply:

"No, not now Cecil; not now Cecil."

It was that. It was also under the two lids of the flour jar the money saved, flour dust on the print of the bills and the bills folded so that her two fists could lift them and take them. Though all her planning meant nothing, because when she decided that afternoon it was as if the decision could have been made years before—it was that when she was out walking, the slight half-warm rain of autumn on her blouse and head, and her shoes scuffed with the mud that had been dust in the ditch of the road it was that something came over her then and there, and she felt weak. She said:

"I'm goin—I'm goin."

She turned and walked through the field—the blue-weed faded and the grass bent and yellowed, the hammock he had strung for her, like some soaked and faded, dyed blanket, the trees listless and waiting.

"If I'm goin—I'm goin now, me and Ronnie is goin and we're goin now—cause I have the money now and in the winter I won't have the money no more."

He had strung the hammock for her—he had strung the hammock for her.

And today outside the bedroom window while she moved the drawers of the dresser carefully, she could see the pine trees where the hammock was attached, and she could hear him in the kitchen over a plate of stew.

"Yes, I'm goin—I'm goin."

She placed the two suitcases on the bed and began to pack and while she packed she watched the door of the room lest it open and he came in. He was still sitting at the table with the stew. There was warm autumn air now and the trees were bright red and golden—the branches of the birches shining white under the light of the sun, the air fresh and clean outside.

When she had finished she set the suitcases on their sides and put them under the bed, hearing the cars passing on the road. Then she smoothed her streaked hair. It was the light through the window that caught the blue suitcases as she lowered them, the metallic snaps. She went back to the bed and took them again, opened them—looked at her folded blouses and skirts and slacks—at Ronnie's toothbrush and socks.

"Christ, I'm goin, I'm goin."

She sat on the edge of the bed. Suddenly her arms began to tremble and the room was cold, and in the kitchen he was sitting. Her arms began to tremble and in the kitchen he was sitting.

She sat for a long time on the edge of the bed. And when she picked the small table-mirror up and looked at herself she saw how white and drawn her face seemed, how large her grey eyes, where wrinkles formed on the skin just under them, where the tiny white mole above her eyelid was becoming visible. Then she thought:

"I'm goin—I'm goin; now—now." Yet her hands were shaking and the naked unpainted nails were coarse, and when she smiled she saw her bared uneven teeth.

She put the table-mirror back beside the wedding picture, and it was Shelby standing beside Cecil and Cathy beside Leah and it was Leah smiling and it was confetti over them—

"Christ."

And it was Maufat when he took the picture, just going to take it until Irene said:

"Tell em ta smile," and Irene was smiling and she said: "Tell em ta smile."

"Ya, smile," Maufat said, and Leah was smiling and Cathy was smiling. Orville stood beside Maufat with a handful of confetti, and Leah said:

"Now don'tcha throw that, Orville."

And Shelby said:

"Orville, don'tcha throw that." So he threw it at Shelby and some of it got into his mouth and he had to spit it out. Then Cecil laughed and Maufat took the picture. So in the picture you could see Shelby's mouth a little puckered and a grin from Cecil breaking into a laugh and Leah smiling and Cathy looking sideways to Shelby with a little bow of flowers in her hands.

He was in the kitchen. She was sitting on the bed.

"What're ya doin?" he said. She could tell by the way he spoke his mouth was full.

When she woke the next morning she said:

"Ronnie—Ronnie," and he rolled over in the bed and looked up at her and smiled. When he smiled she began smoothing the blankets on his bed, and he propped up his knees and laughed. The sun was shining in on his head and when he laughed the morning blueness caught at his pretty face.

"It's time for school," she said.

He shut his eyes tightly and pressed his lips together.

"No, now it's time for school—Ronnie—Ronn—eee."

"I can't hear ya," he said, shutting his eyes tighter.

She sat on his bed and began smoothing his hair, but when she did so he opened his eyes and took his hand and messed it up again.

"Listen," she said. "Listen." He stopped moving his hand around his head and looked at her, the blond hair sticking on end everywhere and the sunlight catching at the blond hair.

"I'm goin and you can stay at Irene's for a while and then you can come too." She kept moving her fingers along the quilt and looking at her fingers moving. He said nothing. She said:

"I'm goin on the train tomorrow—and then you can come too on the train—overnight on the train after a little while."

"Overnight on the train," he said.

"Yes, overnight on the train, real far away, and you can come overnight on the train—because I'm going away and you can come too."

"Where?" he said.

"Real far away," she said.

He said nothing.

"But this is a secret—a secret, I don't wantcha tellin Cecil or no-one else," she said.

He said nothing.

"No-one else," she said.

Then in the afternnon it was warm autumn—it was as if spring had just come, except the road was autumn colour and the trees, and the air had sharpened and the light cast on the trees, that stood in straight stands, and the faint lingering scent of smoke on the road and trees, carried from the lower river fields.

She went out in the afternoon and walked and walked. And as she did so she thought: "I'm goin—me and *Ronnie*."

"I'm goin—me and Ronnie."

She crossed the bridge, the day so warm the sweat was on her forehead, yet the air was cleaner than summer, than spring—a sharpness in the colour of the blue sky, and she walked to the other side of the bridge, staring downward through the loose planking to the black cool silent water—where the black cool silence was, the stillness of afternoon tide washing itself against the shore.

She wished now for that silence, that stillness. And when she was away there would be stillness. She glanced to the river, the bay, light on the water. Because stillness came when you were away. *When Mary went away she just went away, she said to Shelby, "I'm goin soon as summer," and when that summer come she was there at the station with her suitcase and I was there and Maufat was there with Mary's father and Mary looked real good that day with her hair nice, and before she went up to the station we had a beer together in the coolness, because the barn was cool and smelled of the cows in the stalls and smelled of the sweat on the back of the hides and we laughed and I said: "So what is ol Shelby gonna say ta that?" And Mary said: "Don't care." Then I said: "Ya do care, ya do care," and she said: "Why do I care—huh—why do I care?" And I said: "cause," and I took a drink, and Cecil had given us the beer and he come to the door of the barn and said: "What are ya two doin in here, fruitin each other?" "Shutup," I said. "Ha," he laughed. "The two of ya fruitin each other." Then he stood there and looked in and I could see his face only a little bit and his big arms scratching the horse-flies away, and his big arms were twice as big, they were twice as big and his large face. Then he went and Mary said: "Is Shelby there with ya?" And Cecil said back: "No, Shelby ain't here with me." Then Mary didn't say nothing except chip at the label of her beer. "Ya know why?" I said. "Why what?" she said and her eyes were down on the bottle and I wanted to kiss her though Cecil said we were fruitin each other but I wanted to kiss her because she was scared of goin away and I wasn't goin away. I said: "Cause when ya stop lovin someone, when ya stop doin that ya start hatin that person and when ya hate that person it's just the same as lovin that person cause when I get mad at Cecil when he throws me around and thinks it's great I hate him but it's the same, it's the same—and when ya went up ta see Shelby last night and he pretended he weren't home he was pretendin cause it was hate and it's the same as love and he wouldn't let ya in." And she looked up from the bottle and laughed and laughed because I was speakin crazy. "It is, it is." I said: "But I don't know how to explain it right but you told me he threw*

223

away that ring and ever since then ya didn't speak—ya didn't speak ta him, he didn't speak ta you but if ya didn't care ya'd be speakin—cause I don't care one way or the other bout Lorne but I speak ta Lorne." She drank from her beer and said: "Shit—I don't care, I just went ta say goodbye," and I said nothing and she said: "Just ta say goodbye," and I said nothing and she said: "Hey—yer goin marry Cec, aren't ya?" "Don't know—don't care." She laughed and fell on the ground of the barn and her face was red-hot from laughing. "Don't know—don't care," I said.

Leah crossed over the bridge and walked, swinging her arms. When she swung them the coolness came under the sleeves of her blouse and cooled the dampness of the sweat. The road had dust that stuck to the ground—that didn't rise as summer dust rose, that remained almost stationary under her feet. And the day smelled of smoke—like straw smoke or the burning off in barrels, and it affected her, made her breathe deeper and deeper the pureness of the scent and made her remember when she and Cathy played in the barn—with Cathy's skin always so dark and healthy from the summer and the sunlight glancing through the window chinks on Cathy's skin: "Caughtcha," Leah said.

"No, ya didn't," Cathy said.

She came to the church lane and looked down, only the steeple rising in silence was visible, only the large white pines on either side of the lane where Cecil had once tracked a buck deer for five days in succession, missing it—missing it seeing its warm dung, the heat rising from its dung. Missing it.

"It's out there," Maufat said.

"Now I know that," Cecil said. "Tell me somethin that I don't know —tell me where it'll be at 6.30 tomorrow morning."

And the pines rising into the clear fall air, surrounded by the autumn turning. And suddenly she wanted to see the church more than any other place—see the bay off the graveyard and the white siding of the church, and look from the cement steps, arch her neck like she did when she was a girl who lived below the bridge, and look up and up and see the steeple, the naked cross, the sky.

She walked down. There was silence here and then a squirrel darted across the lower branch of a birch and stopped, a hazel-nut in its mouth, its tail up and twitching, its paws clinging deep to the bark. Its tail twitched and she watched it.

"Takin that home for yer family?" she said. "Ppeb," she said trying to make the sound of the squirrel. It flicked its tail. *When Cecil made*

the sound of the squirrel the squirrel wouldn't move, it would stay until
Cecil was almost under the branch, looking down at Cecil with small
doe-like eyes. And yet she couldn't make that sound. She tried again.
It went higher on the branch and then crossed to another tree. She
watched it with her eyes moving, its small grey shape so warm looking
in the sun.

When she came to the churchyard she stopped. Here the sun and
the day was brightest—on the warm blue gravel her shoes made
crunching sounds with every shift of her weight. And she looked, first
to the priest-house, then to the church, then quickly to the graveyard
and back to the church again. It was as if now that she was going, in
her head she didn't want to go. As if now she wanted to go into the
house and put her arms around him. And when she had put her arms
around him she would say:

"I love ya, I guess," and he would laugh and then they would go to
supper in town and Ronnie would buy chicken in the basket in town
and she would buy chicken in the basket in town and Cecil would say:
"Working underground ain't a bad job," and she would say: "Just
makes ya blacker than a nigger is all," and he would say: "Is all."

"Is all," she said aloud. "Is all," she said again. She looked about her
—nothing. Then she walked over to the graveyard, through the swinging iron gate and onto the ground. She knelt at the grave and blessed
herself quickly. It was as if this was why she had come—just to come
to the grave marked: DWIGHT EVERETT, marked ANNIE DUNS-
TAN EVERETT.

She blessed herself quickly. Upon her knees that way looking at the
names, the dates.

Irene said:

"It's just like he were waitin for her all this time—dying on exactly
the same day nineteen years apart—it were as if he was sorta watchin
her."

Leah said:

"Poor old soul."

"She had a good life," Maufat said.

"She was always scared a you Maufat, member that?" Lorne said.

"No, I don't," Maufat said.

"Well, she was always scared a you," Lorne said.

"She was not," Cathy said.

"Just as if he was waitin," she thought. She knelt there a long while
—there was nothing in her but the waiting, the kneeling on the soft

225

October grass, the bay silent, the smell of the breakwater spreading out faint, the opposite shoreline sharp and straight—and then the headstone with the name and the ground above them flat, brownish. "Just as if he was waiting—as if he was up in the sky waiting on a cloud or somethin, and when that day come his ghost or something come off the cloud and went down—and she was rockin, in the chair, Irene said, and outside was real cold and everything and she was rocking, so it's like he come down and just picked her up when she was rockin on the same day and everything."

She stood, the outline of dampness on her knees.

"I'm goin, I'm goin, me and Ronnie."

She turned to the church, looked at it, and in an instant the whole day changed inside her, tears came. And she said aloud: "I'm goin, that bastard what he is," and the church with its whiteness and the bay water with its coldness were empty and tears came. Because she thought: "I'll go down and see that ol steeple," because the steeple when she looked at it as a little girl was so up and up and the cross so good—the doors open on summer evenings and the smell of the inside wood, the warped pews where Annie had put her hands as a little girl and had folded her hands and had prayed with the soft light coming through, and the flowers along the cement siding. Yet now an empty row of withered stems and the day changed inside her. Tears came. She couldn't look at the steeple or the church, and when she walked back over the ground the crunch of the blue gravel filled her with a longing to be somewhere—anywhere, to run anywhere, and she felt sick in the stomach and nervous.

And the one most conscious thing in her was that she didn't hate him—that she felt nothing for him but a sympathy that at this moment when she wanted the most to hate him she couldn't explain. And that sympathy was in her like water on the bay, like a growth at tide, because when she looked at the cold bay it seemed to her that all life was a cold bay, that it was nothing more than when the tide came in, when the tide went out, when the seasons changed and the nights got long or short—and now it was a feeling of strangeness, a feeling of wanting to be little and happy again. Tears came. "Bastard, what he is," she said.

She left the church lane and continued down the highway, at moments stopping short and not knowing where she was going or what she was doing. When she stopped above Irene's, she thought: "The hammock he strung for me," and she was leaving him—and who had she told? No-one—and he would come home tonight from the mines and sit in the kitchen and then she would have to tell him, yet when she thought of it, when she thought of his face and his hands, and the scars on his body from the fire she couldn't move any farther—she could neither go ahead nor turn and go back. She shut her eyes to get the feeling out and her eyes burned. Cars passed her on the road and she thought: "He's workin down in that old underground—and he says it's never past zero down there and black all the time and everything and all he wants is his supper is his supper is his supper."

She put her hands to her face to wipe the tears away, but more and more tears came, as if by the very act of wiping them away she started them coming, and she put both hands over her face and cried. Cars passed on the road and she was crying. She said: "He don't know little Ronnie, he don't like ta go away—he don't know nothing—he don't know nothin." And then Ronnie and Cecil came to her, both in the dry grass at the front of the house and both playing. Cecil lying on his back and throwing Ronnie into the air with his arms, laughing—and Ronnie unafraid, always unafraid—like Cecil the night he fought with Niles and Niles hit him and Cecil never went down, never went down.

"Ya wanta go up ta town tonight?" Cecil said, throwing little Ronnie into the air.

She began moving again—down the highway. "It don't matter, it don't matter, it don't matter." Yet she couldn't see herself *away*—not making his supper or taking the empty bottles from the table in the morning or taking the pan out to wash or taking the vodka from the cupboard and going inside to the bed and lying across it with a cigarette and a glass reading a magazine. She couldn't see herself—and the more she tried the more she saw him coming in from work, unwashed, his face black. The more she tried the more she heard him:

"Ya ain't bought none a them cookies?"

Because she had taken the dollar and put it in the jar.

"Why don'tcha ever buy them no more?"

Because every cent she had taken and put in the jar and now that seemed bad to her and awful to her.

She crossed the road without even noticing and went into the back porch. Irene was washing at the sink and Cathy was sweeping underneath the table, on her knees with the broom outstretched, trying to catch the dust and dirt within the straws. The afternoon was clear and warm and silent. She closed the kitchen door silently behind her.

"That ain't the way ta sweep a floor," she said.

227

Cathy looked up, her hair short, her face full and brown.

"What're you doin here?"

"Walkin."

"Walkin? Where's—Cecil have the car?"

"Yep—he's a working man now," Leah smiled. Then she stopped smiling.

She had come here to tell them. She would have to tell them—Ronnie would be staying with them. Yet she stood by the door and said nothing while they swept and washed and the silent outside lingered with the golden yellow of the trees. It was that everything reminded her of something clean and fresh—the smell of clothes and soap, the afternoon and Cathy on her knees pushing the broom outward and then moving it toward her again with calm assurance that all the dirt would be collected, taken in the dust-pan and thrown away.

"So," she said finally. "It's been over yer graduation by a year and ya ain't doin anything, are ya?" She laughed when she said it and brushed her hair with her hand.

"No—but we're leavin next week."

"Ya want some tea?" Irene said.

Leah said nothing. She looked at Cathy sweeping.

"Whose leavin?" she said weakly. "You and who?"

"Me and Karen is *leavin er*," Cathy laughed. "Goin."

"Where?"

"There's lotsa jobs round here," Irene said. "Don't know why she had ta go gallivantin off."

"Toronto maybe—maybe Vancouver," Cathy said. She stopped sweeping and looked around and her face was flushed and excited, as if she was waiting for Leah to say something. Leah said nothing.

"There's lotsa jobs round here," Irene said.

Leah felt the blood leave her, as if her face had grown suddenly as white as the linen Irene was moving in the blue water. Her lower lip began to tremble, and she shoved at her hair again and smiled weakly. The sound of linen moving in soap and blue water, the broom moving in circles on the floor, the green wall as green as the first of summer.

"So yer leavin?"

"Yep," Cathy said, standing and rubbing the dust from her knees and then smiling again. Her face was flushed and happy.

When Cathy turned to her she saw her face dark and happy, the eyes looking at her as much as to say: "Well then, what then?" Leah felt as if the blood had left her—as if her own face was old and horrible

228

and her own reason for leaving was wrong. That Cathy, with the broom straws bent because of the weight she placed on them, was young and full enough to leave and that she wasn't. That she was only emptiness in a dark room—in a room where the smell of dampness came up from the cellar and attached itself to her. That she would be that darkness in a damp room because she had chosen it—and when she had pictured herself leaving on the road she had pictured nothing but him in his work clothes coming from the mines black and hungry. Cathy stood leaning her weight on the broom. She looked at Leah and Leah turned from her and looked at Irene. Because she had chosen it, as Mary had said: "I'm goin, Shelby, soon as summer." Because now she stood by the white kitchen door in the autumn afternoon and knew that the pain was the pain she *had wanted* and the staying was the thing she *had wanted*, for she had chosen the staying even before she was old enough to realize that what she chose would some day be pain and some day be burden. Though somehow she knew even *before*—before when she was a young girl who lived below the bridge and with his big arms he lifted her and threw her and laughed when she didn't want to laugh. She knew then, perhaps with more understanding than now. She felt hot and weak.

Cathy went to the fridge and said:

"Maufat left a few beer in here."

"Good," Leah said.

She opened the beer and they sat at the kitchen table. Cathy was talking but Leah didn't listen—she was staring beyond Cathy into the field, beyond the field to the level highway that stretched forever. Cathy was saying:

"—so when I hada keep waitin for her cause she kept beggin me an everything and I was gonna go before but by the time she was finished talking to me I decided to wait—and then after her graduation we were supposed to leave in June, and then in July and then in August, but she wanted a summer job to earn some money—and then I got that job at Lorne's keeping house, so now it's October but we're leavin for sure next week."

"Good," Leah said. She drank her beer and the more she drank the more angry she became—she became angry at the sounds of the clothes being rubbed by Irene's hands and at Cathy going on and never seeming to stop—she became angry because Cathy was nineteen and she was old now, 27 now, and her face was drawn. She kept thinking of how her teeth looked in the mirror when she sat on the bed. Nothing seemed good to her as she drank the beer—as Cathy talked and Irene's hands moved in the washtub at the sink.

"—though I didn't think I'd like working down there—and I was sure right."

"He paid ya good enough for the little they have," Irene said.

"—for the little they have—they have more'n you and Maufat ever had—stole mosta it too, everyone knows they stole mosta it."

"What d'ya mean, they stole it?" Leah said, surprised at the harsh brutal sound of her voice.

Cathy stopped speaking and looked at her, not knowing what to say. Her face went scared for a moment and then angry. She said:

"Leah, you know what I'm talkin about."

"No, I don't know what yer talkin about—sayin yer uncle stole things ain't right and ya should know better than that."

"Shhh—now don't *you two* start fightin."

"Well, I'm her sister now and I ain't never said things like that." Irene said: "Shhh."

"Leah, you know what I'm talkin about," Cathy said again, moving forward on her chair. "Leah, you know."

"I do not know."

Cathy began to move in her chair—her face angry, her mouth twisted down.

"Like Maufat helping him with a new room every night after work just after the baby came, and not getting a cent for it—and after Annie died him movin all her furniture down when Mom was entitled ta some of it—and that's what I mean and you know too."

"I do not know," Leah said.

"Now Maufat wanted ta help with that room, and Betty was sick and just from the hospital," Irene said.

Cathy's eyes began to water and she tore at the label of her beer with her head down, her short brown hair just over her ears. Then Leah said:

"He ain't that bad, Cathy."

Cathy said nothing. When she had started to talk Leah became angry—for no reason except that something welled up inside her and she couldn't help trying to find some reason. Cathy sat there saying nothing, with the water coming to her eyes, with her small brown hands chipping at the label of the beer.

"Oh well," she said. "He ain't gonna make us fight anyway."

Cathy didn't answer. There was freshness in the kitchen air that came with autumn, and she breathed it and drank her beer. She wasn't angry any longer—she was sad because Cathy had gone to the fridge and taken two beers for them to sit and talk. The air was clean and fresh in the autumn kitchen and Irene worked at the sink.

"So yer leavin next week anyway—and ya'll be earnin a lot more money where yer goin anyway."

"That's right," Cathy said.

Leah stood and went to the sink. She watched Irene's hands in the water moving the fabric with the sunlight weak through the window. Then she said:

"Listen, can Ronnie stay here for a while?"

Irene kept washing.

"Sure—why?"

"Cause I'm leavin for good tomorrow morning and I wanted ta know that." She drew in her breath as she spoke as if trying to catch what she said. Irene stopped, her hands motionless in the water like two white-bellied fish turned on the tide, flat and lifeless. Her eyes looked and then her head turned.

"What d'ya mean?" she said.

"I'm leavin—I already wrote ta Mary a long time ago and Mary says it's okay."

"Okay for what—okay for what?" Irene said, and then as if answering herself, or stopping Leah from answering, continued while Leah stood there drawing in her breath: "Well, I don't know why everyone has ta go for—run off, there's jobs around here enough and I don't know why anyone has ta go off for." Leah held in her breath—when she saw things she saw them faint and distant—like Irene's hands moving again in the water, rubbing the fabric with some merciless expectation, as if to say, "Goddamn ya, goddamn ya."

For a moment Leah said nothing. She turned and Cathy was finishing her beer. She looked at Cathy, wanting her to speak—but Cathy said nothing, held her beer before her mouth and drank.

"He's got himself a job now, Leah—it ain't like before—fine story they'll have now you runnin off!" Irene said.

"It's been comin," Leah said. "It ain't the job so much as it's been comin every time he gets drunk and everything and it's been comin."

Irene did not look at her. She wanted Cathy to speak. She stood there—her legs so weak, and her stomach with an uncertainty—a building of tightness, so she kept breathing harder and harder and her eyes watered again. In the distance a car came out of the church lane.

"Fine thing now," Irene said. "Cathy's goin away so you have ta go

231

away."

"That ain't it," Leah roared. "That ain't it and you know that ain't it; why are you sayin stuff like that? Cause what did you have ta put up with—what did you have ta put up with and everything? Nothing." She kept stepping away from the sink when she said the words, the words coming from her so fast and strong that she couldn't stop them; and the car pulling away from the church lane, and Irene turning to her with her eyes wide with panic, and Cathy not uttering a sound. Irene's face looked frightened and ill. She turned from her wash, the soap and water on her hands, but Leah kept screaming. She screamed more because Irene was turning to her—more because Irene was frightened of what was to happen.

"Goddamn ya—me goin just cause of Cathy, just cause a her. What! Jesus, d'ya know, d'ya know; she don't have nothing ta put up with—she can go, she can go." She was trying to catch her breath and her throat was paining with the screams, yet she couldn't stop. It seemed as if unleashing something within her was the best way to make them understand, and yet there was nothing that would make them understand—nothing. And then instantly Cathy came to her mind and she hated Cathy again. She turned around. Cathy was rising from her chair and coming to her and Irene, frightened, was putting her arms around her. But she shoved Irene away.

"Shhh," Irene said.

"*That thing* there, ya think I'd go away just cause a *that thing*—ya think that?"

"No, now shhh," Irene said, trying to put her arms about her again. In the distance it was afternoon and silent autumn and through the planking of the bridge it was the quiet stillness of the tide, the longing of the dark water. "Goddamn ya both then—I'll take Ronnie with me and me and Ronnie we'll go away."

"No, now shhh," Irene said. "Ronnie can stay with us for a while—he can stay with us until ya get settled at something." Again she tried to put her arms around Leah and her arms were shaking and her face looked ill—her mouth opened and hollow as if she was about to cry herself. Yet Leah could not stop. She could not stop.

"Sure, I'm sposeta sit around and wait till he wants ta fuck me, I'm sposeta sit around and get his meals and wait till he's horny and wants ta fuck me."

"Now Leah—now Leah."

"Sure—cause that bitch is goin you think I'm goin, you think I'm leavin—ya both turned against me—both a ya!"

"No, we ain't," Cathy said, coming over. "No, we ain't Leah—I wantcha ta leave, I been sayin ta Irene for the last two years that ya should leave."

"Then why are *you* leavin?" Leah said. "Why are ya all *leavin*!"

She was almost sick, the sweat and a choking pain in her throat. She sank to her knees beside the door.

"Shhh now, Leah, you send Ronnie to me down here—cause if yer goin it ain't my business. I just wanta see ya happy."

Cathy put her arms around Leah's shoulders and the shoulders were shaking, they wouldn't stop shaking and the pain in Leah's throat and stomach wouldn't leave. Then Irene bent down and put her face near to Leah's face and began to cry.

Leah lifted her arms—they were so limp now and she could not see, and Irene was breathing and crying and Leah could not see.

"Why do you haveta go—why do ya haveta go, Cathy, huh Cathy, why do ya haveta go?"

"Shhh," Irene said.

2

He was in the henhouse all afternoon—why he did not know except that something, something a long way from him came back at moments when he sat there. There were still the hens themselves, though gone now for the last few years—yet there were still the hens themselves. He remembered them scratching—and when he was home from the hospital, his arms and face still wrapped, he remembered them turning away from his hand and clucking at him through the hole. The hens were *here*, as if hen breath on the air, and outside there was the house in the autumn afternoon, and behind the house the hammock, sagging without weight or width, stirring slightly in the wind. And there was the clapboard and the flecks and chips of wood about, the silence of the dirt, when his boots scuffed at it, making the noise of his boot and dirt.

There was being closed off and remembering—and for long periods of time the peace and tranquillity of only breath, and not the remembering. Then there was himself scratching at his neck when it itched, and scratching at his arms when they itched, and at moments, just to see how long these moments would last, not scratching the itch, the itch growing on the burn scars.

There was the smell of vapour and age when he urinated into the dirt while drinking his beer, for the beer and the urine both gave him that sense of pleasant satisfaction that he had just known. It was of that dim time when he ran out on a June evening, the summer just beginning, the chirping and croaking of things in the marsh along the bog, to the small white outhouse where he urinated then—and in the sun on a June morning the blue flies lazing on the bowl.

All afternoon he sat there drinking, not drinking steadily or quickly, but drinking with the case beside him, the opener beside the stool. He went back to the house at dark.

There he sat in the dark, his large fists closing and opening on the white table, the blue table-cloth that last night she had folded and left over a chair. She had taken it and folded it so neatly, he watching her hands press it in toward her stomach, he watching her hands. Then she laid it over the chair and looked at him. When she looked at him he looked away from her.

"Now don'tcha go burnin this with cigarettes or nothin—remember the last one ya did it to."

He said nothing because he could think of nothing more to say. Then she went about cleaning the cupboards and the sink. Then she took the iron and the board and did his work-clothes and socks. He said nothing.

Tonight his fists folded against the white table. He picked up another beer and opened it, drank it slowly, looking out into the darkness, hearing the wind and leaves against the foundation and frame, hearing the autumn as if it was some force dropping onto the field—the weeds with twisted stems.

Because what was it? Yes, it was the cloth folded so gently into her stomach, much as a little girl would fold things; and it was *her*, last night washing the cupboards and ironing his things, sweat on her forehead and under her arms—and it was absurd, he loved her because of the sweat under her arms and the movement of her thin arm, the movement of the iron over the clothes. When he looked at her that way, doing those things, he said inside, *she's gonna go, she's gonna go.*

He said nothing. After a time when the clothes were done she folded them and sat down. A miller crawled against the glow of the naked bulb, its small powdered wings spreading and closing.

"Ya ever see a miller this late?"

"What?"

"Ya ever see a miller this late?"

He turned and looked about him:

"No, I haven't—I haven't ever," he said.

Then she said:

"Well, I got all yer clothes done and laid out for ya."

"I don't know why," he said. "I don't know why ya'd bother, cause I'm the old scar-faced bastard, cause—" Then he stopped, felt hollow.

And he looked at her but the face wasn't the same face at all—it was turned and small wrinkles showed near the lips. He thought she was going to cry and he didn't look at her for a long time. Then he stood suddenly and left the kitchen, went into the room where he sat on the chair, scratching his fingers against the fabric. After a time she came to the doorway and watched him.

"Ya wanta play cribbage or somethin?"

He shook his head.

"I could skunk ya," she said.

He shook his head.

"Ya don't even wanta be skunked," she said.

"Look—you look—" he said, yet again he never finished and again when he saw her face it was wrinkles and her chin was quivering. "No, I'm gonna go ta bed," he said. Standing, he walked past her and into the bedroom, where the bedroom air was, where she was in the scent and drawers and dresser smell and where she was in the wall and bed and things. Where she was body and form without body and form. She came to the bedroom door as he lay upon the bed, his clothes still on.

"You want tea or toast or something?" she said.

"No."

"You want me ta make up yer lunch for tomorrow?"

"Might quit," he said. "Yep, just might quit."

"Cecil," she said.

"Might quit," he said.

Then he looked at her and laughed.

"Cecil," she said and her voice quivered. "Now yer doing good—now yer doin good back there."

He laughed. Nervous because he was laughing and he couldn't stop —he was laughing and his arms pressing against his stomach.

"Might quit."

"Cecil," she said. And then she began to laugh, for a moment—then she began to cry.

He looked at her shoulders shaking and her face in her hands and her right leg pressed in that way against the door-frame, her thigh and hip so balanced against it. And when she had said, "I'm goin," he had said, "Go then—go on, ya stupid bitch, ya stupid—" but she was calm and her face was calm and she stood. When she had said, "I haveta go now cause me and Ronnie haveta go," the way she looked was cold and calm as if everything was out of her—as if she had already gone. Then something direct and desperate filled him that he thought would never be there.

He lay on the bed watching her shoulders shaking, her hands at her face. After a time she wiped the tears and looked at him, her face reddish.

"Oh I'm stupid cryin," she said.

Again he could think of nothing.

"Stupid old cryin," she said.

"Yes, stupid old cryin," he said, turning his back to her. After a time he heard her in the kitchen fumbling with the cards—as if she would be forever in the kitchen; that in the years and months and days she would be there in the kitchen.

He turned his back to her and closed his eyes.

It was the Christmas before when he and Shelby had taken the Scotch and left the house, travelling downriver. The snow was falling in huge wet flakes against the windshield and on the road and they drank and sang.

"Ya haveta take her ta midnight Mass, don'tcha?"

"Don't if I don't want to."

"Don'tcha, don'tcha?"

"Fuck off now."

"Don'tcha?"

"Fuck off now."

They sang songs they didn't know the words to and made up the words themselves though the words were meaningless at times. Yet the more meaningless they made the words the louder they sang. They went to the wharf and drank—and all along, the houses were lighted and people were inside. They kept the motor running and drank the Scotch.

"Ya know she bought this out of her own pocket," Cecil said.

"Well, we should save some," Shelby said.

"Fuck it," he said. "Outa her own pocket—outa her own goddamn pocket, fuck it."

"Are ya takin her ta Mass?" Shelby said.

236

"Fuck it."

The snow was falling heavy and wet on the wharf road and the bay, and the bay not yet frozen so they could hear it above the sound of the car, swelling and black. Then it was eleven, and then it was after eleven, yet they didn't move.

"Maybe ya should take her," Shelby said. They heard the church bells at the Indian reserve ringing.

"No, now will you screw off," Cecil said.

"It's Christmas," Shelby said.

"I know, ya goddamn stupid son of a whore," Cecil said. Then he took the bottle and closed it. The bells at the Indian reserve were heard so faintly across the swelling water. For a moment they said nothing. He looked at Shelby and Shelby was staring at the huge flakes of snow.

"Christ," Cecil muttered. He turned the car around and headed off the wharf. Then he said: "She's gotcha on her side too—wanting me ta take her ta midnight Mass—I know it's Christmas, ya fucker."

"I know ya do."

"I know it's Christmas."

"I know ya do!"

"Well, shut up about it then."

Shelby didn't speak.

"Well, shut up about it then."

Shelby said nothing.

"Ya fucker."

They drove back along the main road slowly, the branches of the spruce covered with the wet pure snow and the flakes getting larger under the lights. Then Shelby said:

"Ya know what I'd like to do some day?"

"Go out west, ya I heard all about it."

"I'd like ta go sliding some day this winter," Shelby said, as if not hearing what Cecil had said.

"Maybe I can get Ronnie ta go with ya," Cecil said laughing.

"Why not, it's fun sliding—didn'tcha ever slide, ya bastard?"

"I slid more than you did," Cecil said. They rounded Oyster River bridge.

"Maybe Ronnie'll take ya—I'll ask him some day."

Shelby didn't answer. They came around the turn and as they did so a car was coming toward them on their side of the road, and all Cecil could see was lights and the absence of the wet snow—just light glaring out of the darkness on his side of the road.

237

"Pull over, ya son of a whore!" he screamed.

Then his head went down to the steering wheel and in that moment something else took control and he had no thought; yet his head was down and he turned the car in toward the ditch, high banked on his side, and he saw snow again, and when the pole came it seemed to come over the top of the car, and the snow was now in his face and he was wondering why the snow was in his mouth and nose. Shelby was clutching at his arm yet the car wouldn't stop. It had gone through the high banking and there was snow again. Then the pole seemed to go across the top of the car and he felt himself falling to Shelby's side and yet not letting go of the wheel. When falling he was weightless as if he had been picked up and lifted some place by some force over which he had no control. Then he knew nothing except that the car was on its roof.

The car settled on its roof, and then only darkness and silence. "You alright?" he said. He shook Shelby. "You alright—Christ, Shelby, we haveta get out of the car, you alright?" He fumbled with the door-handle in the dark, trying to understand why it wouldn't open, and he kept saying: "Shelby, you alright?"

There was no movement—Shelby's hand relaxed and limp by the shift. Cecil lifted himself again and tried to find the door-handle, using the force of his right arm to free his legs, which were tight and cramped under the dash. When he found the handle he had to push at it again and again before it would open, and all this time he kept saying: "Shelby we haveta get out now, ya bastard, you alright?" Yet there was no movement or answer. When the door opened Cecil lifted himself up. The snow was falling soundless and smooth, the large wet flakes against his face and eyes, and he looked to the sky watching it. It was strange yet for almost a minute he did nothing but watch the flakes, which he couldn't see until they were almost to his face, fall out of the deep onto the gutted ditch. It was quiet. Shelby didn't answer.

He pulled himself out and stood in the soft snow up to his knees and looked about. He couldn't see the other car at all, and they had travelled at least a hundred yards along the ditch and clipped a railing post and all this he didn't understand. He thought they had just stopped and turned over. How had they travelled so far? And what was Shelby doing still in the car?

"Shelby," he said. "Shelby."

"You dead or what?"

"You dead or what?"

What struck him at first was something comic; he felt at first like laughing and slapping Shelby and saying, "Shelby, ya son of a whore; Shelby let's get out and beat that bastard." Because all the time the car was moving across the bank of snow with the snow in his mouth and face he had no fear. It was something *other*—like excitement or nervousness, and if he had any thoughts he thought, "I'll beat that bastard." Then when the door opened and he saw the sky and the snow falling from it and the coolness was on his face, he felt for that long moment a peacefulness, so that he forgot, or couldn't bring himself to move. But now he was running through the snow to the passenger door. He was yelling: "Shelby, Shelby," and he couldn't control his voice. Now what came on the air was the scent of tires and gas—the smell of the winter road, the wood from the post, splintered here and there, and the snow already covering it.

He reached the passenger side and yanked open the door. Inside the splintered glass from the windshield, with snow covering the dash and the roof. Shelby lay slumped, his right arm hanging down across the shift.

Cecil stopped yelling. For a second he stared at everything—trying to comprehend everything—the glass, the snow, the small humped body looking black. The snow falling kept bothering his eyes because he wanted to see everything.

"Goddamn it, Shelby," he said.

Then he reached inside and picked him up as if he were a child. Even though there was no movement, though the body was relaxed, it felt weightless in his arms; even though the snow was deep—to his knees and beyond—the body was weightless in his arms. He carried him to the road, and laid him down carefully.

He took off his jacket and placed it over him and took off his shirt and placed it under his head. He stood bare-chested with the snow falling on him. Yet the snow didn't bother him—it wasn't cold. It burned at his eyes because he tried to see everything and when it hit his bare skin it was warm. He didn't notice it at all any more; he rubbed it away from his eyes and never bothered with it. Then he thought he must go back to the car and take the seat blanket and put it under him, so he ran back again.

He had to lift Shelby once more and put the blanket down—then he placed the jacket and shirt in the same positions. When he lifted Shelby's head to place the shirt Shelby opened his eyes slowly and then closed them.

"Ha ha," Cecil said. "You alright?"

"Ha ha, you alright?"

He stood. The snow was soaked into his pants and boots and coming down on him. The road was empty. He stood there for a while looking down at Shelby and then turned and ran toward the bridge.

The snow was coming at his back as he ran, and he saw his breath on the black air, and when he reached the bridge he saw where the car had gone. Like himself, the driver had swerved to the right in order to avoid the collision and had gone over the ditch and down into the gully. When he stopped running he could see vaguely where the car was—that it had smashed through the snow and naked alders and lay on its side near the water.

"Jesus Christ," he said. He looked up and down the road. There was no sound or movement—no other car, no voice except his own; the snow seeming to fall out of a flat dark sky.

When he looked down and saw the car he didn't want to go to it— something inside him wanted to run, some horror wanting him to run along the road; hide. And yet he knew that he must. He waited. There was no car or sound—the heaviness of his own breathing. He waited.

The gully was steep and the snow, in drifts, sloped downward, gorged by the path of the car. When he stepped from the road and began to descend the snow was at once to his hips, wet and thick, and then above his hips to his belt and waist. Now he felt cold—freezing —and his teeth chattered against each other, and the alders scraped against his naked back and arms and caught at his face. The cold was more one of terror than anything; even though he was bare-chested, even though the snow had gotten inside his pants and boots—it was a cold people feel when sick with expectation. The car lay on its side by the water, frozen over, the underspan of the small bridge brooding with ice and blackness and weight. And still his mind couldn't understand it all. How was it to understand it all?

He was drinking with Shelby—yes, and then they went out the door and down to the wharf and yes, Shelby started talking stupid like Shelby always did because Shelby was always talking stupid about Leah because he didn't know Leah, and then they came back up because Shelby wanted to come back up, he didn't want to stay at the wharf with Cecil drinking. Or was it the other way? Was it he himself wanting to come up and see her—to see her and say: "Ya need more icicles on the tree," and she would say: "Ya, it's pretty sparse," and he would say, "Ronnie, you get ta bed or Santa Claus ain't gonna come."

240

He didn't know. The car had the look of death in the ground where it lay, gorged ground with the snow packed on it—caught on its belly, and the snow still falling gently—unconcerned. What time was it? Leah would be at Mass and then Lorne would drive her home after Mass, and the snowfall. He tried not to look at the car, yet his eyes were continually fixed on it as he went down once or twice, losing his balance in the alders that hung round him, putting his arm out before him. And all the while his eyes were fixed on the car, the four wheels motionless specks—the total body a motionless form. When the day before Leah brought the bottle in from town with a bag of parcels she lifted it out of its bag and looked at him, smiled and said:

"This is for me and you tomorrow."

He said nothing.

"I went and got Ronnie a toboggan."

He said nothing.

Then this evening while she and Ronnie stood on stools and placed the icicles haphazardly on the tree Shelby came in. He took the bottle from the cupboard after they had finished Shelby's wine and he said:

"Here's ta Christmas."

Then they had one drink and then two, and then they left the house and went for a drive. Even though he knew it was impossible—at the hour they left, he hoped for some woman walking the road—for some woman.

"Christ," he muttered. "Christ."

His throat was full, as if at any moment he would burst into tears—with Shelby lying on the road like that. And it was his fault—his because Shelby had wanted to go home, because it was Christmas eve.

Then as he reached the car, with his pants and boots and legs soaked and his flesh red, all those thoughts at once escaped him. He thought and felt at this moment nothing. On the flat hard icy surface of the beach the car lay, the front grille bent and twisted and the roof almost collapsed. He stared at it, and the ever-familiar smell of gas and tires came to him—the scent of something destructive, of death itself in the form of metal and glass. After a moment he called "Hello" softly, as if he would disturb something if he spoke any louder than that, and after another moment he called "Hello" again. Yet there was no sound. He remembered Shelby on the road—with the jacket over him—and wondered if he was alive.

Here he could walk easier, with no more than four inches of snow. He went first to one door and then to the other—looking in. In the driver's seat a body lay forward, the roof pressed on its head. He opened the door swiftly and threw it back, and stepped back himself. Then there was the stove again and the redness when he was thrown back with that desperate energy and force and the blinding scalding on his face and hands.

He left the woman in the seat—couldn't bring himself to touch her. And the thing that struck him most of all was that she had a new coat on, and her small purse still sat upon the dash. That she had a new coat on, stained with the blood from her face.

He turned and looked toward the bridge and then he sat down and put his hands to his face. After a time, he did not know how long a time, he heard a car. He sat up thinking of Shelby again and, turning almost wildly—to leave her behind—began to climb the bank, looking toward the road as he did so, his hands almost clawing at the snow. He saw the light flashing red in the dark air and heard a radio, and a man speaking. He kept climbing the bank—trying to get up the bank, to leave her—to go away, when his clawing hands touched a limp small body in the alders.

He stood quickly and then fell over backwards and, rising again in a second, lunged forward, without idea or motive. He was crying now, and yet in the distance, on the road above came the sound of the man and the radio.

He snatched the infant in his hands and brought it with him, but he didn't look at it, felt it small, like a small animal in his hands. When he reached the top and stood on the road again the snow was falling faster, the wind blowing it to and fro across both ditches into his face and eyes. He carried the small body in his hands and walked toward the police car. Yet at this moment he didn't know whether he walked or ran, stumbled or stood straight. Everything was far away, distant— he saw the dim outline of the young officer in his heavy winter blue, and the patrol-car door opened. The officer was bending over Shelby —and Shelby was just some black hump on the ditch of a snowy road. Nothing now made any impression on him—he felt at one moment that he would throw the infant down and run, and in another instant he wanted to go back to the car and take the woman out. He kept walking—his eyes blinded by the full weight of the snow in his face, his legs so weightless that he didn't know how or where he stepped.

"Hey you," he said. "Hey you," he said louder. The officer stood and came toward him, shining the flashlight into his eyes.

When the officer came closer he lowered his flashlight. Cecil could see a young man—no more than twenty-one, the blue peaked cap with the yellow stripe, the snow scattered and blowing off the peak. He walked very straight and orderly as if he were marching, the only noise the rustle of the coat and his high leather boots.

"How is he over there?" Cecil said.

"I called in for an ambulance—he's alright—he's only—"

The young man stopped speaking and looked at Cecil. He stepped backwards and muttered something that was indistinguishable from the sound of the snow and the trees grating, and his face contorted—his jaw went slack as if a man with no tongue was trying to make himself understood.

"Oh God—God help us."

Cecil stared at him and smiled. He did not know why—but he was smiling and conscious of smiling the way Ronnie sometimes smiled when he was afraid. Then the officer turned away and vomited.

"There's a woman down there, goddamn you, goddamn you stupid—there's a woman down there, when will we get the woman down there—"

The officer said nothing, he was vomiting, and over the car radio came the static of someone calling. Cecil, for the first time, realized that the baby was dead—that what he had felt so much like some tiny animal in his arms was a limp dead child. He stared straight into the snow blinding his eyes, and held it and held it—as if to keep it warm until the ambulance came.

This morning he had taken her to the station. He said:

"Ya'd think ta Christ Maufat'd a got ya a pass."

"I didn't want no pass, Cecil—yer gonna go ta work, aren't ya Cecil?"

"Might, might not," he said. He looked away from her, at the train watering, the steam shooting out at times from its underbelly. Then he fumbled with his watch and took it off.

"Here, you keep this—ta watch the time."

"What," she said, she was staring at the snaps of her blue suitcase.

"Ta keep the time—it never worked on my wrist anyway."

He handed it to her and she looked at him as she took it, placing it in the pocket of her blue coat. The train pulled forward and halted with almost the same sound as if it was shunting.

She got upon the platform of the car and looked at him—their grey eyes level in the cool morning air. The noises of the traffic of the town. She said:

"I'll write ya, eh, and see how yer doin and everything."

243

"Good," he said. There was nothing inside him—regret nor pity nor desperation, just the hum in his ears of a thousand different things, the pigeons scattering about on the naked parking-lot; because the night before when she had come to bed she lay quietly, without a muscle moving, on her side and after a time he reached his hand out quietly and touched her back, and then just as quickly and as cautiously he removed it, and she said "Goodnight," and he didn't answer, and she said, "Goodnight," and he said, "Ya goodnight."

Regret nor pity nor pain. Then she said:

"You'll see about Ronnie until I send for him, will ya?" She looked down at the pavement below the platform where she stood, her right hand on the metal railing. He handed her the suitcase.

Then she bent down quickly and kissed him, not on the mouth but on the side of the mouth, and lost her balance while doing so, so that he grabbed her with his left hand and kept her steady.

"Ya know it's my kid too, ya know—ya know that eh?" he said.

She didn't answer—but something went clouded and dim on her face.

"Never mind," he said. "You get a good job."

He thought she was going to cry again, and he couldn't stand it when she cried; it was as if (when she cried) she was sitting in the room with her best dress on, with her hair done all day long—as she did for three months one winter, and he said: "What're ya cryin for, ya stupid bitch?" "Cause yer not workin—yer not workin." "Well, you get a job, ya stupid son of a whore—get a job." "I will, me and Ronnie'll go away and I'll get a job and me and Ronnie we'll go—"

Tonight he sat in the dark house his large fists closing and opening on the white table. At moments the wind blew so heavily and the rain came so fiercely that he felt sheltered and warm.

3

Orville wondered: *What makes it so good in this air with things rotting, and when I walk over the smothered twigs and leaves it's as if the ground was rising up along me and the trees look better naked.*

What made it so good to him, he had no idea but he felt every day now for the last little while, when he went out with the .22, that he was physically a part of everything he touched—the brown sodden leaves under his feet, the damp branches where the rainwater hung like pearls

244

in the soft air, and the smoke scent within and part of every fibre of it.

At night he walked back through the woods, taking the shore path. He had hunted and had sat on the breakwater—and then he had gone into the woods and had leaned against an aged black spruce, smelled it—the autumn on it, and waited a long while. Because he was so comfortable here and his legs, arms—his whole body ached with contentment.

In the morning the sun shone through a haze that covered the ground, it streamed in light over the birches and alders and came through to him as the very thing his teacher had talked about months before—it came through on him as if he was just one small particle of it—made him infinite. All day he kept thinking of that word as he walked, of what the teacher had said months and months before, of the rooms in the giant hotel. And the light shone on the wetness, and the wetness was on every stem and twig and herb and branch.

Now in the evening something strange filled him. As he walked in the woods, the branches drooping below a black sky, it was as if he wished to be a part of it forever. It was as if all this was the church wax he had used in his room one dark night to get that feeling of removal that he could never explain to anyone.

Rance said: "Stealin candles—what the fuck ya doin that for?" He said nothing. They came along by the river and Rance jumped on an ice-floe purplish and then piss-yellow on the bottom where the black tide moved against it. Rance used a stick to push himself about on the water, his black voice laughing into the black air.

"Stealin stupid candles," Rance said. Orville said nothing. The light brown stick moved the water and Orville could hear the water lapping: lapping. Then in an instant he realized Rance knew nothing and that he knew everything—about the water and the spring air and Rance's legs soaked by jumping too soon. That Rance didn't understand that whatever he did was done by that moving forever in hotel rooms. And yet he knew it himself—when the smoke curled in the room and the rain beat on the window and no-one, only Cathy perhaps was inside.

He walked on the beach, the large black driftwood becoming the large animals—whales or bears, anything he wanted. Then Rance said:

"The devil made ya steal those things—didn't he? Mallory and the devil."

"No," Orville shouted.

"Mallory and the devil," Rance laughed. "Ya can ask my old man, he thinks yer crazy."

"Leave me alone," Orville shouted.

"He thinks yer crazy."

For whole minutes he stood still. And it was different from physical contentment. He gazed at the sky and then at the muddy pathway. He picked up a leaf brown and dead and held it to his nose—and then instead of crumbling it he tried to place it back in the exact same spot —and he could see where he had taken it from, a small film, impression it made on the ground. He was aware that that was where the leaf should be.

"What if I do it now?" he thought, looking about him. He laughed silghtly and breathed deeply—the air fresh and clean. "No," he thought. And then he stopped thinking altogether. He lifted the gun and put it to his face. If he was in the ground among the things in the ground he would be the light forming through the morning haze, he would be the soft earth and the leaf with the overnight film of water—

He put the gun to his face and breathed quietly. Yet he did nothing. He thought neither of hell nor of heaven—only earth and sky and the impression the sun made upon him that morning. He would do nothing.

But he held the gun there for a long time and laughed giddily, unaware of his laughter—only aware of the fragrance of the tiny flower he had picked and smelled that morning. Why did Rance say: "Yer crazy?" He said, "Leave me alone—leave me alone."

Perhaps he could do it whenever he wanted to—it was just the gun and the cool feel of the barrel and the soft trigger, the powder stench and then the quiet. The partridge when it died fell from the tree and fumbled with its wings as if wanting to fly again.

For moments he held the gun to his face, breathing so quietly that he wasn't sure himself he was breathing and the highway was to his left and cars were passing.

Then he began to walk again. He walked out of the woods and into the field. Suddenly fear hit him for what he might have done and he began to run. He ran across the field and into the back lot of Karen's house. Then he walked again. *He wouldn't do it! He wouldn't do it!* Now everything that he had felt at different periods during the day left him. He thought of the leaf and thought there was nothing in it— thought of the sun and couldn't picture it any more. Everything he tried to picture was sour, as if that one instant when the gun was at his face was an explosion of all those things he was feeling, and now they were gone.

They were gone now.

He moved into the yard slowly.

Irene would say:

"Ya shouldn't be out with that gun; yer not old enough."

"Shut up."

"Maufat, he shouldn't be out with that gun."

"I know."

"I was just out huntin."

"Put it away now."

"I was just out huntin is all."

"Put it away now."

When he moved into Karen's yard he went by the back path and came out by the oil barrel. It sweated in the cool evening, and there were stars just breaking among the clouds. He was passing by the oil barrel and glanced into her room. The light was on though he couldn't see her. Then she came over and stood before the mirror by her bed and he could see. She was standing with her back to him, her red hair below her neck. He stood motionless by the window watching. She took off her skirt and then her slip. He was watching. She stood there for moments—the soft purity of her back and thighs.

He stood closer to the oil barrel. She turned from the mirror and was gone to the other side of the room. For seconds he did not move and she did not return. And then she did. She came back to the mirror and the bed, standing naked in the soft warm light of her room. He couldn't bring himself to move—nothing but something alive inside him, spontaneous—as she stood there facing the window. She reached up to the light string and shut it out.

4

She hadn't seen John for months. She had washed it away like a stain on a garment, as if it were something to be cleansed and left to the sun. So the sun would sink its light into the fabric and then only the garment white on a fresh day.

That is how she thought of it. That she was now clean, after the months of not seeing him, or hearing from him—his mouth thinned to nothing, his white skin over the lifting bones of his face. When she thought of him now she thought of him as something distant and ugly that she had come across—as if in the murk of afternoon she had stumbled blindly through the woods and had met him. She thought of him like that and shuddered.

She and Karen were leaving. Yet when she thought of him she thought of the day Orville had turned from her in the woods and had left her to stand alone saying: "I saw Mallory in there—Mallory." It was the same sensation of sickness and dread passing through her, but it was also different—it was the dread of knowing what she thought, the dread of knowing how she had clung for so long to the thought of him.

That when he was drinking he would come to visit and she would wait. Then he would say:

"Christ, when I useta go with Julie—"

And she would say:

"Shut up—shut up—cause why ya always saying that?"

"Fuck ya then—I'm just tellin ya."

"Then why ya always sayin that—"

Because it was as if he wanted to torture himself and her by saying that—that he wished to see his own pain in her face grow and build and the tears starting in her eyes.

"I never cried till I saw you," she said.

He laughed and coughed and swung his arm around, hitting the door so that his knuckles bruised, and when he looked at her again there was something wild in his face, his eyes narrow and cruel. He said:

"Oh I never cried till I saw you." She felt desperate and angry with herself, and yet she clung to his arm. When she clung to his arm he moved to open the door and she said: "No, don't go," and he turned back to her and rubbed his dark hand across his black hair and straightened.

She would say to herself: *He's just talking bout her cause he's drunk —cause he's drunk.*

In the lighthouse it was always dark. It was always dark and the waves formed and washed on the shore. She could smell moisture on the timbers and taste in the darkness the presence of sea-like things, of shells and seaweed and sand—the black heavy salt on her lips and tongue. When they went there he was quiet, his arms and hands strong against her. They would lie in the dark and she would know the presence of sea-like things, of the waves of the timeless ancient bay moving and swelling so far, so far. She would be asleep.

She would say to herself: *He's just talkin bout her cause he's drunk —cause he's drunk.*

248

One night he said: "I useta love her, I suppose I useta but I don't any more—I can't stand the sight of her any more."

She looked up at him and said nothing.

There was spring, and the tide swelled and the ice was breaking, the raging wind of late March, the trees dark and leafless in a changing sky. Something changed with her during spring—after a visit to Karen's the walk along the highway, the snow crusted and broken in the flat fields with the stems and shoots of aged grass solid and reflected in the night. The wind would be against her, her walk would slow, the trees moan. Above the long highway the sky would move and swell and turn, the road itself turned to frost heaves and broken from the winter.

She would stand at the side of her driveway, letting the cold wind blow into her face and open jacket. Motionless. If you asked her why she wouldn't know. She would know nothing but the strange happiness of standing, smelling ice-water in the air.

Snow came again, furious and small, hurting her eyes when she walked into it, mist blowing off the ground and out of the trees. For days it would be the same calm weather, and then the snow again, even into April.

Even into April when he came he would talk of Julie. She would say:

"Ya haven't seen her in so long so I don't know why ya talk about her."

Then for weeks he said nothing about her at all—not even a hint that either she or Andrew existed—had ever existed. They took walks out along the path, the snow still high in the woods, and onto the church lane, dry and brown in the warm evening. At twilight in the field across the inlet they could see Reginald's horse moving like a huge shadow. And when they were in the graveyard the cold from the water.

He said:

"I got something to tell you."

She looked up at him, and then past him where the church was purple with the sinking sun, the pebbles blackened on the shore.

They walked out and up the lane. It was warm again on the lane, the moon pale in the sky and almost full, the late chanting of birds.

"I got the dose," he said and laughed when he said it, turning away from her, staring into the leafless branches where the birds were chanting.

She kept walking.

He turned and walked beside her. The pale moon would brighten with a dark sky, stand out luminous and strong and almost full.

"I said I got the dose."

"What?" she said.

"Ya—off this whore."

"What?" she said. In the evening when the wind blew against her face she could stand outside for hours. In the mud on a warm day it was as if a thousand things were alive, and she held Betty's baby in her arms and cradled it. The sun shone on its small vague eyes and shriveled face.

"Off this stupid whore—I didn't even know her, but here I got these pills for ya and ya got to take them—because you got it too if I got it and—"

"What!" she screamed. She walked away from him faster, and then she couldn't walk. Wanted to hold onto something, to clutch anything and hold on. She stood there and her legs were trembling, her fists clenched together, a vague and distant thing turning brighter in the sky and Venus over her head. *When Reginald took them on the horse he took them round and round, the horse stepping over its own excrement in a muddy field and Karen saying "giddy up," and holding Cathy's waist.*

He came up beside her again. She tried not to look at him but couldn't help the strange attraction she felt for his thinned lips, the jawbones and cheekbones pulling at his face. His height and power over her own smallness. *When the wax smelled from the other room she would put her hand down to it and lay with the blankets tossed about her legs and in the evening the swarm of wind and snow or rain, or the hot stench from the road mingled with the candles in the air, the shadows of the room drawing closer to the lashes of her eyes.*

She looked at him. The birds had ceased chanting, the long rows of still and naked alders, spruce and maple were darkened now, small wet beds of grass showing above the woods' snow, and in the end the sky beyond the inlet and river and rapid brook, beyond the fields; forever. As he looked at her his face changed. For an instant it was as if she could see every human in his mouth and jaw, every person she knew in the small dark beard that was starting here and there—Alton when he shot the deer, or Maufat walking from the copper freight cars in the dusk.

He put his arms around her and for a moment held her—his warm heavy breath against her head. She knew she must tear herself away from him and run, she knew that. And yet for one instant his face so human and his eyes sorrowful as he breathed into her hair. Then she broke free and ran. "I don't care for him or her," she was thinking. "I don't care for him or her." She was crying from rage and fear, the broken frost heaves of the church lane that she could no longer see— the taste of his breath inside her mouth, the taste of all of him inside her, the horror of the taste of the lighthouse and when she went there the waves so far, so far. She was asleep. She felt herself falling and felt the pavement, the motion of her arms and feet and then the sky above her, dark.

She lay on the side of the road crying, feeling the damp mud soak into the bruise and cut on her face. He stood over her looking down.

"Fall?" he laughed.

She said nothing.

"Here, ya better take these," he said, pulling the bottle of pills from his pocket. She closed her eyes. There was no fright when she fell, because she knew as she ran that she was going to fall. There was a lump beneath her eye and the mud was in the cut, the soft salt warmth of the blood.

"Here, ya better take these," he said.

She could see him now. He was like Reginald's horse—a shadow. His hand when it reached to lift her was a shadow coming out of the night toward her. She pushed his hand away. She could feel the wetness soaking through to her back and legs.

"Take these," he said again. She said nothing.

"Goddamn it woman, ya stupid little fucker, take these," he roared. She said nothing.

When Maufat took her fishing he took her to a pool and in the pool the silver thin sea-trout lay resting. When Maufat flicked the fly she could see the head of the trout before the fly and when the trout was landed its glossy opened eyes were sad and waiting, rolling its soft belly in the dust of the river-bank. The pipe-smoke was fragrance on the early June air. She said:

"Let me taste it."

Maufat looked at her and then batted the fish with a small grey stick. The fish was dead.

"Let me taste your pipe."

When she tasted his pipe it wasn't the taste of the smoke, but an unbeautiful harshness. She spit it up.

"Alright, then don't," he said. He kept looking at her—looking. She turned her head to the side so she wouldn't have to look back, and then closed her eyes again. It was such a good feeling to lie in the dirt and cry that all thought passed through her and was gone. The wind and the salt blood and the dirt of the lane all passed through her and was gone.

"If you don't take these I'll throw them in the woods," he said. There was something frightened in his voice that she hadn't heard before— the voice of an old man perhaps. *Reginald when he stuttered turned his head away and cast his eyes down because he was afraid—he was afraid of laughter, and Rance that night when they took the preserves to him, walked the long dirt road into his house, couldn't stop laughing when Reginald said thank you. So Reginald spit and rubbed his boot over the spit and watched the ground when they went away.*

He was watching her. Why didn't he go away and let her lie there— why didn't he? She felt him bending over her now, and when he touched her she didn't flinch or move, the loose strands of hair wisping about her forehead, the grey wet gravel pressing into her left side and making a numbness there.

"Here, take these—ya gotta take these."

She didn't answer him. He tried to lift her up and she thought she would come with him but then, suddenly, she pulled herself away again and rolled on her stomach and began to cry louder and louder.

"Christ," he said. "Ya think I meant to, ya think I did?" he said, grabbing onto her and turning her around. She lifted her head and felt the hot choking in her throat. "Take these and don't be a baby."

"I'm not a baby," she screamed. "And I won't take no pills."

"Christ," he said again, letting go of her. She lifted herself and sat on the road, looking this way and that. Down farther a large white pine towered in the night where Cecil had tracked the buck day in, day out—missing it, missing it.

He stared at her sitting there. For a long time neither of them spoke, the wind growing, blowing at the straight black hair about his face.

"I'm goin," he said.

She said nothing.

"I'm goin," he said louder. "Sit there and rot then," he said.

He walked a few paces up the lane and then turned back to her.

"I'll set the pills here," he said. "Ya take them if ya want, ya stupid fucker."

He walked away.

The man stood close to the door. His beard was long and full, untrimmed, the skin under his eyes leatherlike. When Maufat came in he looked at the man quickly, and at the young woman with him, then at the floor. Lorne followed them inside and the four of them stood in a rectangle in the empty kitchen.

Maufat stared at the floor. The tile was chipped in places but Irene had cleaned it spotless, the smell of floor-wax in the emptiness. The woman stood huddled behind her husband—every little while moving her thin arms about her and looking up at him as he spoke. He spoke softly yet distinctly, as if his voice would carry in that low tone over the fields and into the bright day outside. There was in it—the tone and measure of his voice—something of a flat, *lacking* sound that Maufat disliked. Why he disliked it he didn't know. He only knew the man was standing there, his black beard untrimmed, the hair partially hiding his lips and teeth, the woman beside him in a maternity dress that hung upon her like a drape.

"So you want to buy the place then?" Lorne said.

"We were thinking of it," the man said. There was a pause. The man looked about into the living-room, where the curtains were drawn to the afternoon sun. He had on patched jeans and a faded grey sweatshirt. He put his hands in his pockets and walked away from them without a word, into the living-room, where he stood peering into the upstairs silence.

"Well, I'll show you the rooms then," Lorne said.

"Yes," the man said. "23 acres of land?"

"23 acres," Maufat said. "Uncleared, a lot of it," he said.

They went into the living-room and Lorne began talking. He said that the house had belonged to his mother who was dead and that it was very sturdy, that he and Maufat had done the bathroom over just a while ago—that the upstairs was spotless with five bedrooms and *like new*, that everything in the house was *like new*. Maufat said nothing. He followed behind them up the stairs and into the bedrooms, one by one, the man looking at the ceiling, the floor, the walls, pressing his weight here there and everywhere. The woman said nothing— only now and then nodding her head when her husband spoke. She was slender and her shoulders stooped forward, as if it was awkward for her to carry a child. Her face was narrow and white, yet not unattractive. When they entered Annie's bedroom at the end of the hall,

Maufat said: "This is the master bedroom here," because he had heard the man say at one point, "Is this the master bedroom?" Then he was silent again and stood by the door. He had no ashtray for his cigarette and kept flicking the ashes into his hand, rubbing them like dirt into his palm.

Then they all went downstairs again and stood in the living-room.

"Are these curtains going to stay?" the woman said.

"Sure, why not?" Lorne said.

"And that oak dresser upstairs—but I imagine you'll want to keep that," she said again.

"Oh, we'll throw that old thing in," Lorne said, turning to Maufat and smiling. Maufat smiled and shifted his weight, rubbing the elbow of his left arm. The woman looked at her husband and then looked quickly away.

"Well, my name's Lorne Everett anyway," Lorne said after a pause, putting out his hand. "You were talking ta me on the phone there yesterday—and this is my brother-in-law Maufat MacDurmot—he's gonna be yer next-door neighbour here—if ya buy the place I mean, but I don't mean yer gonna buy the place."

"Ralph Cassidy—my wife Eleanor," the man said. There was another pause and Maufat went into the kitchen to find an ashtray.

He could find no ashtray so he leaned against the counter and flicked his ashes into the sink, running the tap every so often, and trying to hear what the man said whenever he spoke. It was a good house—he had painted it not long ago and if he had had the money maybe he would buy it himself. Because perhaps Irene would like that—perhaps she would. But they didn't need the house. It was far too large for them; and also he had the feeling that even if he had the money— even if Irene wanted the house, Lorne wouldn't agree. He went to the doctor about his elbow and the doctor said:

"Paining you long, has it?"

"Sometimes I can't lift the crates no more," Maufat said.

"Crates?" the doctor said.

"When we have to unload them from the freight-cars."

"Don't they have a fork-lift up there?" the doctor said.

"Yes," Maufat said.

"Well," the doctor said.

"Well, sometimes we use it and sometimes we lift by hand," Maufat said.

"Nothing showed in the x-ray," the doctor said. "But the elbow is

254

a funny joint."

A funny joint, he thought, pressing his right hand into it as if trying to keep the pain inside.

When Lorne took them outside to show them the land he didn't go. He waited by the sink because there was something about the man he didn't like—and he didn't know what he didn't like. Yet something. He went upstairs again and through the rooms once more, alone, looking at the walls and the ceiling and the floor. He went into Annie's room. From the window he could see Lorne leading them into the far fields, turning around now and then to speak, and the man holding a small cane-like stick in his hand. "He don't know nothin bout the land —don't know what yer showin it for," he said aloud, his breath making a haze on the pane. Then he felt stupid for saying that and moved away from the window and leaned against the oak dresser.

In the room, his mother-in-law's. She had used this room in her last years, an existence she was unaware of (except at moments when she would become perceptive of things she had known during the whole course of her life—things such as the kettle on the stove when Irene was there, and suddenly she would turn to that kettle, the steam rattling and hissing from its spout; she would turn to the kettle and then to Irene and smile, innocent with her gapped mouth). And the thought of this filled him. She was afraid of him—why was she afraid of him? When Irene said: "Leah is not Annie's child cause she's my child," he was happy—something welled inside him to know that she had given birth to a child who that afternoon had played with a doll in the centre of the floor. Lorne moved from the chair in the room and went upstairs. And because he loved Irene he loved the child as his own, because what made him love Irene made him love the child. And why didn't Annie know this? Why was she always trying to say things that would please him when he could tell what she was trying to do? Like when she said: "Oh I think Cathy's gonna be far prettier than Leah," and Irene clashed the dishes together just to make a noise, and he said nothing.

Now there was something wrong. It was strange. When he thought of it he laughed, hollow like the feeling inside him. But he remembered her when they went on a picnic and Cecil and Leah were screaming at one another, Leah holding the baby in her arms and Lester staring from his verandah across the way. She was an old woman with a cane walking slowly in a long summer print dress, her feeble white legs bent outward like two rubber sticks, her black shoes making small sliding marks in the sand. She sat on the picnic bench the whole after-noon, surrounded by children and the lobster boiling. The heat tired her, and when she spoke to Orville he shied away and wouldn't speak. Then Maufat took the lobster claws and opened them for her and she said:

"You know, I've lived to see long rafts on this river—I've lived to see long logs on this river—I've lived to see pulp drives on this river —and now I've lived to see nothin on this river."

And he couldn't answer. He stared at the lobster claws, the pink freckled meat, and he couldn't answer. And then she fidgeted with her hands and said quickly:

"This sun is hot, ain't it?"

What did she want him to say?

He cursed under his breath, looked at the small flecks of dust Irene had missed when she swept the upstairs. Across the field they were returning. He could hear the man's deep slow laughter faintly in the distance. As if the voice already owned the property it occupied. As if that. And Lorne would say: "Me and Maufat, we did the bathroom— me and Maufat, we painted the house."

He turned around and began to open the dresser drawers aimlessly. They had to be lifted slightly to be opened and grated and slanted when they were. There was a rich full smell to the wood, the empty vacuum of the inside. Drawer by drawer he opened and closed, his grey eyes scanning the empty thick bottom of the wood. They came into the house and he could hear Lorne calling:

"Maufat, Maufat." He didn't answer.

"Maufat, you here Maufat?"

"Be down in a minute," he said.

When he opened the fourth drawer a photograph fell from the crevice and landed by his feet. He stooped and picked it up, blowing the small particles of dust from its face. It was a picture of Mr. Everett (Maufat had always called him Mr. Everett even though everyone else called him Dwight) and it was the picture of him the day, over 50 years ago at least, when they had shot the sow bear on the upper river. He stood strong, grinless, his eyes still after these years determined in the faded print, his hat clutched in his right hand. In the background the face, a woman perhaps, staring through the window. He put it in his shirt pocket and went downstairs.

"So, they're gonna buy the place," Lorne said.

"Good then," Maufat said. "You people want a beer then or something?"

"We don't drink," the woman said.

He tried to think of her name: "Eleanor." He knew a girl once when he was Orville's age—Eleanor; and she became a nurse in London during the second war, and now she lived somewhere else. Somewhere else, he thought.

He said nothing. For a long moment there was nothing said.

"So, it's $11,000," Ralph said.

Lorne nodded and looked at Maufat and suddenly Maufat felt as if they might refuse and walk out the door—that $11,000 was too much money.

"Maufat here's gonna be your next-door neighbour," Lorne said.

"Yes," Maufat said. "I just live out there by the highway."

"We have the loan arranged from the bank," Ralph said, his voice steady and flat.

"So we can give you the money tomorrow."

"It's a good piece of property," Lorne said. "And we can throw in those drapes and that old dresser—and anything else we have here— we don't need it for sure."

"What do you plan to do then, work around here?" Maufat said. "I suppose you plan to work here and everything."

"My wife's a painter," Ralph said. "I work with pottery and glass— we plan to set up shop here, but it's just tentative—we don't know how many people will relate to our work, as yet none have," he said, laughing in his flat steady voice and rubbing his brown leather-like hand over his untrimmed whiskers, as if spit was on his whiskers and he wished to remove the spit. Maufat stared at the floor and rubbed the elbow of his left arm.

"But if worse comes to worse we can go back to teaching—God forbid," he laughed again, and looked at them so Maufat was forced to look up, seeing the vague black eyes of his face.

"Where are you from then? Not around here—"

"New York," the man said.

"Oh," Lorne said, "New York," and looked to Maufat.

"I knew ya wasn't from around here at all," Maufat said laughing.

"Well, I'll tell you—the States are going to hell in a hand-basket as far as we're concerned—as far as we're concerned any country that claims to be democratic and forces the populace into an unwanted war —then that country is going to hell in a hand-basket and we want nothing to do with it."

257

"Ya," Lorne said. "It's bad like that but you have to beat the communists don'tcha or they'll take over the world—and all the kids are on the dope now and everything, and they all wanta be communists and everything—as far as I'm concerned."

The man said nothing. Maufat turned and stared through the window to where the coloured stone walk was autumn fresh. Then the girl said:

"Oh, I don't agree with that," and Maufat cleared his throat and ran the tap over his cigarette. The man said nothing.

"Well, just watch yer television—just watch yer television on the news every night—some big guy at college here is tellin the kids what to do, and they come from good homes but they look up ta those guys at college—and they're tellin them ta take dope and not ta respect their parents who send them ta college in the first place," Lorne said, his voice loud and carrying through the emptiness of Annie's house.

"Well, Ralph taught in the States and I don't think he ever incited his students into any such practice," the woman said. "But I suppose there can be cases—"

"Cases, cases sure there are cases everywhere ya look, there's cases of this and cases of that," Lorne said.

"Yes," Ralph said, entering the conversation again. "You're right there—but you have to see that it's not any one country's fault—most communist countries are as capitalistic and bourgeois as *America*— for an example, when Eleanor and I went to Leningrad last March the people were affable and friendly—yet we could sense that all (or most anyway) wanted something from you; many of them (and this is no lie) were alcoholic and one poor bastard was willing to trade an icon for a pair of blue jeans—blue jeans, imagine, for an icon—"

"Did you take it?" Lorne said.

Maufat stood near the sink. He remembered the time he helped poultice Reginald's horse and he began talking of trains because Reginald was never on a train, and the more he talked the more he knew that Reginald couldn't answer—because Reginald was never on a train. Yet he talked and talked and Reginald kept saying "Yes," as if he understood. And then on the way home, in the dark, for one instant Maufat believed he knew more about trains than anyone and he said, "I'll take ya up sometime and show ya around," and Reginald said, "Good then—good then." But they both knew he didn't want to go.

"You can't take those things out of Russia," the man said. "They'd crucify you if you did—but for a pair of blue jeans he was willing, begging, to trade an icon."

"They're sneaky like that anyway," Lorne said, moving his hands together and cracking his knuckles outward.

Maufat turned and watched the girl—her white face reddened from trying to explain something—as if everything she was saying was right, and as if her husband, with his beard and patched jeans, was right. Yet there was no sense to it at all, neither what they were saying, nor what Lorne was saying, made any sense to him. He wished to be out of the house and walking—across the stone walk and the field, walking and walking. When Irene said: "I was a young girl—I was sixteen and foolish like that," he said: "It don't matter," and Irene said: "Maufat you have to know," and he said: "It don't matter," and Irene said: "Maufat, you have to know," and he said: "It don't matter," and she said: "But I didn't—" and he said: "It don't matter, goddamn it don't matter, goddamn it," and turned away from her—she thinking he was turning away because it did matter when only he, who couldn't explain what was inside (the way he walked on the snow that night with the thought of Leah playing with the doll), knew that it didn't matter at all.

Eleanor snorted a little, but she smiled immediately and folding her arms again said:

"Well, we think that in Canada people will care a little more than they do down there."

"Oh, we care up here for sure," Lorne said. "There's neighbours up here that'll care when something goes wrong—we're like one big family up here," he said, laughing stupidly and then moving his broad flat hand across the panelled wall.

They were all silent again. Lorne moved his broad flat hand against the panelled wall, muttered to himself. Outside there were sounds of Rance and Jerard.

"Yes, we have a good Prime Minister up here and everything," Lorne said, still inspecting the wall. "Don't we Maufat? A real good Prime Minister up here."

Maufat nodded. *At the town hall the Prime Minister stood with the flag above him and everyone was cheering and screaming, and Cathy was cheering and screaming, and Maufat said, "I thought he was gonna be taller or somethin," and Cathy said, "Oh Daddy—he's tall enough," and Maufat said, "No now, I thought he was gonna be taller or some-thin," and Cathy laughed and she was Irene laughing a long time ago.*

"Yes, a real good government up here for sure," Lorne said again.

Maufat looked at the girl again. The man put his hands into his pockets and yawned—yawning as if already he was in his own house and could yawn in it if he wanted to.

"Anyway, that's enough political speculation and philosophical platitudes for today," he said quickly.

"Ya, that's enough philosophy for today," Lorne said—looking to Maufat, who abruptly turned and started toward the door; because he wanted to be home.

"By the way," the man said. "Is that old sewing-machine in the porch going to stay here?"

"Sure," Lorne said.

"Irene wants that," Maufat said.

"*She* does?" Lorne said.

"Ya, Irene wants that," Maufat said, smiling. "My wife wants that."

"Of course," Ralph said. "Of course—well anyway, we'll all be in touch."

When they left Lorne and he walked back over the field, saying nothing until they reached Maufat's door.

"Ya got a beer in there?" Lorne said.

"Yep," he said.

Lorne came inside and they sat at the table.

"What d'ya think now?" he said.

"They're alright," Maufat said. "It's good the place is sold off any-way."

Lorne said nothing for a moment. He drank his beer quickly and pushed the bottle away, and Maufat handed him another bottle.

"I don't know how good I like them," Lorne said. "They don't know too much what they're gonna do about the land."

"Nothin's been done with it yet in years anyway," Maufat said.

"Well, they don't know too much," Lorne said, and then in the same breath: "I didn't know Irene wanted that old thing."

"Well, she does."

"I didn't know that."

"Well, she does," Maufat said.

It was late in the afternoon when Lorne left. The house was empty and quiet—the cot in the room still pulled out where Ronnie was sleeping, his toy fire-truck upturned at one side of it. He thought of Leah and wondered where she was—what she was doing at that exact instant; and then he thought of Cathy—that she also was leaving. "Goddamn it," he thought.

He finished a beer and pulled his jacket on, went across the field. The trees were naked now, the field hardened stubble, the weak autumn sun sinking beneath the tree-line and a taste of frost. He came up to the house at the other end of the field and stood for a moment at the door. He could think of nothing, the smooth rounded doorhandle of the porch. When Alton came to the door he said:

"Drive me into town, will you?"

"Sure, why?" Alton said, smiling the way he always smiled.

"Because I'm gonna get Irene and me a car," he said, smiling back.

6

When Irene was a young girl Maufat took her out to the black moss— to the place where the moss hung from the bog trees, and the ground had dampness and moisture on it. And he said: "You walk way over there and take them off and I'll be behind this tree." Yet she thought: "Don't he think of the mosquitoes?" She looked at him, her face was bright and happy—yet she looked at him and in the fear throbbing along her temples and in her heart she said to herself: "Now he's gonna do the same thing, he's gonna want it, then he's gonna leave." She said nothing. It was a hot afternoon and the black moss hung from the bog trees. In here it was cooler than on the road where the dust rose in the vapid soundlessness. There was the taste of the brook in here, of the brook rocks.

He said: "It'll be like Adam and Eve."

She laughed.

"Yes, it will—yes, it will." His voice husky and strange, his eyes not really there at all but luminous as if they were the sun that patched and slanted along the bog ground. And at this time the shale pit would be some great burning. The shale rocks would be white heat.

He said:

"Come on now," and putting his white hand outward he touched the loose summerness of her dress, where the top of her dress was opened to the sunburned skin, and where her fine young breasts showed indistinctly with the heaving of her chest.

And he said:

"Come on now," his voice husky, her chest heaving, his voice a whisper.

"No, now Maufat," she laughed. He took his hand back and looked

261

at her, his eyes at once empty—like the shale pit, but that strong immeasurable heating. "Okay then."

"No, now Maufat, mosquitoes will eat us."

"Okay then, okay then."

She could feel her lips quivering and the little sun-hat she wore making her head sweat, and he turned away from her and looked in, toward the low brown water of the brook.

"Okay," she said. "But those old mosquitoes will eat us up."

"Not if you don't want to, never mind," he said.

"Maufat you know, Maufat you know," she said.

"I don't know nothin, I don't know nothin," he said.

It was in the winter and Annie made the cake and Dwight said: "You make that cake good," and looked at her and said: "Irene, now remember it don't matter," and she sat by the wood stove. When her friends came she hid in her room until Dwight said, "Irene, it weren't yer fault and don't be stupid."

"It weren't my fault—ya think it was, don'tcha?" she said.

"I'm not even thinkin of that, why do ya always think I'm thinking of that cause I'm thinking I'm gonna adopt her and everything," he said.

"Ya are? Ya are?" she said. He turned to her again and she felt his eyes on the top opening of her dress where the redness met the white of her small fine breasts.

"What d'ya think, that I'd fuck ya and go like *him*, the bastard, that I'd do that, ya think I'd do that?"

"No," she said.

She turned and walked away from him into the bog.

"You stay there."

"Not if you don't want to now," Maufat said.

"You just stay there," she said.

She went into the bog behind the alders where she could smell the bird cherries on the small dark hedges. She undid her dress and stepped out of it, and her heart was everywhere inside. She saw the whiteness of her belly and thighs, and she was naked, and a trembling came upon her—something vaster than herself came upon her; as if she was the bird cherries on the hedges and the moss sloping limbless on the trees.

It was in the winter and he came down to the corner of the road, and she waded to the corner of the road and she said: "Chuck, Mom made a cake and everything—so Thursday night," and he looked at her. He looked at her and looked at her. She said: "Chuck, Mom made the cake." Then there were tears in her eyes and the cold turned the tears ice-like on her face. "Look," he said. "Look—ya think I'm gonna—ya think I'm gonna—yer only sixteen for fuck sake and ya think I'm gonna—I'm only eighteen, Christ." He looked at her and looked at her, and tears were like ice-water on her face. "Yer ears are gonna freeze, ya should wear a hat," she smiled. "I know, I know," he said.

When she came out behind the alders he was standing in his pants only, at the far side, beyond the path that ran in from the road. And she was in shadow and he was in sunlight that bathed the path and the trees to the left of it. So that she could see his eyes squinting at her, trying to see her form and shape, the darkness there. She went closer to him.

"How are you?" he said. He was in his pants.

"Good," she said.

He laughed.

"What're ya laughin at?" she said.

He laughed again and pointed to her head.

"Ya still got yer sun-hat on," he said. The day was hot yet in here it was cool, mosquitoes at her and she flicking at them with her bare arms, the reddishness of the sunburn above her breasts. The mosquitoes landed on her. She could hear first their whining buzz and then nothing when she flicked her hand at them—then felt the burning sharp sting.

"Damn, Maufat, these mosquitoes are gonna carry us away."

"Yes," he said, not listening. She scratched her legs unconsciously, and he came to her and undid her sun-hat, his eyes luminous as if they were the sun that patched and slanted along the bog ground.

She looked at him.

"Yes, yes," he said.

She ran ahead of him into the bog, and she knew his eyes were on her through the alders and trees and she kept thinking, "Oh Leah, Leah"—the blond face of the child on the floor with the doll. He was behind her—somewhere in the alders, in among it. She turned around and he wasn't there.

"Maufat," she called, "Maufat." *Dwight said: "Everything will be alright an everything if he won't marry ya an everything—I'll go up and see his old man." "Don'tcha do that," Annie said. "I don't wantcha doin that, Papa," Irene said. "Well, why now?" he said, his face flustered as if he had been stupid and was wrong. "Cause, Papa," Irene said. "No, don'tcha do that now," Annie said.*

"Maufat, Maufat," she called.

He came out of the alders naked, carrying her sun-hat in his hand. He said:

"I went back for this—I didn't wanta leave it on the path."

And she said:

"These mosquitoes are gonna eat us."

"Yes," he said. And they moved forward again.

Now and then the birds in the trees, brown and half-hidden, slanted in the motionless limbs and made soft sounds, and the air, breathless, about them without a stir. They came to the spot above the pit. Here she could look down into it and see the sun burning on the rocks, and here also there were no mosquitoes at her flesh. The rocks blazed white in the afternoon sun; the pit a gorged-out gigantic heat, and she thought: *Fire would be no hotter or horribler than stepping on those rocks—fire would be the same as stepping on those rocks.*

He drew her to him. He made no other motion or sound—his eyes measureless when she looked up into them; and the soft turning inside her gut. "Leah," she thought, "Leah, little baby," she thought.

"It'll be just like Adam and Eve," he said.

"Maufat," she said. "Maufat." She was frightened again. He dropped her sun-hat into the soft grass by the path above the shale pit. *Chuck, he said he would, he said: "I'll marry ya Irene, I'll marry ya Irene, and then he said, yer only sixteen fer fuck sake, what am I supposeta do—*

There was a sparrow and it was on a limb of spruce that grew solid in the ground. When she was a young girl it was the spruce smell that she loved in the spring because the air carried the smell along the bog road. And now the poignance of its smell came when he drew his hands on her, and a trembling came upon her—as if she was the bird cherries on the hedges and the moss sloping limbless on the trees. She said:

"How come sparrows don't get stuck ta spruce gum?"

"What d'ya mean?"

The sparrow flitted back and forth on the limb and when he kissed her she kept her eyes open watching the sparrow, its small straw-like legs wisps of nothingness as it flitted from branch to branch.

"What are ya lookin at?" he said.

"Sparrow," she said, and laughed.

They lay in the grass above the shale pit, the afternoon sky a wide and brilliant blue—timelessness of space and motion.

Leah—Leah little baby, she thought.

In the afternoon the white of autumn and the naked trees behind the house, and the flat trampled fields. Maufat would come home and plasticize the foundation and windows of the porch. Yet here, inside, it was warmth from the stove and the occasional sound of the fridge. She was alone.

Leah is gone and Cathy is gonna go—Leah is gone and Cathy is goin.

When she thought of this she was both sad and happy; not understanding why she was either. Because it was better for Leah to be gone and it would be better for Cathy. *Leah turned to the doorway and then slumped in the corner, shaking and sobbing. When she went to Leah she thought: My God, my God, and felt that all her life she had been mean to Leah, that all her life she loved Cathy better. And then Leah lifted her arms as she bent forward and Cathy came over, and by the corner of her eye she could see Cathy's face and see how much it was Leah's face—at that moment and time. She put her arms trembling around Leah's arms trembling and Leah said: "Eh Cathy, why do you have to go, eh Cathy?" and Cathy was crying.*

Now there was silence.

Betty said:

"So she got inta trouble with the nuns."

Irene said nothing.

"What was she doin, smokin or something and the nuns caught her?"

Irene said nothing.

Then Leah came downstairs and Irene said:

"Get upstairs again, Leah," and Leah looked at Betty and her face was saucy and red, her eyes glaring. "Get upstairs, Leah," Irene said, her voice breaking. And Leah went up the stairs again and into her bedroom and slammed the door.

"Well, you tried and you tried," Betty said, as if she was good and right and clean.

Irene said nothing. She rocked her body in the chair and thought of nothing but what the Mother Superior had said when she had phoned: *Leah is a bad girl, Leah is a bad girl—seventeen and a bad girl.*

"I tried and I tried," Irene said, and then she felt awful for saying it.

Betty said nothing.

"But she weren't right for school—she's smart and everything but she just weren't right for it and she's far smarter than ya think, ya know that, Betty, she's far smarter than ya think."

Betty said nothing.

"She is," Irene said. "But just wait'll Maufat hears all this—*she is, Betty.*"

"Oh, I know that," Betty said.

"She can even play the guitar and sing so ya'd think it was the radio," Irene said. She looked to Betty and her eyes failed and she looked away.

"Cathy's doin real good at school though, Irene," Betty said.

Irene said nothing. Upstairs she could hear Leah doing something loudly in her room.

"Maybe she shoulda stayed over with Annie like she was until she was grown," Betty said.

Irene got from her chair and went to the sink and slammed the dishes against one another in the sink.

"Well, just maybe is all," Betty said.

"Now why's that, why's that?" Irene said, turning toward her. Betty said nothing, her eyes staring at her folded hands. "Now why's that, why's that?" Irene said again.

"Well, just maybe yer too kind ta her or somethin, I don't know," Betty said.

"Annie's too old now, Annie's too old," Irene said, almost shouting.

Because they went into the principal's office and the principal was a nun with short grey hair pinned underneath her peaked black hood. There was an Indian girl and Leah, and the Indian girl was crying. The principal said: "Stop your crying, stop your crying this instant, do you hear?" and the Indian girl couldn't stop crying. The principal said: "Reports have come to us that the both of you are seeing men far older than yourself," and Leah said: "What reports—ya got little spies out or somethin?" and the principal said: "Leah, I've never in my life met such an insolent girl as you—now this thing here—this thing," she paused. "Are you sleeping with a *married* man, are you, are you! Stop the crying, are you, are you!" The nun had a white face, like the white knob on the long banister, and smelled of the convent rooms, of beads and sacraments, and Leah looked at her and Leah said: "What do you do, screw yerself with yer finger?" and the nun turned sick-white and slapped Leah in the face.

Because the Mother Superior said, *Leah is a bad girl and we don't want her back here.*

Irene went over and turned the radio on, and tried to listen to it, as if the radio would stop Betty from being there. Then Leah came down the stairs with her old brown suitcase.

"Where are you going?" Irene said.

"To Cecil's," Leah said.

"Now you get back here," Irene was crying. She made a motion with

266

her arm, and Leah turned about, and at the door she said:

"Betty, be sure and run and tell this down the road," and Irene was crying.

Cathy was out this afternoon at Karen's. They both had passes for the train and they would leave in two days, travel west on the train and meet Leah; so it was better.

She went to the stove and poured tea and sat down again. When she was half through drinking it Ronnie came in from school, his small face reddish.

"You want a piece of cake?" she said.

"Good," he said. So she went to the cupboard and got him a piece of cake, and milk; and while he was eating it at the table she thought of Leah—because he looked like her, though he looked like his father also.

"Where's Orville?" he said.

"He won't be back from school for a half-hour yet," she said.

"He's gonna take me huntin," Ronnie said.

"He is?" Irene said.

The boy didn't answer, looked up at her as if he had let go a secret and then smiled weakly. She smiled back at him and then stood and went to him, kissed him on his red cool cheek.

"Now don'tcha rub that away," she said as he lifted his hand to it.

"I'm rubbin it in," he said.

He went outside again, and she went upstairs and lay down.

At first it was Maufat calling to her in her dream. They were in the small cottage at Fundy Park and he was calling to her from the door of the cottage. Outside there was a beautiful dirt lane and it was very green with trees and grass and she came to the door of the cottage to look out. Yet he kept calling and calling. She woke.

She woke to see him standing over her, grinning.

"Now what do you want?" she said yawning, stretching her right arm back and under her head. "Those Americans burn Annie's place down or something?"

"I got something to show you," he said.

"What?" she said.

"Oh nothing," he said grinning.

"What?" she said.

"I said nothing," he said. "Now are ya coming downstairs or what?"

"Is Cathy in yet?"

"Nope."

"She said she'd be back and do supper."

"Are you coming or what?" he said.

She raised herself from the bed and followed him down. On the stairs he took two steps at a time, looking back.

"Fridge blow up?" she said.

"Come on if yer comin," he said. "Come on if yer comin."

He led her through the kitchen and into the porch. She could see his whole body shaking with excitement and when he led her through the porch he grabbed her by the hand, and she said: "Oh Maufat!"

He said nothing.

"Oh Maufat," she said.

"Shut up now," he said.

He opened the porch door and pushed her forward, outside. Then he shut the door behind her and went back into the kitchen.

"Oh Maufat," she said. "It's brand new, oh Maufat."

"Shut up now," he said from the kitchen. "Let a man have a beer in peace."

She looked at it, and looked at it. It was red and brand new, and sat there red and brand new! Then she turned and ran inside again, through the porch and into the kitchen where he was sitting at the table drinking a beer.

"Me and Alton went up the other day and looked er over," he said.

He stood and went to the fridge again and she looked out the window. Then he brought the beer over and went to open it, but she threw her arms around his neck and at first she was laughing and then she was crying, feeling herself sink against him. He put his arms around her. She was shaking and crying.

"Told ya I'd get a fuckin car, didn't I—told ya I'd get a car, didn't I?"

She cried.

Ronnie walked in the drain. In the drain in summer he saw a brown snake slide between the culvert and the rock. It was a hot afternoon and Leah was taking him to the shore, and for an instant, when the snake crossed between the culvert and the rock, Leah froze and clutched his hand. Now as he walked he remembered the clutching hand, large and brown and soft against his own, and his mother's face when she said:

"Oh Ronnie, a snake," and he said: "Ya, a snake," and squirmed out of her grip and chased it. *Snakes could crawl under rocks smaller and littler than them and hide down in them.* And he didn't know why

Leah was afraid, yet she was, and he chased the snake, long and sun brown—it went into the culvert and he crouched on his knees looking in.

"Don't go in there," Leah said.

He didn't answer.

"Ronnie, I'll spank you if you go in there."

"I'm waiting for it to come out," he said.

"No, come on now," she said.

"I'll squash it if it comes out," he said.

He picked up a rock with his two small hands.

"I'll squash her," he said. Not knownig why he would squash the snake—only to see its darting tongue and its brown eye and to hold it. He would kill it and then hold it up and see the yellow brown strip and the white tire-like stomach, and hold it—hold it.

"No, now come on now," Leah said, and took him by the hand once more. They went up over the culvert and onto the road.

Today the sky was bright, the trees bare. He walked along the drain for a time. Orville said:

"Ya know where most birds are?"

"Where?"

"At dusk in the trees along the church path and the church lane—in the birches—we'll sneak out the gun and shoot some after I get home."

So he went along the church path because Orville wasn't home and he wanted to see the birds in the trees along the church-lane path. And when he walked into the woods, where the shadows were under the spruce and pine, and the fall pine smell, he was a captain in the army and he picked up a long stick. At first the stick was a gun because he was shooting the pine-tree boughs and the spruce, and then later it was a spear and he threw it here and there, chasing after it and yelling.

He looked up, into the birches and maples, but he could see nothing of the birds, and he walked on. Orville said: "There are rabbits in the winter hopping all over the path, and when the snow is real light and flaky, you know, and when there's a moon, ya can go out and see them, and so I'll take ya out ta see them when the snow comes—ya know what rabbits look like skinned?"

"What?"

"They look like cats skinned—Rance, he never caught one rabbit all last winter."

Ronnie said nothing.

"Guess how many I caught," Orville said. "I caught seventeen," he said.

When Ronnie came onto the church lane the soft siding pebbles crunched under his feet, the tall white pine above him. Above him also the sky going into night, and a brilliance to the sun beginning to settle. He walked toward the church singing, and now and then, remembering why he was there, looking into the trees. There were no birds, or if there were they were hiding on him in the trees. Orville said there were always birds in the trees, their necks exposed in the naked cool air, their small heads bobbing when you saw them. He said:

"Mosta my birds I get in the trees."

He walked toward the church, and across the open inlet and field he saw Reginald leading in his horse. He saw the horse a far great shadow, its legs immense yet almost invisible in the encroaching dark, and the tall gangly man ahead with his hand on the bridle, and it looked as if his long arm was in the horse's mouth. And Ronnie thought: "I'm gonna get myself a horse."

Then he was down beyond all the trees and he ceased to look for birds. He forgot again why he was outside, and when he looked at the rough waves of the bay water he was a sailor on an island, and the middle buoy was no more than the bow of his sunken ship miles and miles away that he had come from, swimming and swimming.

He was about to turn and go back when the idea came to him. So he went up to the great doors of the church and went inside. Inside, he saw the white statue of Mary, of Jesus with his hands extended, and the brown quiet pews. He was at the altar front and he genuflected and looked at the four burning candles in the twenty-candle stand. They flickered and then were silently perfect—flickered again. He watched the candles glow on the statue of Mary, her silent white face looking down upon him. And Leah said: "When she's lookin at you it's out of heaven, she's seeing you out of heaven because she's up there with God and everything—now Hail Mary full of grace—"

"Hail Mary full of grace."

The Lord be with thee."

"The Lord be with thee—so she isn't inside?"

"Inside where?"

"The statue."

"No, she's with God in heaven but she sees you in the church."

He heard the side door open and when he turned Father Lacey was staring at him, his small old eyes humped out in the middle of a puff of skin. He turned and looked at Father Lacey.

"Hello—who are you now?"

"I'm Ronnie," the boy said, looking up at the old man in his long black thing and his face white and crooked—his eyes humped in the middle of a puff of skin.

"I want to be an altar boy," Ronnie said.

"You can't be until Grade 4," the priest said.

"Oh."

"Well, you don't look like you're in Grade 4."

"3," Ronnie said.

"Then next year," the priest said, talking very quietly. Then he said: "You're Leah's boy."

"Yes."

The priest looked about him, his neck a puff of skin above his tight white collar. Then he said: "Do you want to light a candle to the Virgin Mary?" and Ronnie said: "I don't have no money."

"Well, I just might," Father Lacey said, putting his hand into his pocket and pulling out coins. "Here's a dime," he said. "You light it."

So Ronnie turned, and picking up the long wick lit it off one candle and tried to light another. And as he did so the old man stood behind him, breathing like Annie when Leah said: "You come see Annie." He couldn't get it lit.

"Having trouble?" the priest said. Then the priest came closer and he could smell the priest—he could smell black and the puffed skin, and the old man guided the wick in his hand to light the candle.

"So next year you see me if—" The priest stopped speaking, and closed his mouth that was a black mouth, and moved his teeth together so they made a sound.

"Yes," Ronnie said. "Yes, Father," he said. And moved up the aisle out of the church.

7

He phoned me after months and months—and I weren't gonna go ta the phone cause I weren't gonna go ta that phone for him ever again, after months and months, and those pills. I didn't know. Then Karen said: "Go on ta the phone, MacDurmot, and tell him off—just tell him off on the phone and hang up on him—just do that," and she looked to me as if, if I didn't do it, I was stupid. I said nothing but I didn't know cause I started ta think of it and got madder and madder, cause he just thought he could phone me up and everything. He said: "How are you?"

"Good," I said and then we didn't say nothing. He said: "Did you ever take those pills?"

"What pills?"

"The fuckin pills I gave you, for Christ sake woman."

I said nothing. He said:

"Did you, did you?"

"Yes, yes—and what's it to you?" He said: "For fuck sake, Mac-Durmot," and then we were silent and I could hear the buzz on the line and he said:

"Andy's dead, Cathy—he was killed, Cathy."

I said nothing and got scared and felt weak and scared. I couldn't say anything ta him. I didn't know. I saw Andy drivin the car, I saw him drivin the car. He said:

"Didn'tcha hear?"

"No—I'm sorry, I'm sorry."

"Didn'tcha hear, for fuck sake woman, didn'tcha hear, for fuck sake?"

"No, I'm sorry, I'm sorry, John I'm sorry."

He hung up on the phone and my hand was white on the receiver and my nose and everything and I saw Andy drivin the car like yesterday.

Today was dull looking and she supposed cold, though as yet she had stayed inside, doing the last of her packing. And every ten minutes Karen phoned. She said: "Should I take my blue dress?" and Cathy said: "Yes," and she said: "What'll I wear on the train?" and Cathy said, "Don't know—oh your new slacks."

And all afternoon when she looked at the field out of Orville's window she saw the new people banking Annie's house, the woman tiny and pregnant, the man with a beard. Then she went back to her own room, opened her suitcases again, looked at them—the clothes inside—closed them again, opened her dressers again.

Then Irene said:

"Now when you get up there I want you to get in touch with Leah and Mary as soon as you're in the station."

"Mom, they said they'd meet us there—now don't worry."

"Well, you just don't know how big that place is."

They were silent.

"Mary said she'll be able to get you a job anyway—and take care of

272

yourself up there."

She smiled, and then Irene smiled, placing her white hand on the corner of the sink.

"Ya know there's some rye here," Irene said after a moment.

"Want some?"

"Well, ya know it's a long ride up on that train," she smiled.

"Ya want some?" Cathy said. Irene went to the cupboard and took it out.

They each poured a glass with water for mix and sat at the table. When she drank it Irene was looking at her, and then Irene said:

"Well, I guess selling Annie's was for the best."

"We got new neighbours," Cathy said.

They were silent again.

"I don't know how they'll turn out is all," Irene said.

Then she said:

"I hope Leah is making out good up there."

"I think she'll make out alright," Cathy said. *It was the boy and he stood in the mud, his white animal face streaked with blood and Cecil saying: "You fuck off outa here, you fuck off outa here," and yet it wasn't Cecil's fault.*

"Oh, I don't know," Irene said.

"No, I think she will—because I think that she still loves him and everything, but I think she'll make out."

Irene said nothing. Then Cathy said:

"No, I think she will—you know the last time we had a drink to-gether was when I was eighteen on my birthday."

"Well, we should have a couple more."

"Maufat's gonna come in here and find us drunk," Cathy laughed.

"Piss on Maufat," Irene said, winking. And they both laughed. "That's a great car, ya know he surprised me."

"No, he didn't now," Cathy said.

In the afternoon light and silence of the house, only their voices, the white fridge behind Cathy looking cold, its light shadow on the green wall, and the smell of the kitchen. Outside the window the brownish autumn grass, and Karen's house just visible.

They each drank another glass, Cathy watching the time. Maufat said:

"Ya ain't sittin up on no train."

"We can sit up," Karen said.

He looked at her and said:

"Well, ya ain't sittin up, I got it all arranged."

The train would lull them to sleep, the sound of the wheels beneath them—the outside against the cool frosted glass—

"How far have you been on a train?" she asked.

"Never as far as you're goin," Irene said.

"How far?"

"Halifax, a long time ago—after Orville was born."

"Oh I remember that—you goin away and everything."

"Well, that's as far as we went," Irene said.

She stood and took the glasses to the sink and put the rye away.

"Listen, you're packed and everything?"

Cathy nodded, and stood. The rye had made her light and happy and she wanted to talk to Karen. She wanted to go, and be there all at once —travel without travelling.

In the doctor's office everything smelled too clean. The doctor sat behind the desk and looked into her face so that she trembled, and water started at her eyes. He said: "Well, there's no sign of anything in the blood test." Outside a child with a pea-shooter played on the street, the street hazy. Her eyes watered and the street was gone. "You think I knew—you think—" she began. The doctor said: "Things of this sort will happen." She kept rubbing her small brown hands on her white skirt. Then he said: "But there's nothing to worry about." The child moved farther down the street. She stood—unable to lift her head. The doctor said: "Don't worry now because there's nothing to worry about now."

"Well, I promised Laura I'd go visit—but I'll be back before Maufat gets here ta drive ya up," Irene said.

She left and Cathy watched her walking along the road, until she was to the distant yard, looking small and unwarm under the white sky.

When Orville came in she was sitting on a chair in the room. She had brought her suitcases down and had placed them by the door, and when he saw her sitting there, as if she was to leave at any moment, with her hands pressed together, he began to laugh.

"What're ya laughin at?"

"Nothin."

"Then stop laughin."

"City girl," he said.

"Shut up."

"City girl."

"Shut up."

He went to the fridge and taking out bologna began to eat it, staring at her, looking first at her suitcases and then at her, smiling and walking up and down the kitchen.

"Shut up."

"I ain't said nothin."

"Well then, just shut up."

"Well, I tell ya—Mallory's moved ta Toronto."

"We're not going ta Toronto."

"Where are ya going?" he said.

"Hong Kong."

"Mallory's moved out to Hong Kong last week," he said.

She looked at him and began to laugh and he moved through the doorway and up the stairs. When he was at the top he shouted, "Mallory —Mallory," and was silent. For a long time there was only silence in the house. Then he came downstairs and began talking again.

"Shut up Orville," she said. He was trying to scare her. It was just him and nothing.

"Well, you know for yerself—this guy gets blown up, that guy gets bolwn up, this guy gets hanged in the bathtub, that guy gets hanged in the bathtub."

"Shut up, Orville."

"Just tellin ya."

"Shut up."

When the car pulled into the yard she didn't hear it. Orville was still talking and she listening, laughing at what he was saying. He was moving back and forth in the room and trying to frighten her, but she wasn't frightened. Then she heard the porch door rattle and stood. She looked into the yard and saw a car. The door rattled again, and then John came in.

When she looked at John as he stood in the doorway, his black hair and his white drawn cheeks, she felt a sick throbbing inside. It was as if she couldn't speak; when she tried the throbbing became a lump in her throat as if she were going to cry, or scream maybe. Yet she didn't know.

Orville stopped speaking, stopped pacing the floor. He stood to one side of Cathy and then suddenly he went up the stairs. John stood watching. He weaved now and then unsteadily, his head cocked forward, his arms folded. He said nothing.

"What are ya doin dressed up?" she said.

275

He looked at her and looked at her. It was as if he wanted to see through her, his eyes that dark and cold, his shoulders hunched the way they were *that* night. She looked at the kitchen floor—a piece of straw from the broom resting under the crevice of the stove.

"Just come from a wedding," he said.

"Whose?" she smiled—small and weak.

"Fuckin asshole's, that's whose," he said. He brought his right arm up and leaned against the door.

"Okay," she said. Her smile erased.

"Okay what?" he said.

"Okay, okay," she said. She didn't know. He moved his hand through his hair and she could see burns scarring and blistering his hand. She said:

"Where did ya get them?"

"What?"

"Them burns."

"At a fire."

She went into the kitchen and sat on a chair looking up at him. He turned and leaned against the counter and outside the day was drawn white, the throbbing of the car.

'I had Bruce drive me down here—ya shoulda been at the weddin."

She didn't answer.

"Fuckin good time—we stole a pig and put it in his car."

She didn't answer.

He looked at her and looked away, his thin lips erased to nothing, at the day outside, and the white sick flesh about the blisterings on his hand. She kept staring at the blistering.

"It's a game," he said. "With a cigarette."

At night he jumped into the black dark water of the bay. "I'll touch er," he said. "Boys, yer crazy," she said, and the water a swelling coldness below and beyond the blackened timbers.

"I'm goin away," she said.

He looked at her.

"Today," she said.

"Ya always lose the fuckin game," he said.

"What game?"

"With the cigarette, Christ."

"Okay, okay," she said.

He said nothing. It was that when he spoke, she heard something in him. It was as if it was against himself like the dark pustulation on his hand—against himself.

"Yes, I'm gonna go, me and Karen."

He looked down at her suitcases, muttered to himself.

"And where's *me and Karen* gonna go?"

"Out west—I'm sorry about Andy."

He said nothing for a moment. He looked out the window, stared at her, looked out the window again. And then suddenly he rushed toward her.

"Then why the fuck weren'tcha at the goddamn funeral eh, why not?"

"Cause I didn't know is all."

"Cause ya didn't know—cause ya didn't know!"

"I didn't," she said. She felt sick and weak, and she said: "I'm goin away—me and Karen."

"Well go, ya think I Jesus care?"

"No, I don't."

"Well, why bother tellin me?" he roared. Outside the day was white with an endless sky, the river white, and across the inlet in the field Reginald's horse would snort at the ground, the mud caked to its hooves. And in a circle round and round Karen saying, "Giddy up" and holding Cathy's side.

She heard the car shut off, and in a moment someone came to the door, knocked and came inside.

"You ready, John?"

"No, I'm not ready," John said turning. He took the bottle that was under his jacket and went to drink from it. It was empty. "Christ," he said. "You got anything here?"

"Come on, John," Bruce said.

"You got anything here? Andy's dead—Kevin's married, the gutless son of a whore, the gutless son of a whore."

"There's nothing," she said.

"Come on, John," Bruce said. "We'll go into town."

"You go inta town," he said. "You go inta town." His voice became softer, inside almost, and his eyes widened as he looked at them.

"Ya don't give a fuck, do ya?" he said.

"About what?" Bruce said.

"Anything—either of you, do ya?" He began opening cupboards. "Come on, John now," Bruce said; and when he found the rye he drank from it, looking at Cathy.

She was weak and couldn't think.

"You put that down now, that's Maufat's, it ain't yours."

She heard Orville on the stairs coming down and she felt weak. Bruce tried to grab the bottle from him but he held it away, and then Orville was in the kitchen.

It was because he was drunk—it was because of that.

Orville was in the kitchen; she didn't remember. He was in the kitchen and Orville said:

"Get the fuck outa my house."

John looked at him and set the bottle down.

Orville said:

"You go on out of my house—leave my sister alone, leave my sister alone, you go on out of my house and leave her alone."

"Christ, John," Bruce said. "We'll go inta town."

Cathy stood and walked toward him because he was walking toward Orville. She said: *"Me and Karen, we're gonna go away,"* and she grabbed his arm when he swung.

Orville tried to swing back but he couldn't and John was laughing. He said: "Fuckin one eye, fuckin one eye," and Orville was swinging and John was laughing. She couldn't remember. It was the suitcases and they were going away and Bruce yelled and grabbed John.

Then they were in the porch and Bruce was holding John and Orville was crying. She heard Orville crying out in the yard and he kept saying: "You get out of here, you get out of here and leave my sister alone."

There was silence and then the car was gone and there was silence again. She could hear Orville in the porch and she wanted to go to him but she didn't because he kept crying.

And then there was silence again, the trees stood strong in the dusk, the sharp autumn twilight.

Maufat said: "Now ya ain't sittin up cause I got it all arranged."

"It don't matter ta us, we can sit up," Karen said.

"Well, ya ain't," he said looking at her, then smiling, then looking away.